I0721129

<u>The Ghost Moth</u>

A Red Grouse Tale

Leslie Garland

Published by Noble Legacy Publishing

ISBN: 978-1-911761-02-0

To Anna

<u>The Ghost Moth</u>

"Have pity on such callow fledglings, O Lord, for those who pass by on the road may tread them underfoot. Send your angel to put them back in the nest, so that they may live and learn to fly."

Saint Augustine; Confessions, Book XII: 27

<u>Chapter 1</u>

We had all got our drinks, were seated at our usual table in the bar of The Red Grouse Inn, and that evening already knew that Joe was going to tell us a tale as he had already announced this at our last meeting. Apparently his ex-wife, Elizabeth, had given him an old book that she had found in some antiquated second-hand bookshop and he thought that one of the tales in it would make for an unusual Thursday night story. He did say where the bookshop was - at the far end of a narrow, still cobbled street in the old part of town - and on one occasion, I did try to find it, but was unable to do so.

The book was entitled 'Folk Tales and Legends of Hartstane' and the tale that he had chosen for us that evening was called 'The Ghost Moth'.

Joe took a sip of his drink, opened a very battered-looking leather-bound volume, looked up at us and commenced reading,

"Master Callow joined the Black Acres Monastery as a novice-monk in the early weeks of 1535. He was a thin gangly youth somewhere in his late teens or possibly his early twenties, and in his black monk's habit, which was way too big for him, looked even thinner and paler. The cord at his waist did nothing to assist in the habit hiding his scrawny physique as it gathered the coarse material into numerous folds making it look like an oversized sack hanging from his pinched shoulders, thus emphasizing the puny body beneath it rather than hiding it. He was from a middle class family and so had had a relatively privileged and relatively sheltered upbringing, with the result that he knew little of the world out there which lay beyond the walls of his parents home. No, Master Callow was certainly not street wise; naive would be the polite way to describe him, green or wet behind the ears the less polite way. He was at an age where he would have been self-conscious anyway, but dressed up in that sack of a habit that he'd been given to wear and with his head tonsured to boot, he was a virtual nervous wreck and about as shy and self-conscious as a young man of his years could be."

Having got everyone's attention, Joe then went on to explain,

"You know how it is when you get a book, well a reference book anyway, and I would call a book like this on folk tales and legends a reference book even though one can be fairly certain that most of it is fiction, you open it and idly flick through the pages, or run your eye down the contents page, and end up looking at something that for some reason or other just happens to grab your attention. Well, in this case the something that grabbed my attention was a rather lovely atmospheric pen and ink drawing of a bizarre looking tree with what looked like a face formed in its exposed roots which were hanging curtain-like down a small cliff face. According to the blurb, there was a small cave behind the curtain of roots, and also according to the blurb, it was easy to visit, being just a few hundred metres off the Hartstane road. Intrigued by the fact that the odd looking tree of the illustration did not feature in the title and by the possibility that we could easily go and have a look at it, I started to read the story. It was entitled 'The Ghost Moth.'

Of course, I knew it was just a folk tale. However, as you can see from the obvious age of this book, I also guessed that the story was probably going to be a fairly old one. Still, I nevertheless expected it to be the usual colourful blend of fiction built around the flimsiest of evidence. However, as events gradually unfolded, my then-wife and I came to suspect that the story was possibly all too horribly true, and both she and I had times when we seriously wished that she hadn't bought it for me. However, these misgivings all came a bit later. This is the book," he said, holding up the dilapidated volume, "but I won't bore you by reciting it word for word. I'll just continue reading the first bit and once we've got started will endeavour to recount both the tale itself and the events that occurred while I was reading it."

Reopening the book, Joe recommenced reading, and we found ourselves back in the world of the Black Acres Monastery in the early weeks of 1535.

"A monastic life offered both an education and secure future. So young Master Callow's parents had approached the prior, a stern elderly man who went under the name of Prior Obscurant, and after a suitable donation to the Monastery's funds had been made, it was agreed that their son would enter into the loving bosom of the Church, which would educate and prepare him for his life ahead.

The Black Acres Monastery was part of the Black Acres Priory. This religious complex covered several acres of land just off the road to Hartstane and was so named because the monks wore black habits. So named by the local people that is, because its official name was The Priory and Monastery of Saints Paul and Augustine, as it was the teachings of both that were supposedly the disciplinary yardsticks of the Priory and Monastery, though perhaps it was Prior Obscurant's interpretation of a quotation from The Revelation of St John the Divine that better explained his religious philosophy and hence the actual yardsticks that were used at Black Acres - 'And I looked, and, lo, a Lamb stood on the Mount Sion, and with him a hundred and forty four thousand, having His Father's name written in their foreheads. And I heard a voice from heaven, as the voice of many waters, and as the voice of a great thunder: and I heard the voice of harpers harping with their harps: and they sung as it were a new song before the throne, and before the four beasts, and the elders: and no man could learn that song but the hundred and forty four thousand, which were redeemed from the earth. These are they which were not defiled with women; for they are the virgins.'[1] What Prior Obscurant desired above all else was to be one of the hundred and forty four

---

[1] Revelation 14:1-4

thousand, and those within his pastoral care were also going to be in the hundred and forty four thousand, whether they liked it or not, or else he had failed in his duty.

As well as being elderly and stern, Prior Obscurant was tall and thin. I couldn't help but imagine him looking like some fanatical prophet as depicted by the likes of El Greco," suggested Joe, "with eyes blazing out of an emaciated face and looking fervently towards Heaven. As you can probably guess, he held that faith and belief were about abstinence, penance and mortification of the body. All other aspects of faith, such as love, understanding, tolerance, forgiveness or charity were either a long way further down his list of priorities, or had little or no importance whatsoever. Of course it stood to reason that if a man understood his purpose on this earth and conducted his life accordingly, then he had no need of understanding, tolerance, forgiveness or charity. It was only those who did not understand their purpose in life that had any requirement for any of these. And as for love; Almighty God was the ultimate expression of Divine Love, which was endless and available to all who sought after the true path to Him, and so to have anything which had pretensions to being even vaguely similar to this most glorious love, was both an insult to God as well as being entirely unnecessary. Indeed, anything like this, such as love towards one's fellow man, or worse, indeed unspeakably worse, love towards one's fellow woman, could not only prove to be a distraction to the true believer, but be something that the very Devil might throw in his path to tempt him to stray off the true way and into a life of decadence and debauchery! Man was not put upon this earth by Almighty God to do frivolous things like enjoy himself or plunge himself into sin.

He applied his chosen philosophy to all men, not just those under his guiding hand at the Priory and Monastery of Saints Paul and Augustine, was openly disdainful of all, including the monastery's tenant farmers and trades people, who did anything to bring a bit of colour into their poverty struck lives. How could they expect to achieve any form of enlightenment - of course they could never possibly become one of the hundred and forty four thousand, that went without saying - which might, just might mind you, permit them to enter the outer reaches of the paradise of Heaven that awaits those who have led a pure and abstemious life in seeking after the true path to God? It probably never occurred to him that these peasants had more than enough abstinence and struggle in their lives while just keeping their temporal bodies and souls together, without worrying about their spiritual ones.

The local Duke and his family were a minor exception to Prior Obscurant's black and white view of mankind. After all, it was the generosity of the Duke's fore-bearers that had provided both the land for the priory and monastery, and the finance to build them. That act alone would secure their places in the Celestial Kingdom and so minor indiscretions on this earth such as the Duke's male offspring indulging in the odd drunken rampage through a local village, or siring the odd illegitimate child or two, could be overlooked, as could be the debauched behaviour of the female members of his family with some of the local menfolk. This however was a little harder for Prior Obscurant, as quite simply, women, other than of course the Holy Virgin Mary, the most pure and sacred women to have ever set foot upon this earth, and Saint Bibiana, who had died defending her faith and virginity, did not feature in Prior Obscurant's world other than as whores and she-devils cast down with Satan and his despicable followers to tempt men into sin and away from their quest for truth, enlightenment and attaining the eternal glory of God's Glorious Kingdom. For did The Revelation of St John not clearly state that, 'These (the hundred and forty four thousand) are they which were not defiled with women?'

Now, do not be deceived into thinking that Prior Obscurant was in any way an eccentric, somewhat misinformed kindly old priest, as unfortunately, this was most certainly not the case. He was fanatically serious about both what he believed in and in his role in this life; that of achieving salvation for himself and the others in his care, in the next. Like all Zealots who *know the truth*, he was sour, miserable, intolerant and hard hearted as a man could be. Yes, this bigoted tyrant was in charge at the Priory and Monastery of Saints Paul and Augustine and so it was he who was the man who was in charge of educating and preparing our young Master Callow for his life ahead.

Young Master Callow, though now we should properly refer to him as young novice-brother Callow, was assigned to an older, more experienced brother whose task it was to guide him in his spiritual development, teach him the ways of monastic life and generally be his confidant and guardian. It was novice-brother Callow's misfortune, as it was also the misfortune of all the other novice-monks, to be assigned to the care of a mean spirited, nasty and, as we shall learn later, sadistic little man called Rodiron McBane, the novice-master of the Priory and Monastery of Saints Paul and Augustine.

Novice-master Rodiron McBane was a wizened little specimen with a pronounced chin, sunken cheeks and dark, cold, fierce eyes deeply set in his skull beneath a heavy brow and bushy eyebrows. He had served with Prior Obscurant ever since the Prior had taken up his post and, like a blind disciple, also held that the only way to salvation was through abstinence, penance and mortification of the body; only his interpretation of abstinence was verging on starvation, penance was all-but total humiliation and mortification of the body of course meant mortification of the flesh. Perhaps not unreasonably when seen from his viewpoint, novice-master Rodiron McBane reasoned, though reasoning was not his strongest point, that the novice-monks did not, as yet, have full awareness of what sacrifices and strictures they needed to impose on their lives, and bodies, in order to become worthy vessels of God, attain salvation and join the chosen one hundred and forty four thousand, and so saw it as his duty to 'educate' them is such matters. But more of this an on."

Joe paused, before continuing in a slightly travel guide manner,

"As you all probably know, pieces of the Black Acres Priory and Monastery can still be seen today. The best preserved parts are the original fortified Gatehouse to the monastic complex and the Priory Church of Saints Paul and Augustine, both at the north end of Blackacres village, along with parts of the now upmarket hotel next door to the Church. Also still evident is the square footprint of possibly the cloisters, which is now the village square. Many of the buildings since built around it are in stone, which was no doubt looted from the ruins of the old monastery in the late sixteen, early seventeen hundreds. Indeed, it is the looting of stone that has left the Priory Church looking a little strange architecturally, because of course it was designed as part of the priory monastery complex and not as a stand alone church. After the Dissolution of the Monasteries under Henry VIII, Black Acres fell into disrepair and ruin, and the present day Priory Church was likewise a ruin until rebuilt and repaired at the same time as the rest of the village.

Having been in the hotel I can vouch for the fact that it has a lovely olde worlde dining room and an atmospheric crypt bar with stone barrel vaulting, but as I have never stayed there, I can't tell you about the rest of the building other than to mention that the ruins of the Prior's garden can be seen poking though the grass outside the dining room windows. However, back at the time of our story many of the monastery's tenants would have lived in thatched roofed, wattle and daub huts just outside the monastery walls. These, both the wattle and daub huts and the walls, though with the exception of the Gatehouse, are of course long gone. Whether any of the old peasants' houses were replaced by the current stone built ones is, according to those who purport to know about these things, impossible to say. No doubt some were, but most of the stone houses were probably built at the time the village received a major makeover when mining took off in the area.

And here endeth the local history lesson," said Joe with a smile, "and so now back to young novice-brother Callow."

"He, along with two other new novices, joined the existing three already under the tender guiding hand of novice-master Rodiron McBane, thus bringing the total of novice-monks to six. These novices did not sleep in the main dormitory with the senior monks, as the ever vigilant Prior Obscurant foresaw that young boys in the senior monks dortor, or dormitory, might prove to be a night time temptation towards improper conduct, young boys being just one rung up the ladder from she-devils, and so the novices had a separate, bare stone-walled Spartan cell of a dortor, though cellar might be a better description, directly beneath the senior monks' reredorters, or toilet block, which was located at the end of their (the senior monks) dormitory. Although geographically near their dormitory, the massive stone construction of the building effectively put it about as far away as it was possible to be. And, if the foregoing did not prove to be a sufficient enough obstacle to any impure goings on, the presence of novice-master McBane, who slept in a cot outside but next to the entrance of the novices' dortor, most certainly was!

The novices' effectively subterranean cell wasn't actually below ground, but may as well have been for it was only graced with one small window set high up in its farthest wall and candle light was required if one actually wished to see anything and avoid stubbing one's sandal clad toes on any of the hardwood cots. It might have been argued that as the novices had no reason to be there during the day, why did they need natural light? This cave of a dormitory contained ten cots. Each was furnished with a straw filled mattress, a lumpy pillow and a black rough haired blanket. Unlike the senior monks dormitory, where wooden partitions between the cots afforded some form of privacy, the dormitory of the novices contained no such luxuries. However, as all the novice-monks slept fully clothed so as to be ready for prayer every three hours both day and night, any further privacy was deemed unnecessary and, added to which, the absence of visual obstructions such as partitions, meant that novice-master McBane could keep an eagle eye on those in his care so as to ensure that they did not fall into the last of the temptations that Saint Paul alluded to in his first Epistle to the Corinthians; 'Be not deceived: neither fornicators, nor idolaters, nor adulterers, nor effeminate, nor abusers of themselves, etc., shall inherit the Kingdom of God.'[2] McBane's task was after all, to ensure that the novices *did* inherit the Kingdom of God.

However, novice-master Rodiron McBane not only looked out for and guarded against the weaknesses of the flesh in others, but also in himself and had had a circular brick bath constructed in his cell which was filled with ice cold water into which he occasionally immersed himself so as to 'quench the heat in himself of every vice', as Walter Daniel, the biographer of the novice-master, Aelred at Rievaulx Abbey [3] had so eloquently described such action in his journal as being the purpose for a similar bath used by the aforementioned novice-master at Rievaulx. However, I think we can be fairly certain that the novice-master at Rievaulx did not have, as McBane did, a strange-looking crucifix, which had the disturbing appearance of being part religious symbol and part fertility or possibly Satanic one, secreted in a niche above his cot.

Immediately beyond the entrance to the novice-master's cell and bathroom, a short flight of steps led up to a slype, or corridor, which eventually wound its way to the cloisters and thence an entrance to the priory church, thus obviating the need for a night stairs for the novice-monks, and so to the rest of the monastery. Way before it reached the full light of day and just a short distance beyond the top of the flight of steps, was an

---

[2] 1 Corinthians 6:9
[3] Life of Ailred (or Aelred) by Walter Daniel

opening into a small bare stone built chapel dedicated to St Bibiana, which was for the exclusive use of the novices.

This chapel would have been about five metres wide and about seven long. It was lit in daylight hours by three lancet shaped windows set high up in its far, curved, apse-like wall. Beneath these was a hideously graphic polychrome wooden sculpture of the Crucified Christ, no doubt chosen quite deliberately by Prior Obscurant as he liked to emphasise to those in his care just how much Christ had suffered for mankind and hence how much they, the novice-monks who would use this chapel, would need to suffer if they wished to become one of the blessed one hundred and forty four thousand. This message was reinforced by a blood-soaked crown of thorns which was positioned midway between the sculpture and the windows above it. Directly beneath these two gory artefacts was a small altar, curved at its rear and set flush against the wall. Beneath the altar were two small cupboards, presumably containing religious accoutrements for ceremonies conducted in the chapel. On the top of the altar were set two candles in heavy wrought iron sticks, one at each end. And finally, just in case Prior Obscurant's message still hadn't got home, were four large, square headed, black iron nails arranged in a heap at its centre.

In front of and to the right of this gruesome display was a free-standing polychrome-on-wood statue mounted on a short pillar. One could hazard a guess that it was meant to be of the Virgin Mary; her hands were held meekly in prayer, her gaze averted and thus she looked the very picture of female purity and innocence. However, her all too obviously very thin white and blue robes pulled tightly across and beneath her bust, thus both indicating and emphasising this, and her pronounced fecund belly, rounded hips and thighs, all of which were clearly visible beneath the robes coupled with the all too evident display of female submissiveness, unfortunately did rather suggest that the aforementioned qualities of purity and innocence were possibly not all directed towards God. Just in front of this appallingly kitsch and sacrilegious statue was a tall heavily wrought iron candlestick with a candle positioned so that when lit it would light this tasteless effigy. Opposite her and to the left of the central harrowing image was another free-standing polychrome-on-wood sculpture. This was also mounted on a short pillar and depicted the saint to whom the chapel was dedicated; Saint Bibiana. She also had a candle in a large candlestick, similarly placed so as to light her.

Saint Bibiana? The story ran that under the orders of Apronianus, the Governor of Rome, Bibiana had been tied to a pillar and beaten to death with scourges laden with lead plummets because of her refusal to renounce both her faith and apparently her virginity. No doubt both Prior Obscurant and novice-master Rodiron McBane reasoned that if this dreadful end wasn't mortification of the flesh, then nothing was! Unfortunately she was a woman, but fortunately she was a virgin, which counted in her favour because no doubt there had some misgivings about having a woman as a patron saint to be venerated in this, the novices' chapel. This also appallingly tasteless sculpture showed a well endowed and very curvaceous looking female figure clad in gilded sackcloth - yes, gilded! - with long black flowing hair cascading over white skinned shoulders and in a pose of almost erotic mad ecstasy looking up to heaven whilst clutching a distinctly phallic shaped handle of a blood soaked scourge as if it were the source of her pleasure rather than the instrument of her death.

Indeed, both female figures had a not-so-well-hidden eroticism about them. One would certainly wish to think that neither the Prior or novice-master had noticed the sexuality in the poses when selecting these statues for the chapel, both women had been virgins after all. However, even if these appalling depictions didn't look quite as virginal and demure as they should have done, the ladies themselves were still excellent examples piety. On the other hand, possibly we should not overlook the likelihood that these particular - well, we certainly can't out of respect for the two saintly ladies properly call them likenesses - had been deliberately chosen to test the resolve of the novices, to see if they could keep their minds on their devotions whilst gazing on these portraits of female temptation and wanton abandon. Or, was it that Prior Obscurant knew nothing of these statues, this part of the monastery being the novice-master's terrain, and that it was novice-master Rodiron McBane himself who gained illicit pleasure from looking at them, as it was under his watchful eye that novice-brother Callow and his five fellow novices were required to pray in this chapel and so gaze upon these dreadful artefacts at least once in the morning after rising from their cots and once in the evening before retiring? Whereas the novices may have suffered from either nightmares or 'inappropriate' dreams as a result of praying in this chapel, novice-master Rodiron McBane probably did not have the sensitivity to suffer from nightmares and did have an ice cold bath in his cell in which to 'quench the heat in himself' before retiring.

Thank goodness however, there were other aspects of life at Black Acres Monastery which were altogether simpler to understand and live with, and one of these was working in the monastery's vegetable garden. Each of the young novices was assigned a manual task in the monastic complex so as to free-up time for the more senior monks to devote to their scriptures and tasks of a non-manual nature, and young novice-brother Callow had been assigned to work under a kindly old monk, brother La Roche, who was in charge of the flower and vegetable garden, and the orchard at Black Acres.

Brother La Roche, like novice-master McBane, had served with Prior Obscurant ever since the latter had taken up his calling to be Prior of The Priory and Monastery of Saints Paul and Augustine. However, brother La Roche couldn't have been more different from either the Prior or novice-master. Unlike these two, brother La Roche had no real burning desire to become one of the one hundred and forty four thousand. Oh yes, he wished to go to Heaven if God would be good enough to have him, but, as we shall learn later, his concept of Heaven was not the same as Prior Obscurant's and he held that honest hard work, love, understanding, tolerance, forgiveness and charity was the route to this end, not unpleasant sounding things like self-imposed abstinence and mortification of body. Possibly because of this, he, unlike both Prior Obscurant or novice-master Rodiron McBane, usually had a smile on his round weather-beaten face.

Although not as tall as his Prior, he was about the same height as the novice-master, brother La Roche was certainly physically stronger than both, being a square set, solid man, who in his youth would have been described as being 'as strong as an ox.' However, when young brother Callow joined him in the garden he would probably be best described as being 'as strong as an old ox' for he was well into his seventies. His active life, being both out of doors in the fresh air and the physical work involved in tending the garden, had kept him fit and healthy both in body and soul. So we can imagine him jovially greeting young Callow with a beaming,

"Ah, so you are our new brother Callow. So tell me, do you know anything about gardening and horticulture?"

"A little," might have been the reply of the shy Callow.

"Ah, good, then you will learn quickly. That is why you and I are here brother, to learn, to learn how Almighty God in His wisdom has provided for us. Though in His wisdom He does not simply provide us with our food and sustenance, the simple provision of which would make us lazy, but makes us work for it, so that after the sweat of our labours we appreciate it all the more. Now let me show you round before we start on the business of learning."

And with that and with young brother Callow in tow, we can visualise him setting off round the vegetable garden and its outbuildings at a spirited pace for a seventy-year-old man.

The monastery did not grow all its vegetable requirements and took much of these from its tenant farmers in the form of tithes. What brother La Roche and his team focused on was quality and specialist produce; what these days we would describe as 'high end' produce. This included exotic fruit and vegetables such as various types of apple, pear, peach, damson and quince grown from espalier trees (those with their branches trained along wooden frames in front of sheltered south facing walls), as well as grapes grown on vines which had been trained up and over wooden arches and pergolas that been specially constructed for this purpose in the monastery's joinery workshop. In a large annex to the garden was a physic garden in which were grown the various herbs and flowers that were useful for medicinal purposes. Brother La Roche and his team's responsibility did not actually extend to the making of medicines and potions, that was the metier of a different team of monks, but they were responsible for growing all the necessary ingredients for same.

What would have immediately struck novice-brother Callow was the neat, tidy and ordered layout of everything. Every tree appeared to have its place, every crop type its particular bed, and as brother La Roche would have informed him, young novice-brother Callow's task would be to assist in maintaining this order while he learnt the nature of, the requirements of, and the usefulness of each of the plants he was tending. He was also shown the garden's irrigation system which brought water in at the top of the garden and gradually distributed it via a network of small stone canals and troughs to ponds in all parts of the garden. Brother Callow had never seen anything like this; water cascading over small weirs, being retained and diverted by small gates, and flowing to where it was required in such an ordered and controlled manner, and marvelled at the engineering involved.

"Oh, you will learn about all of this," said brother La Roche, noticing the look of wonder on the young novice's face, "but all in good time. We can't do everything today, or we would have nothing to do tomorrow."

After a quick tour of the garden, brother La Roche then showed young Callow the various buildings in which were stored the variety tools that were used for the multitude of tasks that were required in the garden and very briefly ran through the uses of some of the implements, though he then added,

"The use of each and indeed the design of each will become much clearer when you use them. The form of many of these tools has evolved over years and in some cases centuries. However, that scythe, for example, has probably changed little since our Lord's day."

Poor young novice-brother Callow; his head was swimming with all of this. When he had answered brother La Roche's question about how much he knew about gardening and had answered 'a little' he had never realised that there was so much knowledge required. Each aspect appeared to be an individual discipline in itself. Just knowing about the different trees; how and where to plant them, how to tend them, train them and prune them, what tools to use for each job, what water and fertilizer they required, how to guard them against insects which might cause damage to the tree itself or its fruit, how to protect them against the ravages of storms and winter cold, could take a lifetime. And that was just trees! What of all the fruit bushes, vegetables, not to mention the culinary and medicinal herbs and flowers? Oh goodness, there was so much to learn. Fortunately brother La Roche seemed a kindly and patient man and so although young Callow did feel somewhat daunted by the task in front of him, he also felt that here in the garden he might find some peace and contentment and actually enjoy learning all this new knowledge, whereas he wasn't so sure he could say the same about some of his other studies.

Many of these other studies were undertaken in the cloisters under the supervision of novice-master McBane or even Prior Obscurant himself, and included analysis and interpretation of the scriptures in general, psalms, the epistles of Saint Paul, the teachings of Saint Augustine, with of course particular emphasis on understanding the 'correct interpretation of', for which read, 'Prior Obscurant's interpretation of', The Revelation of St John the Divine. Also included were the laws and rules of the Priory and Monastery of Saints Paul and Augustine, together with ecclesiastic and canon law, and then, if the foregoing was not enough, the understanding of and interpretation of the various papal edicts which arrived from Rome.

Now, it must be remembered of course, that young novice-brother Callow's attendance at the monastery was not as a result of some burning desire on his part to achieve spiritual enlightenment and join God in His Heaven, though he certainly wanted Heaven rather than Hell, but was somewhat more down to earth and practical. Namely, his parents had thought it a good way to secure him both an education and profession whilst at the same time enhancing their family's position in society by have one of their sons in the Church. Becoming one of the 'one hundred and forty four thousand' had never been a factor considered by either young Callow himself or his parents, as none of them had even heard of the 'one hundred and forty four thousand' until young novice-brother Callow had been informed of this by both Prior Obscurant and novice-master Rodiron McBane, and had been left in no doubt by both that this was the ultimate objective of all who served God at the Priory and Monastery of Saints Paul and Augustine.

"If ye are to becometh one of the blessed one hundred and forty four thousand," had boomed Prior Obscurant, who evidently felt that a pseudo-Biblical style of speech added a necessary gravitas to his words of wisdom, "then your lives needeth to be wholly, yea wholly spent in your devotion to God. There can be no middle way!"

A raised right arm with wagging forefinger had emphasised this point to the three new novice monks sitting on a hard wooden bench in front of him, who we can guess, had upon hearing this no doubt wondered what it was they had committed themselves to. It certainly regained the attention of our young novice-brother Callow, who had been momentarily distracted by the shadows cast on the stone floor by the sunlight passing through the cloister arcading. These shadows, like the statues in the chapel, also had an eroticism about them; their profiles wittingly, or unwittingly, suggesting both male and female genitalia, one located above the other.

"Ye must avoideth all temptation. Yea, all temptation, for the Devil will findeth all manner of ways to tricketh ye and tempteth ye into leaving the true, narrow path to Almighty God. And the foremost temptation that the Devil places in the path of man, is woman!"

He stood there with his arm and finger pointing prophetically skywards, his eyes ablaze but saying nothing further so that the full weight of his last proclamation might make its mark on the naive and innocent souls of his three new followers. The general countenance of novice-master Rodiron McBane, who sat ram-rod straight on the same bench as his three new young protégés, was also something to behold. His eyes blazed with the zeal of the blindly converted. Every word confirmed his calling, confirmed his purpose. Indeed, such was his devotion to Prior Obscurant that he would have followed him into Hell itself if so commanded; except of course, they weren't going in that direction, their path was upward, upward to the Divine Celestial Kingdom.

Then, after a theatrical pause, Prior Obscurant continued more quietly and explained,

"For as St Paul stated in his epistle to the Galatians, chapter 5, verse 17, 'For the flesh lusteth against the Spirit, and the Spirit against the flesh: and these are contrary the one to the other: so that ye cannot do the things that ye would.' So my young brothers, mark ye well therefore the words of our Patron Saint Paul and avoideth all temptations of the flesh."

Although Callow was listening, and listening pretty intently, he found his eyes drifting back to the shadow patterns on the stone cloister floor, which so strangely, yet so aptly illustrated the 'temptations of the flesh'.

However, Prior Obscurant couldn't keep the passion out of his voice, or his arm with its wagging forefinger by his side for long and as his voice rose in volume so his arm and finger rose towards God's heaven.

"Heedeth that which is written, for 'the wrath of God cometh on the children of disobedience."[4] And then, no doubt to emphasise this, he continued with, "Mark well the teaching that 'he that overcometh, and keepeth my works unto the end, to him I will give power over the nations: and he shall rule them with a rod of iron.'[5]"

Was this Prior Obscurant's way of letting it be known that he had given 'power over the nations' to McBane to rule the lives of the young novices?

"And you my young brothers, need to not only learn the lessons of our faith, but also learn the disciplines of it and learn to cleanse yourselves, yea cleanse yourselves as St Paul hath written, of 'inordinate affection and evil concupiscence."[6] and with a nod in novice-master McBane's direction, added, "Heed well your novice-master, for he knoweth the sacrifices to be made, he knoweth the hard route to be trod, and his firm hand will guideth you.

Amen."

---

[4] Colossians 3:6
[5] Revelation 2:26
[6] Colossians 3:5

Had this happened today, we might reasonably guess that the three novices might have looked at each other wondering if the fellow lecturing them was somewhat 'off his trolley'. However, we must remember this happened several hundred years ago when attitudes and beliefs were very different. So instead of speculating on the sanity of Prior Obscurant, they were more than likely in awe of and very possibly frightened by his words; he was talking about the fate of their immortal souls after all.

Chapter 2

As we have already learned, life in the monastery was not all about Prior Obscurant, or novice-master McBane putting the fear of God into the ignorant and susceptible young novices. By way of illustrating this, our tale goes on to tell how on the next market day brother La Roche took novice-brother Callow with him to man the monastery's vegetable and culinary herb stall.

The market was located in a large area directly outside the monastery's northern gate. This market square, though it was in fact more of a market trapezium, was clearly indicated as being such by the presence of a splendid market cross at its centre. The right to hold a market at this location had been granted by the Bishop, but the cross had been erected at great expense by the Duke, no doubt part in penance and one suspects also in despair, after a particularly rowdy, raucous and debauched night on the part of his various offspring. Because this charitable act was also an act of penance, he necessarily had had to involve both the Bishop and Prior Obscurant personally in the selection of the somewhat ornate design, the specification of the precise location for it and of course, most importantly, the blessing of it when all the sculptural and construction work was complete. However, all of that had happened before young Callow had joined the monastery as a novice-brother.

The various monastery stalls were given what were deemed to be the best sites, namely those with their backs to the monastery's walls and facing the new market cross. This meant that these stalls were generally more sheltered from the wind than most, except when the wind blew from the north in the middle of winter. They were also more sheltered from the sun, which was good for keeping the vegetables fresh, but not so good for the brothers who were manning the stalls, though no doubt both Prior Obscurant and novice-master Rodiron McBane thoroughly approved of this location both because of the mortification of the flesh it provided (it was cold for the monks) and thus it reduced the temptations of the flesh which the pretty young women who wished to visit the stalls to make purchases inevitably presented, as they (the pretty young women) were not tempted to tarry any more than was absolutely necessary whilst they made their purchases.

Young novice-brother Callow found that he enjoyed these market days, even if his sandal-clad feet did suffer with the cold. We have already noted that he was a shy youth and so talking with young women did not come easily to him. However, armed with his new knowledge about the produce he was selling and his being behind the stall and so physically and metaphorically protected by it, he was able to find a confidence that he had not previously possessed and discovered that it was pleasant to hear the soft voices and tinkling laughter of the young women, to see their radiant smiles, to observe their long silky hair and the way they shook it to show it off to best advantage, to see their large doe-like eyes and how they fluttered their eyelashes. And of course it was nice to see their beautiful faces, soft smooth curves of their necks, their small delicate hands, to infer the smooth rounded shapes of their bodies concealed beneath their brightly coloured dresses and so to generally take pleasure from their femininity. Oh dear, the sap was starting to rise in young brother Callow!

However, when he returned to the monastery and the strict regime of novice-master Rodiron McBane he found himself confused. What exactly was he supposed to think of women? Was their presence upon this earth solely to tempt men into sin and fornication and so deprive them of the glories of God's kingdom and His blessing? But if this was so, why were the Virgin Mary and Saint Bibiana venerated by the monastery? Though when he thought about the two depictions of these women in the novices' chapel it was obvious that there was unfortunately more than just their felicity in their faith on display, as it appeared that even these two saintly women were portrayed as having an undoubted carnality about them. So were all women she-devils sent by Satan to tempt men away from the true path to God as Prior Obscurant had told them in his recent lecture? Even female saints?

This did not make any sense. How could women be she-devils on the one hand and be venerated as saints on the other? And what about all the ordinary women in the middle; all the sisters and mothers? What about his own sister and his own mother? They couldn't all be she-devils, surely? Yes, it had been very nice looking at and talking with the young women at the market, but ..... or was that Prior Obscurant's point, that temptation was 'something being nice'? Wasn't that how the Devil worked, to put something pleasant in your path so that you are distracted from achieving your goal? So are women a distraction to achieving divine enlightenment as Saint Paul had noted, 'so that ye cannot do the things that ye would.'[7]? Are they sent to tempt men off the straight and narrow path to Celestial Glory? And then, in the same way that Callow had suddenly realised that he knew nothing about gardening, he now realised that he knew nothing about women either.

Who could he turn to for advice? For obvious reasons we can presume that novice-master Rodiron McBane was probably not the first person on his list. How about the more reasonable brother La Roche? He found it easy to be with brother La Roche and to talk with him, though most of their conversations had been, it has to be said, directly related to the tree, bush, vegetable that they had been tending at the time. However, there was no doubting that it would be easier to chat with him about such a matter than the severe novice-master, who we could be sure would not understand his dilemma.

"No, my young brother, it is not easy is it?" replied the older monk after Callow had explained his problem to him whilst transplanting seedlings in one of the garden's warming sheds.

---

[7] Galatians 5:17

"When I was young like you, I was, how shall I say, like our Patron Saint Augustine and enjoyed the delights of women. You see, I only came to the priesthood late, after the girl I married was taken from me."

He paused and looked vacantly into the middle distance as the memories of those days, far off in time but still all too recent in his memory, came back to him. Young novice-brother Callow stood awkwardly and silently, probably wishing that he hadn't raised this subject of relationships and in so doing had embarrassed his senior colleague. But brother La Roche wasn't at all embarrassed, even if their conversation brought back some painful memories, and philosophically continued,

"And I realised that such was my love for her that no other woman could replace her, and that if I was not permitted to have her then perhaps God had other plans for me. It is strange my young brother, how your life can suddenly take a turn and you realise how your previous path was shallow, hedonistic even, and mine had been. I had tasted the delights of many women, been like a bee flitting from flower to flower until one day I found the most perfect flower and after meeting her I wanted to taste no other."

Callow looked at him almost in awe. He'd never heard anyone talk like this before. The simple candour of his speech appeared to young Callow to elevate the evident love La Roche had felt, indeed after all this time he still seemed to feel, for this girl of his; his 'perfect flower'. So love between a man and a woman was possible. Women weren't all she-devils; but of course, how could they be? He knew his (Callow's) own mother couldn't possibly be a she-devil, nor his sister. Yes, he had known this, but somehow brother La Roche's words had lifted a weight from him, and to hear this from a fellow brother, and such a senior and long lived one such as brother La Roche, was also reassuring.

"And before you ask, I have wondered if my flower being

taken from me in that untimely manner was a punishment for my dissolute life, but I don't think so. I don't think God is vengeful and cruel ...." He shot a glance at Callow as if to say, but without actually saying it, 'like some in this monastery!' "…. but kind, loving and understanding, and so helps to turn a tragedy in your life into something that does have a meaning after all, that perhaps sets you on your true journey, via a different path. As Christ was resurrected, so God helps us also to be resurrected and put our pasts behind us and start out again anew."

"I'm sorry," said Callow quietly, "I didn't know."

"Don't worry, my young brother. All this happened along time ago, when I was about ….. no, a little bit older than you. But I haven't answered your question have I? And, I am not sure that I can. You see, I had experienced life, tasted life if you like, before choosing this current one and I am content with my choice. However, you are still young and have not experienced life yet and this is why you have your dilemma. You don't know what it is that you are giving up, what it is that you are sacrificing and of course you want to know about it, want to taste it perhaps?"

Young Callow found himself colouring at this last remark of brother La Roche's, because of course he was curious and yes, he did want to taste it even though he knew it was being deemed wrong for him to do so. Brother La Roche was also right to observe that his answer did not satisfy that conflict between the burgeoning man in young brother Callow and the strictures of the monastic life in which he now found himself. So, although young Callow had no desire to seek advice from his novice-master - 'Heed well your novice-master, for he knoweth the sacrifices to be made, he knoweth the hard route to be trod, and his firm hand will guideth you' - this is what he ended up doing.

After he had explained the conflict within himself, Rodiron McBane answered him, though not in anything like the same gentle, understanding tones of brother La Roche.

"Ye are not the first to have such a conflict within yer soul brother Callow, for as St Paul noted in his Epistle to the Galatians, commencing Chapter 5, verse 19," he replied in his broad Scottish accent, adding the chapter and verse for Callow's benefit, "'Now the works of the flesh are manifest, which are these; adultery, fornication, uncleanness, lasciviousness,'" Each sin-laden word was stressed vehemently, before he concluded with a selectively shortened, "'they which do such things shall not inherit the kingdom of God.' So you must purge these thoughts from yer mind young novice-brother Callow. Mortify yer body and drive these unclean thoughts from it!"

And to this end, Novice Master Rodiron McBane prescribed cold baths both morning and night for a week, and additional duties, 'so as too humble him, so that he might see his path to God more clearly'; namely, scrubbing the reredorters (or toilets), every morning before lauds. Whether this was actually prescribed in the monastery's Penitentials is not clear, the cold baths might well have been, but the scrubbing of the reredorters sounds like a novice-master Rodiron McBane addition.

"And now we must pray novice-brother Callow. Pray to St Bibiana to give us the strength to resist the temptations of the flesh. Let us kneel and pray, brother."

And novice-brother Callow knelt and looked up at the curvaceous image of femininity and tried desperately to purge all unclean thoughts from his mind and pray. But the image of the kitsch depiction of St Bibiana with her dark hair tumbling over her smooth naked shoulder and down to her nearly naked and even smoother looking breast, fixed itself in his mind and so whereas the 'appropriate words' were spoken the 'unclean thoughts' were not purged. Indeed, if anything they were nourished - so was this how a real woman might look and could be at the height of ecstasy?

However, at the end of the following week young novice-brother Callow was most certainly not thinking about women at the height of ecstasy. Indeed, he was not thinking about women at all, as he was absolutely exhausted. He walked around in a daze, stumbling on stairs, bumping into door jams, unable to concentrate on anything and barely able to keep his eyes open. He'd hardly slept all week. The usual prayers every three hours, the morning and evening cold baths and the additional task of scrubbing the reredorters had just about purged his puny body of all thoughts other than those of sleep and warmth. Novice-master Rodiron McBane knew only too well how to mortify flesh and 'educate' his novices!

It probably goes without saying that the word 'respite' did not exist in novice-master McBane's vocabulary and so as soon as novice-brother Callow's week of penance was over McBane ensured that Callow was up at the crack of dawn with his fellow novices to pray to the voluptuous St Bibiana in the small novice's chapel before attending lauds and matins in the priory church. The more sympathetic brother La Roche obviously realised what his young protégé was going through and gave him less strenuous tasks to perform in the garden, did not reprimand him when he found him slumped and asleep in a quiet corner, and realised that in such a state of physical exhaustion, young novice-brother Callow would not be in any fit state to man the vegetable and herb stall at the market that week. So he suggested that Callow perhaps might do some reading on the subject of horticulture, though realised and half expected that he, being as tired as he was, would probably take none of it in and indeed rather hoped that young Callow would nod-off in the peaceful surroundings of the monastery's library and so get some very necessary extra sleep.

So in spite of novice-master Rodiron McBane's best efforts to the contrary, young brother Callow did recover from his fatigue, regained energy and unfortunately for him, also regained the dilemma that had got him into all this trouble in the first place. The depicted rounded hips of the fleshy St Bibiana statuette and the sexually submissive, coyly innocent and demure expression on the face of the tastelessly sacrilegious depiction of the Virgin Mary in the small chapel in which he and his fellow novices had to pray each day, were enough to make any young man's mind turn to 'impure thoughts' and raise the temperature of his blood. So young novice-brother Callow continued to wrestle with thoughts of desire and tried, really tried, to quench these with dry extracts from Decretum Gratiani and the Decretals of Gregory IX, with varying degrees of success. Perhaps needless to say, he confessed nothing further to his novice-master and tried everything he could think of to fight such thoughts and keep them out of his head.

When the next market day came round the kindly brother La Roche was unfortunately feeling his age and 'a bit under the weather', as he put it, and so asked young brother Callow if he would mind looking after the stall on his own.

"But," protested Callow, not being at all sure if he would be able to; and no, temptation in the form of pretty young women had not crossed his mind; not at that stage. At that stage he was solely concerned with the heavy responsibility of being in overall charge of the stall. Would he be able to recognise all the vegetables and herbs and know the price of each, be able to operate the scales and weights correctly? Whereas he thought he knew the various vegetables, he wasn't so sure about all the herbs, and the weighing of same was not as easy as he would have liked. The scales were not a simple balance type, but an asymmetric type; those with a hook on one short arm and a sliding weight on the long one on the opposite side of an off-centre fulcrum. Although he had been taught how to use such a balance and thought he understood how it worked, he realised that he didn't really understand the science behind it - that a large load acting over a short distance could have the same force as a small weight acting over a larger one, and hence that a small weight could be used to balance and thus weigh a much larger load. So he was not at all sure that he would be able to both measure the correct weight in the first place and then subsequently calculate the correct price for each purchase, especially when he knew he would have to do these calculations quickly and in his head. "I'm not sure I can," he added, finding himself becoming increasingly terrified at the prospect of having to do all this on his own.

"Don't under-estimate yourself my young brother," said brother La Roche. "I have every confidence in you. You'll manage just fine."

Apparently, one of the other novices, a young man by the name of Venn, Michael Venn, who slept in the adjacent cot to Callow in their subterranean domitory, would help him set up the stall. This it seemed had already been arranged between brother La Roche and a brother Swan. Brother Swan was responsible for the production of the monastery's potions and medicines and just as Callow had been assigned to assist brother La Roche, so novice-brother Venn had been assigned to assist brother Swan. Of course it was understood that once novice-brother Venn had helped Callow to erect his vegetable stall, Callow would be on his own, because novice-brother Venn's presence would be required on the potions stall.

Michael Venn was of a somewhat indeterminate age. He was obviously older than Callow, but could have been anywhere between mid-twenties and a young looking mid-forties, so trying to pin an age on him wasn't easy. He was a little taller than Callow and thinner, yes, it was possible to be thinner than Callow, but was nowhere near as awkward and gangley. Michael Venn was also definitely tougher, both physically and mentally. Indeed, as we shall learn, he was certainly a very interesting young man, seemingly being both unusually worldly wise for his age, though that of course rather depended on what age you attributed to him, and appeared blessed with the inner peace of one who is sure of his knowledge, indeed of himself.

Although having traits of the prophet about him, do not confuse him with the likes of Prior Obscurant, because he did not have the blazing eyes of the zealot even if he did have a rather disconcertingly steady gaze which gave a certain gravitas to whatever he was opining on at the time. He was quiet and thoughtful, though was also quite capable of giving of his opinion forcefully, as we will discover later. As regards his background and why he had chosen to join the monastery as a novice-brother, we know nothing. As said, we shall learn a little more of Michael Venn later on.

The story didn't go into any real detail about the sights, sounds and smells of a medieval market. So as regards the sights, we can only hazard a guess that a market probably looked remarkably similar to a present day one. Of course there would have been no tubular metal frames, plastic temporary roofs or collapsable tables made of hardboard and aluminium. All frames would have been made of wood, the roofing material would probably have been canvas and the tables were no doubt for the major part, timber planks set on trestles. However, given that man's ingenuity was probably alive and well in those days, we can reasonably speculate that some stalls were quite ingeniously designed.

Indeed, young Callow's herb and vegetable stall was one such, being like a long box on wheels with Rickshaw type handles with a bar between them, which extended from both ends of the box. These allowed it to be pulled and pushed to wherever it was required. When in position, two flat sections could be opened out to rest on these handles, thus extending the working surface of the 'box'. Poles, which had been hooked onto its sides, could be removed and placed in holes at the four corners of the trolley and then connected to each other by additional poles over which could be placed a canvas tent-like roof. The produce for sale was stored in trays on shelves inside the box part of this trolley. When the trolley was in position, these trays were pulled out and displayed on the upper surface.

Perhaps needless to say, the whole thing was rather heavy and required two men to move it, which is why it was fitted with the aforementioned two sets of handles. Two pairs of hands were also required to put the poles and canvas covering in position, which explains why fellow novice-brother Michael Venn had been co-opted to assist.

We can also guess that a market of those days would have been a pretty noisy affair, with people haggling and bargaining with stallholders, not to mention catching up on the latest news and gossip with each other, and with criers advertising their produce and wares along with prices for same rising above the general hubbub. And the hubbub would not have consisted of only human voices, as there would also have been the clucking of chickens, honking of geese, bleating of sheep and squealing of pigs all of which were also for sale. Yes, it probably would have been quite a bit noisier than a modern market.

It would also have been a lot smellier as well, and the smell, or smells would have become steadily worse as the day wore on, especially in summer under a hot summer sun, because we would not only be talking about, shall we euphemistically call them 'farmyard smells', but also about butchering smells; the smells that emanate from blood and offal. The poulterers and butchers stalls were situated on the west side of the market where an open drain carried the worst of the waste away from the market area and down to the river. Unfortunately the prevailing wind was from the west and so market goers and stall holders usually had to endure the smells of both the farmyard and the slaughter. Of course it would have made more sense to have had these stalls and the drain on the eastern side of the market, but the priory church already occupied that site so this was not possible.

Although young Callow's mind had been preoccupied with his stall-holding responsibilities and he hadn't given a thought to young women, when at last he did see them walking about the market looking at the various stalls, chatting and laughing amongst themselves, it was too late. Too late to go back and hide in the monastery which is what he desperately wished to do as he saw a couple of delightful young women so obviously heading in the direction of his stall. Oh no! If only he could be somewhere else, somewhere where he did not have to fight this cocktail of desire on the one hand and straight forward nerves on the other. It would have been easier if brother La Roche was with him, he (brother La Roche) could have served them. Whereas as it was, he was going to have to do that. Yes, he, novice-brother Callow, was going to have to talk to them. He was going to have to make direct eye contact with them, see their sparkling eyes with fluttering eyelashes, watch their soft lips move, observe the gentle curve of their necks and shoulders. Oh why couldn't the ground just swallow him up?

Both young women wore long flowing light brown skirts which were gathered tightly about their slim waists, and loose fitting white blouses gathered at the upper arms and across their busts, but leaving a considerable amount of soft smooth skin bare and visible to the eye, and particularly to the eye of young novice-brother Callow! Over the loose blouses each wore a colourful tight fitting laced bodice; a dark almost bottle green colour for the young lady with slightly ginger coloured curly hair and sky blue for the damsel with long straight blond hair. These bodices had the effect, well, for young novice-brother Callow the 'disturbing' effect, of accentuating the slenderness of their wearers' waists and emphasising the roundedness of both their hips and bosoms. And it was the soft, smooth, naked flesh which was visible, coupled with the promise of that which was not, which simultaneously had our young novice-brother's heart racing and nerves jangling. Yes, even after his week of penance at the hands of novice-master Rodiron McBane he found it impossible to simply ignore the curvaceous charms of these two delightful young women. Why hadn't he stayed in the monastery and stayed away from all this? Away from this temptation; this wonderful, beautiful temptation! Oh why did brother La Roche have to be ill today? But as much as his eyes were drawn to their lovely female forms, their pretty smiling faces and flowing hair, Callow did manage to maintain a business-like manner, did manage to concentrate on weighing their chosen produce correctly, did manage the necessary calculations in his head, did charge them the correct sum and did give them the correct change from the leather purse which hung at his waist. Yes, he'd managed! He felt both surprised and pleased with himself. Surprised and pleased that he'd been able to maintain his self-control and to keep things business-like, had been friendly, but not excessively, and had not been distracted; well, not unduly distracted. Yes, all would be well.

And indeed all was well; well that is until a raven haired beauty showed up. Like the aforementioned two young women, this young lady was also dressed in a long flowing skirt, though hers was yellow orange in colour. This was topped by a loose fitting white blouse and tight fitting bright yellow bodice. Like them, the narrowness of her waist and the roundedness of her hips were also shown to the full and her breasts were pushed up by the tight fitting bodice. However her blouse was a little more open at the neck than the other young women's had been, so that one of her shoulders was almost bare and the upper rounded curves of her breasts were, as young Callow noticed only too well, a lot more visible. Tumbling black hair framed her pale face and cascaded on to ivory coloured, smooth skinned shoulders and down her back. Her lips were pale pink and slightly pursed, and so resulted in a small dark diamond being formed at the centre of her mouth where her lips didn't quite touch, giving her an almost hypnotically attractive enigmatic smile. She had a straight nose, high cheekbones and dark, doe-like brown eyes with long lashes.

"Hello. I don't think I've seen you before, have I?" she said in a soft, slow and slightly husky voice, her smouldering eyes focusing directly on the hungry eyes of young Callow.

"Er, no," mumbled the tongue-tied young man, trying desperately to avert his gaze but unable to take his eyes off her.

She was stunningly beautiful, but as Callow also noticed, strangely familiar. He hadn't met her before, had he? Was she a friend of his sister's? No she couldn't be as he would certainly have noticed her before and would have remembered. This was most strange, as he was sure he knew her, but from where?

"You weren't here last week," the raven haired beauty continued, and placed a small rounded delicate hand intimately on the rough wood of the upper surface of novice-brother Callow's stall before turning her body so as to present her almost bare shoulder and curvaceous profile to his nervous, yet feasting eyes. Then she turned just her head towards him - and did she push out her bust? - smiled, fluttered her eyelashes and said, "I hope I will see you next week."

And with that she turned her head and walked slowly away from him trailing a finger idly along the length of the stall confident of her femininity and the effect that it would have on him. Young Callow stood there seemingly unable to move as he watched her departing form; bouncing, shining, black hair flowing down over white shoulders and blouse, golden yellow bodice, trim waist and rounded hips clad in a flowing yellow orange skirt, casually stroll off into the throng of the market. The coarse sounds of the market became a gentle buzz of white noise in his ears as her soft, 'I hope I will see you next week.' replayed in his head. 'Oh yes, I hope so as well.'

But what was he thinking? The dreadful cold baths, the humiliating early morning scrubbing of the reredorters, the continual lack of sleep and appalling tiredness he had endured, all suddenly came flooding back to him. No! No, he couldn't go through that again. He must put this vision of female beauty out of his mind and not be distracted from his spiritual objective. But how could he ignore his desire for this angel - and oh goodness yes, yes he desired her! - a beautiful raven haired angel that he could have sworn he knew already?

But what was it about her that made him feel as if he had

known her all his life, made him feel that it was almost destiny that their paths should cross? 'I hope I will see you next week.' Or ….. or wasn't she an angel? Was she instead, a she-devil; a she-devil sent to tempt him, to tempt him away from the true path? Was that why she had arrived at his stall, to test him, to test his commitment to his calling? But why did she appear so familiar to him? Or was that how the Devil works, to make what is temptation seem to be anything but, to make the victim feel secure and safe so they don't realise what is happening until it is too late and their soul is undone? So which was this beauty, an angel or a she-devil? And even if she was an angel, should he embrace her. No, no not physically of course! Or should he shun her? How should he handle this? No, what was he thinking? No, not handle the young lady either; though that is exactly what he wanted to do! No, what he meant was …. er, handle the situation. Poor Callow's thoughts were all over the place and all the wrong words were tumbling round in his head. Stop! Stop. Think. Just what should he do? Oh goodness, he must be careful.

Although his mind continued to wrestle with the problems and contradictions that this meeting with the beautiful raven haired girl in a golden yellow bodice had thrown up for him, he nonetheless did manage to continue to serve other customers who came to his stall without making any mistakes, though there were a couple of occasions when he almost had to tell himself out loud to focus on what he was doing and ignore the torment in his head. And then thank goodness, at last, the market came to a close. No bell was rung. No crier announced the final minute, but all seemed to know when it was and within a surprisingly short space of time a bustling, noisy market place thronging with people rapidly changed to a deserted area of cobbles strewn with rubbish and somewhat bedraggled looking stalls. It could not have come soon enough for young novice-brother Callow. At last his ordeal was over. He stacked the crates with unsold produce into his trolley, and with the help of novice-brother Venn dismantled the stall, placed the poles onto the hooks at the side of the trolley, positioned the role of roof canvas on top and then between them they pulled and pushed the heavy contraption across the cobbles and in through the monastery gate, back into the monastery's safe environment where temptation did not lie in every pretty face that passed in front of him.

For the rest of his day young Callow was kept busy. Firstly, totalling up the day's takings and taking these to the Treasury; secondly, taking all unsold produce to the kitchen; thirdly, unloading the trolley and tidying it away ready for the next week, and then it was time for prayers. While his mind was occupied he was fine, but when he had those idle moments, walking back after having completed a task and before he was focused on the next, or while he was waiting, then he couldn't help himself from recalling the shape of her nose, her pale pink lips with their enigmatic smile, her silky black hair, or the plunge of her blouse and ….

And why did he think he knew her? What was it? If only he could pin that down. It worried him that she appeared so familiar to him, yet he was unable to say from where. For some illogical reason he felt that if only he could answer this, perhaps his desire for her would abate? If she was a friend of his sister then that would be alright. He could talk to her as a friend. That would be fine. No, there would be nothing untoward in that. Indeed, it would be rude not to talk to her in a friendly manner. So …. so, was she a friend of his sister's?"

Chapter 3

"It wasn't until later that same evening," said Joe, "that I was able to continue with young Callow's story and, as you have probably guessed, he met up again with the beautiful raven haired girl on the next market day.

"Hello again," she said in what we can imagine was a sexy, sultry tone. "Have you missed me?"

"Er, yes," might have mumbled a shy and nervous Callow without thinking about what he was saying or how it would be interpreted.

"You do like me, don't you?" she added, placing her small, rounded hand on the rude wood timber of the stall table, and then, after leaning forward towards him and making a pretence of picking up an apple whilst knowing full well that her loosely tied blouse would fall open and so present her pale skinned rounded breasts to Callow's hungry gaze, added,

"You do like what you see, don't you?"

And oh yes, Callow certainly did like what he saw! Oh goodness, yes!

"What is your name?" she asked smiling at him and tilting her head to one side.

"Er, Callow. Novice ..... novice-brother Callow," he stammered.

"No silly. Your Christian name."

"Um, Adam."

"That's funny," she said.

"Funny?" he replied a bit taken aback with her response.

"Yes, because my name is Eve. We were obviously meant for each other; Adam and Eve," she remarked with a sweet smile, whilst gently swinging the apple to and fro by its stalk and turning her head so that her shining black hair rippled over her smooth white shoulder. Eve with the apple in her hand. Though whether Adam Callow actually made any connection with his namesake's temptation in The Garden seems unlikely, because when she asked, "Will you walk with me Adam, when the market is finished?" it was simple nerves on his part which prompted his, "Er. No. No, I can't."

Everything was moving far too quickly for comfort for our young Callow, because of course he could walk with her; there was nothing stopping him. The monastery was not a prison and he was free to come and go. Yes, part of him wanted to walk with this pretty girl, to walk with Eve, but .... but he didn't feel in control. He felt as if his choices were being made for him, rather than he making them and .... and he couldn't put his finger on it, but .... but something .... something didn't feel quite right. Perhaps it was the picture of Eve standing in front of him with an apple in her hand that was subconsciously troubling him? Or was there something else?

"Alright," she said taking her hand off the wooden table and turning as if to leave, though still holding his gaze with her beautiful and bewitching dark eyes. "Suit yourself. If you don't want to."

But Callow did want to! But then again, he didn't. Oh, what did he want? Should he, or shouldn't he? He didn't know, except that he didn't want to decide right there and then. He needed to get this sorted out. To know what .... but he had no idea what it was he wanted to know.

"Your name is Eve?" he asked quickly and nervously in an attempt to cover up his confusion and cowardly refusal of her offer.

"Yes. Eve Lilith," she replied, seemingly not put out by his stupid question. "I hope I will see you next week Adam Callow."

And with that she slowly and gently replaced the apple, turned and flouncing her hair, walked off into the throng of the market without a backward glance.

As he had done on the previous occasion, Callow just stood there, a numb tangled knot of conflicting nervous emotions and desires, unable to move. The sounds of the stallholders shouting their wares, the conversations of the market-goers and general bustle of all that was around him faded into an unobtrusive white noise as his eyes followed her; a raven haired, pale skinned beautiful angel, until he lost her in the crowd.

"How much are the potatoes, brother?"

"Uh! Sorry!"

"How much are the potatoes, brother?"

And the spell was broken and young Adam Callow was back to the reality of what was actually going on around him. However, snippets of conversation came back to him, as he weighed out the potatoes. 'No silly! Your Christian name.' Oh why did he answer, 'Novice-brother Callow'? What a fool. 'Have you missed me?' 'You do like me, don't you?' 'You do like what you see, don't you.' Of course he did! But why couldn't he admit to it? What was holding him back? Had …. had she been trying to tempt him? Her Eve offering his Adam the apple? Yes, he recalled that she had been literally offering an apple; swinging it to and fro in a …. was it rather blatant fashion? Had she been brazenly offering him the forbidden fruit; and if he ate of it, would he, like his namesake, be undone, be barred from God's Paradise? What exactly had been going on during those minutes he'd spent with her? He felt uneasy, felt as if he had failed to grasp something which everyone else would have understood, only he had missed.

And …. and there was something else. Now he knew her name, it wasn't just her appearance that was disconcertingly familiar; so too was her name, Eve Lilith. For her to have the name Eve when he had been christened Adam, seemed a strange coincidence, almost too much so to be true, and he knew the name Lilith from somewhere, but from where and in connection with what, he couldn't remember. This feeling that he knew her, but was unable to pin down exactly how, confused and troubled him. Who was she; an angel, or .... or a she-devil; a she-devil sent to tempt him, to lure him off the straight and narrow road? Oh God, what should he do? His desire for her coursed through his veins; her smiling beautiful face, her tumbling shiny black hair, her curvaceous form and her soft white skinned flesh. Oh how he wanted her, but oh how he also feared that desire! Where would it lead him? Where might she take him; down which hidden paths? Indeed, down which forbidden paths! And so would his soul be damned if he chose to go with her? For hadn't Prior Obscurant so clearly pointed out to him and his fellow novices that 'no man could learn that song but the hundred and forty four thousand which were redeemed from the earth. These are they which were not defiled with women?' He must take care not to become defiled.

Callow's head was churning and unfortunately for him wouldn't stop churning. Later on, even in the middle of one of the evening's chants, his mind was so distracted that he completely lost the tune of the chant and had to make a conscious effort to refocus and rejoin his fellow brothers in their devotions, and then, as a result of this lapse of concentration, he gained the additional worry of whether the eagle-eyed novice-master had noticed and this added itself to the turmoil in his head. Oh goodness, how could he stop this; stop this conflict between desire for a beautiful woman and the almost certain knowledge that if he gave in to it she would lead him off the straight and narrow path to God's heavenly paradise?

Even when he lay in his cot, he still couldn't get the image of the young woman out of his head. An angel! The most beautiful and desirable woman he had ever seen. Her lovely pale skinned face framed with black silken hair. Oh to run his fingers through it, to smell it. Her dark brown, sparkling eyes, her full pink lips; warm and wet and made to be kissed! Her soft pale, smooth skinned shoulder, the low set blouse and the mounds of her breasts .... No! Stop thinking about her. She is a she-devil sent to tempt you! Can't you see, you fool? A temptress sent by the devil himself, who has taken on the guise of a friend of your sister's so that she can work her evil ways with you, lure you off the straight true path so that .... what was it that St Paul had said? .... 'ye cannot do the things that ye would." He lay there in the dark wondering what exactly were 'the things that he would?' But all he could think about was her warm smooth skin, shapely body, soft breasts, rounded hips and bottom, and .... oh yes, he knew 'the things that he would.' Such delights! Such pure delights that only she, a woman could offer. He could almost smell her hair, feel her soft, silky skin as he slid his hand down beneath his habit .... and .... and then all was shattered with,

"Novice-brother Callow, I think you had better come with me."

Novice-master Rodiron McBane, with a candle in one hand, was standing right above him. Such had been young Callow's distraction that he had not noticed the approach of McBane. What noise had he made to attract the novice-master's attention? And if McBane had noticed, what of his fellow novice-brothers? Although it was dark, he could 'see' them, wide awake, lying still in their cots, looking in his direction and listening to every word. Oh the shame! If only he could curl up into a ball and die! He'd thought that he'd wanted the earth to swallow him up back at the market, but that was nothing compared to this. Now he really wanted it; wanted to be anywhere other than where he was with McBane towering over him.

"Come with me brother Callow," repeated the novice-master in an ominously flat tone.

Fortunately for Callow, he was dressed in his habit and so was not humiliated further by having to rise naked in the blinding light of the novice-master's candle. And then the two of them left the novices' dormitory and walked along the slype to the small chapel.

"It would seem brother Callow," continued the novice-master in the same flat tone, "that you are having difficulty adhering to the advise of our patron saint. Do you nay recall his advice, brother Callow? That which he gave in his first Epistle to the Corinthians, Chapter 6, verse 9," which he then, while placing stress and contempt in equal measure on the appropriate words, paraphrased to, "'Be not deceived: neither effeminate, nor abusers of themselves, shall inherit the Kingdom of God?' Kneel brother Callow! Kneel here in front of Saint Bibiana and pray," he continued, his voice starting to rise as the zeal of his mission - to bring wayward young novices like young novice-brother Callow back into the fold, back on to the true straight and narrow path to God's Celestial Kingdom - caught hold of him.

"Pray for forgiveness, brother Callow. Pray for forgiveness of your shameful sin."

'Nor abusers of themselves, shall inherit the Kingdom of God,' screamed in Callow's head as he knelt on the cold step in front of the tasteless statuette. How had his life brought him to this; being dragged from his bed in the middle of the night and humiliated in front of his fellows, being forced to kneel in front of a tasteless statue and ….? Oh goodness. What had he done that his life should have arrived at this point?

"Pray to her," continued McBane, "she who died rather than give up her virginity. Pray that she may intercede on your behalf. Pray that you will see the error of your sinful ways. Pray that the demon in you will be cast out and that by God's boundless grace your soul will be purified and you will regain the true path to Him."

Lit only by McBane's solitary candle, the chapel had taken on a claustrophobic and frightening look, its flickering light casting giant, dancing, grotesque shadows of the sculptures onto the bare stone walls. Almost in despair Callow looked up at the portrait of the near orgasmic, voluptuous woman on her pedestal, her hand clutching the phallic shaped handle of the scourge and .... and as well as wondering what fate now awaited him on this occasion, also possibly wondered how had such an appalling depiction of a saint ended up in a chapel of a monastery? Yes, it was appalling, but actually was it so inappropriate when one knew that Saint Bibiana's patronage is also given to the mentally ill and insane?

His initial crusading message over, novice-master McBane then knelt down beside young Callow and continued in a quieter, more intimate and menacing tone,

"You will remember brother Callow, that our beloved Prior referred you to the words of Saint Paul in his epistle to the Colossians, 'Mortify therefore your members which are upon the earth.'[8]? What our Prior did not explain then, but I will tell you now is that our Saint also explained how we should do this, how we should cast out devils that are sent to lead us astray. In his First Epistle to the Corinthians, chapter 9, verse 27, he wrote, 'I chastise my body and bring it into subjection: lest perhaps when I have preached to others I myself should be castaway.' You are in danger brother Callow, grave danger of being castaway. So we must bring your body back into subjection."

Mc Bane, his eyes ablaze with the fervour of his task, continued quietly,

"As your novice-master I will teach you this, and as your novice-master I will suffer with you and help you purge this demon from your body. Bare your back novice-brother Callow."

---

[8] Colossians 3:5

By this time young novice-brother Callow must have been quaking in his, well, his bare feet as he hadn't had time to put on his sandals before leaving the dortor, and as meek and helpless as a frightened lamb loosened the upper cord of his habit and let it fall to his waist. Novice-master Rodiron McBane rose and turned to the small table just inside the entrance to the chapel and picked up the leather thonged scourge that he had placed there earlier.

Chapter 4

"You'll appreciate," said Joe, "that the tree with the cave hidden in its head-shaped roots that I'd talked about earlier, had not even been mentioned up to this point in the story and so you can also probably guess that I was wondering what it had to do with the story that I was reading. According to the book blurb the tree and cave were easy to visit, being just off the Hartstane road. So I suggested to Elizabeth that perhaps we could all go for a walk and see it at the weekend. Harry thought it a great idea; a hidden cave, wow! Elizabeth, who didn't hide the fact that she didn't like the picture, wasn't quite so keen,

"It doesn't look right, Joe. It looks as if is haunted," and was at pains to point out to me that as I hadn't come across either the tree or cave in my story yet, we still had no idea of the history of either and so no idea how these were connected to the folk tale, and that we could be certain that the tale and hence the tree and cave, would have something sinister attached to them.

"Why do we need know? It is just a folk tale," I pointed out. "What do we need to know the story for?" And then unfortunately in all innocence I added, "Look, if you hadn't given me the book, we wouldn't even know there was a story associated with them."

"No, and we wouldn't know where they were either," she fired back, though I have no idea why she said this, as it was she who had bought me the book.

We had only just moved here back in those days," Joe explained to us, "and all I could guess was that perhaps the reality of country life wasn't quite the same for her as the dream of it and she was already missing the city?

"True," I replied to Elizabeth, "but we do know, and by the sounds of it and if the map is anything to go by, it will make a nice walk. Come on, it'll be good fun and will help us get to know the area."

So on the Sunday morning we drove up the Hartstane road, found the parking spot mentioned in the book, donned our walking boots and the three of us set off up the path towards this mystery tree.

It was one of those late autumn, early winter mornings. The previous night's frost was still on the ground covering everything with a glittering sprinkling of fairy dust. The birch trees stood with their white and black scarred trunks and drooping twigs bedecked with small sparkling crystals hanging still in the cool morning air, waiting, waiting as if for 'the off,' the day when spring would be officially announced. The dead grass of the summer lay tumbled in frost covered heaps about our feet like a choppy sea. Overhead was a clear blue sky spreading from horizon to horizon and a bright yellow sun which bathed all beneath in clear bright light and a surprising amount of warmth. Indeed, the frost and frozen droplets of water on the birch twigs had already started melting as we set off up the path.

Part way round our first corner Harry discovered a frozen dead mole in a drainage ditch. The little black corpse was just lying there on the sunlit sloping earth side of the ditch completely undamaged. We stroked its still damp dark velvet fur and inspected its disproportionately large strong hands.

"They are almost blind you know," I explained to Harry, "because they spend all their time underground in the dark."

"So how do they know where they are going?" he asked.

Yes, I thought, how do they? And how do we? We have eyes, but being able to see doesn't appear to make us any better at knowing where we are going. Indeed, given the mistakes we all seem to make in life, we might as well be as blind as the mole.

"I have no idea," I replied, "but they always seem to be able find our lawn, don't they?"

Harry looked at me and smiled.

"Come on dear, put it down," said Elizabeth, with a terse edge to her voice and an unstated, 'it's dirty,' because I could bet that that was what she was thinking. For reasons which eluded me, she had become one of those women who wanted nothing to do with anything that had not had 99 percent of all known germs removed from it, and a frosted dead mole was probably unlikely to meet that strict criterion. She then added somewhat pointedly,

"Let's go and see this head of daddy's."

Oh yes, this was *my* head. Not the head in the story, or the head in the picture, but *my* head. And we were out on this walk on this cold day, not because anyone else wanted it, least of all Elizabeth, my darling wife, but because *I* wanted it.

The deceased 'velvet coated gentleman' was placed back on the side of the ditch. Harry then went careening up the path in front of us playing some part in a game of his imagining.

"You shouldn't encourage him," said 'darling wife' when she judged he was out of earshot.

"But he has to learn about these things. We moved out of the city to be closer to nature, for precisely this type of experience. To see nature, red in tooth and claw," I added, putting my arm around her and giving her a squeeze. She made a very half-hearted attempt at feigning a laugh and pulled away from me. Oh dear, it looked like it was going to be one of those days. What was the matter with her? I genuinely had no idea, though guessed it was something to do with our recent move from urban to rural living. Elizabeth had seemed as enthusiastic as I had been to move from the city out to the country, but ever since we had moved she has started to find any reason to be miserable, find fault, and generally not enjoy anything, and of course, it was all my fault. This was usually implied rather than stated, but it was obvious enough.

Fortunately for me, just at that moment a large black Labrador with a short, stocky middle aged woman in tow, made an appearance and captured Harry's attention. She, the woman not the dog, had a slightly middle eastern appearance about her; olive skin, fine features, dark brown eyes, and could have been possibly Lebanese or Egyptian? She was dressed in one of those knee length waxed cotton raincoats, with a matching hat; so popular with city dwellers who profess to love the countryside even though they don't choose to live there.

"Good morning! Lovely day for a walk," was how she greeted us, with not a trace of an accent. "I'm just taking Ben, or rather Ben is been taking me," she said, "up to High Black Crag. Where are you off to?"

"Oh we are not going that far. We're just going to have a look at The Head. We haven't seen it yet and ….."

"Ah," she said rather flatly and I think both of us noticed that the sparkle in her eyes and beaming smile on her open and friendly face seemed to fade a little.

"You have heard of the story of The Ghost Moth?" she asked.

"Yes, of course," I replied. "I'm reading it right now. That's how we know about The Head or The Tree, or whatever name it goes under."

"So you know about The Cave then?" was her next slightly disconcerting remark.

"Well, I'm not sure I would say know about, but yes, we have seen a drawing of it," I replied.

Well, although I felt certain she hadn't intended to alarm us, her, 'So you know about The Cave then?' did unfortunately have that effect, as the slightly ominous edge to it was of course immediately picked up on by Elizabeth. Possibly Ben's owner noticed that her probably well intentioned remark might not have been received quite as she had intended it, because she then added in a jaunty manner,

"Oh, that's good. Look, don't mind me. Enjoy your walk. Come on Ben" and set off down the path with Ben both on and in the lead, smiling at Harry as she departed.

"I don't think we should. You heard ...," Elizabeth said anxiously, as soon as she deemed the woman out of earshot.

"Please darling, I think she was just enquiring if we knew what the cave would look like, and we do. What I am reading is just a story. I haven't come across anything that is remotely untoward yet. The Tree, or The Cave, or whatever it is called, hasn't even had a mention. I wouldn't be surprised if she works in the local tourist office and earns her money selling the very book I am reading. You know how all places love to have their own myth, legend, ghost story, or whatever? It brings the punters in. I'll bet you a £1 there are postcards of this Head for sale in the tourist office.

Now, come on."

Elizabeth smiled somewhat lamely and said nothing, so I guessed that she was not one hundred percent convinced. However she did start walking, albeit somewhat sullenly, along our path in the direction of daddy's head. Had she now decided that she was going to play the martyr card? Oh these so unnecessary, silly and annoying games. Why do some women seem to gain a sort of perverse enjoyment from playing them and the innocent party, or parties have to put up with them? I didn't want a row, I just wanted a nice day out, but felt as if Elizabeth was deliberately trying to provoke me into arguing with her. However, in spite of these, er, distractions, we did go on and fortunately didn't have to go on too far. Just round the next bend a small path with birch trees growing on both sides of it, led off the main one, just as described in the book blurb. This was obviously our path. It wasn't that long and soon gave way to a now frost free gently sloping open area of ground. On the downhill side was rolling tussocky grass with a lovely open view across the valley, and on the uphill side was shorter cropped and still wet, green grass. Beyond the green slope of the uphill side could be seen the top of what was obviously a large tree.

"This must be it. Come on Harry, I think we're here. Race you!" I cried in an attempt to inject a bit of fun into our day out, and we both ran up the incline until the full height of the tree came into view. I have to admit that my first thoughts upon seeing it were, oh dear, if it isn't already, now it most certainly is going to be, 'one of those days'! How on earth am I going to explain this to Elizabeth in her current mood?

"Is that it daddy?"

"Yes, I think it is. And I think we had better wait here for mummy."

Where does one start to describe the sight that was before us; perhaps with the easy bit? The slope that we had run up gave way to a flat area of ground that spread out in front of us like a small amphitheatre to the base of a little sandstone cliff, well, outcrop some two to three metres high which stretched about ten to fifteen metres in each direction from the huge tree that was located at about its centre point. So far so good. But what Elizabeth was going to see was .....

A tree that was obviously extremely old and growing, well it may not have been as it could just as easily have been dead and so not actually growing, directly above the lip of the outcrop with about half of its roots cascading down the rocky face. The remaining roots were no doubt spread out behind it buried in the earth on top of the rock layer. Its trunk was possibly a couple of metres in diameter and not much more in height. At this point it almost literally exploded into branches heading off in all directions, looking as if it had suffered the most almighty electric shock. The deformed limbs shot out from that stump of a trunk and at each change in direction and at each bifurcation there appeared to be an ugly arthritic looking knuckle. The trunk and lower sections of the larger branches were for the major part covered in either dark green moss or lichen. Further up, the more arthritic looking branches, complete with their swollen knuckles, were festooned with strands and clumps of pale green lichen, which, from where we were standing had all the appearance of ancient cobwebs. Its deformed shape, coupled with both the moss and lichen covering made it impossible to guess as to its type. Possibly it was beech? I don't think it was oak. I honestly don't know. However, that was not all. Its roots cascaded in a jumbled tangle down the scarp of this small rock outcrop and were as twisted and deformed as the branches. Behind these was obviously a cave of sorts which one could enter via a large opening which extended upward from the flat soil forming the base of the natural amphitheatre.

OK, those were the facts which described that tree, but how do I describe the nightmare image that it presented? Have you ever seen one of those weird surrealist paintings, or psychological ink blot tests, which can appear to be two things at the same time depending upon how you look at them? Well, this arboreal freak took on the appearance of three things. The first was that of horrendous arthritic witches arms, hands and fingers stretching upwards towards, indeed, clawing at the very sky. The second was that of looking like a huge malevolent octopus sitting on the edge of the small cliff with its twisted tentacles reaching down and squeezing the life blood out of some victim. And the third, which you couldn't pull your eyes away from once you'd seen it, was that of the roots having formed the image of a skull screaming in anguish and despair across the valley in front of it; det uendelig skriket (the endless scream) as Edvard Munch might have described it. Indeed, the image presented by those roots had a remarkable similarity to that portrayed in his famous painting The Scream.

"Oh my goodness! That is ghastly!" said Elizabeth when she joined us.

"Yes, it is, isn't it?" I replied. There was no point in my trying to deny this. The whole thing, though it sounds a little illogical saying this about a tree, looked so totally devoid of any hope or salvation on the one hand and so horrific on the other and so a living (if indeed it was living) example of the subject matter of a worst nightmare.

"And you brought us here to see this?"

"Well I had no idea what it looked like!"

"But you've seen the picture."

"Yes, but it didn't look anything like this in the picture."

In my defence, I should add that the drawing that I'd seen suggested a rural curiosity. It most certainly did not suggest the vision of horror, hopelessness and despair that was standing right in front of us. I don't think I have ever seen anything that was so emotionally draining.

"I've only read the opening chapters," I continued in a vain attempt to justify why I had suggested we should come and see this ghastly sight. "The tree hasn't been mentioned yet. But I think we can definitely guess why folk stories have grown up around it! Have you ever seen anything like that?"

"You're enjoying this, aren't you?" said my wife with a not so well hidden sarcastic edge to her voice.

Such was the emotional impact of this weird looking tree, that even young Harry had been standing still and just staring at it without saying anything since he and I had first set eyes on it. But then he obviously decided that enough of standing still was enough,

"Can I go and look in its mouth?"

"No, you certainly can't!" snapped Elizabeth.

"Steady," I said as I put my arm round her.

"Don't you 'steady' me!" she retorted, pushing me away. "You bring us out here and…..". Her voice trailed off in frustrated anger. Was she finding it easy or hard, this act of being so unreasonable, of finding fault with everything? I knew I was finding it hard trying to handle her unpredictable mood swings on the one hand and provide a fairly up-beat and happy emotional feel to the day on the other, and so had to tell myself to try and let it pass and not to dwell on it.

The small amphitheatre in front of the outcrop was covered in short clipped green grass, there were obviously sheep around somewhere, though we didn't see any that day, and was also decked with a liberal sprinkling, if that is the way to describe such things, of variously sized dice shaped sandstone rocks, which had no doubt been eroded from the small cliff face over the ages.

"Let's go and sit on that one over there," I suggested pointing to a large rock that was more the shape and size of a garden bench than a die, "the one in the sun, then we can look this way at the view and have our sandwiches. Yes?"

"Okay," she said quietly, and so we made our way over to the rock, got the mats out and sat down, pulled the Thermos and sandwiches out of the rucksack and made ourselves comfortable.

"Do you want chicken or ham, Harry?" I asked.

"Chicken!"

"Why do I always end up getting the ham?" I said in an attempt at jocularity.

Harry took his chicken sandwich and pulled a face at me.

"'cause you do."

"You've only packed two cups," said Elizabeth the martyr, who, oh-so-stoically, was making a start on pouring out a warm drink.

"Er, yeah, I'll take the Thermos top."

Oh dear, things were tense! And, as ever in those days, I

really had no idea why.

"That way you'll get more than us," said Harry, who had obviously noticed the difference in size between the cups and the top of the Thermos flask, though fortunately didn't appear to have really noticed the differences between his parents. Or perhaps he had, and he, like I, was trying to pretend that they weren't there; trying to pretend that we were one happy family out for a pleasant day's walk in the country.

"No I won't, because mummy will pour the same amount into each cup," said his pretending-to-be-happy father, who quite honestly was getting towards the end of his tether at trying to keep a lid on things. I'd really had no idea what that tree would look like. So why on earth was Elizabeth blaming me for it as if I had planned this day out just to spite her? What was the matter with her? However, I knew it wasn't the tree, that much was obvious, even if it was a dreadful sight. Something else was niggling at her, but I had no idea what.

In the way that kids are, Harry had eaten his sandwich and drunk his close to boiling hot Ribena before Elizabeth and I had barely made a start on ours.

"Can I go and play?"

"Yes," Elizabeth said, "but don't go inside that skull of daddy's."

Oh, it was 'that skull of daddy's' now. This bickering was wearing. She and I sat on our hard stone bench, said nothing to each other and looked stonily at the view. The view was in fact a glorious one, looking almost due south across the valley which was spread out in front of and beneath us. The birch trees, which had stopped at the opening to the small amphitheatre in which we sat, provided a pretty and delicate frame to each side of a landscape picture of hills covered in yellowed grass, brown heather, bare deciduous trees and dark green conifers which rolled away into the distance. Above was a pure blue sky and a lovely warm sun.

"Isn't that gorgeous?" I ventured. "Beats the Town Moor, doesn't it? Glad you came?"

"Yes, it is lovely," she grudgingly concurred. "I'm sorry, I'm not feeling so good today."

"Not to worry. Are you enjoying yourself now?"

"Umm," she sighed in what I took to be agreement, though I realised might not be.

We could hear Harry running about behind us making alternate aeroplane and machine gun noises. As we sat there soaking up both the view and the sun, I took hold of her hand in an attempt at reconciliation and hoped that both this gesture and the warm sun would in some way help to thaw out the frosty atmosphere between us. Just as I did so, a bright orange flash against the grey shade of the birch trees caught my eye.

"Look at that," I said pointing to a bright yellow and orange moth, which had just settled on a nearby dead piece of wood. "What a beauty, but what's it doing out at this time of year? If it had any sense it would still be hibernating."

I don't think moths are well known for their hearing, but no sooner had I said this than it took off and disappeared off to one side of and behind us. We continued to sit, hand in hand, enjoying the warmth of the sun, until suddenly we both noticed a lull in Harry's war games and turned to see what he was doing only to find that he wasn't there.

"Harry! Harry, where are you?"

We got hastily to our feet and almost ran across the small natural amphitheatre.

"Harry!" screamed Elizabeth.

"Yes, mummy," he said as he ran out of the opening of the silently screaming skull.

"Oh my God. You didn't go in, did you?" she asked somewhat inanely, having just seen him come out.

"I was trying to catch a yellow butterfly and it flew inside."

"And did you catch it?" I asked in a tone which I hoped might help to defuse what I foresaw was likely to become a return to our pre-lunchtime tension.

"No. I couldn't find it. There's a big cave in there."

"Is there?" I said. "Let's have a look." And Lillibeth (my nickname for Elizabeth) and I walked over to what had been 'that skull of daddy's' to have a look at the cave which lay inside it.

"Are you going in?" she asked me.

"No, no," I reassured her. "I am just going to have a look though one of the eyes sockets."

By this time I was right next to the entrance to the root covered cave and looking in through the gap in the roots which formed the left-hand eye socket to this 'skull-cave'.

"There's nothing in here," I said, as indeed there wasn't. Actually, it was not that big a cave, but I suppose it must have appeared big to young Harry. The back and side walls were the native sandstone of the outcrop, the front wall, or front screen perhaps is a better description, was comprised of a tangle of tree roots. The floor looked sandy and had a few cuboid sandstone boulders lying about on it. The air smelt a bit damp and musty. No, not exactly what one pictures as a dramatic cave associated with a mysterious local story; more of a damp hole in a rock.

"There was," said Harry indignantly.

"Well, there isn't now," I replied. "No moth as far as I can see."

And then to my complete surprise, Elizabeth ducked down and entered 'that skull of daddy's' and proceeded to walk around inside it. Of course I was surprised; she had spent the preceding hour or so pouring cold water on my proposal to come and visit this natural oddity and now, there she was playing about inside it like a naughty school girl!

"What's it like?" I asked her through the 'eye socket'.

"Cool and a bit damp," came the reply.

"Can you see the butterfly, mummy?" asked Harry.

"No."

And with that, Harry lost all interest in the cave - he had already been in it after all - and ran off across the flat amphitheatre. My eyes followed him. When I turned back, Elizabeth was still in the cave.

"Are you going to stay in there?" I enquired in the manner of a joke.

"I might," she replied a little coquettishly. Perhaps things were thawing between us? "Will you come and join me?"

"No. Come on out you naughty girl. I think we ought to be heading home."

"Spoil sport," she said as she emerged from behind the curtain of roots. "We could have had a little kiss and cuddle in there."

Elizabeth's unexpected lunchtime change of mood did come as a bit of a surprise and the very fact that I can still remember it is testament to that. Although I really didn't know what to make of it, to be honest I wasn't too bothered about analysing the 'whys and wherefores' as it was just nice to have her back happy again. I remember that she took my arm and as a couple again we set off down the sloping hillside to find Harry.

Chapter 5

If the earlier penance of cold baths and scrubbing of the reredorters hadn't had the effect of purging any thoughts on Callow's part of confiding in novice-master Rodiron McBane, the subsequent flogging most certainly did. Indeed, we can reasonably speculate that the experience had not only been extremely painful, with McBane's zeal for his task way exceeding that which might be deemed reasonable, if indeed one considers it reasonable to flog a young man for having thoughts about young women, but also extremely traumatic, with guilt about things sexual having been carved into Callow's soul just as the scourge had carved into the flesh of his back. The purity of the love that La Roche had described for 'his perfect flower' must have seemed to Callow as if it were some unattainable dream.

Fortunately however his experience didn't stop him from feeling desire for beautiful women, but now that this perfectly natural desire had been definitely designated as 'wrong', it was also now tainted with guilt and sin. McBane had made it perfectly clear that the Devil, or a devil, though in this case a she-devil, had been tempting him, trying to drag him off the pure and narrow path to salvation and that necessarily he had had to be 'corrected'; 'his body brought into subjugation.' We have mentioned that Adam Callow hadn't joined the monastery with the desire of becoming one of the hundred and forty four thousand, which were to be redeemed from the earth. Indeed, he'd known nothing about this until Prior Obscurant had enlightened him. None-the-less at the time of this story the saving of one's soul was a serious matter and so subjects such as 'being castaway' and not becoming 'defiled with women' could not be idly dismissed. Hence the problem of whether Eve Lilith, the raven haired beauty who had inadvertently got him into this emotional mess, was an angel or a she-devil continued to haunt him and remained unresolved.

Such were Callow's wounds at the hands of McBane, that the monastery apothecary, brother Swan, the senior brother that novice-brother Venn was serving under, arranged with brother La Roche for Callow to be transferred to the infirmary and for Michael Venn to attend to him. We can speculate that while together thus, he and Venn might have explored the apparently very complex nature of male / female relations and indeed how any relationship with a woman could possibly be justified or explained given both the strictures and teachings of the Priory and Monastery of Saints Paul and Augustine, and when it was crystal clear from The Revelation of St John the Divine that 'no man could learn that song but the hundred and forty four thousand, which were redeemed from the earth. These are they which were not defiled with women.'?

Somewhat to his relief, relief in that he realised that he wasn't the only one who couldn't make any sense of this, Adam Callow found that Michael Venn gave the impression of being just as confused about it as he was. During one of their conversations La Roche's name came up and without breaking La Roche's confidence, Callow was able to tell Venn a bit about the conversation he'd had with La Roche and so suggest that he had a sympathetic ear and, most importantly of course, was nothing like McBane. As Callow worked under La Roche in the garden, it was agreed that when Callow had recovered, he would ask La Roche if he and Venn might visit him for some teaching and discussion on this subject.

Although it was not the case, it seemed as if no sooner had Callow and Venn decided to consult with La Roche on the subject of women, that suddenly a woman was the subject of the news which swept through the monastery. Without any hint of warning and so to everyone's surprise, a woman had been charged with being a witch, of witchcraft and dabbling in the Black Arts, of blasphemy, and of selling potions. As Prior Obscurant vehemently explained to the sea of tonsured heads in front of him,

"We hath a disciple of the Devil, a disciple of Satan amongst us! Yeah, in our very midst; a whore of the Devil! It behoveth us, we, we who have the seal of God in our foreheads, to cut this viperous she-devil from our midst! For does it not say in Nahum 3:3-4 that, 'The horseman lifteth up both the bright sword and the glittering spear …..'" and needless to say, the thin arm was raised aloft brandishing 'the bright sword' as this selectively edited quotation was continued with, "'….. because of the multitude of the whoredoms of the wellfavoured harlot, the mistress of witchcrafts!'"

At this point he paused briefly, having placed so much emphasis on each of the words starting with a 'w' that he required the pause to regain his breath before recommencing, "And does not St Paul say in his Epistle to the Galatians, even though all in the monastery must by now have known this quotation off by heart as he had said it so many times, 'Now the works of the flesh are manifest, which are these; Adultery, fornication, uncleanness, lasciviousness, idolatry and witchcraft?'[9] With great emphasis being placed on the word witchcraft, as adultery and fornication weren't the main subjects for disapproval today.

"This is why, my beloved brothers, our Holy Father, Pope Innocent VIII issued his Summis desiderantes affectibus (Desiring with supreme ardour). So that the foul heresy of witchcraft can be cut out like a cancer from our midst."

Callow, who had heard of witch trials but that was all, his parents having told him that they had occurred in the past but hadn't been that common, listened to this in amazement. It was only later that he discovered that the quoted papal bull only applied to inquisitors in northern Germany. Needless to say, it had never occurred to him that a witch could be responsible for

---

[9] Galatians 5:19

so much evil, though in the relatively short time that he had been in the monastery he had begun to learn that evil was all too often directly linked to women. Perhaps McBane had been right to try and purge his flesh of the Devil, or devils, of Rosier[10] or even Asmodeus,[11] who were trying to lead him astray? Perhaps? However, he wasn't entirely convinced, as his treatment by McBane had, as well as removing some of his skin, also removed some of his naivety and he was now a little more sceptical and less inclined to immediately believe everything he was told. Was there not a verse in Genesis which said something like 'the Lord God said, It is not good that the man should be alone'?[12] And, although he couldn't remember the rest of it, did recall that God had also made woman and so reasoned that if God had made woman, then women could not all be evil.

So were witches evil? Did Callow also think it a little strange that witches, who were invariably female, and witchcraft were also mentioned in the same sentence as whoredoms and harlots, not to mention fornication and lasciviousness, and hence that all evil appeared to centre round sex and women? According to Prior Obscurant the single greatest problem to achieving salvation and entry into God's Divine and Celestial Kingdom was the temptation posed by women. It couldn't be clearer. But it wasn't just Prior Obscurant who thought this. Obviously St John the Divine must have thought so as well, or why else would he have written, 'no man could learn that song but the hundred and forty four thousand, which were redeemed from the earth. These are they which were not defiled with women; for they are the virgins,' in his Revelation? And why did Paul write, in effect, that a relationship with a woman meant 'that ye cannot do the things that ye would,' and after that St Augustine continue with the same theme stating that, 'I found it irksome

---

[10] Patron demon of tainted love and seduction
[11] Demon of lust
[12] Genesis 2:18

to be forced to adapt myself to living with a wife'?[13] There was obviously something that he (Callow) was not understanding and so was comforted that he and Venn had agreed to seek brother La Roche's guidance.

Prior Obscurant continued to boom on, selectively quoting from Revelation,

"And it was commanded them that they should not harm the grass of the earth; but only those people which have not the seal of God in their foreheads. And to them it was given that they should not kill them, but that they should be tormented five months; and their torment was as the torment of a scorpion, when he striketh a man. And in those days shall men seek death, and shall not find it: and shall desire to die, and death shall flee from them."[14] and then use this to justify his, "The witch shall remaineth incarcerated until found guilty and burned. Consumed by the Fires of Hell, from whence she hath come!"

There was no acknowledgement of the possibility that she might just be innocent. Nor any mention that, if she were guilty, of her soul being in anyway cleansed by the fire and so not even the vaguest likelihood of redemption or forgiveness for her so-called sin. While Callow was no doubt left wondering whether anything relating to some form of a fair trial had been over-looked and hence whether her guilt was already deemed a foregone conclusion, Prior Obscurant continued,

"But we are not pagan savages and she will receiveth a fair trial, even though she hath come amongst us in this fiendish manner to spread her foul blasphemies. She will be tried in our inquisitorial court under Canon Law. As I couldst not in all conscience burden another with the onerous responsibility of being Lead Inquisitor," for which read, Judge, and although he might as well have added 'and jury', he didn't, "I have taken it upon myself to fulfilleth this role. Our own sub-Prior, brother

---

[13] St Augustine, Confessions, Book VIII:1
[14] Revelation 9:4-7

Arriviste Grees will lead the prosecution against this whore of the Devil."

The sub-Prior, Arriviste Grees, who was also the priest in charge of the Treasury, was of medium height and, for one in the hard line Prior Obsurant camp, surprisingly portly in build; he obviously liked his food and wine. This sub-Prior Grees had a round head set on a fat neck. On this round head was a fleshy face which protruded forward from his brow to his upper lip thus giving his nose an almost snout-like appearance. Beneath the snout were set two small, thin wet lips and on each side of it were two small, dark and forever darting porcine eyes. Indeed, his whole face had the appearance of an untrustworthy, cunning pig. However, his cunning was not the brute animal cunning of McBane, but carefully calculated cunning, the sort of cunning to beware of, like .... well, like the cunning of sub-Prior Arriviste Grees. He was quite a bit younger than both Prior Obscurant and novice-master McBane and more ambitious for 'things temporal' than both of the aforementioned, and one could visualise him taking over as Prior before Prior Obscurant was even cold in his coffin, let alone in the ground, if he (Grees) could possibly arrange it. Power and money were Grees' objectives and an ecclesiastic life was the route to these; of that he had no doubt. And as for 'things spiritual'? Yes, he knew such things existed, but rather like McBane, though on a totally different intellectual level, he didn't let that bother him. He was doing God's work after all, and so rewards in this life were not incompatible with paradise in the next. Prior Obscurant had obviously observed the naked ambition in Grees and had decided that it would be best to hold his enemy close and so had taken him as sub-Prior even though he self-evidently had wildly different views on abstinence, penance and mortification of the body, and hence the correct route to God's Celestial Paradise. It was obvious to Prior Obscurant that his sub-Prior would not be amongst the one hundred and forty four thousand, but realpolitik suggested that if he, Prior Obscurant, wished to be amongst those who would be redeemed from the earth, then he would have to somehow accommodate the porcine sub-Prior Arriviste Greeses of this world.

Obscurant continued,

".... and the inquisition of this harlot from Babylon will be undertaken by our novice-master, brother Rodiron McBane." So no surprises there. Then after a brief pause, he necessarily had to ask, "Is there anyone present who will speak for this harlot of Satan's against these heinous crimes?"

The priory church was absolutely silent. No doubt all the brothers realised that defending a 'whore of the Devil' or a 'harlot of Satan's' would not go down well with either their Prior, or sub-Prior for that matter. So was their silence due to fear? Possibly all had, in their time, been flogged, both to bring their bodies into subjugation just as Callow had been, and so had this also resulted in their wills having been brought into subjugation as well? Even the young, but now not so naive Adam Callow noticed a pervading air of submissiveness, of acceptance, a lack of any real will to question, or object. So were the brothers afraid, or had they simply lost any will that they might have once had, lost all desire to think for themselves and so were content for others to decide for them?

It was also obvious, even to Callow, that both Obscurant and Grees had no idea of the concept of impartiality and so no intention whatsoever of listening objectively to evidence before pronouncing on the case, and let us be clear about it, pronouncing sentence. Of course this woman was guilty. She was a woman and that alone was good enough for Prior Obscurant. And in addition, she was a witch and so couldn't be anything but guilty. However tiresome though, justice had to be seen to be done, so the judicial process had to be gone through.

Prior Obscurant then went on to explain that the trial would not take place in the secular courts but in a closed inquisitorial court under Canon Law. This struck Callow as a little odd, because from his limited readings to date on such matters, he was under the impression that witchcraft could only be tried in secular courts. Of course it didn't cross his mind that the reason why Prior Obscurant and his sub-Prior might have chosen this was to ensure that the legal process could be fairly and faithfully followed to its just conclusion, the final burning, without any unnecessary distractions such as objections from those who would most certainly not be amongst the one hundred and forty four thousand, the illiterate herd, who so obviously would not fully understand the intricacies of the law or grasp the gravity of the offence.

"It pleaseth me to see that none of you wish to soil your souls with foul association with this blasphemer," boomed Obscurant, who then so considerately added, "I will appointeth someone to full fill this unenviable and unpleasant role when the date is set, as there is no need for anyone to burdeneth themselves with it now."

Callow looked around the cold cavernous interior of the priory church for brother La Roche, not in any connection with this up-coming witch trial, but because in spite of he and Venn thinking it would be easy for him (Callow) to ask brother La Roche about the apparent conflict between their religion and male / female relationships, it had in fact proved harder than expected and Callow had still not managed to find brother La Roche to do so. Consequently, he was hoping that he might catch him at this assembly. However, a somewhat disappointed Adam Callow found that his mentor didn't appear to be there.

Having finished his announcement, Prior Obscurant then offered up a prayer requesting that God make his Divine Justice manifest upon this earth through the good offices of the inquisitorial court. With the 'amen' the assembly finished, and the black habited and cowled monks shuffled out carrying their stench of cowardice and / or indifference with them.

Although it seemed like an age to Callow, he did eventually manage to catchup with brother La Roche the next day. Perhaps needless to say, he found him out in his favourite vegetable garden.

"Unfortunately, my young friend," explained brother La Roche, "when you get older you aren't always on the best of form all the time, and just recently I haven't been feeling so good."

"You aren't ill, are you?"

"Oh no. Not unless you define old age as an illness," he replied in a jocular manner, and then in a more philosophical tone added, "Perhaps it is. Perhaps that is what old age is; an illness from which one doesn't get better. The only possible recovery, if you wish to call it that, is death." There was nothing self-pitying in the way he said this, it was stated simply and unemotionally as though a statement of fact.

They continued to walk slowly up the path from the point where they had met.

"But no matter. It comes to us all, young Adam, and it's coming to me now, so I mustn't complain. Let us hope that it is God who is calling me," he added with a smile, and without saying, though it was abundantly clear that he meant 'and not the Devil'.

Callow smiled. He liked brother La Roche. There was something solid, dependable and trustworthy about him. He had no pretensions. Did young Adam Callow see him as something of a role-model even though the pair were like chalk and cheese; Callow, a puny, shy young sparrow, gangly, inexperienced and unsure of himself and with his life ahead of him; and the older man, well, although old, still reasonably physically strong, with a lifetime of experience and it seemed possibly his life now behind him? And there was no doubt that brother La Roche for his part enjoyed the refreshing nature of his young protégé.

"And how are you, my young brother?" he asked. "I have heard that our novice-master has been taking an interest in you."

"Oh, not too bad," replied Callow, putting on a brave face, though his wounds were still troubling him and giving him a nasty twinge from time to time.

"You're young and strong. You'll be alright in a week or two. However, do promise me that you will try and not upset your novice-master again," he added with a wink and smile.

Adam Callow smiled back.

"Shall we?" said La Roche indicating the wooden bench that they had just reached. "Now, I can see that you have been managing very well without me," he said looking around the garden, "but you must tell me what I missed yesterday."

Callow described how all the brothers had been summoned to attend an unexpected meeting in the church and how Prior Obscurant had then told them that a witch had been caught and was about to be put on trial. He found it pleasant to be talking to brother La Roche again. He felt relaxed. In fact perhaps a little too relaxed, as he even permitted himself the luxury of a gentle mocking of Prior Obscurant's use of language and hand gestures. Although brother La Roche made no comment, as soon as it became apparent to Callow that the senior monk was not amused by them, he felt a flush of embarrassment, restrained himself and stuck to reporting just the bare facts.

"Um," said brother La Roche, when Adam Callow had finished.

"Did you see this witch?" he then asked.

"No."

"So you have no idea who she is?"

"No."

"And Grees is to prosecute, eh?" said La Roche pensively, "and I suppose McBane will take his usual role as inquisitor?"

Callow nodded and also noticed that although brother La

Roche had not been amused at his gentle mocking of Prior Obscurant, he himself (La Roche) had most unusually for him referred to both senior clerics just by their surnames, having omitted their official titles. If Adam Callow hadn't already realised, this was the first hint that he'd had that this business was serious. It had to be so for La Roche to be so lost in his thoughts about it that he had evidently forgotten that he was having a conversation with a novice-brother.

"And did no-one offer to defend this poor woman?" enquired La Roche in the same quiet and pensive manner.

"No." replied Callow, a little taken aback by La Roche's use of, 'this poor woman.' Was this when at last Callow began to appreciate that perhaps a witch was not as Prior Obscurant would have it, some whore of the Devil's who had been granted fantastical powers to wreak havoc in this world, but instead might just be a poor normal, ordinary, flesh and blood woman?

"Our Prior said he would appoint someone nearer the time," continued Callow.

"Thank you," said La Roche.

Then, after a reflective pause, he added more breezily, "How selfish of me? I have been keeping you waiting. Now you must tell me what it was that you were wanting to see me about."

After Callow had told him the subject of the conversation that he'd had with his fellow novice-brother Venn, La Roche didn't answer immediately which made Callow wonder if he had presumed too much and over-stepped some mark of propriety and so was just about to start apologising for his presumption when brother La Roche said,

"Of course. Why don't you and Michael Venn meet me after prayers this afternoon and we can go for a little walk outside. God has given us such a lovely day, hasn't He? We mustn't waste it. Yes, a little walk in the countryside would be nice and we three can discuss this."

At this point Elizabeth and I heard a cry from Harry upstairs. So I put the book down and she and I went up to attend to him.

"My head hurts," he sobbed.

"There, there," said Elizabeth, putting her arms around him. "you've probably caught a cold, what with all that running about today. You didn't have your hat on, did you, sweetie?"

"Didn't want it."

"You've probably got a head cold, my darling." Then, turning to me she added, "I'll go and make him a hot lemon and honey." She then left the room and went down stairs to attend to the drink.

I sat down on the bed next to Harry.

"Not feeling too good, old lad?" I asked.

"The butterfly was there," he said, no doubt thinking that I still didn't believe him when I'd said that there was nothing there after I'd looked inside the cave.

"It was a moth, not a butterfly," I corrected him.

"So you did see it!"

"No, not in the cave. I saw it while mummy and I were eating our sandwiches."

Henry visibly brightened at hearing this. Perhaps his father did believe him after all?

"And you followed it into the cave, even though mummy had told you not to go in?"

He fell silent and looked down at the bed covers.

"Never mind," I said putting my arm round him.

"My head hurts, dad."

At this point Elizabeth returned to the room with the hot

lemon and honey, and an aspirin.

"Now don't worry, darling. Drink up and take this," said Elizabeth, offering Harry the hot drink and aspirin. "After a good night's sleep you'll feel better in the morning."

The warm drink and aspirin seemed to do the trick and it wasn't too long before Harry was breathing the regular breaths of one who had dozed off. We shut the door quietly and left him.

Once back downstairs again, I tried to assess whether our day out had been a success or not. It had certainly not started off well, but after lunch Elizabeth had brightened up quite considerably and at the cave had been in the best mood I'd seen her in for a long while, and, fingers crossed, it seemed to be holding. As I have already mentioned, although the decision to move from the city to the country had been jointly agreed upon, it seemed that no sooner than we had moved, Elizabeth had decided that she didn't like the country, that it was dirty and uncouth, and that it was my fault that she was missing the shops, visits to the hairdresser, etc. So what was I to make of today; had a milestone been passed? If so, it was a pity that the day should now end on a down note, with Harry having a head cold.

I confess I was a little curious to know why he had gone into the cave, especially when his mother had expressly told him not to, as this was unlike him. I also realised that my thinking about this suggested that I believed, at least in part, that which the lady with the dog had suggested to us by her, 'so you know then,' which although not stating, certainly implied that there was something untoward about the cave. Perhaps I was over-reading things, you know, adding two and two and making five for no good reason, but let's just say I was curious about the whole business. Consequently, I wanted to continue reading the story which obviously featured the strange tree and cave, even though so far, neither had had a mention. However, my plan to do this evaporated when, as I was settling down on the sofa, Elizabeth walked into the room clad only in her dressing gown, came over

to me, sat on my lap and whispered in my ear,
    "Are you coming to bed?"

Chapter 6

On the following evening and back in our story with young novice-brother Callow, it was a lovely spring afternoon with a warming sun shining in a clear, rich, cerulean blue sky. A gentle breeze whispered through the twigs of the nearby beech trees breathing life into the buds which were already pregnant with leaf but had not yet burst forth into delicate bright green. Primroses shone like small yellow suns in the newly greening grass. Yellow headed daffodils nodded in that same gentle breeze which, like an invisible messenger, was passing through and awakening the valley from its winter torpor.

As the three brothers passed though the monastery gates and out into the village square they must have looked a strange sight; the huge steady bulk of La Roche, flanked on each side by the slight, gangly and awkward forms of sparrow-like Callow and the tall, thin and lanky Venn.

"Good day to you brother," greeted one man, addressing himself to La Roche and touching his hat with his hand, as they met part way across the square.

"Good day to you David, and may God go with you."

"Good day to you brother La Roche," said another.

"Good day, Roger Kirkermous. And tell me, is your wife better than when we last spoke?"

"She is indeed, thanks to you."

"Don't thank me, Roger. Thank our good God. I merely provided His medicine. It is He who has made your wife well."

"I gave him a little potion ….." he explained to Venn in a conspiratorial manner, when they were out of earshot of Roger Kirkermous. La Roche knew of course that novice-brother Venn worked under brother Swan who was responsible for preparing the monastery's potions which were on sale in the market on every market day. "..... as they are a poor family and could never have afforded our prices."

It was obvious that La Roche was liked and respected by the villagers and observing this again reminded Callow of when he first saw brother La Roche talking to a crowd outside the monastery about loving one's neighbour, doing unto others as they would have done unto them, etc., and how this influenced both his and his parents decision for him to go into monastery. They all realised there was some 'good' in there and not just the rumoured hard line Obscurant view of life and religion; because at that time, they really had no idea just how narrow and hard-line Prior Obscurant's view of the world was.

"Let us go up this road to Hartstane," said brother La Roche. "There is a nice flat area part way up, with some boulders to sit on and a lovely view if I remember correctly. It's been a while since I last visited it and I would like to see it again before ....." but he didn't finish his sentence and instead added, "We can have our discussion there."

And so the three of them set off up the road.

As it gained height, smooth grey barked beech trees and rough flaky, rust-coloured mature Scots pines which lined it on its northeastern side, gradually gave way to pendulous birch and scrubby gorse. On the other side of the road was a drystone wall which separated the road from the adjacent fields. A grassy verge of varying width filled the gap between the wall and the road which meandered slightly as it made its way up the hill.

Had Callow noticed the slight difference in brother La Roche's manner after his little bout of 'not feeling so good'; how he seemed to be more pensive and hesitant in his replies, as if weighing each before responding? And did he now notice that La Roche was wishing to revisit a place that he obviously had known from before, as if he was needing to confirm that it was still as he remembered it, to see it again in case this was his last chance to do so? Unlikely, as Callow was full of the energy and certainty of youth, whereas brother La Roche had probably realised that his recent bout of 'not feeling so good' meant that perhaps God was closer to calling him than he might have wished.

"I think this is it," said brother La Roche when they arrived at a point where a small path led off the road to the left.

The path wound through some birch trees laden with long claret coloured twigs, which like the beech trees further down the valley were ready to burst into leaf, but not quite yet. The trees ended and the path opened out onto a slightly sloping hillside which led to a large flat amphitheatre with a small sandstone outcrop to its rear. On the short cropped grass of this small, round field were scattered a number of rectangular flat-faced sandstone boulders. Yes, it was as brother La Roche remembered it, and in case you are wondering," added Joe looking round at all of us, "sounded very much like a description of the same flat area in front of the tree and cave that Elizabeth, Harry and I had visited just that past weekend. At last the story I was reading was beginning to tie in with what we had seen."

"Shall we sit here, my young brothers?" suggested La Roche indicating a couple of boulders bathed in sunlight and surprisingly conveniently arranged so when they sat down they both partially faced each other, and the view over the valley and the sun.

"This afternoon," said the old man, slowly, "out here in this beautiful spot, we are equal under God's Heaven. So we shall be Adam, Michael and Stephen. Mind you," he added with a hint of a smile and a twinkle in his eye, "when we return to Saints Paul's and Augustine's you will again address me as brother La Roche."

Adam Callow and Michael Venn smiled. Could either of them imagine Prior Obscurant or any of his cronies saying such a thing? So this afternoon, thought Callow, they were to be equal brothers, brothers in arms, brothers fighting, or about to fight an evil which although he and Venn didn't understand, he rather hoped that brother La Roche, or, as he would be known that afternoon, Stephen, did.

"So what is it that you want to know?" the elderly brother asked.

Callow and Venn looked at each other wondering who should ask the first question on this somewhat difficult, indeed, what some might have described as an almost heretical subject.

Taking the initiative, novice-brother Venn ventured, "Er, we are wondering why our religion is so anti-women and so anti-sex?"

"Don't worry my young brother. We all question. So don't be afraid to ask," replied Stephen La Roche. "What we speak about today will remain in confidence between just the three of us. I can't promise that I will be able to answer all your questions, but we can discuss them and maybe God will grant us the wisdom to answer some of them.

I am just a simple monk," he continued. "and so the way I look at this is that the Bible is the word of God as interpreted by man and as written down by man. So we can see that there is plenty of room for error in that alone. Firstly, there is man's misunderstanding of God's Word. Then there is man's inability to actually put that Word, as understood by him, into words. Then last and not least, man simply getting it wrong. And if that does not leave enough room for error, there is then the reading of what is written and the understanding of that, or the misunderstanding of it. So it seems to me that it is not only very possible for God's Word to be misrepresented, but almost impossible for it not to be!

Man is very good at getting things wrong," he added with a smile.

"Now to answer your question; as you both must be aware, there is plenty in the Bible about love, about love in marriage and indeed about sex in marriage."

"Yes, but ….." commenced Michael Venn.

"Yes?"

"So why is our Prior constantly telling us that we must avoid temptation and that 'the foremost temptation that the Devil places in the path of man, is woman'? And he is not the only one. Our very own patron saints, Paul and Augustine are forever talking of celibacy and I don't think either of them married. Augustine also cites men and women who were promised in marriage, giving up their promises of marriage and dedicating their virginities to God.[15] It is almost as if for a man, knowing women and having sex precludes any possibility of salvation,"

"Oh, I am not sure that is strictly true, my young friend. Paul certainly wrote several passages in his various epistles extolling the virtues of marital love and as I was married once myself, I hope I won't be precluded from the possibility of salvation because of that!"

"But how can we be one of, 'the hundred and forty four thousand, which will be redeemed from the earth', if we have been with a woman? St John's Revelation clearly states, without any ambiguity whatsoever, that it will be, 'they which are not defiled with women.'"

"Umm," mused the elderly brother. "The Revelation of St John the Divine. So, tell me Michael, what do you know about it?"

Venn looked at him.

"Set out the facts, Michael, as you know them and we will see if we can move on from there."

---

[15] St Augustine, Confessions, Book VIII:6

"The Revelation of St John the Divine is traditionally attributed to John the Apostle, who is also known as John the Evangelist," commenced Venn, somewhat hesitantly, wondering why it was he had been asked the question.

"Yes," said Stephen La Roche, but sensing that Venn was struggling, helpfully continued with,

"You did know that John was the youngest of the apostles, outlived all of them and was the only one to die in old age of what might be described as natural causes? Now, as to 'The Revelation'. There is some debate as to whether John the Apostle did in fact write this. The Johannine works, as they are known, consisting of the gospel and the three epistles, are currently considered to be his work, but 'The Revelation' is markedly different in style and message, and so it is thought might have been written by a John of Patmos, or John the Presbyter. Now, I realise that doesn't answer your question, but I hope explains that there is considerable debate about the origin and authorship of that book."

"But what our Prior quotes is written," ventured Callow, who had learned of several other quotations via the good teaching of McBane, who had reinforced his lesson on this subject with the scourge.

"So, is it not entirely possible that the views he (Prior Obscurant) expresses of women and sex are not solely his, but stem from what is written?" added Venn. "If, as Adam has just suggested, it wasn't written, it couldn't be quoted. So the fact that it is written is important, as that colours the views, or opinions, of those who subsequently read it. However, one cannot also help but notice that so much of what our Prior quotes seems as if it has been deliberately selected to support his views of women and sex."

Did Stephen La Roche smile a little?

"Do you think the views of those who wrote the scriptures

might have allowed their personal opinions to colour what they were writing?" asked Michael Venn, wondering if he might have hit upon a reason.

"They were only human, so I think it could be possible," suggested La Roche.

"So, are Saint Paul's views on women his views, rather than God's views?" ventured Callow.

"Very likely," said La Roche. "But tell me Adam, what do you know of our patron saint?"

"Well, I know he was born in Tarsus," commenced a somewhat nervous Callow, who like his fellow novice-brother, was also wondering why he had been asked his question. "He was a Jew and a Roman citizen, was named Saul, and was a tent maker by trade. His family must have been fairly rich because they sent him to Jerusalem for his education under the noted Rabbi, Gamaliel. Later he became a zealous nationalist and was probably a Pharisee."

"Yes?"

"Well, he initially tried to suppress Christianity, was 'consenting' to Saint Stephen's stoning and was responsible for incarcerating many early believers. He famously underwent his conversion to Christianity whilst travelling to Damascus, and after this took the name Paul. He travelled and preached a lot, wrote many epistles and with Peter and others took a major role in setting up our church?"

La Roche nodded.

"But none of that explains the perceived misogynist slant to some of his writings," observed Michael Venn.

La Roche raised his eyebrows, but said nothing.

"Did he reject women?" asked Callow.

"From what I have read," said Venn, "he apparently retired

to a remote area for thirteen years to learn our faith. That seems like a long time to be away from society and possibly women? And if he did, why? And it would mean that he would have been in something like his mid-forties when he started his journeys and his writings. I seem to recall that there was one passage in one of his epistles that could be interpreted that he either was or had been married, but it is very ambiguous. Also I think Augustine might have suggested that he'd had children. However, as the word children could mean followers, that is also ambiguous."

"There is indeed very little recorded in the Bible about his private life." confirmed La Roche.

"But the very absence of hard evidence, means that we do have to speculate based on the evidence that we do have," posited Venn. "Choosing to be without women is not normal. Indeed, in Genesis God is quoted as saying, 'It is not good that the man should be alone' and made woman and 'bought her unto the man.'[16] Why would God say and do that if he meant men to live alone? So if Paul was living a celibate life without women, why was this so?"

"You said Paul's choosing to be without women is not normal," observed La Roche. "That depends a little on how you wish to interpret this. At the time of Paul, there were many, often uneducated people, who gave up life in the cities and went out into the desert to lead simple, humble lives with the aim of finding some form of salvation. Although there were also some women in their number, they were known as The Desert Fathers. So what Paul did, by living a life of solitude out in the desert, was by no means 'not normal' in his day. Indeed, for anyone seeking after God, it could be argued that it was 'very normal'. However, Michael, I do take your point that a celibate life does appear to contradict God's Will, as expressed in Genesis."

---

[16] Genesis 2:18-25

"I know my sister doesn't like him," said Callow.

"I didn't hear that," said Stephen La Roche, "and neither did you Michael Venn."

Callow cringed with shame at realising how he'd so easily nearly condemned his beloved sister for heresy. He hadn't intended to, it was simply that ….. Oh goodness, he must be careful, and 'thank you God' that it was only brother La Roche and Michael Venn who had heard him.

"No" confirmed Venn, who then added, "But I heard a group of women saying that they didn't like him and agreeing that they wouldn't have wished to marry him."

"Really?" commented La Roche. "However, as there is no doubting that women have different views to men, perhaps, for the purposes of our discussion, we should consider these. What can you remember of that conversation, Michael? However, no names please and we don't want to know where this overheard conversation took place either. It might however be useful to know how old the ladies were and whether or not they were married."

"Some were and some weren't," replied Venn, now more aware than previously that the subject matter of their conversation was potentially dangerous not only for them, but also for anyone who might be mentioned in it. If the young novice-brothers hadn't realised earlier, this of course was why brother La Roche had suggested that they have their discussion out of the monastery, out in the country where there was almost no chance that they would be overheard. Heresy was undoubtedly a serious offence in those days and the three of them were probably committing it.

Michael Venn continued, "and they were between twenty six and thirty six."

"Sorry, for being so inquisitive, Michael. I just wanted to ascertain whether we were about to learn the opinions of girls or of adult women, that is all."

"It was a typical female conversation," recalled Venn, "lots of silly giggling and they were grown women! However I remember one of them cited a text entitled 'Acts of Paul and Thecla' and in this apparently Paul is described as 'a man of middling size, and his hair was scanty, and his legs were a little crooked, and his knees were projecting, and he had large eyes, his eyebrow met, and his nose was somewhat long.' Another woman suggested that he was bald and had a red face. There was general agreement among them that he wasn't very handsome and that he seemed somewhat obsessed with celibacy and virginity, and teaching 'that one must fear only one God and live in chastity.'[17] As I recall these observations were one of the causes of much of the giggling. It was universally agreed that none of them would have liked to have married him."

"But he did have women friends," observed Stephen La Roche in his usual quiet manner. "Indeed, you will find quite a list of them mentioned in Romans[18] and several of them, such as Phoebe, Priscilla, Junia and others, helped set up the Church in Rome."

"Yes, I know," said Michael Venn, "but having women friends and women patrons is one thing, having a woman who you desire and who desires you is another. The two are nothing like the same."

Did our young Adam Callow warm inside when he heard Michael Venn talk of a woman desiring one and did his imaginings drift off to picturing a beautiful Eve Lilith smiling at him? 'I hope I will see you next week Adam Callow.'

"Yes, that is true," said the old man in response to Venn's observation, his thoughts possibly having drifted back to the days when he was happily married with his 'beautiful flower'.

---

[17] Acts of Paul and Thecla
[18] Romans 16

"However," continued La Roche, with a smile and a twinkle in his eye, "if you don't mind my saying so my young friend, you profess to know an awful lot about this sort of thing for a young man of your tender years. So what are you suggesting?"

"I am suggesting," said Venn, without batting an eyelid at Stephen La Roche's observation about his knowledge and age, "that perhaps Paul was not the type of man that women fall for, fall in love with that is, and that he knew this and was conscious of it. Conscious that women didn't really desire him and so, as many in this situation do, sought escape in his work. It would not be a big step to then also justify his not having sex as being what God desired, and then if this were the case for himself, why not for all men?"

"But Paul wrote some most beautiful passages about marriage and how couples should care for and love each other," Stephen La Roche reminded him.

"Yes, that is true. So doesn't that beg the question that if he did see marriage as beautiful, why wasn't he married? The very fact that he wasn't and chose not to be would suggest that his writings were about what he wished to have had, namely, the love of a woman, a loving relationship, but did not have."

"So are you suggesting that his, as you word it 'perceived misogyny,' was as a result of his reaction to women not finding him attractive," said La Roche, "and think this might have affected his attitude towards life and women?"

"His *perceived* misogyny, yes, possibly. His attitude to life and women would be bound to be affected wouldn't it? To feel rejected and not desired would not be pleasant. We all like to feel desired, to feel loved. So to see that others enjoyed this, but realise that it is denied to yourself would have been hurtful, would make you feel a bit sad, lonely, somehow not connected to the rest of humanity, feel on the outside of life, rather than in it. But other thoughts have occurred to me."

"Yes?" said brother La Roche.

"Possibly Paul simply didn't like women, or was in a bad marriage and wanted out, or that he secretly perhaps ….. no, I'll come to this later. As I have already suggested, you must have noticed that people tend to throw themselves into their work and / or travel when their private lives are either going through a rough patch, or are in turmoil. So why did Paul travel so much? What was he escaping from? What other explanations can there be for a man eschewing women to the extent that he did?"

"His love of God, perhaps?" answered brother Stephen La Roche quietly, but not entirely convincingly.

"So is finding God and loving Him only possible if one abstains from loving women and sex? Is this what, in effect, Paul is saying? To me that makes God seem like a strange sort of god. Sorry, but I cannot believe that a god who said 'It is not good that man should be alone' and made Eve to be his companion, would then turn round and say, 'It is good for a man not to touch a woman.'[19] But of course, God did not say that. Paul did. So why?"

La Roche smiled at his young protégé. Whether he agreed with him we don't know, but we can suspect he was pleased that Michael Venn was thinking. The young radical then continued,

"In the four gospels there is very little talk of sex being sinful, or of the need to remain celibate, etc., and Paul, as I have already said, is remarkably tolerant on the subject. Indeed, he suggests that to avoid fornication 'let every man have his own wife and let every woman have her own husband'[20] but puzzlingly he concludes his thoughts on this subject with, 'for I would that all men were even as myself. But every man hath his proper gift of God, one after this manner, and another after

---

[19] 1 Corinthians 7:1
[20] 1 Corinthians 7:2

that',[21] which you have to agree is about as close as it was possible for him to admit that his 'gift of God', as he put it, was different from the accepted norm and hence that he *had* to remain celibate.

When Paul talks about marriage, he unambiguously states that husbands should look after wives and wives look after husbands. So why does he say, 'it is good for a man not to touch a woman', which I hope you will agree is most certainly ambiguous? Is he suggesting that 'it is good that men do not touch women'? However, in the light of his views on marriage, this seems unlikely. Or is he saying 'it is good for a man, *like me,* not to touch a woman'; possibly because he has no desire to anyway and so it is *good* that he does not? Whichever is the case, there is no doubting that Paul's ideal is celibacy. Why? Why doesn't he say 'I would that all men were even as myself and have a loving wife and be in a happy marriage?' No, there is something missing that he could not say and my contention is that it had something to do with his 'gift of God' as he euphemistically puts it, and it is *this* which drove his personal need for celibacy. Thus I find myself concluding that perhaps Paul liked men rather than women. It could certainly explain his Platonic friendship with women, who would not have felt sexually threatened by him, could explain his idealised views of marriage, and could also explain his guilt about sex and his personal and absolute need to remain celibate.

So was his passionate, almost fanatical belief in a god that loves him, a type of substitute for that lack of human warmth and human love? Might it have been a kind of escape from the hard reality of not being desired, not being wanted, or, if one was desired, of having to publicly and privately deny that desire? And if that was so, would it not also be logical to then think that the only way one could truly *see* that loving god would be if one was celibate? So does Paul assume that his

---

[21] 1 Corinthians 7:7

knowledge of God comes from either his chosen or forced abstinence from sex and preaches and writes this, even though, logically, this cannot possibly be true, because if it were that would suggest that those who do have relationships and sex cannot know God, when of course they can? God is not exclusive.

Unfortunately his continual mentioning of sexual abstinence, and his urging of others to be as he (celibate), has the effect of forcing this, as an ideal, into our religion. The linkage between virginity, abstaining from sex and Godliness keeps being cited. In the 'Acts of Paul and Thecla' that I mentioned earlier, Thecla's entire life seems to be one non-stop round of defending her virginity and being miraculously saved from almost certain death. Our own St Bibiana died horribly defending her virginity. Why is virginity deemed so important? Surely, it ought to be the having of children that is more important? From the emphasis placed on this one can almost infer that anyone who is not a virgin has no hope of salvation. It is Paul who, if not introducing all of this talk of celibacy, magnifies it out of proportion, so that it almost becomes part of the doctrine of the religion and our Church, and hence what our Prior and his fellow fundamentalist fanatics are picking up on. Indeed, our beloved Prior never stops reminding us that 'the one hundred and forty four thousand who will be redeemed from the earth will be virgins who have not been defiled with women.' In the eyes of so many, Adam and Eve were damned for simply having eaten of the apple when it was the most logical and natural thing to do!"

Did our Adam Callow startle at hearing his friend Michael Venn mention his and Eve's name thus? Was he, Adam Callow, already damned? And how did Michael know about himself and Eve? Had he seen them talking together? No, no …. thank goodness …. as he realised that Michael had been talking about his and Eve's namesakes in the Book of Genesis. But he must have thought, am I, like the first Adam, already on the way to tasting the apple, as he would have been unable to easily forget Eve holding one up at his market stall, 'You do like what you see, don't you?' Had she been tempting him, in the same way that the Biblical Eve had tempted her Adam? Would he, Adam Callow, be damned as Michael Venn had just suggested?

"Yes Michael," said La Roche slowly. "As I have already told Adam, I took Holy Orders after my young wife was taken from me and I have often questioned my motives for doing so. Was I trying to escape from my loss and seeking sanctuary from the travails of life in the safe confines of a monastery; safe from the danger of having my heart broken again? Did I find comfort and solace and learn to know God better because I was lonely and did not enjoy the company of and pleasures of a woman? Or was I a better person for having suffered a loss and this loss put my life in perspective, and hence it was because of this that I was open to discovering God? I don't know the answer. All I do know is that one goes through life and tries one's best to do the right thing at the right time. At times 'the right thing' is obvious, at others it is not."

The two young men said nothing. Although neither had experienced the love, loss and heartbreak that Stephen La Roche had described, they could tell from the tone of his voice that it had obviously hurt him and that the pain of it was still with him.

"But we are not here to discuss me," La Roche added in a breezier manner, before continuing,

"Your thesis Michael; I grant you has a logic to it. However, may I suggest that prevalent attitudes to women and their place in society at the time of Paul might have also had some bearing on his thoughts and writings? And may I also suggest that not a great deal has changed since then either. Even these days women are still married with dowries, which can certainly give the impression that it is a payment or bribe to the husband to take the woman off her parents' hands, and so does make one wonder if some husbands do actually want their wives simply for themselves, for who they are, rather than just for some easy money?"

"Certainly," said Venn, "But haven't our current ideas come from Paul's? Those expressed in his First Epistle to Timothy - 'Let the woman learn in silence with all subjection. But I suffer not a woman to teach, nor to usurp authority over the man, but to be in silence. For Adam was first formed, then Eve. And Adam was not deceived, but the woman being deceived was in the transgression.'[22] - are hardly ones which regard women as equals! Jesus didn't talk like this. All of this came later. Indeed, if I have not misunderstood what I have read, there are some who say that Paul misrepresented Jesus' word. Prior Obscurant and his like don't have to make things up, all the proof he needs for his warped opinions are there, already written down," concluded an emotional Michael Venn.

"You may think our Prior's opinions 'warped', as you put it, but I can tell you there are many in our Church, going right to the very top, who think exactly the same way. Be very careful of giving your opinions too freely my young brother," cautioned La Roche.

"Now, on a scriptural point," he continued, "there is some debate as to whether St Paul actually wrote the Pastoral Epistles, as they are sometimes known (the First and Second Epistles to Timothy and the Epistle to Titus) and that these may have been written on his instruction, and hence the views expressed are possibly not quite as he had intended. You will have appreciated that there is nothing like this in any of his other epistles. However, I grant you that there is perhaps an over emphasis on celibacy and that there is some current debate as to whether Paul truly represented Jesus' word. However in Paul's defence, I think the quote you cited from "Acts of Paul and Thecla" also continued to describe him as a man 'full of

____

grace and mercy; at one time he seemed like a man, and at another time he seemed like an angel,' which, I hope you will both agree is pretty complimentary."

La Roche then added with a smile, "And with that thought, shall we give St Paul a bit of respite for this afternoon?"

"Thank you brother Stephen", said Callow and Venn almost simultaneously and hence to the amusement of all three.

"No, it is I who must thank you, my young brothers. It has been a long time since I have had such a stimulating discussion. It is you who have given me much to think about. We must do this again sometime."

"Might we meet like this again?" asked Michael Venn enthusiastically. "There is so much we haven't talked about; St Augustine, for a start."

"Yes, I don't see why not. I will look forward to it. In the meantime however, I must caution both of you again not to say a word to anyone. *We know* that we are discussing, debating if you will, but others could and would so easily misinterpret our discussions as heresy and we know the consequences for that. So please for all our sakes, not a word."

The two young novice brothers nodded their understanding.

"Oh dear me!" exclaimed brother La Roche. "Would you mind helping me up? I seem to have got a bit stiff sitting on these hard rocks."

As the three made their way back down to the monastery, three different trains of thought were tumbling in three different minds. For the young, or not so young firebrand, Michael Venn, it was getting to the bottom of what he saw as the false teaching, false representation of Christ's message of love and tolerance and an over emphasis on chastity and celibacy by the Church. For Adam Callow it was still the contradictions of young love against the backdrop of being torn between the supposed need for celibacy coupled with not wishing to damn himself on the one hand, versus the beautiful face and figure, coupled with the anticipated pleasurable charms of Eve Lilith on the other. And as for brother La Roche? He was pleased at having spent an hour or so in the presence of two young lively, questioning minds, glad to have had his mind re-awakened, to notice the new buds on the trees, to feel the wind on his face anew with all the innocence and joy of a child who is experiencing such delights for the first time; to feel vital again, to feel alive again. Only we can suspect that for brother La Roche he may have realised that such days, such vital days, may not be his forever and hence that it was up to him to live, truly live whatever life God was still prepared to grant him.

Chapter 7

Two days later we find young novice-brother Callow manning, though perhaps 'youthing', if there is such a word and so might be a better way to describe his endeavours, the vegetable stall at the market. He was not quite as shy and awkward as he had been on the first occasion but his confidence was not exactly over-flowing either. Of course the beautiful Eve Lilith showed up and our young Adam Callow was both pleased and awkward in equal measure at seeing her.

"Hello Adam Callow. I hoped I'd find you here."

"Hello, Miss Lilith."

"No silly, call me Eve," she replied, leaning across the stall at him so that her loose blouse fell open and the plump roundness of her breasts were displayed to him. Oh yes, this was no accident; she knew exactly what she was doing!

"Are you looking Adam? You naughty boy," she said, standing upright again, tossing her silky black hair and making an extremely half-hearted attempt at adjusting her oh-so-wayward blouse, so as to ….. preserve her modesty? ….. hardly?

"I, er ….."

"Don't make excuses, Adam Callow, I know what you were doing," and just in case Adam Callow wasn't feeling uncomfortable enough, she picked up a large orange carrot, held it upright by the greenery in one hand and ran a finger of the other hand slowly down it, while at the same time looking sideways at Callow with big dark, soft eyes and a cheeky, suggestive grin on her lips.

"Oh, this is nice," she said.

In a hopeless attempt at trying to defuse what was so

obviously going on, Callow stupidly asked,

"Would you like to buy some of those?"

"Oh yes please Adam. Can I buy yours?"

Poor Callow. He had absolutely no idea how to deal with this, was almost writhing with embarrassment and in a fruitless attempt at hiding this, set-to frantically rearranging some of the other vegetables.

"I'm sorry Adam. I was only joking," she said softly, realising that she had obviously gone just that bit too far with him. He was still a bit of a boy, wasn't he? A sweet boy. But she would make a man of him. Oh yes, she would do that!

"You do still like me, don't you? I haven't upset you, have I?"

"No. Er …. no you haven't. And …. yes, I do still like you," he stammered.

"Good. I am glad we are still friends. Will you walk with me, Adam. I would like that."

"Well I …. I can't this afternoon. The market doesn't finish until …. and then after that I have a lot to do when I get back …."

"Will you walk with me tomorrow, Adam?"

"Yes, er yes," he replied, more because he was unable to think of a reason why he couldn't than because he'd actually decided that he did wish to.

"Good. I'll meet you here. When?"

"No! No!" said Callow as visions of the craggy countenance of McBane armed with his flagellum flashed through Callow's mind. No, he couldn't possibly meet her here in the market square just outside the monastery. "We can't meet here," though a part of his thoughts were also wondering why was he going to meet with her anyway? This was madness.

But …. but McBane was prosecuting the witch, wasn't he? Thank goodness for that, reasoned the now slightly wiser Adam Callow, because in the meantime he'd come to learn that what McBane possessed in zeal and sadism was balanced by what he lacked in intellect and general mental capacity. One task at any one time was about all McBane could handle; or, to put it more accurately perhaps, making one person's life a misery at any one time was about all he was capable of if he had to do the thinking. So yes, he (Adam Callow) could walk with Eve, but they would have to meet away from the monastery, away from where prying eyes might see them together. She seemed to understand, because there was no need for Callow to explain why they couldn't 'meet here'. Possibly she had heard one of Prior Obscurant's sermons, or perhaps the general reputation of the Black Friars Monastery was more widely known than Callow had realised.

"Do you know the Hartstane road, Adam?"

He nodded.

"Just before you get to the top of the hill, there is a turning on the left hand side. A small path leads off through some birch trees and comes out at a flat area with some large boulders."

"Yes, I know it."

This must be fate he thought; he, Venn, and brother La Roche going to the very same place just a couple of days earlier. If they hadn't done so, he would never have known of its existence. This happy geographical coincidence reassured him that their (Eve's and his) plans were moving forward into at least partially known territory. With bolstered confidence on Adam Callow's side, they agreed the time for their rendezvous and then parted.

"Goodbye, Adam. Until tomorrow. Don't be late."

"No, I won't. Until tomorrow, Eve."

Oh goodness; was Adam Callow in love? Did he really know what he was getting into, where a relationship with this girl /

young woman was going to take him, how it might change his life forever? But do any of us know these things at the outset? Can love ever be logical, or is it almost by definition illogical, unexplainable, blind and thus to put it somewhat unpleasantly bluntly, leads to probably the biggest gamble that any of us are likely to make in our lives? Hence perhaps it is not only as well that we don't know how things will work out, but also probably necessary that we don't know!

After praying in front of the wanton image of St Bibiana, which surprisingly he hardly noticed that evening, Adam Callow slept well. He might have mentally chewed over some of the subject matter that he, Michael Venn and brother La Roche had discussed a couple of days earlier, but for him the most important thing that came out of that day was learning where he would meet his new sweetheart on the morrow. So full of warm feelings of love rather than hot feelings of lust, he drifted off into a peaceful sleep. Peaceful that is until he was dragged out of bed three hours later to go and pray, but even the nocturnal rituals of monastic life didn't prevent him from dropping off again almost as soon as he had re-settled himself in his cot in the novice-monks' subterranean dormitory.

After a morning of trying to concentrate on some of the finer points of Canon Law, the afternoon came round and a nervous Adam Callow set off up the road to Hartstane. Would he fail to recognise the turn-off and so miss his tryst? Would he have to explain how he had simply not seen the path? Yes, he'd known where it was, but somehow he'd missed it and by the time he had realised that, it was too late. Too late! Oh no! But his attack of panic subsided when, there was the path, in fact just as he'd remembered it, leading off through the birch trees. He felt the urge to run, but resisted it and walked on until finally he left the birch trees behind and reached the open hillside just beneath the boulder strewn amphitheatre. He walked up the incline, but where was his Eve? He couldn't see her anywhere. Had he arrived too early? Or had she decided that …. but just as this last ghastly thought was beginning to form in his head he heard, "Over here" and saw her waving from behind some scrub-like bushes which were growing in front of the small cliff at the back of the natural amphitheatre. He walked over and joined her behind the bushes and beneath a small overhang of the cliff. This hidden, roofed recess wasn't quite a cave, but with the bushes forming a barrier in front of it, it was the next best thing to one. No wonder that he hadn't seen it when he, Venn and brother La Roche had visited this place a few days earlier.

He also noticed that Eve had evidently thought a lot more about the practical aspects of this rendezvous than he had and felt a little embarrassed and annoyed with himself that he hadn't put more effort into this meeting of theirs. She'd had the foresight to bring a blanket for them to sit on and Callow could see that she had obviously moved enough of the cuboid boulders which littered the floor of the semi-cave, so as to spread it on the resulting area of flat ground. She'd also brought what looked like a bottle and two plain goblets.

"Come and sit with me, Adam Callow," she said, smiling at him and patting the blanket beside her.

However, instead of doing that, he remained standing and looked at her. Goodness, she was more beautiful than he'd remembered. Her black hair tumbling down over smooth silky white skinned shoulders. Her pale face, with dark doe-like eyes set about a straight nose and above high cheek bones. And those lips; pale pink with that almost hypnotic small dark diamond between them in the centre where they didn't quite meet. Oh how he wanted to kiss that enigmatic mouth! She was wearing the same orange and gold dress again, which was spread out like a large fan on the blanket. He noticed that her gold coloured bodice wasn't as tight as he had seen it on earlier occasions and the white blouse likewise appeared looser fitting. Having observed this, he sat down beside her.

She handed him a goblet of wine. "Welcome, Adam."

They touched their goblets.

"Welcome, Eve," he replied nervously.

They sat there looking at each other, each a little unsure of what to do next. They drank their wine.

"Would you like some more?" she enquired.

"No, no I shouldn't," he replied.

"Oh, come on," she said with a smile, "this afternoon is just for us," and refilled his goblet.

Callow felt the warm glow of the wine course through his body; but he probably didn't notice it dissolving his inhibitions as it did so. She stroked his hand and then his face. And then it was as if they both knew the next part of the script, or screenplay, as both turned away and put down their now empty goblets, turned towards each other again and fell desperately into each other's arms.

Those pink lips tasted wonderful to Adam Callow, the smooth ivory skin of her neck likewise, and then he discovered that the gold yellow bodice was definitely looser than it had been previously as it came off without much difficulty at all! And the loose fitting blouse? Before he knew it his eager hands were feeling her soft firm breasts and his lips kissing her hard pink nipples. Their blood was up and it did not take long for Adam Callow's habit and Eve's beautiful golden orange dress to be discarded and for the apple to be well and truly tasted. And yes, it tasted good. No, not just good, wonderful; the nearest thing to heaven on this earth. But their first taste of heaven on this earth did not last long and all too soon their tiny, elusive taste of it was over and they lay back breathing hard.

So what had happened? Oh yes, we know that they had made love, had sex, if you think that sounds less ambiguous. But what else had happened?

Adam, bathed in post coital euphoria, felt a peace that he had not known in ages, if indeed, ever. All the troubles in his world had evaporated and he felt at one with all that surrounded him. He had done it. He was now a man! A proud masculine man. He had known a woman. And pride at this and the accompanying contentment that it brought flowed through him. Had his namesake felt the same euphoria after he had tasted the apple in the Garden? In which case, why was shame, stigma and sin attached to something so beautiful? However, no sooner than he had posed this question of himself than his perfect peace was shattered with both a question and was it also an answer? Oh good God, had he made her pregnant? A cold chill of fear crept over him, fear of what this would mean, fear of an unknown future, a future over which he would have no control. Was the die cast? The die of his life. Had it been cast in those few glorious moments? What price was he going to have to pay for straying into God's Paradise? And so Adam Callow began to feel his world starting to collapse around him.

He looked across at her. Eve; Eve the first woman made from a rib of Adam was lying there with a peaceful and contented smile on her face. She was now a woman. However, although supposedly made of the same flesh, she, the woman, was the female, and her life's agenda was not the same as his. She had succeeded as nature had intended her to do, to get her egg fertilised. She would now breed, she would have a child; the entire justification for her life as a woman, as a female. She was now past the first hurdle; for in this sexual act she had not only ensured the fertilisation of her egg, but had also simultaneously secured her mate, her man, her husband, who would love her and toil for her and her offspring because she provided him with the sex that nature required him to need. This man (Adam Callow) would be educated and rich, rich enough to look after her and her young; her baby. No wonder she had a peaceful and contented smile on her face! Was life in fact so basic, so pagan ….. so ….. so animalistic?

And if she would have a child, his child, would he have to

leave the monastery? He certainly could not stay there with maniacs like Obscurant and McBane; goodness knows what would happen to him if they got to know of this whilst he was still there as a novice-brother! Would he have to marry this girl, who he suddenly realised, he hardly knew? What would his parents think? Would they take him back after this? Indeed, could they take him back after this; his 'having had carnal knowledge of a woman outwith wedlock' and having left the monastery in disgrace? The heavy sounding words sounded so much heavier now, like those of a judge solemnly passing sentence; a life sentence! 'In the sweat of thy face shalt thou eat bread, till thou return to the ground; for out of it wast thou taken: for dust thou art, and unto dust shalt thou return.'[23] He would have to get a job in order to support his wife and child, but who would employ him? He'd only been at the monastery a few months and so learnt next to nothing, and he'd have 'for getting a girl pregnant' hanging round his neck for all to see! Oh, Good God what would he do? What could he do? Certainly not 'that which he would.' The possibilities of a life that he and his parents had talked about, now lay in ruins. Ruins, as the result of daring to spend a few euphoric minutes in a paradise that he now realised came at a dreadful price for mortal man.

And what of his immortal soul? That must also now be in ruins as it was inconceivable that he could possibly become one of the 'one hundred and forty four thousand with the seal of God in his forehead,' for he was now most definitely defiled. Defiled by woman! And his sin was a hundredfold worse than that, because he'd known the woman outside of Holy Wedlock. Oh Dear God, he was damned! What had he done? Adam Callow; no, not a god, just an ordinary young man and already in ruins.

But was it all his fault? Hadn't Prior Obscurant almost incessantly warned them that, 'the foremost temptation that the Devil places in the path of man, is woman'? Yes, he (Adam

---

[23] Genesis 3:19

Callow) had failed, he had been tempted just as his namesake had been tempted, but was this all his failing or was it in part the work of the Devil? After all it was the Devil in the form of a serpent that had tempted Eve and it was Eve who had tempted Adam. What was it that his friend Michael Venn had quoted from Paul's Epistle to Timothy? 'And Adam was not deceived, but the woman being deceived was in the transgression.' So had his Eve, Eve Lilith, in her turn, tempted him?

He raised himself on his elbows and looked at her lying there with her contented enigmatic pink lipped smile set on her so beautiful ivory skinned face. Yes, it was she who had brought the wine and she who had given it to him, ... no, not as a sacrament, but as .... Oh no, 'The nectar of Satan'! Had she offered him the wine knowing that it would reduce his will, reduce his ability to resist her charms? Was she .... and a dreadful realisation began to dawn on him .... was she a she-devil sent by the Devil to lead him astray? And he, poor innocent fool, had succumbed, had been tempted, tempted by the joys of the flesh, tempted by a disciple of Satan! He had to get away from her, escape her evil influence, get away right now! He sat up, frantically reached for his habit and pulled it over his head.

"I .... I, I must go," he stammered.

"So soon? Hold me Adam," she purred.

Tempted! Tempted by the delights of the flesh!

"No, no. I can't," came his strangled reply.

"Why not?" she asked crossly, her mood suddenly changing upon hearing this rejection of her. "Ah. You've had what you want and now you just ....." as she reached for her yellow orange dress and pulled it to her to cover her nakedness, to cover her shame - just as her namesake in the Garden had similarly reached for fig leaves? "You are just like the rest Adam Callow! All you men want is sex. And now you have had it ….."

But Adam Callow hadn't just wanted sex. Well yes, he had wanted sex, but not *just* sex, and right now, if only she knew it, sex was the last thing he wanted and he was wishing as fervently as he could that he'd never had anything to do with sex! But no, it hadn't been *just* sex. He had felt something for her, something that he couldn't define. Was it love? Because if it wasn't love, what was that warm, contented feeling that had enveloped him over the preceding days and immediately after their lovemaking? But right now he had no time to muse on what constituted love, he had to try and get a grip on what had just happened; come to terms with it. He needed space, and time, to think.

"No. That's not true," he managed and leaned across in an attempt to kiss her, but she pushed him a way.

"Go on. Run away. Go back to the safety of your monastery."

And so, shamefacedly, Adam Callow stood up, let his rough dark grey habit fall about him, picked up the cord and tied it round his waist, turned and walked away, back to the supposed safety of his monastery."

"At this point I had to stop," said Joe, "because again I heard Harry crying upstairs. Putting down the book, I went up to see him.

"Hey, steady on old lad. Can't sleep?"

"It hurts, dad, and I can't see straight."

"Yeah," I said impotently, knowing that there was absolutely nothing I could do to help, other than comfort him.

"What can't you see straight?" I asked.

"It's like I see two of everything," replied my sobbing son, and then to my surprise he suddenly came out with,

"There was a woman there, dad. A beautiful woman in a golden dress."

"Where?" I asked.

"In the cave."

Now please don't forget it was after midnight, I was tired and debating with myself whether I would creep into bed with Elizabeth or hunker down on the sofa and so it took me the proverbial 'two ticks' to grasp what Harry was talking about.

"Are you sure?" I asked as calmly as I could. "I thought you said you went looking for that pretty moth?"

"Yes, I did. It flew into the cave."

"But when I looked in the cave, Harry, it wasn't there and neither was there any beautiful woman. Honestly. And mummy went into the cave and she didn't see a moth or a woman. There was nothing in there, except a few square looking boulders on the floor. Now, try and sleep, there's a good boy. Everything will be better in the morning."

Where had Harry got this 'beautiful woman in a golden dress' from? There had been nothing in the cave. I had looked into it and Elizabeth had actually gone right in and neither of us had seen anything. Then the penny dropped. Possibly Harry had taken a little peek at the story I was reading, trying to find out about the cave and the strangely shaped tree, just as I was trying to do? The book had just been sitting on the coffee table in the living room after all. He could have easily picked it up. Yes, I thought, that was probably it. And then of course I realised that it wouldn't have been only the 'beautiful woman in a golden dress' that he would have read about and made a mental note not to leave the book lying about.

After a minute or two with my arm around him I noticed that his eyes had closed and his breathing had become more regular. He might have been surprised to learn that his father's breathing had also become a bit more regular now that I'd realised how he had come by his little story, and that my concern about that had reverted to the decision of whether to creep into bed with Elizabeth, or, rather like young Adam Callow, 'go back to the safety of my sofa?'

<u>Chapter 8</u>

Whether Adam Callow was safer in a monastery under the watchful eye of Prior Obscurant and the gentle guiding hand of novice-master Rodiron McBane than he was out in the real world was a moot point. As this of course rather depends on whether one considers it safer to be constantly told of and reminded about the temptations presented by women and how defilement by them would preclude one from entering God's Celestial Kingdom, not to mention, of course, the risk of being flogged for momentary lapses of concentration, or to be left to make up one's own mind about such matters.

Although we have no idea of the mental torment novice-brother Adam Callow went through trying to mesh spiritual objectives with more basic temporal matters such as pregnancy back in the safe confines of his monastery, we can guess that he could and did tell no-one; neither Michael Venn nor brother La Roche. What had happened between him and Eve had to remain his secret.

After his initial panic as to whether his actions with Eve would leave his life in tatters, he calmed down and realised that the end of the world hadn't arrived just yet. He recalled having heard a conversation between his mother and sister about friends of theirs who were wishing to have a baby but had not been successful and from this reasoned that having sex did not necessarily result in the woman becoming pregnant, and so partially convinced himself that it didn't have to follow that Eve would become pregnant just as a result of that one liaison. Oh how he wished he knew more about all of this as there was just so much he didn't know; but who could he ask? Certainly not his mother or sister because they would immediately want to know why he was asking and / or guess and then his family would know and this was precisely what he was wishing to avoid. The only other person that came to mind was brother La

Roche as he had been married once and so might know about these things, but for much the same reasons he couldn't ask him directly either. Perhaps though, he might manage to slip his question in during one of their discussions? Yes, that might be possible.

Subsequently he learned that Venn and La Roche had arranged a date for the next of these discussions and, fortunately for the three of them, when the day came round it was another fair spring day. Fortunately, because it meant that they could use their previous venue again; well away from the cold stone, but porous walls of the monastery.

The buds on the trees had begun to burst, releasing their small delicate bundles of green out into the fresh spring air. Even Callow, whose mind was rather preoccupied with other matters, was surprised how this alone made such a change to the stone road, effectively enclosing it with soft green on one side so that now the only open view was out over the drystone wall to the fields. Likewise, the small path leading through the birch trees to the grass covered amphitheatre had become transformed and was now more akin to a tunnel of new young leaves leading through to the bright sunlight of the open grassy area beyond. A physical manifestation of hope for our young Adam Callow? However, even in its new spring guise, going back to that little natural rock amphitheatre could not have been easy for him. The sandstone blocks upon which the three of them were sitting were just a few metres away from where he had lost his virginity to Eve on that afternoon of hot passion. Almost inevitably he would have been reliving the memories of this and trying at the same time to be oh-so-careful not to let anything slip which might give himself and her away. Luckily, the three of them were facing the wonderful view across the valley and not the rock outcrop and cave, so at least he didn't have to sit there looking at the location of his taste of Paradise - or was it sin and subsequent shame? - of that day.

"Now where had we got to?" asked brother La Roche when

they had all made themselves as comfortable as was possible on the cold, hard sandstone blocks.

"Oh yes. As I remember Michael, you had been giving our patron saint St Paul a bit of severe scrutiny."

"Had I?"

"Yes, suggesting that you thought his perceived misogyny was a reaction to women not finding him attractive," said La Roche with a hint of smile.

"Well, I think I suggested that it could have been for a number of reasons," replied Michael Venn, a little surprised at Stephen La Roche's remark.

"And your argument Michael, was that our religion and Church took on an anti-women and anti-sex stance because Paul had in your opinion, had difficulties with women and sex?"

"Yes. Well you can't deny that he did," replied Michael Venn, "and then Augustine carries on where Paul left off."

"Oh? But please don't forget my young friend, how both Augustine and Paul, were in many ways the prime movers in establishing our Church and spreading the word about our religion."

"No I don't, and that is why their views and opinions are so important. However, both had serious problems with their relationship with women and sex, and it is because of this and their undoubted influence on our religion, that I am suggesting that their opinions have resulted in an unnatural bias against women and sex."

"Yes Michael? And you blame Augustine as well? And there was I thinking that a red blooded young man like yourself might have let him off the hook for his asking God to 'Give me chastity and continence, but not yet',"[24] said La Roche with a

---

[24] St Augustine, Confessions, Book VIII:7

mischievous grin.

"No, I don't see why," said a much-too-serious-for-himself, Michael Venn. "But Stephen, wasn't he supposed to have said that when young? So perhaps one should forgive him and put it down to a bit of bravado?"

"True and possibly," conceded Stephen La Roche.

"However that said, I don't know whether to dislike him, or feel sorry for him. I suspect he was spoilt by and was probably dominated by his mother, Monica, as his writings suggest that she had a, what some might describe as, an unhealthy influence on him well into his thirties, and it was not until she died that he finally felt free to do as he wanted. There was no doubt that her death hurt him and he felt her loss as he wrote in his 'Confessions', 'It was because I was now bereft of all the comfort I had had from her that my soul was wounded and my life seemed shattered, for her life and mine had been as one.'[25] She was without doubt the woman with whom he shared his thoughts, in whom he confided. However his, 'her life and mine had been as one' is the type of sentiment that is usually expressed about a wife, not one's mother."

"But don't all young men regard their mother as a female role model and use them as a sounding board for their future relationships with women?" suggested La Roche.

What might have passed through young Adam Callow's mind when he heard his mentor observe this? Had he thought of his dear mother as a role model when he had agreed to meet Eve? The honest answer was probably 'no' as the only thought that he'd seriously entertained about her (his mother) was that of trying to ensure that she did not find out about his liaison with Eve, or if Eve had become pregnant. However, it must have even crossed Adam Callow's mind that if this were to be the case, a lot more people than just his mother would get to

---

[25]St Augustine, Confessions, Book IX:12

know about it. After a moment of mild panic at this prospect, he remembered that he must try and ask his question of Stephen La Roche as soon as the opportunity presented itself. In the meantime might he have also consoled himself with the somewhat convoluted argument that if he could make some sort of connection with his sister, namely, that if Eve was a friend of hers, then that would mean that Eve had the approval of his sister and, as he was sure his mother would know his sister's friends, then that would suggest that Eve also probably had the approval of his mother? Er ….. didn't it? But of course he wasn't at all sure of any of this because he didn't actually know if Eve was a friend of his sister's, he just vaguely recognised her from somewhere and so was simply presuming this connection. Oh why couldn't a relationship with a woman be simpler? And why hadn't he been a little more circumspect and found out a bit more about Eve before rushing off and getting her pregnant? But he hadn't 'rushed off and …..' It had ….. it had just happened. What a fool! But no, calm down. He didn't actually know that she was pregnant. It was just, if she was. What he needed to do now was try and get his question answered. So with this uppermost in his mind, he sat there in silence only partially listening to his mentor and fellow novice debate, whilst not daring to open his mouth for fear of letting his guilty secret out.

"Yes, young men certainly," agreed Michael Venn, "but Augustine was still having his life ruled by his mother when he was in his thirties. As most men develop relationships with other women of their own age, the use of their mother for this purpose fades and instead of continuing to confide in her they start to confide in their new female partner, so by the time they are married their wife should have completely superseded their mother in this role. As I am sure you know Stephen, Augustine was all-but married. He'd had a mistress for something like fifteen years and had had a son by her. He was in his thirties when his mother died. Of course he wrote his 'Confessions' considerably later, so possibly was reminiscing a little when he wrote them. Though quite why he felt so kindly towards his mother is surprising considering that it was she who had arranged his marriage to a twelve year old girl, who, of course, was from the right social class and so was the cause of his having to split with his mistress, who obviously was not, and send her back to Africa. As he wrote, 'the woman with whom I had been living was torn from my side as an obstacle to my marriage and this was a blow which crushed my heart to bleeding, because I loved her dearly,'[26] this suggests that this proposed marriage was not of *his* choosing, that breaking with his mistress had really hurt him and so I would have thought that he would have found it difficult to forgive his mother for that. Indeed, I would have expected him to have ignored his mother and married his mistress, for whom he obviously did have strong feelings."

Again, we might wonder what novice-brother Adam Callow was thinking as Michael Venn related this? Might it have been how his Eve would be seen in the eyes of others; as his mistress? Would he, like Augustine, be forbidden to marry her because she was beneath his station in life and would he have to disown her and send her away? His ears must have been burning and his heart must have been sinking at the prospect of this as a future. Oh goodness, what was he going to do? Would he fight for Eve? Though more importantly, could he fight for Eve if he left the monastery and his parents disowned him? And hot on the heals of this question came the next; namely, did he actually love Eve? Yes, he was sure there was something special between them, a spark which he could not define, but was that love, or was it simply lust? What did love feel like when it struck you? How did you know when you'd fallen in love? Poor young Adam Callow must have realised that he knew nothing of any of this.

"And," continued Venn, "when this future saint (Augustine)

---

[26] St Augustine, Confessions, Book VI:15

discovered that the woman, sorry, young girl that his mother had selected for him was still two years too young to marry him - she was only twelve and so he would have to wait two years for her - he took another mistress! Augustine's relationship with his mother, although not quite like that of Oedipus to his mother, was certainly that of a spoilt 'mother's boy'. He was so obviously the apple of her eye, and she was to all intents and purposes his wife, with his mistresses only being there to gratify his sexual desires."

'Gratify his sexual desires;' was that what he, Adam Callow, had been doing; simply gratifying his sexual desires and was Eve just his plaything? Oh what a low, selfish specimen he was? But he didn't *not* love Eve, he just wasn't sure that he *did* love her. But if he didn't know what love was, what it felt like, how could he know? And while thoughts, or rather excuses such as these were seething in his head, it suddenly struck him that Venn had been talking about mistresses, and hadn't he just said that Augustine had lived with one for fifteen years yet had only had one son? They must have had sex more than once, so yes, it would seem that having sex did not automatically result in pregnancy. Perhaps he should put his question now?

"But with all these mistresses ….." Callow blurted out, cutting across Michael Venn's train of argument.

"All these?" said La Roche. "Michael has only mentioned two."

"Well, um, but why did he only have one son?"

The old man looked at him, no doubt a little annoyed at his having so rudely interrupted his friend, though must have realised that years previously this aspect of life had been a mystery to him and so kindly replied,

"Knowing a woman does not automatically mean that she will become with child. When you are married, some of these mysteries will become less mysterious, though I don't think men, or man will ever fully understand how new life is created."

Was Adam Callow's mind put at rest by that answer, or did he then start worrying about a possible distinction between being married and not being married? After all, La Roche had said 'when you are married,' but he, Adam Callow, was not. If being married made a difference to one's immortal soul then why should it not also make a difference as to whether or not Eve would become pregnant? But was marriage so important? Did it in fact make a difference to one's immortal soul? Augustine had had a mistress and had had a child with her, and subsequently had gone on to become a saint. And as a saint, indeed as the patron saint of their monastery, he must have had the seal of God in his forehead and must be one of the one hundred and forty four thousand who would be redeemed from the earth because a saint couldn't possibly be left out! But Augustine, by his own admission, was not a virgin, had been 'defiled by woman' and had *not* been married. So perhaps he (Adam Callow) had nothing to worry about; his immortal soul was not in danger after all? He must have breathed an enormous sigh of relief at coming to this conclusion. It wasn't inevitable that Eve would become pregnant, and if Augustine, a revered saint, had both had mistresses and a son born out of wedlock, then he, Adam Callow, could also reasonably assume that his immortal soul was not in danger either. Phew! And so with this immense weight off his puny shoulders he mentally rejoined the discussion between Michael Venn and Stephen La Roche.

"You were saying, my young friend," said La Roche to Michael Venn.

"It seems that keeping his mistress, the mother of his son and the woman he professed to love dearly, was not at the top of Augustine's list of priorities. And neither were the feelings of the girl to whom he was betrothed to marry, who he 'liked her well enough'[27] though obviously didn't love, as he saw nothing

---

[27] St Augustine, Confessions, Book VI:13

wrong in taking another mistress in the interim. Nor were the feelings of that second mistress important to him, as he would have known right at the outset that he was only going to have a relationship with her for those two years prior to getting married. No wonder he was subsequently so disgusted with himself."

"Yes," replied Stephen La Roche somewhat pensively, "Augustine did admit to being 'more a slave of lust than a true lover of marriage.'"[28]

But Michael Venn wasn't finished yet.

"Exactly! But for him to then go on and write that the reason he subsequently broke his promise of marriage to the young girl to whom he was betrothed was because 'the voice of Truth told me'[29] .... The voice of truth had told him! In the very next paragraph in his Confessions, he witters on about 'I have found you, our Creator, and your Word who is God with you, one God with you,' and so he sycophantically drones on. There is no mention of his treatment of his first mistress, the mother of his child that he dispatched back to Africa, or the poor girl that he was to have married, or his second mistress, or of any desire on his part to try and make some form of amends to them. The only sin he admits to is that of not seeing God earlier! It is as if his treatment of those women simply doesn't register with him. He expresses no remorse for his actions, other than the purely selfish how these hurt himself, and of course, 'my sin'; 'Oh how wrong of me that I failed to see you Lord'. It is *not*, 'Oh dear God forgive me for treating those poor women so badly, what can I possibly do to make some form of amends to them?'"

Michael Venn fell silent for a minute, perhaps wondering if he had said too much in anger? However, the older monk said nothing. But, who can blame young Michael Venn for being angry? He, and no doubt the older Stephen La Roche, would

---

[28] St Augustine, Confessions, Book VI:5
[29] St Augustine, Confessions, Book VIII:1

have realised that we all make mistakes. That in itself is not the problem; however, failing to acknowledge one's mistakes and then doing nothing to try and rectify them, most certainly is. So we can reasonably speculate that Michael Venn must have been wondering how such a man could become a saint and be revered by a religion that preaches about love of one's fellow man? Or is it that *that* is the problem; the religion is for men, and so are we to infer that for some reason women don't count and so remorse for actions against women is not necessary?

His self control back in check, Michael Venn continued.

"I think there can be no doubt that his domineering mother tried to force the marriage on him and so has to take a lot of the blame for breaking up the long standing relationship he'd had with his first mistress. After his mother had died, and so pressure on him from her was no more, he probably felt no longer obliged to go through with a marriage to a girl so many years his junior who he obviously didn't love. I also suspect that he probably hadn't got over the break-up with his first long-time mistress, because he does say, 'Furthermore the wound that I had received when my first mistress was wrenched away showed no signs of healing.'[30]

Perhaps however, he should have taken more note of his own words on truth? Namely, that a man 'pretends to himself that what he loves is the truth, and because he hates to be proved wrong, will not allow himself to be convinced that he is deceiving himself. So he hates the real truth for the sake of what he takes to his heart in its place. Men love the truth when it bathes them in its light.'[31] So Augustine's sin, according to Augustine, is his failing to see God sooner, and acknowledging that 'truth' bathes him in light. So is his interfering mother and his treatment of the women in his life, 'the real truth,' which is displaced from his heart by this? Oh yes, he certainly 'pretends

---

[30] St Augustine, Confessions, Book VI:15
[31] St Augustine, Confessions, Book X:24

to himself that what he loves is the truth.' Why did it never once occur to him that his observation applied to himself and that he was deceiving himself?

In fairness to him though, I do wonder if he was hurt more than he admits? He would have been in his mid-thirties at the time of losing all those dear to him[32] and so must have felt very alone. I also wonder if, when he looked back over his life when he was writing his 'Confessions', he felt disillusioned with the seeming futility of it all. What had been the point of his relationship with his mistress of all those years; a relationship that had been cruelly cut by his mother? What had been the point of their having had their son, when he had died early? Sadly, it seems that he could not actually bring himself to say that he'd loved his mistress, even though his writings suggest that he had, because no doubt that would have been to have put blame on his mother for the break-up. He was obviously disgusted with himself, but for what; for not blaming his mother, or at himself for being so weak willed and not standing up to her? Was he really disgusted at himself for having had sex in what seems to be a perfectly reasonable relationship; other than the fact that his partner was not, according to his mother, from the right social class and they were not married? Or was it that after the break-up with his long-term mistress he foolishly thought that another mistress would somehow console him and subsequently felt he had debased himself with her? At every turn he seems to have made the wrong decision. So perhaps it is little wonder that he seems disgusted with himself about everything. He even went on to describe his son, yes, his own son Adeodatus, as 'my natural son born of my sin, for there was nothing of mine in that boy except my sin.'[33] What a dreadful way for a father to describe his son, and why? Or are we back to the 'the real truth' again, and that in fact he did love his son,

---

[32] His long standing mistress, his mother and finally his son, all in relatively quick succession.
[33] St Augustine, Confessions, Book IX:6

still missed loosing him, and this loss is being displaced from his heart by his ludicrous self-loathing; 'Oh my God I have been so sinful!'?"

The three of them sat silently until Stephen La Roche broke it by asking,

"So, in your opinion Michael, how do you think this effects our religion and Church?"

"Well, I am inclined to feel that it was Augustine's taking his second mistress after breaking up with the first that really disgusted him, as that action could only be attributed to base lust. So rather like an alcoholic who cannot drink responsibly and so has to become teetotal, Augustine decided to give up sex and women altogether and become celibate. And, just as Paul had done, because Augustine saw total abstention as that necessary for him to truly discover God, he assumed that it must be the same for all and hence that *all* should do likewise. Indeed, he then goes on to associate sex with sin and even goes so far as to suggest that man's original sin is passed on during intercourse; 'God created man aright, for God is the author of natures, though he is certainly not responsible for their defects. But man was willingly perverted and justly condemned, and so begot perverted and condemned offspring.'[34]

So hard is Augustine trying to suggest that his ideas are correct, that later he even suggests that God is responsible for the corruption of intercourse and childbirth! 'Now a woman's sex is not a defect; it is natural. And in the resurrection it will be free of the necessity of intercourse and childbirth. However, the female organs will not subserve their former use - there will be no lust in that life - but freed from corruption that which He had created.'[35] So according to Augustine, God is to blame for the 'corruption that which He had created'! Did it not cross Augustine's mind that as God had created man and woman and

---

[34] St Augustine, City of God, Book XIII, Chapter 15:14
[35] St Augustine, City of God, Book XXII, Chapter 17

their means of reproduction, that perhaps sex, intercourse and childbirth were not a corruption, and that it was he, Augustine, who was wrong to assume that they were? By allowing his own experience of loveless, lustful sex to cloud his judgement, he assumes that love, desire, passion and lust are all one and the same and so assumes that *all* sexual action is motivated by base lust. Whereas that may well have been the case for himself with his second mistress, and he freely admits to it, just because that was so, it does not follow that perfectly normal desire and passion within a loving relationship cannot also motivate sex."

"And I confess, though that isn't quite the right word in the circumstances,' said La Roche with a smile at his unintended joke, "that having had a loving marriage myself, I find myself concurring with you on this. Why Augustine went and took a second mistress has always puzzled me, as I know from my own experience that I had no desire whatsoever to even contemplate a relationship with another woman after my wife had died."

But Michael Venn had the bit between his teeth that afternoon and ploughed on.

"However, in spite of Augustine happily citing Romans 14:3 'Let not him that eateth despise him that eatheth not; and let not him which eateth not judge him that eateth,'[36] he does not apply this sound advise to himself on the subjects of women and sex. He wishes to abstain from sex for his own personal reasons, but instead of heeding the foregoing advice, which he had advocated, and keeping his opinions to himself, he feels compelled to comment on and judge others. Paul appears much more insightful and makes no such assertions about the baseness of sex. Indeed, he almost goes out of his way to advise couples to love each other and render conjugal rights to each other and in so doing evidently sees nothing shameful about sex within marriage. Hence it seems that Augustine's views on sex are so tainted by his own behaviour as to be almost worthless.

---

[36] In St Augustine's Confessions, Book X:31

So unfortunately, both Paul's and Augustine's religion is not just about a loving, tolerant God and what flows from Him, but about what they, as flawed men, needed to do in order to overcome their own weaknesses and failings. Hence for them, abstaining from sex, because that is what they for their different reasons chose to do, becomes part of *their* interpretation of religion. And if one has gone that far, it then follows that if abstaining from one worldly pleasure is a route to Godliness, then abstaining from other worldly pleasures must also be routes to Godliness. So their whole interpretation of religion and God becomes one of abstemiousness and self-denial. So Godliness becomes associated with self-imposed misery. Misery on this earth and in this life with the hope of salvation and paradise in the next."

"Um," said La Roche with a wry smile. "I think you might have some difficulty explaining all of that to our Prior."

"You are not going to deny it are you?" asked Venn quietly. "Just listen to him when he gets going; his sermons are all on the subject of sin on the one hand and abstaining from anything which is vaguely pleasurable on the other."

"Just what I meant," said a still quietly amused La Roche.

"But what is their view of this paradise?" Michael Venn asked. "Hell always appears to be easily depicted; monsters, demons and devils gleefully tormenting and torturing sinners," and he couldn't resist adding, "our novice-master would be well suited there," which caused Stephen La Roche to raise an eyebrow.

"Although that pictorial view is somewhat dramatic and simplistic, most of us have a pretty good idea of Hell. However, Heaven is not so easy depicted, probably because each of us has a different idea of it. For a man whose life has been one of hard work, poor food and no enjoyment, his idea might be that of a place where there is no work, where there is an abundance of food and fun all day. For the woman whose life has been one of drudgery, scrimping and saving, and bad clothes, her idea might be that of a pampered existence, an adequacy of everything and wonderful clothing. So, do they find these things, or even these types of things in God's Heaven, in His Paradise? Is what one finds in Heaven so much better than that experienced in this life? If this is so, then God obviously approves of it, in which case why are we told by our saints and religious leaders that this present life on earth must be one of self-denial and abstemiousness, and that only by living in this manner can we hope to make our way to God?

Of course, mercenary, mortal man might reasonably argue that putting up with misery in this life is fine *if* there is reward in the next, but, if Paradise is no better than this present life, why should man stoically endure the present misery? So is Heaven just full of angels and harpers harping as our Prior seems to imply? Do we honestly think God, or rather Saint Peter, is standing at Heaven's Gate handing out free passes to Paradise to those that have been good? This is not only far too simplistic, but is, I would suggest, an insult to God. Yet this seems to be what our Church is implying, which should make us wonder what *exactly* does our Church think is the Paradise in which it believes?

Our two patron saints seem to have inadvertently got our religion and Church into an awful bind," continued Michael Venn, "all because they had their own personal problems, were unable to live their lives normally and hence thought that the solution that they found for themselves was also required of others. Their masochistic self-denial quite logically led on to the masochism referred to by Paul in his Epistle to the Corinthians, 'I chastise my body and bring it into subjection: lest perhaps when I have preached to others I myself should be castaway.' (A quotation which was probably all too horribly familiar to Adam Callow!) But why the need for this? Why does Paul have to bring his body into subjection? What is he afraid of? If, as I postulated earlier, he preferred men to women, then we can understand this, because discovery of his persuasion would have meant certain death. So, yes, he would have had to be constantly on his guard against his own feelings and it would be logical for him to use every means possible so as to ensure that his secret was not discovered. However, this has erroneously led on to others suggesting that self-inflicted physical pain is following Christ's example, as if he, our Lord, believed in self-inflicted physical pain and practised the same on himself, which he most certainly did not. The pain which he suffered was not pain inflicted on himself by himself, it was inflicted on him by others. From there unfortunately, it is only a small step from inflicting pain on oneself to inflicting pain on others in the misguided belief that 'the inflicting of pain' is doing God's work. Hence the actions of sadistic monsters like McBane are, in effect, given religious approval."

"And so what do you believe is God's message, my rebellious young friend?" asked Stephen La Roche.

"Perhaps, that 'the kingdom of God is within you.'[37]? Which means that Heaven is also within you, as is Hell; for 'whatsoever a man soweth, that shall he also reap.'[38] We make our own heavens and hells. So it is up to ourselves to redeem ourselves, because when we die we take them with us. Augustine's view of Heaven as a place where all his sins are going to be miraculously annulled and his soul returned to a pure and innocent state, is just a dream.

I can see no need for any ridiculous abstaining from this or that. God created all. If He hadn't meant us to enjoy it, He would not have created it for us. That is not to say that we should indulge to excess, but likewise it is not saying that we need to abstain to excess either; and celibacy, as Paul and Augustine have preached, is abstaining from sex to excess. This is why I suggest that they took our religion down a wrong road.

---

[37] Luke 17:21
[38] Galatians 6:7

Their personal problems or negative views about women and sex have given a prominence to these which is way beyond that which is reasonable. Just look at the ludicrous dictates that our Church issues to married couples about when they can and cannot have sex; all detailed in our Church's Penitentials. Aren't there now something like one hundred and forty days in the year when married couples are forbidden to have sex? Neither Jesus, or to be fair to him, Paul, said anything about this. Yet Paul's constant referring to celibacy has resulted in our religion and then our Church linking sexual behaviour with Godliness. What business is this of our Church? It now appears to be far more interested in poking its nose into peoples' private sex lives than it ever does in actually practising love, tolerance and forgiveness. Indeed, I would suggest that its only real interest seems to be in power and money, and holding people to ransom over their sex lives is simply a means to this end."

None of them said anything for a moment or two until Stephen La Roche broke the silence with,

"Possibly we should conclude today's discussion at this point?"

"You are not angry with me? I have not spoken out of ….." asked Michael Venn in a slightly worried voice.

"Oh no, Michael. However, as I said earlier, do be very careful about to whom you make your opinions known. No, I am not angry. Indeed, I feel that perhaps I ought to congratulate you on your very thorough study of the lives of our patron saints. And how about you, Adam, how are you getting on?"

Though before an embarrassed Adam Callow could answer; he was only too well aware of where and how he had been spending his time; brother La Roche held out his hands and added with a smile,

"Would you be good enough to help me up, my young brothers? Thank you."

<u>Chapter 9</u>

Although slightly embarrassed at his evident lack of studies, Adam Callow obviously came away from his afternoon discussion with brother La Roche and his fellow novice-brother Venn, both with a sense of relief and renewed confidence that all would be well vis-s-vis himself and Eve. If a man such as Saint Augustine, who had been a self-confessed fornicator and had had a child, could become a saint, then Callow reasoned that he had little to worry about his immortal soul even though his Prior was suggesting otherwise, and there was also every reason to suspect that Eve was not pregnant just because they'd made love on that one occasion. On this last point though, Adam Callow would just have to wait and see. However, even if Eve was pregnant, if St Augustine had managed with a child outwith wedlock, why shouldn't he also manage somehow? Consequently, when the next market day came round and he saw Eve approaching his stall he did not exhibit the near terror that he'd felt when all the dreadfully negative aspects of his having made love with her had hit him that earlier afternoon when up at the cave just off the Hartstane road.

"Hello Adam Callow," said she in a very formal manner.

"Hello Eve."

"Oh, so you are talking to me now, are you?" she replied. "I am not totally beneath you then?"

"Please Eve. I'm sorry. I really am. Everything just …. just …. I needed to have time to think." He realised that he was treading water, but couldn't bring himself to explain in detail all that had gone through his mind as a result of their having made love.

"And so now you've had time to think," she continued in the same sarcastic tone, "what are your great thoughts?"

"I would like to meet you again. If …. if you would like that."

"Oh?" she said, "If I would like that? I can have any man I want Adam Callow. So tell me, why should I want you?"

"Um ….. "

"Maybe I will and maybe I ….." she continued, the arrogant tone in her voice having softened. She smiled, turned her head to one side and looked at him coquettishly with her big dark eyes. "So do you love me?"

"Er ….. yes," replied Callow.

"I need to be loved a lot, you know. Do you love me a lot, Adam Callow?"

"Um ….. yes," said Adam Callow, who didn't really know what to say.

"Will I see you as before? Same place, same time?" she asked, in a tone and tempo which might have suggested that she had paid no attention whatsoever to Callow's reply.

"Yes. That would be nice."

"You know, you had me worried Adam Callow. I thought you didn't love me any more, and you need to love me, you know."

"I'm sorry if I gave that impression, it's just that ….." and it was his turn to let his sentence trail off. "Same place, same time," he added a little more breezily.

"Yes," she replied, evidently happy that she had secured another rendezvous with the naïve young monk who she had singled out as her preferred mate.

She kissed a small slightly chubby, pale skinned hand and blew him that kiss before walking confidently off into the market throng, her hips rolling and her silky black hair bouncing as she did so. Adam Callow's eyes followed her -

'You have captivated my heart with one glance of your eyes.'[39] It feels so right, he thought, so God must have meant it to be so; and with a smile on his face and warmth in his heart, he continued to complete his session at the market. However, when the market was over and he was back in the monastery, he was back again in the repressive regime of Prior Obscurant, back again in a regime where true followers after the glories of God's Kingdom did not need distractions such as warmth in their hearts.

The following morning's sermon to the brothers and novice-brothers was, as usual, on the subject of fornication, though this time with a slightly different slant.

"And I talketh to you again of fornication!" The word 'fornication' rattled round the bare, intolerant walls of the priory church, its echoes of debauchery and whoring diminishing with every ricochet until all was finally obliterated by Prior Obscurant's next pronouncement.

"Hath our patron saint, St Augustine, warned us not in his writings, that knowledge of a woman even in marriage, yeah even in marriage ...." and as ever the bony arm was raised and a thin emaciated finger was pointing towards the Heavenly Paradise, ".... 'carries shame.'[40] Yeah, shame upon the head of he that endulgeth in such base acts. But, ..." continued Prior Obscurant, with a level earnest voice, but no raised arm now, as both bony hands were gripping the sides of the lectern, ".... in His great wisdom our Almighty God hath decreed that knowledge of a woman purely for the purposes of procreation is not sinful. However, and mark this well, that no pleasure is to be derived from the act. There are many in our very village, my brothers, who faileth to observe this. So I say unto you, hear their confessions well for any satisfying of base animal sensuality and desire, even with one's lawful wedded spouse is

---

[39] Song of Solomon 4:9
[40] St Augustine, City of God, Book XIV:18

a venal sin! Hark well the words of our patron, Saint Augustine, 'The sins of the flesh which defiled my soul'[41] for defile it they willst, and forget not that those that are defiled by women will never enter the Divine Purity of the Celestial Kingdom of Almighty God."

At this point, the man on this earth appointed by God Himself to lead the undeserving miserable sinners to His Everlasting Paradise, paused to allow time for his message, without doubt received directly from God, to be fully 'understood' and 'appreciated'. He then continued in a more subdued manner.

"However, it beholdeth us to acknowledge that our revered fathers hath decreed that those who commit the sins of the flesh within the sanctity of their marriage are only guilty of venal sin ....." A drop in the volume of his voice suggested that this decree was not of his choosing, and so we can probably safely assume that Prior Obscurant would have much preferred it had these undoubted sins been classified as a mortal sins, ".... and they will be cast down ...." the bony arm pointed downward towards the pit of everlasting flames and torment, which is where he would have wished to cast these undeserving sinners, ".... to where, on the Seventh Terrace of Purgatory [42] they may contemplateth their undeniable guilt of their licentious actions!"

After another brief pause, he added in a calmer voice,

"Brothers, our sub-Prior Grees will explaineth the Papal encyclical that hath come through to us."

An imperious Prior Obscurant then let go of the lectern and made his way back to his burgundy coloured satin covered throne. There he sat down, the human embodiment of moral superiority, without a trace of doubt on his hollow cheeked and chiselled face. But why should he have doubt? He had just

---

[41] St Augustine, Confessions, Book II:1
[42] Dante, The Divine Comedy, Inferno, 7th Terrace reserved for the Lustful.

imparted the Divine Truth after all.

The corpulent figure of sub-Prior Arriviste Grees rose and waddled over to the lectern.

"As our beloved Prior hath explained," commenced sub-Prior Grees in a similar pseudo-Biblical manner of speech as Prior Obscurant, though whether this mimicking of his Prior was meant as flattery or mockery, or whether he also thought it gave a gravitas to his high pitched utterances, wasn't clear.

"Our Church is merciful and so makes it possible for these miserable souls to partially redeem themselves and so reduce the punishment that they have brought upon themselves ....." (the time they have to spend in Purgatory) "..... by purchasing an indulgence. So it beholds you my brothers, to listen to your confessions well, the confessions of both men and women, though particularly those of the women, because as we know, it was Eve who tempted Adam and so therefore we also know that it will be the wives who have tempted their husbands, so that we may *assist* those that have strayed."

Again like his Prior, sub-Prior Grees paused so as to let this oblique message sink in. Namely, that there was a lot of easy money to be made from the sins of the flesh, especially from those who were married, because their sin was venal and so could be in part expurgated by the purchase of an indulgence, whereas fornication between those who were not married was a mortal sin and this could not be expurgated so easily with a paid-for-with-cash, simple indulgence. We can be fairly certain that novice-brother Michael Venn would know, even if Adam Callow did not, of the somewhat flippant maxim attributed to Tetzel, the Grand Commissioner for indulgences in Germany; 'as soon as a coin in the coffer rings, a soul from purgatory springs,' and that it would also be safe to wager that sub-Prior Arriviste Grees had more interest in ringing coffers than he ever did in the souls of the miserable sinners from whom these indulgences would be extracted.

Perhaps needless to say, the Church had decreed that there was plenty of scope for venal sin. Married couples were only permitted to use the missionary position, or possibly side by side for love making, both of course assuming that absolutely no pleasure was derived from same or that this took place on any of the dozens of forbidden days; Holy days, saints days, etc., and indeed, there were over one hundred and forty such days! However, so called 'lustful couplings' such as sex a tergo (from behind), or if the woman was on top, were to be punished with three years penance on this earth and for however long God deemed necessary in Purgatory. As sub-Prior Grees explained, a purchased indulgence would help to reduce that time in Purgatory. It also, though he conveniently omitted to mention this, would help to pay for the likes of building works; as, for example, it had done for the construction of St Peter's Basilica in Vatican City in Rome a few years earlier.

As Callow listened to his sub-Prior explaining the importance of ensuring that those who needed indulgences were both ascertained and issued with same - for the sake of their immortal souls of course - a worm of doubt suddenly inserted itself in his mind. Namely, was Eve a virgin? Because if she was; 'If anyone commits fornication with a virgin he shall do penance for one year'[43] and then, before Callow could stop it, the worm, like a hydra, sprouted a second head. If she was a virgin, he was damned, and if she was not, then she was damned, and so also was he for knowing a woman that was already damned! A cold sweat started to break out over him. Oh dear God! There was no way out; he could feel the whirlpool of sin circling around him. And if that wasn't enough for poor Adam Callow, the hydra grew yet a further head! What if …. what if she was married? No, no he was sure she wasn't. So the, 'if with a married woman, he shall do penance for four years, two of these entire, and in the other two during the three forty

---

[43] Medieval Handbook on Penance – Book One, II of fornication

day periods and three days a week,'[44] was surely not relevant? However, the worm bored yet further in, as Callow couldn't help but recall that Eve did seem to know far more about what to do than he did, so perhaps she was …. was what? Er …. was already a damned woman or …. or was already married? Married! Oh Goodness! He'd thought that he'd just excluded that possibility. This was not a whirlpool of sin dragging at his soul, it was a stinking mire, and he was both right in the middle of and up to his spiritual neck in it! How could he possibly confess to any of this and so unburden himself of the sheer weight that was pulling him down into this pit of slime? And if he did not confess, his soul would most certainly be damned and he, without doubt, would be excluded from the sublime peace of God's Heaven and cast into the bottomless fiery pit, tossed into the everlasting damnation of Hell!

Fortunately for Adam Callow, as the day moved on so his confused burning hot tangle of guilt and soul-searching did gradually pass, and by the time he set off for his rendezvous with Eve his mind was far less troubled. Indeed, it was almost peaceful in a resigned sort of way. What was done, was done and er …. he told himself yet again that if Augustine could become a saint after having had at least two mistresses and an illegitimate son then …. then, where was the problem? Augustine hadn't been damned, so why should he be? Unfortunately, this very logical argument did little to actually alleviate his worries and so, with confidence built on sand, he plodded up the Hartstane road to meet his newly beloved Eve.

As previously, she had arrived before him and had already arranged the blanket on the ground beneath the small overhang of the outcrop and behind the screen of bushes in front of it. She was kneeling on the edge of the blanket and this week wearing a lovely emerald green skirt and matching bodice. Oh goodness, she looked beautiful, beautiful enough to set any young man's

---

[44] Medieval Handbook on Penance – Book One, II of fornication

heart racing, and Adam Callow's soon was.

"Why are you always late?" she greeted him.

"Am I?" he replied, both puzzled, for he was sure that he was on time, and somewhat absently, as he was still trying to convince himself that his soul was not in danger of everlasting torment.

"Yes, you are always late, Adam Callow. I didn't think you were coming."

"But ….. " started Callow, about to point out that they had only met once before.

"We must get started," she said with a twinkle in her eye as she pulled at the rope around his waist and habit. The emerald green bodice was, as Callow couldn't help but observe, already well loosened and her white blouse was just about hanging on to her smooth ivory skinned shoulders.

"Come here you naughty man," she said as she pulled him to her. She then kissed him full on the mouth and gently bit his lip.

"Oh how I have missed you, Adam Callow," she purred as she pulled him down on to the blanket, before pushing him back and straddling herself over him pulling up his habit and spreading the emerald green skirt over them both like a small tent. "Do you have any idea how much?"

"But …," managed Callow, who still had a part of his thoughts focused on boiling brimstone.

"No buts, Adam Callow. I want you …. and I will have you," she playfully snarled at him before removing her bodice, letting her blouse fall to her waist and revealing her pert, round soft white breasts with their rose pink nipples.

What resistance could Callow put up? Even Prior Obscurant's dire warnings of Hellfire and damnation were no match for those divine breasts! 'To love and to have my love returned was my heart's desire, and it would be all the sweeter if I could also enjoy the body of the one who loved me'[45] were Adam Callow's revered patron Saint Augustine's thoughts on such matters, and he (Adam Callow) was not about to disagree. He looked up at her as she leant forward over him, taking her weight on her arms whilst gently lowering herself onto him. Her black hair tumbled down over smooth skinned white shoulders and gently swaying soft white breasts. Her soft, smooth white belly moved rhythmically over his, slowly at first but gradually increasing in tempo and vigour. Heaven on this earth!

At times she looked down at him and smiled, and at others she gently threw her head back in a gesture of ecstasy which suggested that she too was enjoying this taste of heaven on earth. As he looked at her it struck him that there was something vaguely familiar about that gesture; the head thrown back, the black hair on ivory skinned shoulders. What was it? Unexpectedly and disconcertingly Callow once again found himself feeling that he already knew Eve from somewhere .... but, as before, he couldn't say from where, or for that matter precisely what it was that was so familiar. However, the increasing pleasure of their union pushed that slightly uncomfortable and intrusive thought from his mind before his consciousness finally exploded into an ecstatic bliss that filled his whole being.

After their exertions she took the weight off her arms and lay down on top of him, her head resting on his shoulder and her shining black hair spread out over his chest. She purred softly with contentment. With one finger she traced the outline of Callow's tonsured hair. Could she be certain that she was definitely pregnant now and would have her child? Had she now finally caught herself an educated, rich husband, and so would have her house, her beautiful clothing, maid servant and her carriage? He would be a fine catch even if he was weak and malleable. Indeed, these qualities would be ideal in a husband,

---

[45] St Augustine, Confessions, Book III:1

making it so much easier for her to control the marriage, and she could always take a lover if she needed to. It would all work out. Just wait.

However, none of the foregoing was going through Callow's mind as he gently ran the fingers of one hand over the small of her back, whilst with the other he toyed with her hair, curling it over his fingers and feeling its silky softness. He breathed steadily and it has to be said, thought of little, other than how wonderfully nice it was to lie like this with this beautiful raven haired woman in his arms. No, this time he didn't get a fit of the panics and want to rush off. He was peacefully at ease. Whether he would be damned or not, or whether he would avoid this fate as Saint Augustine had done, had fled his mind and all that was now occupying it was the present; the beautiful, peaceful present and he wanted, so wanted to hold on to that, to absorb it into his very being, to prolong the sublime experience of this all too brief a taste of Heaven on earth. He leaned his head forward and kissed her and she opened her eyes with a start, smiled at him and kissed him back with those soft pursed pink lips that had that hypnotic dark diamond at their centre. He ran a finger slowly over them and she smiled.

And then the time came when they had to climb down from their very different euphoric cloud nines.

"Oh goodness! It's late and I must get back for prayers," he said, not as an excuse this time, but as a statement of fact. He stood and got dressed.

"Don't worry about that," she replied, as he started to fold up the blanket. "You go on. I'll tidy up here."

Our Adam took his Eve in his arms, she still half naked with her blouse round her waist, and held her semi-naked pale skinned body against the rough dark hair of his habit.

"I love you, Eve Lilith. I love you."

"Yes, I know you do," she said. "Now go."

Chapter 10

"Although the characters in our story don't know this yet, their story is about to take a turn," explained Joe. "However, before this happens we need to make just one more visit to the little amphitheatre with brother La Roche and novice-monks Venn and Callow. So, what follows now is a record of that visit.

It was one of those truly beautiful summer days as the elderly brother La Roche and the much younger Venn and Callow, made their way up the Hartstane road to what had de facto become their regular meeting place at the grassy amphitheatre. A large bank of Rosebay willowherb, which graced a section of the roadside between the road and drystone wall of the adjacent field, swayed gently in the breeze, the beautiful, delicate pink flower spikes set above bright green leafed stems moving in unison as though a fantasy wave on a lake in some imaginary paradise garden. Beyond them and the rough grey and green lichen covered stones of the drystone wall, lay a sea of soft cream coloured Meadowsweet, the fragrant scent of which was carried on that afternoon's breeze over the stone barrier to the three monks as they made their way up the road.

"Just look, feel and smell, my young friends," said brother La Roche.

"And does this not suggest that Heaven could in fact be here on earth?" asked Michael Venn.

"Very true, Michael. We don't need a lot, as 'more' does not equate to 'happiness'. We just need to be able to fully appreciate and enjoy that which we do have, and this afternoon God has given us this," said Stephen La Roche with a sweeping gesture of his hand. "What more could we wish for? What more would make it better?"

Adam Callow looked around him. That which surrounded them was beautiful; indeed, *was* beauty. Could Paradise in

Heaven be more beautiful than this Arcadia here on earth? He ran his hand through a sea of waving grass stems and felt their soft seed heads brush over his skin; soft like Eve's hair playing through his fingers. Looking across the road he saw the gently undulating sea of pink Rosebay willowherb. Pink, pink like her lips with that strange diamond at their centre. The sweet scent of the Meadowsweet that wafted past him on the warm breeze conjured up memories of her sweet smell and the idyllic time that he had spent with her. Then, as he passed the old gnarled pine trees with their rough bark, like plates of flaking rusting metal, he noticed their sweet resinous smell; something that he had taken for granted previously, but today he noticed it. He also noticed the thick carpet of lush green grass growing beneath the pines and the spikes of Foxgloves, some pink, some white, and some a mix of the two, rising up through that green carpet like forest-edge sentinels keeping an eye on who was passing along the road.

Michael Venn was already discussing something with Stephen La Roche, but Adam Callow was only partially hearing it as he was so lost in his own thoughts and his realisation that since his last seeing Eve, the world seemed to have taken on a new sparkle. A sparkle as if he was seeing all that it contained for the first time, as if a veil had been lifted from his eyes and that all had suddenly become crystal clear, was new, bright and shining, as though indeed, he was looking at a real Garden of Eden, a real tangible paradise, and felt slightly amazed that it was in fact here on this earth. Was it possible that Heaven could be on earth, that Paradise was in fact all around us if only we could open our eyes and see it? Did being in love have this effect on everyone; that of opening their eyes, heightening their senses and making them more aware of the beauty that is already all around them?

Had his companions also noticed the beauty of the world around them? Indeed, he realised, they had probably noticed it, or at least voiced it before he had. So were they in love? And if so, in love with whom …. or …. with what? He knew, or thought he knew he was in love with Eve. She was a woman and so that seemed natural to him, even if he was being told that it was wrong, was sinful, and would bar him from entering God's Heaven. But was it possible to also love life, to love the world that surrounded one, to love God independently of the Church and its doctrine? And if so, was Heaven actually much nearer than the likes of Prior Obscurant suggested it was? Possibly Heaven was not a place that 'one went to', a place 'up there', but was in fact within each individual as his friend Michael Venn had suggested during their last discussion? Possibly that's it? So might it be that Heaven and Hell are not external to us at all, but are in fact within each of us here on earth, and we experience one or the other depending on how we interact with and see the world around us? What was it that he thought Stephen had just said? 'We don't need a lot, as more does not equate to happiness. We just need to be able to fully appreciate and enjoy that which we do have.' So could Heaven be what you want it to be, whereas Hell is what you find it to be …..? And at that point Adam Callow's train of thought began to elude him, rather like a fleeting dream that continually changes so as to always be just out of reach.

Eventually the three monks arrived at the little amphitheatre and took their seats as though they were attending some ancient Greek forum at a man made example of this little natural wonder.

"Now Michael, were you wanting to have another go at our Patron Saint Augustine?" commenced Stephen La Roche with a smile.

"No, not just yet," Michael Venn replied, "though I thought I 'might have a go,' as you call it, at Saint Jerome, because he, possibly more than any other, has set our religion and Church against women and sex. So I think we must discuss him."

"Yes, why not?" replied Stephen La Roche good

humouredly. "He is another revered Founding Father of our Church, so it would be a shame to miss him out. Do you have any objection, Adam?"

Callow shook his head to indicate that he did not. He was quite happy to let his firebrand friend do the talking. Although he would probably never have admitted it, least of all to himself, he was in fact quite content to let others take the initiative in most things. He didn't hold strong opinions about anything really, was quite happy to sit and listen, and, as we have probably already realised, let others make decisions for him.

Although Adam Callow had learnt a bit about the monastery's two Patron Saints, that was almost obligatory after all, he hadn't even started on St Jerome and secretly marvelled at how Michael Venn had managed to find the time to read up on and learn so much about the early saints that he and brother La Roche had been discussing. However, in fairness to young Callow we must concede that his involvement with Eve made a subject such as the private lives of others, something which he might prefer not to talk about for fear of giving himself and Eve away. At times it must have been hard enough just listening to Michael Venn and perhaps wondering if his mentor, brother Stephen La Roche, had noticed his discomfiture and hence had realised his secret. However, if brother La Roche had, he gave no indication of this.

"Jerome, like Augustine," commenced the young firebrand, "also allowed his own sexual experiences to cloud his views on both sex and marriage, and likewise completely forgot, or over-looked the vital fact that God created both 'male and female created He them and that God blessed them, and God said unto them, be fruitful and multiply.'[46] He did *not* instruct them to live lives of celibacy, ignoring each other because the act of procreation was in some way shameful or guilt-laden.

---

[46] Genesis 1:27-28

Jerome, like Augustine, had been subsequently appalled at his own earlier sexual behaviour. Only in his case it was not sex with women but with other men when he was a student in Rome. And so he, like Augustine, also associated sex with shame and guilt. He cites in particular Psalm 55:15 'Let death seize upon them, And let them go down quick into Hell: for wickedness is in their dwellings, and among them,' which no doubt conveyed both his feelings about the debauched practices in Rome at that time and his guilt at having involved himself in them. Of course the next line in that psalm reads, 'As for me, I will call upon God; And the Lord shall save me,' and I think we can guess that Jerome was fervently hoping that this would be the case for him!

However, as Jerome is so anti-marriage and anti-sex, perhaps the first question to ask is, when did God decree that sex purely for the purposes of procreation was not sinful, whereas sex which also gave pleasure within a caring loving relationship, was? And no, I am not asking about the writings of some saint, or saints, two of whom so obviously had huge personal problems about women and sex, I am asking when did God decree this?"

Venn let his question hang, before continuing,

"Yes, Augustine describes his experience of sex as, 'love and lust together seethed within me. In my tender youth they swept me away over the precipice of my body's appetites and plunged me into a whirlpool of sin,'[47] but, as we discussed last time, Augustine was reminiscing about base lust in a loveless, selfish, exploitative relationship, not about sex in a loving relationship or marriage."

What might have gone through Adam Callow's mind upon hearing about love and lust, and a whirlpool of sin? Was what he felt for Eve also just base lust as described by Augustine? Or

---

[47] St Augustine, Confessions, Book II:2

were his feelings for Eve more sincere, more profound, as Michael Venn had described and Stephen La Roche had obviously experienced? Or was he (Adam Callow), as his novice-master McBane had suggested, in danger, grave danger of being castaway, of being sucked down into that whirlpool of sin? He had no idea, but simply considering these possibilities was enough to bring his worm of doubt back again. Oh goodness, what was he doing? Why, oh why was he getting involved with Eve? He should never have agreed to meet her again, but .... and that was Adam Callow's dilemma; Eve was that lovely girl, that beautiful woman, *his* Eve; his Eve with silky black hair and soft white skin, his lovely Eve, who made him feel like a man. No, the truth be told he didn't really understand what he was doing, though was fairly sure that he didn't feel ashamed, except that, actually, he didn't really want others to know about himself and Eve, because what he did know was that he felt terrified of what others would do if they did find out about them, which was not …. er, was it? …. quite the same thing.

"Whereas Augustine accepts that procreation is God's Will and is good," Michael Venn was saying, "he attempts to assert that the act which brings it about is sinful whilst conveniently forgetting that God made both man and woman *and* their mode of procreation. Whereas he purports to know, though gives no explanation of how in fact he does know, 'of the bliss that existed in paradise,'[48] he singularly fails to explain how man was going to 'be fruitful, and multiply' had man not disobeyed God's commandment. He simply avoids this subject with a bland 'they (presumably those who do not hold with Augustine's convoluted argument) suppose that children could not have been begotten except by the means with which they are familiar,' and of course has to add his own usual biased, base opinion, 'namely, by means of lust, which as we observe, brings

---

[48] St Augustine, City of God, Book XIV:1

a sense of shame even in the honourable state of matrimony.'[49] He then tries to justify his stance by suggesting that God's blessing of 'be fruitful, and multiply' was given to Adam and Eve before their fall and so therefore stood, whereas the means of achieving this, which involved Adam and Eve's eating of the fruit and so gaining knowledge and hence sexual desire for each other, was after they had disobeyed Him, as if this explains everything.

He also seems to assume that man and woman were created to live in Paradise and that it was *only* because of their sin that they were banished from it. Whereas it is true that their sin resulted in their Fall and banishment from the 'garden eastward of Eden',[50] God had already created the rest of Earth. Why would He have done that if man and woman were destined to live only in Paradise? What would have been the point?"

"Have you forgotten our earlier conversation already, Michael; the one we had while walking up here?" asked Stephen La Roche.

"No, Stephen. But as both Augustine and Jerome have taken the early books of Genesis literally rather than metaphorically, I was responding to their literal assertions. It is they who presume a Heaven 'somewhere up there' and a Hell 'somewhere down there' and their writings point to their literal interpretation of the Creation. Of course the 'up there' and 'down there' might be no more than useful ways of describing man's attempts at aspiring to high ideals on the one hand and of course, his failure to reach them and his falling down if you will, on the other. And so perhaps Paradise, the 'garden eastward of Eden,' is an analogous way of describing a life of childhood innocence? This in turn suggests that banishment from it is not a physical thing, not one of being removed from a place, but a spiritual one, banishment being from the paradise

---

[49] St Augustine, City of God, Book XIV:21
[50] Genesis 2:8

provided by a life of innocence?"

"Go on Michael."

"Because, didn't God say, 'Behold, the man is become as one of us, to know good and evil'[51]; and with that knowledge, peace, contentment, serenity are, if not totally banished, unable to ever again be enjoyed as they were in a state of innocence? And it is that 'state of innocence', that state of contentment, state of inner peace that both Augustine and Jerome were so anxiously trying to recapture. Both wanted a religious philosophy which condemned that which they felt guilty about, namely sex, and one which granted the lifting of that burden of guilt from their shoulders, namely divine redemption, and so one which restored their states of innocence. Thus Heaven had to be a place where one would 'go to' and be free of worldly sin and guilt; hence their obsessing about original sin, and trying to make a wonderful analogy fit what they wanted from *their idea* of our religion. Why did they not pay attention to Paul's writings - 'Husbands, love your wives, even as Christ loved the Church'[52] and 'The husband should give to his wife her conjugal rights, and likewise the wife to her husband. For the wife does not have authority over her own body, but the husband does; likewise the husband does not have authority over his own body, but the wife does.'[53]? We can only presume that Paul's advice was taken by both Augustine and Jerome as tantamount to encouraging sin within marriage, which perhaps explains our Church's current attitude towards sex and its sale of indulgences? However, as Augustine had dismissed love from his life and did not subsequently love either his second mistress or his fiancée, and Jerome was simply so ashamed of his actions, these words from Paul would have fallen on deaf ears and no doubt would have been seen as a contradiction of their biased views of marriage. And it is their biased views that

---

[51] Genesis 3:22
[52] Ephesians 5:25
[53] 1 Corinthians 7:2-4

have come down to our Church today; their views, which completely ignore the advice given by Paul, and instead advocate that sex should only be for procreation and certainly not for any form of enjoyment.”

“So do I gather correctly, Michael, that you condemn St Augustine and now absolve St Paul?” asked a curious Stephen La Roche.

“A bit of both. Paul obviously had his problems, but on balance I think he gets unfairly criticised. It is clear from his writings that he recognised love within marriage and did not see sex as a sin; saw it as part of marriage and not just for procreation. I have wondered if his oft quoted, ‘If I have the gift of prophecy and can fathom all mysteries and all knowledge, and if I have a faith that can move mountains, but do not have love, I am nothing,’[54] should in fact be interpreted as a cri-de-coeur. Namely, as relating to the need to receive love as well as the need to give it. We all need love and his writings make it abundantly clear that he realises this, but he seems to have had a very lonely personal life and I get the feeling that this was not entirely of his own choosing. No, on balance I think he was a good man. As you pointed out, Stephen, he was described as being, ‘full of grace and mercy; at one time he seemed like a man, and at another time he seemed like an angel.’[55]

However, whereas I cannot wholly condemn Saint Augustine, because his life was one of classic tragedy and it is that which influences his writings, nonetheless those writings have influenced our religion and Church. In my view much of the blame for his experiences must lie with his mother (Saint Monica), though he steadfastly refuses to acknowledge this. The perfect storm of events - the forced break-up with the love of his life, the stupid decision to take a mistress he didn’t love, the death of his mother followed by the death of his son - that

---

[54] 1 Corinthians 13:2
[55] Acts of Paul and Thecla

overtook him all within a few years, were probably enough to drive any man into wanting to live 'a life of peace away from the crowd.'[56] His observation that 'is not man's life on earth a long, unbroken period of trial?'[57] also suggests that all the joy seems to have been driven from his life. For some reason he seems to attribute this to his sin of not finding God earlier, rather than his sin of taking too much notice of his domineering mother, not making his own decisions and living his own life, and quite possibly more than his fair share of bad luck. However, opting out of life and hiding himself away in Hippo, whereas it is understandable for the short term, so obviously could never be a long term solution to his life, and strikes me as the actions of one who is afraid of living."

There was a brief pause. Although completely unintentionally on his part, we might wonder if Michael Venn's observation had inadvertently hurt Stephen La Roche, as he had also 'hidden himself away' in his monastery following the death of his wife? If it had, La Roche gave no indication of this.

"But, I mustn't place all the blame on Augustine," continued an enthusiastic Michael Venn who then produced a slim volume from his leather shoulder bag, "because Jerome should also take his fair share, which is probably more than that deserved by either Saints Paul or Augustine. Indeed, I think I am correct in assuming that much of our Church's current attitude against women and marriage is based on Jerome's writing, 'Against Jovinianus.'"

This indeed was the slim volume that Michael Venn now held in his hand. Brother Stephen La Roche smiled to himself, because he had anticipated that Michael Venn would probably wish to comment on this tract which is probably one of the most blatantly anti-women, anti-marriage and anti-sex to have ever been produced. There is no doubt that it greatly influenced both

---

the then formative religion in the fourth century and, when it was subsequently revisited, the medieval Church, when it was used to justify the negative influence of women and sex on those wishing to achieve Divine Enlightenment and hence their entry ticket to Almighty God's Paradise. As Michael Venn explained, probably for Adam Callow's benefit, as it might be reasonably assumed that Stephen La Roche was well acquainted with both Jerome and Jovinianus and their respective works,

"Jovinianus was an opponent of the asceticism favoured by Augustine and Jerome and their like in the fourth century and so was, in 390, condemned as a heretic. He did not hold with their ludicrous notions that abstemiousness in all things was what God desired. Indeed, he openly stated that a virgin was no better in the sight of God than a wife, and that abstinence from food was no better than partaking of same in the right disposition, both of which seem perfectly reasonable. However, Augustine and Jerome had already established that virginity and abstemiousness on this earth was what God desired and so branded him heretical. Unfortunately, some of Jovinianus' other ideas were a bit strange. For example, that a person baptized with both the Spirit and water could not sin - oh that this were true! He also rather illogically suggested that all sins were equal and then that there is only one grade of punishment or reward in the future state, be it Heaven or Hell. Unfortunately, Augustine and Jerome were just as illogical, or false if you prefer, in taking Genesis literally and hence tying themselves up in knots whilst attempting to justify their arguments. In addition, and which is a far greater sin, they ignored what is clearly stated in the Gospels about God residing in each and everyone of us; 'God dwelleth in us, and his love is perfected in us.'[58] or 'For, behold, the kingdom of God is within you.'[59], and instead presented Heaven and Hell as 'geographic places',

---

[58] 1 John 4:12
[59] Luke 17:21

'up there' and 'down there', as both had a desperate need of a 'physical' Heaven to 'go to' where they would be freed of their burdens of guilt. This claim was in direct opposition to both the Gospels and the teachings of both Jovinianus and Pelagius.[60]"

Michael Venn opened his book.

"Jerome commences his examination of Jovinianus' work not by logical argument, but by pouring scorn and derision on him because he does not hold with the same opinion as Jerome. 'The style is so barbarous, and the language so vile and such a heap of blunders, that I could neither understand what he was talking about, nor by what arguments he was trying to prove his points' and, 'To understand him we must be prophets. We read Apollo's raving prophetesses. We remember, too, what Virgil says of senseless noise. Heraclitus, also, surnamed the Obscure, the philosophers find hard to understand even with their utmost toil. But what are they compared with our riddle-maker, whose books are much more difficult to comprehend than to refute? Although (we must confess) the task of refuting them is no easy one. For how can you overcome a man when you are quite in the dark as to his meaning?'[61] What sort of logical argument is that? It is no better than a rant.

Having thus derided Jovinianus, Jerome then asserts that 'we have read God's first command, 'Be fruitful, and multiply, and replenish the earth;' but while we honour marriage we prefer virginity which is the offspring of marriage,'[62] for which we perhaps should read; Jerome prefers virginity and celibacy, and holds this preferable to marriage. However, having asserted his preference, he, like Augustine, does not then explain how his desired virginity fulfils God's command to be fruitful and

---

[60] Pelagius, British theologian who advocated free will, asceticism, the goodness of human nature and hence that good works did not require divine intervention. As a consequence he was branded a heretic by St Augustine.

[61] St Jerome, Against Jovinianus, Book 1:1

[62] St Jerome, Against Jovinianus, Book 1:3

multiply. He continues in a not dissimilar fashion to Augustine, to ramble on about 'virginity is to marriage what fruit is to the tree, or grain to the straw,'[63] an illogical analogy which ignores the fact that the fruit or grain only comes about because of procreation and that both exist solely for the purpose of procreation. How can virginity and celibacy be compared or be preferable? If mankind had remained in Jerome's preferred state Adam and Eve would have died childless in the Garden!

Although completely illogical, I think what Jerome is saying, although he is not actually saying it, is that *he* would have preferred to have remained virginal, rather than having defiled himself in the way that he did, and *this* is why to him virginity is preferable. It is his guilt and shame about his experience of sex that is directing his thinking rather than analysing God's Will as is clearly stated in our Holy Book. Jerome then has the bare faced effrontery to go on and describe Jovinianus' writing as 'nauseating trash,' when his (Jerome's) is no better. He dares to waffle on about marriage, even though he has no experience of it, and concludes his tirade by illogically suggesting that 'if we abstain from intercourse, we give honour to our wives: if we do not abstain, it is clear that insult is the opposite of honour.'[64] What does Jerome suggest is the point of marriage? He obviously forgets God's first commandment given to Adam and Eve, and also Paul's advice. For Jerome loaded with his guilt and shame, virginity and celibacy is the ideal state. However, this was *not* God's command to mankind!" exploded an exasperated Michael Venn.

And what did poor Callow think? Had he dishonoured his Eve by having had sex with her? He wasn't married to her. So had he defiled her; defiled her body and her soul? And just as this thought had occurred to him, Michael Venn continued to quote Jerome,

---

[63] St Jerome, Against Jovinianus, Book 1:3
[64] St Jerome, Against Jovinianus, Book 1:7

'"For there are virgins in the flesh, not in the spirit, whose body is intact, their soul corrupt. But that virgin is a sacrifice to Christ, whose mind has not been defiled by thought, nor her flesh by lust.'[65] Jerome, like Augustine, simply cannot help associating sex with lust rather than love. Jerome talks of guilt, Augustine talks of shame, but is there really much difference between them? And so Jerome, like Augustine, obsesses on abstinence, celibacy and virginity. Phrases like; 'When they have tasted the sweets of chastity', 'although they had not the benefit of virginity', 'we prefer virginity', 'and thus the crown of virginity is expressed', 'a holy man of spotless chastity', 'the prize of virginity', etc., are all trotted out with boring regularity, even though to Jerome, this ideal state would, as he admitted, 'do away with the seed-plot of mankind.'[66]

Having made it eminently clear that *his* ideal is that of virginity and celibacy, he then asserts, 'he that is unmarried is careful for the things of the Lord, how he may please the Lord: but he that is married is careful for the things of the world, how he may please his wife, and is divided', thus implying that one has to choose between women, marriage and sex on the one hand or God on the other, before asserting that 'Marriage replenishes the earth, virginity fills Paradise.'[67] Whereas his assertion that 'Marriage replenishes the earth' is certainly true, is he now suggesting that it is acceptable to dishonour our wives, as he indicated would be the case for the sake of replenishing the earth, or are we, as he suggested, to 'abstain from intercourse (and) give honour to our wives?' In which case how is mankind going to replenish the earth in accordance with God's Will?

Jerome also conveniently forgets, though Augustine remembered, both that God gave his blessing 'be fruitful and multiply' and that Adam and Eve were already married, *before*

---

[65] St Jerome, Against Jovinianus, Book 1:13
[66] St Jerome, Against Jovinianus, Book 1:12
[67] St Jerome, Against Jovinianus, Book 1:16

they sinned, as is evidenced by 'and they were both naked, the man and his wife, and were not ashamed.' [68] So their 'replenishing of the earth' was God's Will and anything vaguely akin to mankind trying to get back to Paradise, is mankind's hubristic will, or rather Jerome's hubristic will; his trying to assuage his guilt and return to his oh-so-desired, but lost state of innocence.

And all of this," said Michael Venn with a flourish, "brings us round to our Prior's favourite dictum, 'And I looked, and, lo, a Lamb stood on the Mount Sion, and with him a hundred and forty four thousand, having His Father's name written in their foreheads. And I heard a voice from heaven, as the voice of many waters, and as the voice of a great thunder: and I heard the voice of harpers harping with their harps: and they sung as it were a new song before the throne, and before the four beasts, and the elders: and no man could learn that song but the hundred and forty four thousand, which were redeemed from the earth. These are they which were not defiled with women; for they are the virgins.' This no doubt is where Jerome found his justification for claiming that 'virginity fills Paradise.' Likewise, it also gives our Prior all the justification he needs to pursue his misogynistic philosophy."

"And so do I presume correctly Michael, that you do not agree with Jerome's line of argument?" asked Stephen La Roche with a wry smile.

"No, most certainly not. I think he is self-righteous and arrogant. God did not tell Adam and Eve to leave the Garden and advise them that if they remained virgins they would be readmitted at a later date. So why does Jerome presume that only virgins, of which he is not one by the way, will be readmitted? He thinks that as long as he denies himself, God will forgive him and grant him readmission. This goes right back to his time in Rome, his guilt and his then adopted fervent

---

[68] Genesis 2:25

plea to God to atone for his debauched behaviour, 'As for me, I will call upon God; And the Lord shall save me.'

However, he goes from bad to worse, stating, 'does he (Jovinianus) imagine that we approve of any sexual intercourse except for the procreation of children?'[69] Obviously Jerome didn't approve because his guilt was still hanging round his neck like a millstone, but how could he assume that God didn't approve when he (Jerome) knew that God created woman? Whereas Paul correctly realised that there was nothing wrong with sexual joy within marriage, shame-laden Augustine and guilt-racked Jerome did not wish others to enjoy that which they, because of *their* shameful actions, were subsequently unable to face, let alone enjoy. Jerome even goes on to assert that 'all sexual intercourse is unclean.'[70] The man is obsessed by his own guilt and has completely forgotten God's original blessing and, as already mentioned, Paul's advice to married couples. Having told us this, Jerome then goes on to inform us that 'a wife is classed with the greatest evils'[71] and that, 'like a worm in wood, so a wicked woman destroys her husband. But if you assert that this was spoken of bad wives, I shall briefly answer: What necessity rests upon me to run the risk of the wife I marry proving good or bad?' and cites Proverbs 21:19, 'It is better, he says, to dwell in a desert land, than with a contentious and passionate woman in a wide house. How seldom we find a wife without these faults, he knows who is married', to justify his opinion. Goodness! What an assertion, and on what evidence? Jerome wasn't even married and so could have known nothing of marriage, or of a loving wife."

"Yes, my young friend," said La Roche quietly, "This assertion of his does appear to be based purely on speculation, though no doubt it is also coupled with hearsay from those in unhappy marriages, as those who are happy don't tend to

---

[69] St Jerome, Against Jovinianus, Book 1:20
[70] St Jerome, Against Jovinianus, Book 1:20
[71] St Jerome, Against Jovinianus, Book 1:28

complain about being happy and contented."

Michael Venn and Stephen La Roche smiled at each other, the younger man appreciating the older man's joke and implicit in it, if not his full approval, at least not his disapproval of his line of argument. There was an air of kinship between them, a meeting of minds, something which Callow noticed he could not share. He wanted to, but he just wasn't on their wavelength. He so wanted to be, and to say, 'I have met and know this wonderful girl, this wonderful woman and so I, like you, know what love is' ..... but did he really know what love is? Did he *really* know, or did he just think he did? A bit like Jerome in fact, though he hoped not as bad as Jerome? And this doubt about the sincerity of his feelings played on his mind, disconcerted him and so kept him from joining in the conversation with his fellow novice-brother and his mentor. And of course, as much as he wanted to say something he couldn't, indeed, dare not say anything because of his fear of being discovered.

"However," continued Michael Venn, turning to the correct page in his copy of 'Against Jovinianus', "it is his Book 1:47 that contains his piece-de-resistance on the subject of marriage. Here he quotes, as he says from, 'A book On Marriage, worth its weight in gold, passes under the name of Theophrastus. In it the author asks whether a wise man marries. And after laying down the conditions - that the wife must be fair, of good character, and honest parentage, the husband in good health and of ample means, and after saying that under these circumstances a wise man sometimes enters the state of matrimony, he immediately proceeds thus: But all these conditions are seldom satisfied in marriage. A wise man therefore must not take a wife. For in the first place his study of philosophy will be hindered, and it is impossible for anyone to attend to his books and his wife. Matrons want many things, costly dresses, gold, jewels, great outlay, maid-servants, all kinds of furniture, litters and gilded coaches. Then come curtain-lectures the livelong night:

she complains that one lady goes out better dressed than she: that another is looked up to by all: 'I am a poor despised nobody at the ladies' assemblies.' 'Why did you ogle that creature next door?' 'Why were you talking to the maid?' 'What did you bring from the market?' 'I am not allowed to have a single friend, or companion.' She suspects that her husband's love goes the same way as her hate. There may be in some neighbouring city the wisest of teachers; but if we have a wife we can neither leave her behind, nor take the burden with us. To support a poor wife, is hard: to put up with a rich one, is torture. Notice, too, that in the case of a wife you cannot pick and choose: you must take her as you find her. If she has a bad temper, or is a fool, if she has a blemish, or is proud, or has bad breath, whatever her fault may be - all this we learn after marriage. Horses, asses, cattle, even slaves of the smallest worth, clothes, kettles, wooden seats, cups, and earthenware pitchers, are first tried and then bought: a wife is the only thing that is not shown before she is married, for fear she may not give satisfaction. Our gaze must always be directed to her face, and we must always praise her beauty: if you look at another woman, she thinks that she is out of favour. She must be called my lady, her birth-day must be kept, we must swear by her health and wish that she may survive us, respect must be paid to the nurse, to the nursemaid, to the father's slave, to the foster-child, to the handsome hanger-on, to the curled darling who manages her affairs, and to the eunuch who ministers to the safe indulgence of her lust: names which are only a cloak for adultery. Upon whomsoever she sets her heart, they must have her love though they want her not. If you give her the management of the whole house, you must yourself be her slave. If you reserve something for yourself, she will not think you are loyal to her; but she will turn to strife and hatred, and unless you quickly take care, she will have the poison ready. If you introduce old women, and soothsayers, and prophets, and vendors of jewels and silken clothing, you imperil her chastity; if you shut the door upon them, she is injured and fancies you suspect her. But what is the good of even a careful guardian, when an unchaste wife cannot be watched, and a chaste one ought not to be? For necessity is but a faithless keeper of chastity, and she alone really deserves to be called pure, who is free to sin if she chooses. If a woman be fair, she soon finds lovers; if she be ugly, it is easy to be wanton. It is difficult to guard what many long for. It is annoying to have what no one thinks worth possessing. But the misery of having an ugly wife is less than that of watching a comely one. Nothing is safe, for which a whole people sighs and longs. One man entices with his figure, another with his brains, another with his wit, another with his open hand. Somehow, or sometime, the fortress is captured which is attacked on all sides. Men marry, indeed, so as to get a manager for the house, to solace weariness, to banish solitude; but a faithful slave is a far better manager, more submissive to the master, more observant of his ways, than a wife who thinks she proves herself mistress if she acts in opposition to her husband, that is, if she does what pleases her, not what she is commanded. But friends, and servants who are under the obligation of benefits received, are better able to wait upon us in sickness than a wife who makes us responsible for her tears (she will sell you enough to make a deluge for the hope of a legacy), boasts of her anxiety, but drives her sick husband to the distraction of despair. But if she herself is poorly, we must fall sick with her and never leave her bedside. Or if she be a good and agreeable wife (how rare a bird she is!), we have to share her groans in childbirth, and suffer torture when she is in danger. A wise man can never be alone. He has with him the good men of all time, and turns his mind freely wherever he chooses. What is inaccessible to him in person he can embrace in thought. And, if men are scarce, he converses with God. He is never less alone than when alone. Then again, to marry for the sake of children, so that our name may not perish, or that we may have support in old age, and leave our property without dispute, is the height of stupidity. For what is it to us when we are leaving the world if another bears our name, when even a son does not all at once take his father's title, and there are countless others who are called by the same name. Or what support in old age is he whom you bring up, and who may die before you, or turn out a reprobate? Or at all events when he reaches mature age, you may seem to him long in dying. Friends and relatives whom you can judiciously love are better and safer heirs than those whom you must make your heirs whether you like it or not. Indeed, the surest way of having a good heir is to ruin your fortune in a good cause while you live, not to leave the fruit of your labour to be used you know not how.'"

Michael Venn paused and smiled, as did Stephen La Roche. They were evidently in on some joke, whatever it was, whereas he, poor Adam Callow was not, and instead was taking all that Michael Venn had just recited very much too literally. Would his beloved Eve want costly dresses, gold, jewels, all kinds of furniture, and not just a horse, but gilded coaches? What was it that they found amusing about that!?

"Ah," mused Stephen La Roche, "the thoughts of Theophrastus. Perhaps for the sake of male sanity, these should be taken with a bit of a pinch of salt?"[72]

"Unfortunately though, Jerome does not appear to have a sense of humour," proffered Michael Venn, "and so rather than taking this piece in a tolerant spirit, he takes it way too seriously as it seemingly concurs with his views on marriage. In this same 'Against Jovinianus', he then tries to tie us up in intellectual knots by saying of Adam and Eve, 'if you object that before they sinned there was a distinction in sex between male and female, and that they could without sin have come together, it is uncertain what might have happened.'[73] Indeed, what might have happened is uncertain, but why do we, mortal men, need to consider what is entirely hypothetical to us? What we do

---

[72] Theophrastus was a Greek Peripatetic philosopher and pupil of Aristotle, and was not connected to the Church. So whether this piece was written as a serious tract or as a bit of fun, does rather depend upon how one wishes to interpret it.

[73] St Jerome, Against Jovinianus, Book 1:29

know is that they were referred to as 'man and his wife, and were not ashamed' so the distinction in sex was absolutely certain, as was the fact that they so very obviously were married whilst still in Paradise and before their expulsion. What might have happened had the 'man and his wife' not tasted the fruit, we, and that includes Jerome, don't know, because as we all do know, they *did* taste of the forbidden fruit. So to then assume 'so that from the very earliest days of humanity virginity was consecrated by Paradise, and marriage by earth,'[74] as Jerome does, does not follow at all. Firstly, as we have already said, Adam and Eve were referred to as 'man and his wife,' before their sin, so marriage had already been consecrated by God, in Paradise. Secondly, virginity was only lost after they had eaten of the tree. So virginity is not dependant upon Paradise per se, but on innocence, or ignorance if you like, because Genesis 3:7 makes it abundantly clear that after they had eaten of the tree, 'And the eyes of them both were opened.' And all of that is assuming Jerome's, and it has to be said Augustine's as well, very literal interpretation of Creation."

"So do I take it, Michael, that you don't go along with a, as you describe it, literal interpretation of Creation as cited in Genesis?" asked Stephen La Roche.

"Of course I don't. How can it be literal?" replied Michael Venn indignantly.

"I think there will be many who will disagree with you."

"Let us assume then, that what is written is literally true; that Adam and Eve were the first man and woman and that all mankind can trace their lineage back to them, which is what Augustine and Jerome believe."

"And our Church believes, Michael," added La Roche.

"'When I was a child, I spake as a child, I understood as a child, I thought as a child, but when I became a man, I (should

---

[74] St Jerome, Against Jovinianus, Book 1:29

have) put away childish things.'[75] However we have *not* put away childish things; we *continue* to think like children!" exploded a frustrated Michael Venn.

"Suppose we start with Adam and Eve. They have two sons, Cain and Abel. Although there is no mention of daughters, perhaps we can assume that Cain and Abel had sisters and that perhaps they were not mentioned in the text. However, crucially, there is no mention of *any* other couple, who could have had children; of *any* other couple other than Adam and Eve. So if we believe the story as literally true, who did Cain marry? Who were the father and mother of Cain's wife? All we have recorded is that 'Cain knew his wife; and she conceived and bare Enoch.'[76]

Augustine and Jerome appear to be taking everything literally. All their theories of the origin of sin and it being passed from one generation to the next, assume that all of mankind is descended from Adam and Eve. So are they suggesting that Cain married his sister, that theirs was an incestuous marriage? Yes, that certainly does sound worthy of being an 'original sin'! Who else could Cain have married and who else could have been Cain's wife's parents, if they were not Adam and Eve? However, that is *not* the 'original sin' cited; indeed, there is no mention of it. And personally, I find it all-but impossible to imagine God sanctioning an incestuous marriage at the first generation of mankind and so I suggest this story should *not* be taken literally, but taken as an analogy. An analogy of mankind moving from innocence and security, from an ideal existence into a world with all its unfairness and brutality; rather like the transition we all make from childhood into adulthood," posited Venn. "When one has eaten of the apple and become an adult, the world becomes very different to the world one knew as a child."

---

[75] 1 Corinthians 13:11
[76] Genesis 5:17

Although Adam Callow said nothing, did he find himself concurring with Michael Venn's observations about the world pre and post 'tasting of the apple' as his friend had so poetically put it? There was no doubt in Adam Callow's mind that the world had changed, and changed quite dramatically, since he had known Eve (both socially and biblically). So he understood that part. However, the concept of 'analogy' was new to Callow and so if the story was an analogy and hence Adam and Eve were not the first man and woman, who were? Unfortunately, Adam Callow's powers of reasoning were not ready for Michael Venn's radical new and, which some would certainly describe as, controversial way of looking at the long held norms of their religion.

"Could these early saints not grasp this?" asked an infuriated Michael Venn.

"Evidently not and nor have thousands of others," said La Roche quietly.

"How could they and our church have wasted so much time arguing about piffling details which a mere modicum of logic would indicate cannot possibly be true and so miss the main messages; one of which is that God made both man *and* woman? And so in His eyes women must be just as important as men. There is no doubt that what has been written has been written by men primarily for men, so that our religion has become a 'male religion' and Augustine and Jerome have simply reinforced this bias as a result of their shame and guilt about their sexual relationships. How could they not grasp that God's Grace could be, indeed most certainly can be experienced here on earth? Likewise of course, so can Hell. Did they not realise that the hells they were living in, their own private hells, were hells of their own making, and instead of doing something about them, sat wallowing in misery and self-pity hoping that God would redeem them and whisk them off to some shame and guilt free paradise of their imagining?

I suppose we should feel some pity for Jerome at his almost desperate attempts at trying to claw his way back to a life of virginity and innocence, as this inevitably suggests that his guilt about his sexual behaviour must have weighed terribly on him. But why didn't he stop and question how God's Will could possibly be fulfilled by men living lives of misogyny, abstinence and celibacy? These two, Augustine and Jerome, instead of trying to right their wrongs, took themselves away from the world and polluted a religion with self-loathing, anti-feminism, anti-matrimony, anti-sex, abstemiousness and misery and as a result have without doubt given the current fanatics in our religion all the justification that they need to hold their extremist views."

Michael Venn slumped forward, possibly a little exhausted from his dissertation, though probably also in frustration and resignation tinged with despair, that all that he had said, whilst appearing so obvious to him, was so evidently not at all obvious to others. He need not have worried though, because brother Stephen La Roche leaned forward, squeezed his hand and said simply,

"Well done, Michael. However, please don't under rate the contribution that these saints have made to our religion just because you don't agree with their views on women and relationships."

"No I don't Stephen," replied a now much calmer Michael Venn. "I know Paul's and Augustine's writings and Jerome's translations were extremely important. However, just because much of their work was good, so important, that does not mean that *all* of it was. There can be no doubt that their views on women, relationships and sex were extremely biased by their own experiences of same. Whereas Paul paid heed to the advice given in Romans 14:3 ('Let not him that eateth despise him that eatheth not; and let not him which eateth not judge him that eateth') and adopted a fairly neutral stance on these matters, Augustine and Jerome did not and forced their biased opinions on sex into our religion and on to others. And have you noticed that whereas they are happy to cite Adam and Eve and weave all sorts of theories about whether and when, etc., to justify their anti-relationship, anti-sex stance, they make little or no mention of the various married couples also mentioned in the rest of Genesis? This no doubt is because those relationships cannot be held up as examples of those who failed to follow God because they were married. So they are quietly forgotten about because they do not fit into the Augustine and Jerome ideal of 'celibate followers of God.'

And their ideal of 'celibate followers of God' has been adopted as a necessary condition for those of us who now wish to become monks, priests, and nuns; wish to follow God. We in the Church, are expected to be and remain celibate, to be apart from the other sex, remote from the other half of society. How can this be right? And furthermore we know innately that it is not, and that such an unnatural way of living creates all sorts of problems. Indeed, the very fact that whole sections of our Church's Penitentials lay down a vast array of penances and punishments for any of us who transgress this code ought to be indication enough that an enforced celibate lifestyle is unnatural.

I trust you understand Stephen, that I am not saying that Augustine and Jerome are not entitled to their opinions, but am saying that they should never have thrust them to the fore and forced them into our religion, where, in the original texts any relationship between virginity, celibacy and Godliness hardly gets a mention."

"I certainly take your point Michael," concurred La Roche, "but as I have already said, there are and will be many who will not agree with you. Right now, as you both should be well aware, St Jerome's views on women and marriage are held in very high regard by our Church, so I strongly urge you Michael, and you Adam, to keep you opinions and what you have heard today to yourselves. I have no doubt that in time Michael, things will change and, who knows, the day may come when others might at least agree with you in part, but that day is not now. So we must keep this discussion between ourselves.

Now my two young friends, God requires that I need you to lift this old man to his feet."

Chapter 11

"Marketh ye well that the foremost temptation that the Devil places before you is woman!" Prior Obscurant boomed, with the usual raised arm and Heavenward pointing finger. Oh yes, we can be fairly sure that he had read Jerome's 'Against Jovinianus; Book 1:47'; though not for possible warnings about marriage as he'd probably never had any intention of doing such a Godless thing!

"The Devil lays cunning snares to trap the unwary and indeed I have learned that many of our fellow brothers have been led astray! Fornication is rife in our very Church!"

Poor Adam Callow's heart must have missed a beat when he heard this. Had they found out about him and Eve already? How? Oh Goodness, what would happen? An icy cold finger of fear crept up his puny spine. When would he be summoned? Oh Dear God, what had he done? Would he be accused of concubinage and have to endure all the penances that went with such a sin? - and he could be certain that McBane would not limit these to just those specified in the monastery's Penitentials. And what would happen to Eve? Excommunication without a doubt, and then …..? He tried to steel himself for what might be coming next; steel himself that is, until he belatedly realised that 'our very Church' was not the same as 'this very monastery,' and indeed, it transpired that 'our very Church' was not even 'our very Church in this very country', but was in fact the Church in far off Germany. Our near terrified novice-brother Adam Callow must have breathed a huge sigh of relief upon belatedly realising this.

"Grave news hath reached us, brothers, from the city of Münster (in Germany), where there art already so much heresy," thundered Prior Obscurant.

"Of late I hath told you of that viper Luther and his fellow serpent Melanchthon who dwelleth in the city of Wittenberg, and of their heresy against our Church and our Holy Father, of how they hath denied the venially sinful of their right to expurgate their sins (through the sale of indulgences), how their cancerous wiles have even reached the shores of this Kingdom and hath resulted in our Holy Book being printed, not in the language that God ordained for it to be known, but in the sacrilegious and base language of the common people. The very language of the Devil!"

Perhaps needless to say - though we will say it! - Prior Obscurant conveniently forgot that the Bible was not originally written in Latin and that the Vulgate version, which he implied was in the 'language that God ordained for it to be known,' was in fact made by Saint Jerome from various Hebrew and Greek sources[77] for much the same reason as it had now been printed in 'the sacrilegious and base language of the common people.' Namely, in order that it could be understood in Rome. However, whether it was because he'd realised that what he had just said wasn't strictly speaking true, or whether he simply needed to re-collect his thoughts having realised that he had inadvertently strayed off the main subject of today's morning-missive, or perhaps a bit of both, he was, after a brief pause, soon back on message and with his bony arm raised above his head.

"Heretics! Heretics who calleth themselves Anabaptists, hath both ousted the beloved Bishop and our Catholic brothers from the city, and hath proclaimed that *all* hath the seal of God in their foreheads! Proclaimed that all men are equal and lay claim that this vile heresy comes from our Holy Book!" All men were equal! All had the seal of God in their foreheads! All might find a way to God's Celestial Kingdom and Paradise! The absolute absurdity of these notions was so utterly incomprehensible to Prior Obscurant that he stood there in front of the brothers, his arms uncharacteristically lowered and in

---

[77] The Hebrew Bible, Septuagint and Greek Hexapla.

front of him, his palms spread and with a stunned look of incredulity on his skeletal face.

"Hath they not read its message?" he inquired. "Couldst it not be clearer that only the one hundred and forty four thousand who art not defiled by women will be redeemed from this earth?"

And then in a calmer voice, but one laced with sarcasm, he continued, "They calleth it a New Jerusalem. New Jerusalem? Pah! A New Sodom and Gomorrah!" The bony finger was wagging again and beginning to move skyward.

"The Devil is truly amongst us! He hath even driven out the Viper's (Luther's) adherents from that Godforsaken city; for now it most certainly is Godforsaken, having descended into iniquity, depravity and vice. Not only hath many sacred objects and holy relics have been destroyed by these devils my brothers, but we have it on good authority that several of them, these so called Anabaptists, hath taken several wives and that fornication is rife. The town is now descending into a mad pit of whoring and debauchery! A New Kingdom of, 'Babylon the Great, the mother of all harlots and abominations of the earth'[78] and, in our own time!"

Although his initial fear had probably passed, Callow's heart was also probably descending as he listened to this. OK, he was not a priest just yet, he was only a novice-brother; he was only training to be a monk. However, he was conducting an illicit love affair with a woman with whom he was not married and had had knowledge of her not just once, which might just be considered a mistake or accident, but twice, when it most certainly could not be dismissed so lightly. Sodom and Gomorrah, depravity and vice, whoring, fornication and debauchery. Babylon! Oh Goodness; what was he doing? Would his soul end up being thrown into 'the lake of fire'[79] and

---

[78] Revelation 17:5
[79] Revelation 20:14-15

suffer 'the second death'? And what about the first death, how would that be at the gentle hands of McBane?

"But the forces of God will triumph over the forces of the Devil," Prior Obscurant was explaining. "The Bishop himself[80] is commanding the siege of the city and already one of the heretics, a devil called Matthys, hath been killed and beheaded, and his genitals nailed to the city gate as a warning, a warning to all of the sins of lust, sins of the flesh and of fornication!"

'The sins of lust, sins of the flesh and of fornication!' echoed round the cold intolerant stone walls of the abbey church. Well, if not literally, then most certainly metaphorically for Adam Callow, as we can imagine a further cold shiver of fear must have run through him upon hearing this. There he had been naively thinking that somehow he could get away with a dalliance with the beautiful Eve Lilith, that somehow St Augustine's transgressions coupled with his subsequent canonisation would, for some undefined reason, miraculously result in absolving him (Adam Callow) from what he had done; indeed, was still doing. Genitals being nailed to a city gate must have sounded about as far from miraculous absolution as it was possible to get, and no doubt he suddenly woke up to the brutal fact that what had happened in Saint Augustine's day, was not quite the same as what was happening right now in his! Oh dear God, what would happen to his genitals if any of his transgressions with Eve ever became known? An horrendous vision of a gleeful McBane, with hammer and nail in one hand, and a bucket containing his - oh goodness, no! - making his way to the monastery gate must have flashed through his mind. However, as much as that vision probably made his stomach turn, picturing what might have happened a few minutes earlier was probably so ghastly as to be all but unimaginable; him still alive and held fast, and that sadist McBane with a cold steel knife about to slice-off ….!

---

[80] Franz von Waldeck

He felt sick, weak at the knees and cold. Oh dear God help me! He must terminate his relationship with Eve before it's too late. It can only end in disaster. He really *must* stop seeing her! But did he? No, no he didn't, because no, he couldn't. It was the delightful Eve, or the prospect of meeting with her, that kept him going through the week. How else would he have put up with being dragged out of his cot at three hourly intervals to chant and / or pray either in the main church or in that subterranean cave of a chapel containing those two disgustingly erotic portraits of two saintly ladies, followed each day by physical toil in the monastery garden and mind-numbing slaving over dry texts which had to be memorised almost, if not completely by heart? For Callow, the promise of Eve was like the promise of a particularly juicy carrot to a work-weary donkey. And so he buried the dangerous reality of what he was doing to the innermost recesses of his mind, denied to himself that there was any danger and, led by the nose by his desire, continued to meet his beautiful lover who took him to heaven every week with her uninhibited and adventurous love making.

Of course we shouldn't forget that he also had the intellectual delight of his weekly discussions with brother La Roche and fellow novice-brother Venn. These he also looked forward to and enjoyed even if he didn't contribute much to the discussion. Michael Venn usually did most of the talking, but Callow found it mentally stimulating to listen to other ideas, different interpretations of those that were forced on them by the regime of Prior Obscurant, sub-Prior Grees and novice-master McBane. However, as brother La Roche had both informed them and warned them, the strictures applied at the Priory and Monastery of Saints Paul and Augustine, were most certainly not unique and could be found, though perhaps less zealously applied, throughout most branches of the Church at that time. Indeed, one only had to read the Church Penitentials to observe that the absurdly intrusive rules relating to sexual relationships and behaviour were not made up by fanatical lunatics such as the three aforementioned - as novice-brother Venn might have described them - but were, so awfully, a normal part of the then mode used by the Church to hold power over the population and extract wealth from it.

Unfortunately, nothing lasts in life and these stimulating meetings enjoyed by Adam Callow, Michael Venn and Stephen La Roche were no exception, and, as has already been mentioned, inevitably the time came when brother La Roche announced,

"I am afraid my two young brothers that we will have to halt our meetings for a while."

"Oh?" said a disappointed Michael Venn and a likewise disappointed Adam Callow.

"You are aware that a poor woman has been accused of witchcraft and that no-one has volunteered to defend her."

"But, she is a witch," said Callow hesitantly, as if that definition was definition enough, but then realising that perhaps it might not be, added, "isn't she?"

"What do you think a witch is, my young friend? Some supernatural devil that has a black cat, eats babies and casts evil spells?" answered a controlled, but evidently angered brother La Roche.

"Well, er ....."

"Has it not occurred to you, to both of you, that a witch is an ordinary woman who has been branded a witch by others? You have heard of the expression 'a witch-hunt'? It was not - I say 'was not' as I had hoped that we were past that sort of thing, though evidently not - just a hunt for so called witches. It is the 'searching for' and the 'hunting down' of those whose views and actions do not conform to the orthodoxy of the day. What are her crimes? What has she done? We don't know. All we do know so far is that 'she is a witch' as if that explains all we need to know, and so she has already been found guilty in the eyes of all, simply by being accused. The Greek philosopher Plato said,

'The penalty good men pay for indifference to public affairs is to be ruled by evil men' and I fear we are being indifferent and are being ruled by evil men.

We three have a wonderful life in our monastery, even though it may not seem like it at times. We have good food, we have excellent accommodation, we have learning, our physical work is not too arduous and we have medicine. Possibly only the Duke and his family live better than we do. And as a result of this luxurious lifestyle we live longer than most of the rest of the population. Their lot is one of almost continual drudgery, poor food, cold and damp living conditions and no medicine unless they can afford the rates that we charge, or, they manage to get them from a so-called witch, who in fact is doing nothing different to ourselves, only her medicines are branded evil potions and Black Magic, whereas ours are sold as medicines and are referred to as White Magic. And if all of that wasn't enough, our Church then goes on to do its best to remove any enjoyment from the lives of ordinary people and takes every opportunity that it can to take what money it can from them for concocted so-called sins and offences, which it then offers to expurgate! How does our Church dare to pretend that it knows God's Will and that it can do anything remotely connected to His Will on this earth?"

Adam Callow and Michael Venn sat there aghast at what they were hearing. They knew that brother La Roche was open minded to alternative theological narratives, but had never heard him be so openly critical as this. Indeed, they had never heard any senior monk talk in such a way and so had never suspected that brother La Roche would do so. They had always assumed that the older monks agreed, to a greater or lesser extent, with the general philosophy expounded by Prior Obscurant and the Church in general. So to hear an older, senior monk, condemning the Church in such violent terms came as quite a surprise. Michael Venn in particular must have felt considerable relief at knowing that his somewhat radical opinions of some of the fathers of their Church and religion had been heard by someone who was similarly disenchanted by and critical of the present regime.

"I owe the pair of you a debt of gratitude for opening my eyes for me," continued La Roche. "I realise now more than ever that when I came into the priesthood after the loss of my beloved wife I did need to escape from the world in order to come to terms with my loss, rather like our Patron Saint, Saint Augustine did when he retired to the monastery at Hippo. Like him, I needed to find a new purpose in life, a new direction, something to devote myself to, and serving God in this monastery seemed to provide those needs. But I realise now that serving God within the confines of this monastery is a selfish way of serving Him, because I gain all the advantages of such a life of ease and luxury, but what good do I do to others? This so-called witch has probably done far more good than I have.

I thought I would serve God by following His example and creating a garden, a Garden of Eden if you like, a small piece of paradise on earth. It was a labour of love, but I now realise one born of vanity; the vanity that I could ever in my small way create something that would emulate God's Paradise. It was when you talked about how St Augustine had wronged the women in his life and then retired to Hippo, Michael, that this came home to me. It is all very well us confessing to God that we have sinned, but that only eases our conscience, it doesn't put things right, or even attempts to put them right. Retiring to the spiritual, intellectual and physical safety of a monastery, hiding oneself away from the real world is I now realise a cowardly way of facing life. What God requires is that we do something about our sins; do what we can to rectify the damage that we have done as a result of our thoughtlessness and do something about what is wrong in the world. How can we do that hidden away in a stone walled monastery theorising about who is and who is not going to join God in His Heaven? Almighty God will decide that, not us! And His love is not perfected by burning women!" he concluded vehemently.

"But won't Prior Obscurant ....?" commenced Callow.

"You'll be taking a big risk," added Michael Venn.

"Not as big as all that," said La Roche modestly. "Don't forget I have been at Saints Paul and Augustine's just as long as our Prior and he and those who support him know that. But don't you two get any foolish ideas. Even I could end up burning, but that won't be too easy for them. However, there won't be any qualms about throwing either of you on the fire if they feel the need to. So you keep your heads down," and with a very pointed look at Michael Venn added, "and keep your opinions to yourselves. You may not realise it my young brothers, but the tide is changing. Luther has challenged the greed and dominance of the Catholic Church. William Tyndale has translated and published The Bible in English so that now all can read and understand it, and our King, King Henry VIII, is rumoured to be splitting from the Catholic Church and creating a new church; the Church of England. Huge changes are taking place and our Prior and those like him must realise that their days in power are numbered and so they, like cornered animals, will fight to the last to retain a hold on what they can. Indeed, these last ditch struggles appear to be happening in the Church right now. I have heard rumour, though I have no idea whether it is true or not, that William Tyndale himself has been arrested and charged with heresy. If this is true and even a great man such as he is not safe, my advice to you is don't get involved in the immediate battle. Young men like you will be required to rebuild our Church after the dust has settled."

Callow and Venn looked apprehensively at each other. Had it struck either of them that their lives both were and had been not so dissimilar to having lived in a paradise on earth before suddenly 'the eyes of them both were opened'[81] to reveal the

---

[81] Genesis 3:7

real world that lay beyond the shelter and protection of the walls of their monastery? Whereas we might reasonably hazard that Michael Venn may not have known precisely what was happening in the greater world outside, we can guess that he probably would not have been surprised or shocked by it. However, the same could not be said of Adam Callow, who in all probability had no idea at all, and so did not appreciate what a protected life he had been and was leading.

"Who is the witch?" asked the naive Callow cautiously, still not entirely convinced that she could be a normal flesh and blood woman and not some mad she-devil of Prior Obscurant's imagination.

"You will find out soon enough, my young brothers. In the meantime, I think it is best that you don't know."

"And when will her trial be?" asked Venn.

"In about a months time. The date is not fixed just yet."

Chapter 12

The next morning Harry's head was still hurting him and a little later I learned from Elizabeth he'd been sick again. At that stage she hadn't heard about the beautiful woman in the golden dress, but she soon did.

"Why didn't you tell me?" she asked angrily.

"Lillibeth, I've only just got up. We've hardly seen each other yet and I've been making breakfast," I replied in my defence, though in truth I had completely forgotten about it. Whereas this had shocked me when Harry had first mentioned it, once I'd realised that in all probability he'd read about it in the book I was reading I'd ceased to attach any importance to it. However, poor Harry really did inadvertently drop a bombshell when we took his breakfast up to him and he told us that not only had he seen the beautiful woman in the golden dress in the cave, but also that she had spoken with him and had asked him to come with her.

"But I said 'No, no I wouldn't,'" said Harry, "and she got cross and said, 'You will come with me little boy. I need a child!' But I said, 'I don't want to, you're horrible!' and I ran out of the cave, and as I did she then said in nasty voice, 'You have come into my head little boy, so now I will go into yours.'"

Oh goodness! Can you imagine the look on Elizabeth's face upon hearing this? However, it wasn't quite the look of horror that I was expecting; more a look of surprise or a look of guilt at having been found out, almost as if she already knew about it but hadn't expected to hear it from Harry. But ....? And I had to consciously remind myself that Elizabeth *had* just asked me why I hadn't told her about Harry's mention of the woman in the golden dress, which of course suggested that she hadn't known. So feeling somewhat confused, I asked Harry,

"Are you sure?"

All the while I was frantically trying to recall the events of Harry's departure from the cave, because, as I remembered, he'd come out straight away after he'd heard Elizabeth and myself calling him and hadn't seemed the least bit put out or frightened, which is what I would have expected after the experience that he'd just described. However, I didn't want to press him on this as I felt sure he wasn't going to want his dad having a go at him when he wasn't feeling so good. So I left him to his breakfast.

"What do you make of that?" I asked Elizabeth as soon as I deemed we were out of earshot of Harry. "'You have come into my head, so now I will go into yours,'" and was about to add, 'and he is complaining of a head ache,' but though better of it. "It certainly is a little odd that he should say that now though, when he said nothing about it at the time," I continued. "And when I looked into that cave there was no one there, and you went in and ...."

"You wanted to go to that cave. It would be a nice day out you said. Now look at what you have done!" was what I received in reply.

"Me?" I could hardly say that I didn't know about the woman in the golden dress, because, yes, I had read about one, but that was subsequent to, not prior to our visit. However, it was certainly a strange coincidence Harry claiming to have met what appeared to be a very similar woman to that mentioned in the story. "I am not blaming you." I explained to Elizabeth. "I was just about to say that when you were in the cave you didn't see anyone either."

Elizabeth didn't answer me.

"What do you think she meant by ....." I commenced.

"Who?"

"This beautiful woman in the golden dress."

"Oh ..... nothing," said a now very disinterested sounding

Elizabeth. "He's probably had a dream as a result of the temperature he's running,"

"I was wondering if he's been having a peek at the book I'm reading," I offered. "as it does mention a woman in a golden dress. But where do you think he's got the idea that his cave dwelling woman should talk about 'my head' and tell him that she was wanting a child? I haven't read anything about either of those."

"Goodness, Joe! Can't you talk about something else? He's obviously read that book of yours, you've left it lying around all over the place, he's got a temperature and a head ache and you've just said yourself that he was fine when he came out of that cave, that cave that *you* took us to. Is it surprising that his imagination ….. ?" she let her sentence trail off, before coming back with, "Did you know, he's been sick this morning? And all that concerns you is 'what did she mean by this?' 'what did she mean by that?' and why 'she wants a child.' What about *my* child?"

Yes, perhaps Elizabeth was right. Perhaps I was paying too much attention to what Harry had claimed he had seen and heard. And in case you are wondering, yes, I did note Elizabeth's possessive, 'what about *my* child?' as opposed to a more reasonable, 'what about our child?' Harry is also mine after all. However, in fairness to Elizabeth, it is interesting to note that whereas all women expect men to 'contribute their fair share' to the up-bringing of a child, they do tend to continue to regard the child as theirs; especially upon divorce. It was, let us say, academically interesting to note that St Jerome and Theophrastus also observed how this female trait of grasping all that is potentially 'within reach' extends to how women regard '*their* house, *their* furniture, *their* dresses and *their* carriage' all of which are also supplied by their husband, but that is perhaps being a little too cynical! What is yours is mine, what is mine is my own. However, if a woman has carried a child for nine months before it is born, then a degree of possessiveness is to

166

be expected, and for the child's sake is probably desirable, especially in a world where some fathers might take no responsibility whatsoever.

"I think we should take Harry to the doctors," I said as calmly as I could, as I was seething inside at Elizabeth's callous possessiveness. I hadn't known that Harry had been sick again and to me this suggested that his condition was a little more serious than just a head cold.

"I'll take him," answered Elizabeth.

"No, we'll take him."

"And we'll say nothing to the doctor about our visit to the cave," she added assertively, "other than we had a day out at the weekend and so we thought he'd caught a head cold. Agreed?"

What had brought about this volte-face on what had previously been 'that cave of daddy's'? I confess I was more than a little bit taken aback by her reply as I had been half expecting that she would wish to continue to imply that Harry's illness was somehow my fault. No doubt I was being unkind. However, it wasn't that I disagreed with her suggestion and of course we needed the doctor's objective medical opinion, but it was curiously obvious that she wasn't wanting anything mentioned about the cave.

"All right," I replied.

The three of us drove down to the doctors' practice and fortunately were able to see a lady doctor after a relatively short wait. She asked Harry a few questions and then asked us if we had a car. When Elizabeth said that we had, it became apparent that she (the doctor) wanted us to take Harry down to the main hospital for a head scan as soon as possible as it would only be after that that any diagnosis could be made. We were advised to pack an overnight bag for Harry, just in case it was required. The doctor then made a phone call to the hospital to tell them that we were coming, that we had a car and that an ambulance wasn't required. After that we left.

Once back home we packed Harry's bag and headed down to the hospital. It had all happened so quickly. One minute we'd been sitting round the breakfast table and the next we were sitting in a hospital waiting room. A simple head cold had morphed into something a lot more serious. Then the waiting began. Yes, the hospital had known that we were coming, but there were several patients before us that also required the use of the scanner and so Harry had to wait his turn until they had been dealt with.

Aren't hospital waiting rooms dreadful places? All that everyone there wants is to 'get on with it', whatever 'it' is. Yet that is what doesn't happen. There is no 'getting on' with anything. Your entire life is put on hold until, at last, whoever it is that you are waiting for is free and deigns to see you. In this case we were waiting for a scanner, a certain MRI scanner, to become free so that it might give wholly of its attention to our Harry's head. I found myself musing if things had changed so much from the times I had been reading about in my tale of The Ghost Moth? In those days people went on a pilgrimage to a cathedral and waited for a saviour or saint to come and lay hands on the damaged part of a body. These days we go to a hospital and wait for an MRI scanner. The individual remains as powerless and helpless today as in the past. Oh yes, we kid ourselves that an MRI scanner is of course nothing like a saint - it was all superstition in those days! - but most of us have no idea how an MRI scanner works any more than our predecessors knew how the saint's healing hands worked. So are we, as individuals, any the wiser, given that today we are still totally dependant upon some external source of miraculous healing? It is just that perhaps 'the miraculous healing' is understood a little better by some who are in the know; those who our ancestors would have said were closer to God?

So would waiting in Purgatory, waiting for one's venal sins to be forgiven, be like sitting in a hospital waiting room, with the odd angel popping in now and then and calling out a name? Yes, such a conception of Purgatory sounds trite, but as Michael Venn in our story had observed, 'what is Heaven like?' and the truth be told, although we, mankind, know how to make an MRI scanner these days, we are still no nearer to knowing what Purgatory, or indeed God's Paradise is like. So the three of us sat, and we waited. I toyed with the idea of picking up and skimming through one of the obligatory waiting room magazines as a means of killing the time. However, I decided not to. It was poor Harry who was doing the real waiting, not Elizabeth and I, and so I opted to try and keep him amused. We tried a bit of 'I spy' and did a bit of 'people watching' on others, who, like us, were waiting to be summoned to the inner sanctum. Gradually the waiting area emptied and we were the only ones left; the only ones left in Purgatory waiting for an angel to arrive and summon us.

"Hello, I thought I might find you here."

To our surprise a nurse had appeared, seemingly from nowhere and was addressing young Harry; his angel had arrived. However, the nurse's arrival wasn't the only surprise, because we immediately recognised her as the woman with the dog that we had met on the way to the cave and tree at the weekend.

"Hello," I said, "it certainly is a small world."

"Did you have a nice day out?" she asked.

"Actually ….," began Elizabeth.

But before she could say anything further, the nurse cheerily introduced herself,

"I am nurse Senoy and I will look after this young man. So don't worry." And then turning to Harry, added with a smile, "If you don't mind waiting just another couple of minutes, I'll go and see if we can scan you now."

"She's the woman with the dog, isn't she?" said Harry.

"Yes, isn't that strange meeting her again, so soon after bumping into her on our Sunday walk?"

Elizabeth didn't say anything. Although I couldn't put my finger on what, or produce any evidence, I got a strange feeling that for some reason Elizabeth had taken an almost immediate dislike to nurse Senoy. Why, goodness knows, as we'd only met her once before and as far as I could tell she seemed a cheery enough soul? What is it with women, their immediate and illogical likes and dislikes? Anyway, a couple of minutes later nurse Senoy was back with a cheerful,

"Now young man. It is Harry isn't it? The scanner is free. So we can go through now," and she held out her hand to him and to my surprise, because Harry is usually a little shy of strangers, he rose, smiled at her, took hold of her hand and went off with her to the room containing the scanner as though they were old friends; an angel with a trusting soul.

I looked at Elizabeth as if to say 'Wow, that must be a first', but from the look on her face gained the impression that she was more probably of the opinion that nurse Senoy was the beautiful woman in the cave trying to abduct young Harry. Her earlier possessive remark of that morning, 'what about my child?' came back to me. Of course we were both worried about Harry and so quite possibly Elizabeth's seeming possessiveness and my observing this in her were nothing more than each of us over-reacting in our own ways. I tried to dismiss these negative thoughts from my mind as we followed Harry and nurse Senoy along the corridor, and instead tried to remember if we had in fact introduced ourselves that day, as I was pretty sure we hadn't. So how did this nurse know Harry's name? Ah, of course! The hospital knew we were coming and she would have seen his name on the practice's referral notes. 'Oh dear' I sighed, as I realised that I was getting as jumpy and suspicious in my way as possibly Elizabeth was in hers.

Nurse Senoy stopped outside the room and turned to Harry,

"We are here now. All they are going to do is take a picture of your head, so the doctor can see what is hurting you. Be brave and I will see you when you come out." Turning to us, she added, "Yes, please do go in with him. They are ready for you." And with that, she turned and walked off down the corridor.

I won't bore you with details of the MRI scan, other than to say that it must be a rather claustrophobic experience, that young Harry was very brave, kept his head still as instructed and all went well. That done, we went back to the waiting room anticipating that a doctor would come and give us his verdict on the scan. Instead however, nurse Senoy returned. She smiled at Harry.

"I heard that you were very brave in there," and then, addressing Elizabeth and I, added, "I am afraid Harry is going to have to stay in overnight so we can keep an eye on him. The consultant will have a look at both the scan and Harry tomorrow morning."

"So you can't tell us what is wrong?" asked Elizabeth somewhat shrewishly as though this was the nurse's fault.

"I am afraid not," and then to Harry, "So it looks like you will be staying with us tonight. That will be fun won't it?" Turning again to us she added, "A nurse will come and show you Harry's room and settle him in. Please don't worry, he will be in good hands. I will look after Harry. The best thing you can do for him is to go and get a good night's sleep."

Of course back in those days it wasn't possible for parents to stay in hospital overnight, so we were going to have to say goodbye to Harry and leave him on his own, a prospect which didn't appeal to Harry, or it seemed, Elizabeth. I had to smile at nurse Senoy saying 'Harry's room', when I was certain that what she meant was Harry's ward.

"I'll say goodbye now. A nurse will be along in a minute. See you later Harry."

Nurse Senoy left us and another arrived almost as soon as she'd left.

"Hello, you must be Harry. I am nurse Catherine. I am afraid Harry is going to have to stay in overnight so we can keep an eye on him. The consultant will have a look at both the scan and Harry tomorrow morning." She then turned to Harry and added, "So it looks like you will be staying with us tonight. That will be fun won't it?" after which she said to us, "Please don't worry, he will be in good hands. The best thing you can do for him is go and get a good night's sleep."

Did I hear all of that correctly? Because if so, it sounded to me like an almost word for word straight repeat of what nurse Senoy had just said. I wasn't sure if Elizabeth had noticed, which was possibly just as well, but it certainly struck me as odd. Was this just a strange coincidence, or .... was I beginning to see, or rather hear, mystery and imaginings in things that were in fact perfectly, well perhaps not perfectly, but relatively normal? I felt uneasy. Perhaps what Harry had told me about the woman in the cave had made me a little more jumpy than I'd realised. Or was it both that and Elizabeth's unexpected insistence that we didn't mention the cave that had got my nerves rattled, so that now I was noticing 'strange things' without any real need of prompting?

"Shall we go and find your room, young man?"

And with that, nurse Catherine turned and walked towards the exit; waiting rooms don't really have doors, do they? And yes, before you ask, I had noticed that this nurse Catherine had also used the words 'your room.' Harry looked up at us with a question mark on his face, but I think Harry's 'question mark' was more to do with 'what do we do now?' rather than questioning his sleeping arrangements.

"Let's go and find this room of yours," I said to him. And the three of us followed nurse Catherine out of the room.

We trailed along various corridors, got into a lift at one stage, then more corridors and then to my complete surprise arrived at a room, which was going to be Harry's; I really had expected that he would be put in a children's ward.

"And this is your room, Harry," said nurse Catherine as we arrived at what looked like a very nice private hospital room. Harry looked around, somewhat wide-eyed and apprehensive.

"Hey! You're a lucky chap," I reassured him. "A room all of your own. What have you done to deserve this?"

I have to admit that I wasn't so sure whether this was a good thing or not. A private room sounds like a nice idea to an adult, but I was wondering if Harry would have preferred the company of some other boys of similar age when in this strange new environment of a hospital. Would he feel a bit 'all alone' and frightened in this 'very nice room' all on his own?

"You can put his clothes in here," explained the nurse opening a cupboard door. "Perhaps if I show Harry where the toilet and bathroom are and then I'll leave you to settle in?"

Harry looked at us, but didn't say anything.

"Go on Harry. Do a bit of exploring with the nurse. We'll still be here when you get back."

Poor Harry, his head was obviously hurting and I presumed he was also a bit worried about the prospect of spending a night on his own away from us and in a strange hospital room.

"It's a nice enough room," said Elizabeth, once the nurse and Harry had departed on their toilet and bathroom expedition.

"Very."

"When that first nurse ….."

"Senoy," I said. "Such an unusual name."

"Yes," said Elizabeth coolly; well, coolly enough so that I couldn't fail to notice her all-too obvious dislike of her. "When she said room, I thought she meant ward," she added.

"Yes, me too. Do you think he'll be OK in here on his own? He does seem a bit apprehensive about it. But I'm sure nurse Catherine will look after him, and nurse Senoy said she would as well. So he'll have two nurses fussing over him."

Elizabeth took to busying herself by inspecting the cupboard and table, and then looking out of the window as if looking for someone or something. Probably just nerves, I told myself. When Harry returned he was hand in hand with Nurse Catherine and did appear happier than when he had left us.

"We've had a look round, haven't we Harry."

"Yes," he replied quietly.

"I think Harry could do with a rest," she said to Elizabeth. "He's had a long day and so could do with some sleep. If you could get him into bed and ....." Although she didn't say it, it was fairly obvious that she wanted us to leave.

As Elizabeth tended to Harry, Nurse Catherine came round the bed to me and said quietly,

"He's been sick again and he's not too steady on his legs. He just needs to rest." She then left the room.

We got Harry into bed.

"We are going to say cheerio now," I said, "and let you get some sleep. We'll be back in the morning."

Oh, such goodbyes are difficult. You tell yourself that it is for only one night, but the duration is not what is important, it is the act of parting which is; that cold blooded severing of an emotional link which binds the two of you. You are horribly aware that you are 'wielding the knife.' So how do you explain either to the one you are leaving or yourself that this is a 'good thing' when it feels anything-but to the both of you? Of course it is not a 'good thing', it is a 'necessary thing'. So is it an irrational fear of 'potentially losing' that upsets; the fear that you might not see the person again and so might lose their love for you and yours for them, that they might be lost to you forever, and as a result of losing that love, you will lose something of yourself? A heart, a soul, stripped of love is a cold barren place and something buried deep within you tells you that you don't want to go there.

"Sleep well, darling," said Elizabeth with tears in her eyes whilst pulling the bed clothes up around Harry and giving him a kiss. "Mummy loves you."

"You have two lovely nurses looking after you. You'll be just fine," I contributed, whilst fighting to retain a 'stiff upper lip.' "Until tomorrow. Sleep tight, old lad."

We both kissed him and left, shutting the door to his room gently behind us.

"Here is the best place for him," I said as reassuringly as I could, for both Elizabeth's benefit and I admit, for mine. "Here he has nurses and doctors on hand."

"Yes," she said, taking hold of my arm, "Let's go home and have an early night."

We started strolling along the corridor. My thoughts though were still with Harry, so I didn't immediately notice Elizabeth's sudden change of mood and show of affection, or register her totally unexpected, 'Let's go home and have an early night.' It was as I did and when we were just turning a corner, that there was nurse Senoy, right in front of us. Goodness! Where had she come from?

"Hello again," she said in her usual breezy manner. "Is Harry nicely settled in? Will you find your way out alright?"

"I think so," I replied somewhat vaguely to both questions as I was preoccupied with totally different subjects; all the slightly odd things that had happened since we had arrived at the hospital, whether Harry would like being on his own and would manage OK, what had prompted my wife's unexpected change of mood, and finally, no, I wasn't actually sure whether I would find where we'd parked our car.

"Don't worry, I will take care of Harry," said nurse Senoy in a manner which I felt didn't have the usual glib reassurance about it, but somehow sounded weightier, as if it were a statement of fact rather than of reassurance. Was I now imagining this as well, or was it simply that she had said something like that before? I couldn't remember. It had been a strange day and I couldn't shake off the feeling that things weren't quite normal, that there was something odd going on that I wasn't privy to.

"I'll pop my head in and see if he is asleep," nurse Senoy added. "Goodbye."

She left us and set off down the corridor towards Harry's room.

Throughout that little exchange I noticed that Elizabeth had not once looked at the nurse, which I thought was a bit rude, especially as she was obviously one of the nurses responsible for looking after our son, but as I've already mentioned, women's moods, or perhaps I should be more accurate and say Elizabeth's moods, were a total mystery to me.

Much to my relief we found our way out surprisingly easily; a different entrance, or exit in our case, took us out to the car park without having to retrace our steps through the waiting room.

Once home I felt I had to find out if there was any linkage between Adam Callow, Eve Lilith and the cave, and what was happening to our young Harry's head. The ominous sounding 'You have come into my head, so now I will go into yours!' can easily be dismissed as a bit of melodrama if you don't have a member of your family involved, but when this comes against a backdrop of your son complaining of an aching head, having been sick on several occasions and various medical people have deemed it necessary for him to go into hospital because of same, it is not quite so easily dismissed as mere melodrama. Indeed, it becomes quite worrying. Was Harry's malady connected to the beautiful woman he claimed to have seen in the cave, or was that episode a figment of his imagination brought on by the onset of whatever it was that was ailing him? I had no idea. However, in the circumstances, as I'm sure you understand, I wanted to check out just what had happened in that cave in the past to learn if it did have any bearing on our Harry's present condition.

I picked up the book and started to read. However, I had barely opened the pages when Elizabeth arrived in the living room again clad in a new silky, Chinese-looking dressing gown, which I observed did look remarkably good on her.

"And I thought we were going to have an early night, Joey."

"Well, I ….," I commenced

"Come to bed you naughty boy. It is not every night that we have the house to ourselves," and with that she let her dressing gown fall open. Yes, my then wife may have had her faults, but her body wasn't one of them. She came over to me, sat on my lap, gently took the book from my hand and put it on the coffee table, and then pushed me back onto the sofa.

<u>Chapter 13</u>

Such was young novice-monk Adam Callow's preoccupation with his own affairs that he simply forgot about the impending witch trial and so hardly noticed the polarising effect that this was having on opinion in the monastery. Total control of body and soul was what the Church required according to Prior Obscurant, because how else could any of the wretched sinners stand a chance of not spending a minimum of an eternity in purgatory, even if, in Prior Obscurant's opinion, most of them were deserving of a far worse fate, let alone getting the slightest glimpse of Heaven on a distant horizon if left to their own devices? Someone had to lead them for their own good, and that someone was Prior Obscurant.

There was no doubting that a gruesome spectacle such as a witch burning would certainly put the fear of God into all and establish beyond any doubt that those who opposed the word of God, as interpreted by Prior Obscurant and the hard-line faction, would not be tolerated. According to them this would only be 'carrying out God's Will on earth', the purging of their society of a witch and she-devil. Of course it would also reinforce the power of the Church, though as those advocating this were not seeking personal power after all they could hardly be accused of doing this for personal motives, such as 'clinging on to power'. They were serving God and it was projecting His power on earth that mattered. However, whether the 'undertaking of God's Will on earth', such as burning a witch, would actually benefit the standing of the Church in the eyes of the population at large and in the longer term, was very much another matter, and the more progressive elements, which included brothers La Roche and Swan, thought that it would do nothing but harm and alienate the population at large.

Now, we might be tempted to think that novice-master Rodiron McBane headed-up the supporters of this so self-evidently righteous and Godly stance, but that would be to forget that animal cunning and human intellect are not the same thing and that McBane had more of the former than the latter. In fact, somewhat surprisingly, it was sub-Prior Arriviste Grees who appeared to be the chief supporter in the Obscurant camp. Indeed, it might even have been Grees who was pulling the strings and using his Prior to promote his (Grees') own ends - a small political insurance on his part in case anything went wrong, when it would be Prior Obscurant who would be in the immediate firing line, not him, and that ought to lead to his promotion to Prior? Only the detractors of the Obscurant / Grees philosophy, those who patently did not understand what was required to gain access to God's Celestial Kingdom / ascend the greasy pole, would describe such a philosophy, entirely erroneously of course, as ultra-conservative, hard-line, or even fanatical or extremist.

When Prior Obscurant had appointed his sub-Prior Grees to prosecute the witch and novice-master McBane to interrogate her, no one had any idea who the accused was and possibly, partly because of this, none had had the courage to put themselves forward to defend an unknown woman who Prior Obscurant had described as a 'whore of the Devil' and a 'harlot of Satan's'. So at that stage Prior Obscurant quite reasonably assumed that his sub-Prior and novice-master would be able to present the case and carry it forward unimpeded to its desired conclusion; a spectacular burning in the Market Square. However, since then the name of the accused had become known to the more senior monks and many had realised that the lady in question was most unlikely to be a witch and that the accusation was extremely doubtful. Indeed, they knew her to be well educated, kind hearted and liked by all. As La Roche had explained to Callow and Venn, she was knowledgeable enough to grow her own herbs and make up potions, but because she was doing this outside the 'protective cloak of the Church' her acts were deemed 'the dark arts of Black Magic' and her products 'evil potions'. However, her potions sold for a fraction of the prices charged by the monastery and so we can reasonably assume that the villagers weren't that concerned about the fact that they hadn't been blessed by Prior Obscurant's god and by extension had been cursed by the Devil! They worked as well as the more expensive White Magic, Holy Potions, and that was all that concerned them.

Unfortunately, this kind and charitable lady was also a physically attractive and desirable one. She was also one who had chosen to remain single rather than get married, so in Prior Obscurant's eyes was already a temptress and she-devil using her feminine wiles to lead men astray. It stood to reason of course; she was unmarried and so therefore remained 'available' and so must be tempting men to improper thoughts and, most certainly to improper actions! And if the foregoing wasn't enough, she was outspoken and critical of inequalities, unfairness and the dominance of the Church. This fierce independence of hers and her lack of respect for conformity most certainly would have put Prior Obscurant's nose out of joint and indeed the Church's nose out of joint. However, her cardinal sin (if we can excuse the pun) were her views on the hypocrisy of the Church and how it seemed to be far more interested in money and power than it ever was in doing good and saving souls. Prior Obscurant no doubt felt deeply insulted by this, as his whole existence was devoted to the saving of souls; though only those worthy of saving it goes without saying, only those with the seal of God in their foreheads, so hence only those who comprised the one hundred and forty four thousand. He couldn't save everyone after all! Sub-Prior Grees however was probably less concerned with this aspect and more concerned about her verbal assaults, as he would have seen these as being potentially politically damaging, and no doubt foresaw that they had the very real possibility of turning the population against the Church and so undermining the privileged lifestyle he enjoyed and, far more importantly, potentially damaging his personal career.

However, 'all her faults' did not make this woman a witch in the eyes of many of those in the village, or indeed in the eyes of many of the monks. As far as the villagers were concerned, anything and anyone who put Prior Obscurant's nose, or that fat pig Grees' snout out of joint, had quite the opposite effect, as in equal measure the villagers both feared and loathed the pair of them. In their eyes, this woman was a real-life angel. There were also many inside the monastery who both acknowledged her perhaps somewhat unconventionally presented goodness and were also only too well aware of her standing in the community, and so realised that burning this 'angel' would not go down well. They were hence secretly relieved when brother Stephen La Roche threw his hat in the ring and offered to take on the role of her defence.

This news must have been received by Prior Obscurant with a mixture of annoyance and concern. There was no doubt whatsoever that brother La Roche's taking on this role was an open act of defiance; it couldn't be interpreted as anything else and so it would inevitably be expected that Prior Obscurant would be annoyed that anyone would dare to openly defy him. However, his annoyance was also tinged with concern, because he was only too well aware that although La Roche modestly pretended to be otherwise, the learned brother might well be able to hold his own with the Machiavellian Arriviste Grees. This was probably the more troubling factor because as Prior Obscurant would have seen it, that heretic of a vegetable grower, La Roche, was far more popular with his fellow monks than ever the porcine sub-Prior was, and so both aspects might influence the outcome. There was now the very real possibly that this inquisition would not be quite as straight forward as Prior Obscurant had hoped it would be.

While God's Prior was attempting to work out how to get this trial back onto his idea of the right track, a totally unexpected incident blew up. A young man called Frank Artless had been caught supposedly attempting to steal lead from the monastery roof. He had been doing no such thing of course and had in fact been doing his best to stop the real perpetrator, by shouting at him. This had the desired effect of frightening off the thief, who dropped his roofing hammer as he fled, but the undesired effect of attracting attention to himself. He had then foolishly picked up the hammer, and so when others arrived they found him with it in his hand and so had erroneously jumped to the conclusion that it was he who had been trying to steal the lead. It was his further bad luck to be recognised by novice-master McBane as he passed by the throng that had gathered round him. Whereas by this time there were several in the group who were listening to Frank Artless' version of events, it never crossed McBane's small mind that master Frank Artless might be the wrong man. Soldiers were sent for by McBane, arrived and escorted master Artless away even though he and several of the assembled crowd were now vehemently protesting his innocence[82].

Prior Obscurant must have felt that this incident was Heaven sent. Of course, God was on his side. Why shouldn't He be? After all, God's Prior on Earth was leading the pure life ordained by Him, following the true straight and narrow path to Salvation and His Heavenly Paradise, and so why shouldn't God recognise this by delivering up to him (Prior Obscurant) this wretched soul, Master Frank Artless? This Master Artless was so obviously guilty. He had been found with the hammer in his hand by none other than Prior Obscurant's trusted novice-master. Hence, a formal trial would not be necessary and the sentence, public flogging, could be carried out as soon as was practical. Most fortuitously this would have the desired effect of reasserting the Church's authority as well as giving him (Prior Obscurant) the necessary time to work out how to sidestep the troublesome problem thrown up by that vegetable grower La Roche taking on the role of defence of the she-devil

---

[82] Loosely based on St Augustine's story of Alypius, cited in Confessions, Book VI: 9, though with a totally different outcome.

witch. The date for the flogging was set for the following Saturday.

Gradually this latest news filtered through the monastery. When it arrived at the ears of novice-monks Venn and Callow they simply couldn't believe it. Both knew Frank Artless personally. He and his family were friends of both of them and their families. He couldn't possibly have done this. There had to be some mistake. To Callow the world seemed to be going mad; apparently some innocent woman had been locked up and was awaiting trial as a witch, he had his own troubles, both in this world and of the next concerning his relationship with Eve Lilith, and now his childhood friend, who hadn't got a drop of felonious blood in his veins, had been found with a hammer in his hand apparently trying to steal lead off the monastery roof! Was he living in a world where conventional logic and morality had been turned on its head, where what was good was being deemed as wrong and sinful and now where the good and innocent were being branded as wicked and guilty?

One of the rumours going the rounds had it that the sadistic little novice-master, McBane, had actually caught master Frank Artless in the act of removing lead. However, another suggested that McBane had caught him with the hammer in his hand, which wasn't quite the same thing as many reasoned that Frank Artless could have simply picked up the hammer after it had been dropped by the escaping would-be thief. They also knew McBane well enough to know that it would be totally impossible for him to even consider the possibility that he might have made a mistake, might have jumped to a false conclusion and so apprehended the wrong person. So Callow and Venn were not the only ones in the monastery who thought that this was looking like, what we might call today, a 'stitch-up'. However, unlike La Roche, many had not joined up the dots in the larger picture and so had not grasped why it was that their Prior was so keen to pass judgement and pronounce sentence so quickly.

But it wasn't only those in the monastery who felt that something wasn't quite right. Many in the village knew master Frank Artless, and / or knew a member of his family. This was one which had a reputation for propriety and honesty, his father was a cloth merchant, and they were rich, so there was no financial reason for young Frank to go stealing lead. And furthermore, to attempt such an act in broad daylight was deemed, even by the more criminally minded of the villagers, to be so downright daft that they couldn't believe that a well educated, intelligent young gentleman such as Frank Artless could be so stupid. Then of course there were the testimonies of those partially involved in the incident, many of whom felt that McBane had acted too hastily and not heard all the evidence. No, something definitely wasn't right. Unfortunately, no one, both inside and outside the monastery, had any more information, so it was all-but impossible to mount any form of logical defence against the sentence handed down to the young Frank Artless. To the hard-line faction in the monastery, the case against him was so obviously an open and shut one, and so of course, he would be publicly flogged in the Market Square on Saturday afternoon. That was that.

The day after market day a group of men, under the watchful eye of an armed guard, started erecting a raised platform, with a whipping post at its centre, in the middle of the Market Square next to the market cross. The prompt erection of the platform and whipping post had very little to do with the timetabling of the labourers who erected it and everything to do with the psychology of striking maximum fear into the population, because once erected it was simply left there, a visual testament of what was to come in a few days time; a visual warning to all that the law would run its course, would be obeyed, which was another way of saying; 'we are in charge and don't you forget it, you will obey our laws and God help those who do not!' There was no doubting that McBane was good at his job.

As soon as lunchtime prayers were over on the Saturday,

novice-monks Adam Callow, Michael Venn and their four fellow novice-monks, together with all the senior monks, assembled in the cloisters and, with one of their number, a young novice-monk, Peter Lamb, holding aloft an ornate crucifix on a pole at their head, filed out of the monastery. Immediately behind young Peter Lamb was sub-Prior Arriviste Grees, dressed in his sub-Prior's finery, a scapular and cowl of ecclesiastical claret over his usual black habit, and behind him novice-master Rodiron McBane with lash in hand. All the senior monks were clad in their black habits and cowls. Callow and his fellow novice-monks also wore cowls that day. The solemn procession was so evidently intended to strike God's justice, power and fear into the crowd that a human face was neither desirable nor required; it was the impartial anonymity of justice that was on display. Justice had to be seen to be done, not because there was anything 'just' about it, but quite simply to put the fear of God into everyone. That, after all, was the principle aim of this 'display of justice'.

The monks made their way to their side of the village square; the one they usually occupied on market day and the one which - and was it coincidentally? - resulted in their backs being protected by the monastery wall. Set in that same protective stone masonry wall was a sculpted stone fronted balcony resting on projecting stone corbels. This was reserved, safely out of harm's way, for the Prior and the Duke to oversee proceedings. A small doorway containing a heavy wooden, iron coach-bolt studded door, gave access to and from this balcony. Adam Callow glanced up at the balcony and noticed that it remained empty.

That day on the village square Adam Callow found himself standing just a few paces away from where he had stood on the previous market day and must have pondered how strange it was that the scene witnessed from almost the same spot could be so different on two different days. Even with all his worries, he must have appreciated that the market day had had a sense of freedom to it, with people being there because they wanted to be, enjoying meeting up with friends, chatting happily to each other. Whereas today they had no desire to be there and only were so because messengers had been sent round the houses advising all that it would be 'wise for them to attend'. Some may have ended up standing next to friends, but their meeting thus was not one which brought forth a smile and a joyful greeting, but one which might have resulted in a silent nod of acknowledgement and that was all. Acknowledgement that they were also there under duress to witness the barbaric enforcement of a law which had been prescribed by others and which was imposed on them without their consent. Four uniformed guards armed with halberds, stood at each corner of the raised platform. Several more, similarly attired and armed, stood in a group at the corner of the square off to the left of Callow. It could not have escaped his notice that the almost full Market Square was surprisingly quiet.

Although out of Adam Callow's field of view, it was evident from the reaction of the crowd on the west side of the square that something was happening. And thus the ghastly spectacle began. The hapless pawn in Prior Obsurant's game of wishing to restore Church authority, master Frank Artless, was marched into the square flanked by two guards. He looked almost totally exhausted and was having difficulty walking. Had he been tortured in an attempt at getting a confession out of him? As he came near to where his parents and siblings were standing, his mother started screaming. Two of the guards positioned themselves in front of his family members, their halberds crossed. Callow clearly heard young Frank Artless say,

"I didn't do it. I didn't."

"We know, son," said his father who was holding his distraught mother so as to stop her from rushing headlong at her son. His two brothers and four sisters quite simply didn't know what to do. Two of his sisters were already crying. Why was this so blatantly gross injustice happening?

As Frank Artless and his two guards reached the steps to the platform, ascended them and proceeded to the pole, the crowd became more restless. Some jeering and booing could be heard above the general hubbub. This of course would never have happened a few years previously; the crowd would have had more respect, or more fear, and it was re-establishing fear that this charade of justice was all about because, as Prior Obscurant had suspected, the Church had obviously been far too lax recently. This sort of insubordinate, indeed insolent behaviour illustrated perfectly why it was necessary for the Church to re-establish its authority and bring some discipline back into society. However, what was deemed disgraceful to Prior Obscurant must have been reassuring to Callow and Venn, as they must have realised that they were not the only ones who thought a grave miscarriage of justice was about to be committed. The cords which were already attached to Artless' wrists were taken and threaded through the projecting iron loops on the pole and tied off. The guards then descended the wooden steps leading to it and took up positions on each side of them.

The noise from the crowd suddenly increased. Callow looked along the row of monks to his right and saw sub-Prior Arriviste Grees and novice-master Rodiron McBane with lash in hand, walking towards the platform. A quick glance behind him also showed that Prior Obscurant and the Duke, both in their full regalia for the occasion, had taken up their positions on the stone balcony. Grees and McBane climbed the steps to the platform. McBane took up a position on the south east corner of the platform facing the majority of the villagers and with his back to his fellow monks. Sub-Prior Grees, Bible in hand, moved to the front centre of the platform facing the crowd and with his back to poor Frank Artless.

"We are here today," commenced Grees in his unfortunate high-pitched squeaky voice, "to witness punishment exacted on this wretched sinner ....."

There were some boos and jeers from the crowd.

"..... this wretched sinner, who hath broken God's holy commandment; 'Thou shalt not steal'..... " and yes, Grees was even talking and acting a bit like Obscurant, the same pseudo-biblical style of speech and the same arm, though not a long bony one, but a shorter chubbier one, aloft brandishing a Bible in a small pudgy pink hand as he said, 'God's holy commandment'.

Callow must have felt himself shiver under his cassock. Oh goodness, if these lunatics ever find out about ..... - 'But I have broken with her now. I have seen the error of my ways, just as Saint Augustine did. Yes. Listen, Saint Augustine did the same!' 'But novice-brother Callow, you wretched man, you not only fornicated out of wedlock, but also on a day specifically prescribed by this Holy Church as a day of celibacy! Your sin bears no comparison to that of our revered saint. How dare you taketh his name in vain? You shall be taken from here and .....' Did Callow feel the cold sweat running down his back?

"..... and not only was he stealing," squeaked the flabby necked Grees, "but stealing from God's very own house!"

There were more boos and jeers from the crowd.

In true Prior Obscurant style, sub-Prior Arriviste Grees lifted his arm, shook his Bible and looked round the crowd with the apparent unshakable confidence possessed by those whose self-belief trounces everything. He certainly did his best to make his confidence look apparently unshakable, but he must have noticed the boos and jeers from the crowd, and the crowd must have noticed the resulting rising pitch in his voice as he continued with,

"Stealing from God's own house! To those of you who know not the facts, they are these. This wretched sinner was caught in flagrante delicto committing his heinous crime; he had the hammer in his hand!"

There were yet more boos and jeers from the crowd, which suggested that they did not feel that this alone proved his guilt. There had been no trial. Even the hardened villains of the village, who thought Frank Artless a stuck-up little rich boy, knew that he was not capable of such a thing, knew he was not a thief; it was blindingly obvious to them, a little rich snob like him hadn't got the bottle for it!

"Commence the punishment!" squeaked Grees evidently almost in relief that his part in this was all-but over.

The volume of booing and jeering rose as McBane stepped forward, took hold of Frank Artless' shirt and with one sweep of his arm ripped it from his back. And then the true horror began. Lash after lash from McBane. At first Frank Artless screamed as the lash struck him and then gradually his legs began to give way and his cries of pain changed to a pathetic sounding whimper. Finally his legs gave way completely and he was left hanging from iron hoops of the whipping pole and all that could be heard was the sound of McBane's lash striking his bleeding back. The crowd was in uproar and the guards were beginning to look nervously at each other for moral support. How would so few of them ever manage to contain this crowd which was beginning to look as if it was about to explode with rage at the injustice of the so-called justice being meted out.

Then suddenly the whole mood of the crowd changed, the braying and booing gave way to a huge cheer as brother La Roche strode purposely forward mounted the steps and, pushing McBane out of the way, bared his back and stood with his hands on the top of the whipping pole, his huge bulk shielding the body of Frank Artless, and said in a clear voice,

"This man has had enough. I will take the rest of his punishment."

Callow couldn't believe what he was seeing and nor probably did any of the crowd. McBane didn't either and had no idea what to do. Was he supposed to publicly flog a fellow brother and one of the most senior brothers in the monastery? And would he dare to actually flog brother La Roche who was twice his size and possibly still twice as strong, and likely as not, might still be able to take McBane apart with relative ease in a two man contest? He looked around for his sub-Prior for moral support and instruction, only to find that he had already departed the platform. No doubt sub-Prior Grees had sensed that it might be wise to leave a scene that was beginning to look so decidedly ugly, as the crowd was now both cheering and jeering in equal measure. Prior Obscurant signalled from the safety of his balcony to the group of guards to the left of Callow and six of them moved forward to the raised platform. No sign was given to McBane. The loyal novice-master was left on his own.

Brother La Roche's, 'Even I could end up burning' came back to Callow. Oh goodness, had it actually come to this already? 'Don't you two get any foolish ideas. There won't be any qualms about throwing either of you on the fire if they feel the need to. So you keep your heads down and keep your opinions to yourselves.'

The guards reached the steps and as they started to mount them the crowd started booing again. Brother La Roche took his hands off the top of the pole and half raised them to the baying throng and amazingly, well, Callow thought it amazing, they fell silent. La Roche then turned to face the guards and raised his left hand to them as a signal to stop, and again to Callow's surprise, they did. La Roche then went to the whipping pole and untied the wretched Frank Artless, signalled to two of the guards to come forward and gave them his limp body to carry away, presumably to where it could be tended. The other four guards mounted the rostrum, but did not advance towards brother La Roche who turned his back on them and, facing the crowd and in what could only be interpreted as an open public act of defiance to Prior Obscurant, started to say, for the very first time in the village, the Lord's Prayer in English.

Adam Callow glanced round at the balcony. The Duke had already left and Prior Obscurant was evidently just about to do so, but had turned upon hearing Stephen La Roche's clear steady voice. He must have realised enviously that he could never hold the crowd like La Roche was doing right now. Damn the man! Why had God given him the ability to do this, when it was he (Prior Obscurant) who knew the true path to God's Heaven and Glory? What did that vegetable planter, La Roche, know of this? It was he (Prior Obscurant) who needed the talent to lead the earth's miserable sinners to their Divine Maker and Redeemer. But he would show them. He would lead them to God's Kingdom even though none of them deserved it. Then he turned and disappeared from view.

Callow looked back at brother La Roche and saw the four guards, standing still, with heads bowed, as were all in the now silent crowd. None present had ever heard anything like this. A prayer, which they all could understand. Not a prayer in some foreign language, owned by a self-selected elite which they then magnanimously handed down to them. No, they could own this, it was their prayer. Their prayer, which they could personally offer up to their God. So there was no longer any need to have the likes of Obscurant interceding on their behalf, acting as some sort of divine broker between them and God and extracting a fortune from them for this 'service'.

After the final 'amen', brother La Roche turned to the guards and walked towards the steps, pausing to permit two of them to descend first. He then followed with the other two behind him and the five of them walked off through the crowd, the guards gently moving people out of the way in a manner more akin to their being La Roche's personal body guards rather than those sent to arrest him.

It was only after brother La Roche and his entourage had moved out of sight that Callow thought of looking for McBane. Where was he? Somehow that little weasel of a man had slipped away unnoticed.

Chapter 14

The first thing Elizabeth and I did the following morning was phone the hospital about Harry. We were informed that the consultant would be looking at him that morning and were asked if we could come in after lunch when he would discuss Harry's case with us.

Good news, I thought. However, immediately after that phone call and to my complete surprise given that we had had a lovely romantic night together, Elizabeth in effect indicated that this now counted for nothing and that the gloves were off again between us. I had no idea what brought on this latest sudden change of mood. All I knew was that it was wearing trying to keep up. So that morning I discovered that I couldn't do anything right. After making the coffee too strong, I then .... yes, possibly did drop a bit of a clanger by telling her that I had researched the orange coloured moth that we had seen at the cave that day and knew which type it was.

"Do you honestly think I need to know about that!" she snapped back.

"Well, I thought you might like to. It is called a Ghost Moth, Hepialus humuli."

"Is it? Well it didn't look very ghostlike to me. Ghosts aren't usually orange, in case you haven't noticed."

So now she was suddenly an expert on ghosts. Not wanting an argument, I answered as patiently as I could,

"No, traditionally they aren't. However, the male ghost moth is white. What we saw was the female."

"Yes," she answered in a non-committal sort of way.

"Don't you think it a strange coincidence that the female ghost moth is orange and yellow in colour and that the woman that Harry saw in the cave was wearing a yellow and orange dress?"

"But, there was no woman. You saw that for yourself."

"Yes, true. But it is odd that Harry should come out with a story of this woman asking him to come with her and of her needing a child."

"Did you see this woman?" she asked. "well, did you?"

"No. You know very well I didn't. So why are you asking me?"

"Because you keep talking about her. You have done nothing but talk about her since we got up."

She seemed to be trying to provoke another totally unnecessary argument. Why? We'd had a lovely night together, which is what she had wanted …. well, she had wanted it last night …. and now she just seemed to want a fight.

"But we both saw that moth," I offered hoping that this change of subject might defuse the tension.

"And what has that got to do with it?" she fired back at me. "Maybe that area just happens to be an area favoured by, what were they, ghost moths?"

"So you think this story I'm reading has been tailored to fit what is already there?" I suggested.

"Didn't you suggest that yourself, Joe?" she replied angrily. "That all tourist boards like to have a story that 'brings the punters in'?"

Yes, I had, hadn't I? Nonetheless I groaned inwardly at Elizabeth's unwillingness to engage with me on what I thought was an interesting and strange coincidence. However, I had to acknowledge that 'my coincidence' theory wasn't as convincing as I would have liked it to have been, because although Harry's account of what he'd seen and heard could be deemed to tie-in vaguely with what I had read in the book, neither Elizabeth nor I had seen or heard anything of Harry's beautiful woman in an orange dress.

Although Elizabeth seemed to be giving the impression of being totally disinterested in what I'd been talking about, she was obviously irritated by it, because suddenly she almost snarled out,

"And now my lovely son is in hospital and being looked after by ….. "

Of course she meant 'that woman'; nurse Senoy. Quite why had she formed such a dislike of her, a dislike so intense that she couldn't even bring herself to say 'nurse', or even 'woman', was still a mystery to me and ….. why had she suddenly brought Harry's nurse into our discussion? What had she got to do with the ghost moth at the cave? But, I realised, why was I assuming that she had? There was no reason at all why Elizabeth's outburst had to be anything to do with anything other than her dislike of nurse Senoy. However, her reaction struck me as if it was not a simple 'nurse thing' and almost as if there was something personal between them from way back when, but there couldn't possibly be, we'd only just met the woman.

While I was trying to pull these various strands together, the phone rang. It was nurse Catherine telling us that the consultant had looked at Harry's scan and would like to talk to us as soon as possible.

"You do know we have an appointment for this afternoon?" I replied, concerned at this apparent sudden urgency.

"Yes, I do," she said. "There is nothing to worry about. Harry is fine. It is just looking as if we have a cancellation and so can possibly bring Harry's case forward, that is all. Can you come in?"

"Certainly," I replied, breathing an inward sigh of relief. "It will take us about an hour. No, you'd better allow a bit longer, parking is always such a problem. Let's say an hour and a half to be on the safe side. Will that be OK?"

"Just come through to Harry's room. I'll meet you there."

After an uneventful drive and an unusually easy location of a parking spot, we arrived at Harry's room in the hospital well in time and found Harry and nurse Senoy sharing what must have been a joke as both were laughing.

"Come away from my child," blurted out Elizabeth upon seeing the pair of them so close and obviously enjoying themselves.

Goodness me; what was the matter with her? Did she think every woman was trying to kidnap 'her Harry' and take him away from her just because of what Harry had told us he'd heard in the cave that day?

Fortunately, nurse Senoy didn't take offence at this rude instruction from my wife and instead turned and said,

"Hello. You're early. Harry and I were just having a little chat."

I'd seen Harry's face the minute we'd walked into the room and couldn't help but notice how it fell upon hearing Elizabeth's rude and totally unnecessary instruction to nurse Senoy. Was he happier when we weren't around? And I felt a touch sad inside and a little envious of this nurse; was Harry happier with her than he was with his own parents? Where had we gone wrong? And then I went on to wondering if all parents have these pangs of guilt, or is it simply that children just enjoy new company; new company that is not as old and boring as their parents?

Nurse Senoy moved away from Harry's bed and came across to greet us. Elizabeth however just ignored her, walked straight past her, went and sat on the bed next to Harry and put her maternal arm protectively around him and kissed him, much to his embarrassment. He didn't exactly push her away, but it was fairly clear from his body language that he didn't want to be kissed and cuddled by a soppy mother.

"And how has he been?" I asked nurse Senoy.

"Oh, just fine." she replied.

Turning to her and away from Elizabeth who was still on the bed with Harry, I tried to quietly apologise for Elizabeth's behaviour without actually saying 'sorry, my wife is so rude,' and instead said something like,

"I am sorry. We've been a bit anxious."

"Of course. It's quite understandable," she replied, "but please don't worry. I will look after Harry."

Then she added quietly and with a conspiratorial wink, "I have given him a lucky amulet. It has my name on it. I know it's a slightly difficult name to remember. So now, if he needs me he can always see my name and call for me. I hope you don't mind."

"Of course not," I replied. What possible harm could such a gift do? However, when I thought about it later it did strike me as slightly strange that a nurse should give Harry something like that, as it was more something that sweethearts might do and, although Harry and nurse Senoy were obviously getting on well together, their relationship was certainly not of that type. But, there seemed no reason to make any sort of fuss over a little present. Having observed the illogical antagonism that Elizabeth seemed to feel towards nurse Senoy, I decided I would keep this bit of information to myself for the time being.

"If you will excuse me?" said nurse Senoy, and then with, "I'll see you later Harry," she left the room.

No sooner had she departed, then there was a knock at the door and the other nurse, nurse Catherine came in.

"Hello," she said to Elizabeth and myself, possibly a little surprised that we had arrived so early and perhaps a touch embarrassed that we had arrived before she had. Turning to Harry, she asked,

"Hello, young man, and how are you?"

Harry smiled at her, but didn't say anything.

She turned back to Elizabeth and I. "If you are ready, the surgeon will see you now."

"See you later old lad," I said to Harry across the room whilst feeling a bit annoyed that I hadn't been able to have a word with him as a result of my trying to cover for Elizabeth's moods and behaviour. "We are just going to have a chat with the doctor."

We followed nurse Catherine out of the room. As I closed the door I gave Harry a little one-fingered salute and was pleased to see that he raised his hand and smiled back at me. Perhaps he didn't hate his parents after all and was just enjoying a change of company.

Nurse Catherine led us along the corridor until we arrived at what was obviously the surgeon's room. I say obviously, because it had a sign on the door upon which was written Mr D. Brain, rather than Dr D. Brain, followed by a string of qualification initials. I confess, I nearly burst out laughing at learning that a surgeon, who was evidently the man who had looked at Harry's scan and was going to tell us what was medically required to relive his headaches, was actually called Mr Brain. And of course my imagination raced on to the classic 'Brains' characters as portrayed in cartoon strips; you know, dressed in white coats, with large round heads, wearing wire rimmed glasses and speaking in pseudo-German accents; and I wondered what this man would look like. In the event it turned out that he looked nothing like these comic book cliches. He was tall and thin, his suit jacket was hanging over the back of his chair and he spoke with a very affable and reassuring English accent.

"Ah, you must be young Harry's parents. I'm Damien Brain,

the surgeon looking after your son, Harry."

We went through the formalities of shaking hands.

"Please. Sit down," he said, indicating two chairs which I thought looked rather too nice for a hospital. When was the last time I had been in a hospital? I asked myself. And realising that it was a good few years ago, came to the conclusion that things had probably changed and for the better since then.

"Now, your son, Harry. He has what we call cerebral cavernous hemangioma. Don't worry, medical names always sound a lot worse than the actual condition they are naming. This cerebral cavernous hemangioma takes the form of a malformation of some of the blood vessels in the brain, which results in their bursting and bleeding, and it is the blood inside his skull which is putting pressure on the brain and it is this which is giving him the headaches, the dizziness, the nausea and is affecting his vision."

As this was explained to us, it struck me; could these symptoms explain Harry's thinking he'd seen a woman in a yellow and orange dress in the cave, when Elizabeth and I had seen nothing? Had what he'd thought he saw simply been the result of perhaps his recalling what he secretly gleaned from my book in the form of an hallucination brought on by the pressure of blood on his brain? Perhaps things were a lot more explainable than I had imagined.

"This is a relatively rare condition, but not that rare. It is perfectly treatable and once the hemangiomas are completely excised, there is very little risk of their re-growth or of any re-bleeding."

"So what do you recommend?" I asked.

"We will need to deal with the hemangiomas and stop the bleeding."

"And how is that ….," I commenced.

"We will need to open his skull ….,"

At this point Elizabeth gasped.

"Please don't concern yourselves," he said, looking at Elizabeth. "This type of operation is very straightforward these days. We will cut just by the hairline, so when it is all healed you won't even see the scar. He will look just as handsome afterwards as he does now," he added with a smile at Elizabeth. "Once we have opened up the cranial cavity we will be able to excise the affected blood vessels with laser surgery. We then close everything up and, as I said at the start, there is very little risk indeed of any re-growth or of any re-bleeding. Of course he will have to be careful with his head until the bone has married back together again. So no sports or anything involving physical contact until then."

"And how long will that be?"

"Just a few months. Think of it like a broken arm or leg. He is a fit and healthy young man and so I would expect him to mend very quickly. Now, as to why I asked you to come in early. We have had a cancellation and so we could operate on Harry, first thing tomorrow morning if you are willing to give us the go-ahead. Obviously, we will need your consent as Harry's parents. Once we have that we'll make a start on what has to be done here so that we are ready for him first thing tomorrow. Is there anything you would like to ask me?"

I looked at Elizabeth and she at me, as I think neither of us had any idea what to say. We were both completely out of our depth.

"Would you like a minute or two on your own?" he asked, getting up out of his chair and starting towards the door. He left the room and closed the door quietly behind him.

"Well what do you think?" I asked Elizabeth.

She looked at me and shrugged.

"I don't think we have much choice. The poor lad is suffering. If this op. has got to be done, I can't see anything is to be gained by delaying. Indeed, perhaps this cancellation is a stroke of luck. Perhaps he does have a guardian angel looking after him after all?"

Elizabeth continued to say nothing.

"Any thoughts?" I asked.

She shook her head. "No," she said without looking at me.

"We are we agreed?"

Elizabeth nodded her approval, after which I went and invited Mr Brain back into his office.

We then completed the necessary paperwork and went back to see Harry, only somewhat unexpectedly to find nurse Senoy in the room with him again and shooing something out of an open window,

"Get you gone! And don't come back."

She obviously heard us entering and, after closing the window, turned to us.

"Just a moth," she said with a smile, "perfectly harmless, but a pretty colour though."

She crossed the room and as she opened the door, turned and smiled at Harry. Then, turning to us she said,

"Mr Brain is an excellent surgeon. Harry will be just fine. Please don't worry, I will look after Harry."

'Perfectly harmless, but a pretty colour though.' Perhaps needless to say, I had recognised the moth instantly and I could be certain that both Harry and Elizabeth had as well, if they had seen it, as it was the same type of yellow and orange female Ghost Moth that we had seen at the cave that day. Perhaps it was the time of year for them? Although I tried to remind myself of the 'logical explanation' that I had just heard a few minutes ago and convince myself that this was just a strange coincidence, it was nonetheless disconcerting to see this second moth so soon after the first, and, I felt, odd that one should be in Harry's room.

"Did you see the moth?" said Harry pretty excitedly for a sick child. He had obviously seen it. "It's the same one I saw at the cave."

"I don't think it is the same moth, old lad. The same type, yes, but not the same one," I said, more for Elizabeth's sake than Harry's.

"I know that, dad," he replied, with an edge to his voice which implied, I'm not that stupid.

"No, it definitely isn't the same moth, darling," said a very certain sounding Elizabeth, who then all-but rushed over to the bed, put her arms round Harry and pulled him to her.

"My head, mum!" wailed Harry.

"Oh sorry darling," she bleated, having of course completely forgotten that the reason why Harry was in hospital was because of head aches, and there she was crushing his head to her breast in an exhibition of motherly love. What is it with women, that any thought and common sense is totally displaced by their emotions; I love him, I must show it, irrespective of anything and everything else. Ah goodness, I give up! Poor Harry, I think he would have hit her if his head wasn't hurting so much. Instead, he just sat there enduring the pain with his head held gently in his hands, watched by his foolish mother who now had a hurt 'how-was-I-supposed-to-know?' expression on her face.

"Mr Brain ….," I commenced and Harry started laughing; well not out loud, it was more of a titter.

"What a funny name he has," said Harry.

His mother remained sitting on the bed, not sure of what to do, or what to say, now that her demonstration of motherly affection had gone so wrong. However, I couldn't help wondering if it was it simply motherly affection that had motivated her action, or if …..? I don't know as I couldn't put my finger on precisely what was bothering me, but some of the things Elizabeth had said and done lately disconcerted me more than I would have wished and unfortunately they niggled away at me. Why her insistence that we didn't mention our visit to the cave when we first took Harry to the doctor? So was there perhaps an element of guilt at play now; a feeling on her part that Harry's being in hospital was somehow something to do with her, to do with something she had or hadn't done? But it wasn't her fault that Harry had gone into the cave. Indeed, she had specifically told him not to, and, added to which, I wasn't at all sure that Harry going into the cave had anything to do with his now being in hospital anyway.

If it was guilt, much the same accusation could be levelled at me. Was I being dreadfully unkind to Elizabeth? Were her actions and of course my reaction to them, simply just the pair of us being unable to hide our anxieties and nerves? In which case, had this latest show of motherly love been bought on by her noticing, the same as I had, that Harry appeared to be happier with nurse Senoy than he was with us and, given the obvious antipathy Elizabeth felt for nurse Senoy, was her demonstration of love more to do with straight forward female possessiveness; a reclaiming of *her* child? This did not seem an unreasonable possibility and perhaps was quite understandable. Only had she just been a bit too, er, demonstrative and clumsy? With these confusing thoughts churning in my head, I thought it best to join her on the edge of the bed, both to give her some moral support and to indicate to Harry that his parents were together in wishing the best for him.

"Yes, he has, hasn't he?" I replied. "But we are told he is a very good doctor and he told us he can do the operation to get rid of your headaches tomorrow morning. That'll be good, won't it."

The look on Harry's face suggested that it wouldn't be good, and I thought that, well, if I'd been in his shoes, I wouldn't exactly be looking forward to some doctor cutting my head open even if it would result in stopping my headaches.

"We'll both be here."

"You will be?" he asked apprehensively.

"Yes darling, we'll both be here tomorrow," Elizabeth confirmed.

Trying to reassure someone when you know no more about what they are going to experience than they do, is not easy, and so trying to keep up the pretence that all will be well begins to sound a bit hollow after a while. I hoped Harry didn't notice and that he took some comfort from the fact that we explained that we had both been in hospital before and had survived to tell the tale! So of course, he would be OK. He'd nothing to worry about.

"I'm tired," he said at a certain stage.

"Would you like to sleep?"

"Yes," and he sank down into the bed.

Elizabeth leaned forward and pulled the covers up to his chin.

"Probably best if we let him sleep," I said to her.

It did cross my mind if Elizabeth had seen the amulet that nurse Senoy had given Harry as she tucked him in, but I guessed she hadn't, because I felt absolutely certain she would have said something if she had.

"OK, Harry old lad. You have a good sleep and we'll see you tomorrow."

Chapter 15

Back in our story in Adam Callow's monastery; it was apparently after lunchtime prayers on the following day that Prior Obscurant announced to the assembled monks,

"It grieveth me to tell you that our beloved brother Stephen La Roche, hath passed away during the night and hath been taken into Almighty God's Eternal Kingdom. Let us pray for his soul."

There was no mention of the previous day's events, and no sign of grief on the face of Prior Obscurant. All was as if nothing of importance had happened. But of course something had happened and it was important. As much as Prior Obscurant might have wished otherwise, perhaps to turn the clock back, he could change nothing. His staged and totally unjustified public punishment of an innocent man had taken place and had been publicly halted, but not by him, but by brother La Roche, who was now dead. All in the monastery knew this. And all, both those in and outside the monastery, had also heard the anger of the crowd the previous day, something which even a year ago would never have been the case. Brother La Roche may have died, but his defiant stand had put down a marker that all had seen. Prior Obscurant and his Church could be defied. Indeed, had been defied. He was no longer omnipotent, he was vulnerable and in spite of his fanatical conviction, very probably knew this to be the case.

Probably as a result of this and hence a desire on his part to, as we would say these days, air-brush brother La Roche out of existence, Prior Obscurant made no mention of how La Roche had died and so unfortunately made matters worse rather than better, as the cause of brother La Roche's death was speculated upon. Inevitably the question arose; had Prior Obscurant, or that Machiavellian second lieutenant of his, had him secretly killed in his cell so that he would no longer be a thorn in their sides?

Such a course of action made sense, as not only did it remove someone who'd had the courage to stand up to the Prior Obscurant camp and their hard-line approach, but it also eliminated the problem of the defence getting the upper-hand in the forth-coming witch trial and thus jeopardising the reassertion of the Church's and with that Prior Obscurant's authority. And furthermore and probably just as importantly, it sent out a clear message to the woolly-minded moderates in the same camp as La Roche, that dissent would not be tolerated.

Of course there was no denying that it was also perfectly possible that La Roche had simply died of what might be described as old age, possibly brought on by the physical and mental stress he had endured whilst making his courageous stand. Several knew, Adam Callow amongst them, that he had not been well for a while and was prone to having his 'days when he didn't feel so good' and so the actions of the previous day might have quite simply been the last straw for him.

However, there was a further unexplained aspect to this; namely, why had this news not been relayed to all in the monastery first thing in the morning, or at least as soon as was possible after it was known? Why was it not until after the lunchtime prayers that this news was finally broken? The fact that no-one knew for certain how, or precisely when brother Stephen La Roche had died created what we might describe as an information-gap for various conspiracy theories.

All dutifully bowed their heads, sub-Prior Grees and novice-master McBane included, and sincerely prayed for the soul of their departed brother monk. Though whether they were praying to thank God for having 'rid them of that turbulent priest,'[83] or thanking God that such a speculated upon grisly fate hadn't been visited on them in the witching hour, or whether they genuinely cared for his soul as in fact many did,

---

[83] Attributed to King Henry II of England, which led to the murder of Thomas Becket, Archbishop of Canterbury in 1170.

was not as clear as perhaps we and young Callow, might have liked it to have been. Prior Obscurant's hard line rule at the Priory and Monastery of Saints Paul and Augustine was not universally liked and so did not have universal support, and all knew only too well that 'if a house be divided against itself, that house cannot stand'[84] and so an ominous foreboding hung in the air. The house was going to fall, but when and with what damage? Brother La Roche's demise had the effect of suggesting that that date had possibly been brought forward.

La Roche's death, coupled with the events of the previous day, must have had a devastating impact on young Adam Callow, for not only had he seen his mentor, someone who he'd looked up to and had felt understood him, die in somewhat unknown and mysterious circumstances, but had also seen his friend, who was almost the same age as he was and from the same social group as he, a group which was usually well remote from subjects such as crime and punishment, nearly flogged to death. And if all the foregoing wasn't enough, as we well know, his own personal life was in complete turmoil as well. As much as he tried to reason that Augustine had done much the same as he had and in spite of that had become a saint and therefore all would be well, Augustine had not had his genitals nailed to a city gate back in the fourth century. Yet this was exactly what was happening now in this century to those who were deemed guilty of being fornicators!

If the temporal problems weighing on young Adam Callow were not enough, there were also his spiritual ones. Was he already damned? Would he be spending eternity on the Second Circle of Hell, the circle specially reserved for the Lustful, or would he only end up on the Seventh Terrace of Purgatory, also reserved for Lust?[85] As it was impossible for him to confess his sins - just the thought of what McBane would do to him ruled

---

[84] Mark 3:25
[85] Dante, The Divine Comedy

that option out - and so gain some measure of remission, he might end up having to spend eternity in Hell. Which was worse, Hell or Purgatory? Probably Hell, but Adam Callow didn't fancy spending eternity in either of them.

Whereas he had managed to push some of this spiritual turmoil to the back of his mind, to pretend to himself that somehow it would all work out, that all would be well, there was now much too much weighing on him, too much dragging him down. Problems were beginning to erupt in his mind like the pools of boiling brimstone in Hell, and he was finding it harder and harder to retain some sense of reason, some sense of sanity. As much as he had no desire to, he concluded that while there was still time he must try and deal with some of these problems, and after much soul-searching and heart-ache came to the painful decision that he must break with Eve Lilith. Augustine had broken with his mistress and he had already had a child with her, so yes, breaking with Eve was possible. It would be horribly painful, just as it had been for Augustine, and Adam Callow didn't want to do it, but it was possible. That simple, singular act would solve many of his problems, both temporal and spiritual, at a stroke. No, it wasn't too late. He resolved he would tell her at their next meeting. It had to be done. He really had no choice, he had to do this.

The simple act of making that decision appeared to have the effect of lifting a weight from him. Yes, that is what he would do. All would be well. However, in spite of telling himself the foregoing, when the day came round and he walked up the road to Hartstane, it was with a heavy heart, because, the truth be told, he had no desire whatsoever to break with Eve. Only what Adam Callow considered to be cold reason, reason that completely ignored the joys and delights of physical love as well as something else which he sort of sensed was there but hadn't managed to categorise, or was it rationalise, something perhaps called love, indicated that he must do so. His head may have told him this, but his heart was most definitely not in it.

However, he had to get out of this spiral of problems that were close to dragging him under, get out of this cesspool of sin that he felt was beginning to close in over his head. So it had to be done.

When he met Eve she must have realised straight away that something was wrong, because he could not, and so did not, immediately take her in his arms, crush her to him and kiss her. Instead, he kept his distance and his face was expressionless and dead as he said,

"Eve, I .... I have something to tell you."

"Has something happened? You look dreadful."

"I ...." commenced Callow.

"What is it, my love? And I have such wonderful news to tell you."

"Wonderful news?" Callow repeated. Oh how he wanted something positive and joyous, something wonderful to lift the gloom which seemed to have surrounded him ever since he had made his decision.

"Yes. I am pregnant. We are going to have a baby. Our baby!"

Can we even start to imagine just how the bottom must have crashed out of Adam Callow's world upon hearing this? 'I am pregnant. We are going to have a baby. Our baby!' It must have felt like his worst nightmare had come true. Well no, not his worst nightmare, as that no doubt involved McBane with a bucket, a rusty nail and a hammer, but his one-from-worst nightmare.

"There, feel," she said, taking his hand and placing it on her belly.

Callow had no idea what he was feeling for and frankly no interest whatsoever in feeling for anything, but even in his state of shock he could not fail to notice that Eve's belly was perhaps a bit larger. Oh goodness, how was he going to tell her now;

now, when she was so evidently full of joy at this, for her, wonderful piece of news? But he had to. It had to be done. He had no choice. He had to break this spiral of fornication and debauchery, this downward spiral that only led remorselessly down into the depths of the bottomless pit. If he did not take action now, he would never escape.

"But we can't ...." he started, rapidly removing his hand as soon as she stopped pressing it to her.

"Can't what?" she fired at him, even though she had a pretty good idea of what he was about to say; she wasn't that daft or naive.

"Can't what?" she repeated angrily.

"Can't have a baby," Callow managed at last.

"Why not?"

"Because ...."

"Because you don't love me! I'm not good enough for you and your hoity-toity family. You stuck-up snob, Adam Callow. You coward!"

How could Callow possibly answer this? He did love her. Well, he thought he did. He loved sex with her. He knew that much. It was just that he couldn't envisage giving up his post in Saints Paul's and Augustine's Priory and Monastery, or being disowned by his family in order to marry her and bring up her baby. Oh dear God, was she right? Did he only *think* he loved her? And now, now that it had come to the crunch, perhaps he didn't? Was he a snob and was he a coward? Although he had no desire to acknowledge either accusation, he couldn't stop himself feeling sick and ashamed at something he had or hadn't felt or done. Without his wishing it so, his mind must have flashed back to Venn talking about Saint Augustine's disgust at himself. Augustine had not loved his mistress enough to marry her against the wishes of his mother, even though she had borne him a child, a son. Was he, Adam Callow, now in much the same position? And of course the baby would not just be her baby, it would also be his baby. It would be, as she had just said, *their* baby. If previously he'd had no idea of what the saint might have felt like, he certainly was beginning to have a much better idea now!

"Look, I'll …."

"Don't you 'look me', Adam Callow! You spineless ….. spineless coward!" she cried back at him, her voice cracking with hurt emotion and her eyes filling with tears. "Oh yes, you were happy to use me, to have your way with me, and now you don't want the consequences of your actions. Doesn't your bloody god tell you about that?"

Yes, his bloody god had told him! Well, not his god, but his bloody Prior and bloody novice-master most certainly had on numerous occasions, and they had also made it abundantly clear that, 'the foremost temptation that the Devil places in front of man is woman.' Hadn't anyone told her about that?! Well no, probably not, he realised, because she was a woman after all.

"You faithless man!" 'the foremost temptation' screamed at him.

Him, faithless? How could she say that, when there he was desperately trying to serve his faith, desperately trying to resolve the problems that seemed to be being thrown in his path, desperately trying to climb out of the cesspit of sin that *she* was dragging him into? 'And I looked, and, lo, a Lamb stood on the Mount Sion, and with him a hundred and forty four thousand, having His Father's name written in their foreheads ….. and these are they which were not defiled with women; for they are the virgins.' How could he explain to her, she, a so obviously uneducated woman, about faith, about being redeemed from the earth, about the crucial importance of being one of the one hundred and forty four thousand?

"You spineless, faithless man!"

Oh dear God, was he? Had he been so faithless to God? He knew he was no longer a virgin, so …. so yes, he was defiled …. defiled by a woman. And not just any woman, but by the very woman who was standing there right in front of him right now, the very woman whom he evidently didn't love enough. So was he faithless to her as well? And then, at last, it hit him; was *that* what she meant by faithless? Not his being faithless to God, but his being faithless to her?

"You ungrateful, faithless man!" she screamed at him, her dark eyes blazing as she pounded him with her fists, "and after I have given you everything."

After she had given him everything?!

What had she given him? Yes, she had given him some wine and yes, she had had sex with him and he with her, but that was what they both had wanted. She had wanted their sex as much as he. She hadn't 'given' him anything over and above what he had 'given' her. So why was her having had sex with him, 'her giving him everything'? Whereas his having had sex with her was 'him using her'? What kind of twisted, one-sided logic was that? Do all women try to blame men for everything, try and make men responsible for actions that they (women) have chosen? Or was this casting of blame in fact far more to do with the possible failure of her plans to secure, no not secure, but get her claws into an educated rich husband who would provide her with her desired lifestyle of dresses, a house and a carriage, and that it was this dream of hers that was now evaporating in front of her eyes, and her realisation that having had sex with him was not yielding the rewards that she had hoped she had secured by it and felt were justly hers?

Theophrastus' warnings about marriage must have been ringing in our Adam Callow's ears, as must also have been Prior Obscurant's favourite warning about the 'foremost temptation'. The 'foremost temptation'? And suddenly that strange feeling that he knew Eve Lilith from somewhere came back to him.

What was it that was so familiar about her? A quiet horror crept over him as he wondered who, or was it what, was standing in front of him and berating him; an angel or a she-devil? He felt the hairs on his neck start to rise and a chill come over him. Yes, 'the foremost temptation that the Devil places in front of man is woman!' A she-devil! It had been *she* who had made eyes at him at the market. It had been *she* who had suggested they meet at the cave. It had been *she* that had given him wine, *she* that had tempted him! And it had been *she* that had straddled him in this very cave, *she* that had been on top, *she* that had led him into fornication, debauchery and the pit of sin! Oh dear God, it was all so suddenly clear!

"Get away from me!" shouted Callow, as he tried to avoid her flailing fists.

The blank look of shock on Eve's face suggested that she couldn't believe what he'd just said. She recoiled from him, took a step or two backwards before her foot hit one of the rocks on the cave floor, she lost her balance and almost as if in slow motion, twisted round and fell full length, her belly landing with a horrible dull thud on one of the other small rock cubes that littered the ground. She lay still for what seemed like an age to Callow, before she rolled herself off the boulder, and with her face as white as a sheet, said quietly,

"Oh God. Look what you have made me do."

Chapter 16

We can presume that Callow must have felt absolutely wretched after the appalling accident at the cave. Appalling in so many ways. Whereas his mind may have rested easier on the subjects of sin and fornication, in their place he had potentially added murder of an unborn child, all be it accidental murder, and he could be sure that at the Day of Judgement that would be deemed a far more grievous sin than sex out of wedlock. Not that he had to concern himself with the possibility of wedlock after this, as no doubt his romantic lovemaking trysts with Eve Lilith were at an end. However, his desire to draw a line under their relationship had not been achieved, all he had succeeded in doing was to change the nature of it, and for the worse. Was the unborn child dead or damaged? Might it still be born horribly disfigured and crippled? In which case Adam Callow would have responsibility to it and its mother. Oh why did he hit her? How could he have done such a thing? But he had, hadn't he, though he could not recall it, but must have done as why else would she have fallen? Everything that stemmed from that fateful moment was now the lot of the pair of them. So all he had succeeded in achieving was terminating all the joy in their relationship while binding them closer together in potentially miserable responsibility. Possibly he would still have to marry her and bring up their crippled child in a loveless marriage and so might still be disowned by his family? And furthermore, as priests in the Prior Obscurant camp had made it abundantly clear to all, any child resulting from a coupling outwith wedlock, or as a result of having been conceived on any of the one hundred and forty or so days specifically forbidden by the Church would be born deformed, epileptic, or otherwise incapacitated. So if he and Eve had a crippled child all would know why and judge this as God's punishment for their having had carnal knowledge of each other in this forbidden manner. No seal of God in Adam Callow's forehead, just the emblazoned seal of a fornicator! He had hoped to rationalise his future, get it into some sort of order, get it to a state where he thought he might be able to have some sort of control over it, but instead .... Oh goodness! It was now far worse than he could ever have imagined.

Thus Adam Callow found himself in a purgatory of his own making. He had no-one he could talk to. La Roche was dead, not that in all probability he would have had the courage to talk to him about this and no, he dare not involve Michael Venn. He felt so dreadfully alone, dreadfully isolated and distanced from those that surrounded him, felt as though he were marooned in the middle of a barren, rocky plateau with nothing but the vastness of the barren land stretching into the distance in all directions ..... and he had no idea what to do. Whichever way he looked he could not see even the vaguest sign of a way off this bare joyless plain, or even the slightest hint of a path leading off towards any golden sunlit uplands. The only routes that appeared open to him were cold, dark and damp holes in the ground with dripping rock walls bereft of sunlight. Dark, damp holes leading remorselessly downward into what Milton would subsequently describe as 'Regions of sorrow, doleful shades, where peace and rest can never dwell, hope never comes.'[86]

Although Adam Callow might have thought of seeking death, he did not. He was quite simply, too numb to think of anything, including death, and death did not come his way either. He had to live, or rather endure the life that he had. His life was not one of living, not one of grasping life and truly living it, but one of existing, being alive but unable to see any future, feel any joy or appreciate any beauty in the world around him; a life of purgatory. His days passed in a slow uneventful blur; he did what had to be done, but felt nothing and gained no pleasure from any of it. He didn't even think about quitting the

---

[86] John Milton, Paradise Lost, Book 1

monastery. Yes, that was an option that was open to him. It would probably not have been initially welcomed by his parents, but he should have realised that any disagreement on this would more than likely eventually have blown over. However, whereas leaving the monastery would have got him out of the immediate grip of the religious fanatics who appeared to be in the ascendancy at that time, it wouldn't have changed anything vis-a-vis his relationship with Eve and their unborn child and it was that which was now dominating and hence determining Callow's life. And so, a very uncomfortably numb Adam Callow thought of none of the possible options that might have been open to him.

If he did ever actually pause and think, it would have been strange for him to look back at what would have seemed like those far distant early days, though in fact they were only a few months previously in the spring, when he had first enrolled at the monastery and then started with the market days. Yes, those early days had been a bit of a trial for him; his seeing all the young women with their shapely figures, lovely soft features and beautiful dresses, and he feeling awkward and tongue-tied. However, that paled into insignificance compared to the trials he was now facing. He didn't wish to see or talk to anyone and certainly not have friendly conversations with any pretty young women of the village. No, now he wanted absolutely nothing to do with women; they were nothing but trouble as Theophrastus had made abundantly clear in his writing cited by Saint Jerome, and why, oh why hadn't he heeded the advice of his Prior, 'And the foremost temptation that the Devil places in the path of man, is woman!'? If he hadn't understood the wisdom in this previously, he certainly did now, because all Adam Callow really wanted to do was to crawl into his shell and hide there until everything, whatever it was that constituted 'everything,' had blown over. But he couldn't hide in his shell, or even hide in his monastery, as Eve would have had him do, and so the next market day saw him out on the square going through the motions of manning his stall.

All went as well as could be expected for the first hour. Garden produce was weighed, money was taken for it and the conversation during that exchange was kept at a minimum. That last element was relatively easy, because quite simply, he had nothing to say and found nothing in others' attempts at starting a conversation that he wished to talk about. So although physically present in the bustling market, he remained at least for the major part, safe in his shell. Safe that is until he saw a girl with dark hair and dressed in a bright green bodice making her way towards him. Oh goodness, it was Eve! What was he going to say to her? How was she? And the baby? A cold sweat started to break out over him. Why did she have to show up now? Why couldn't he be anywhere else than where he was? It did cross his mind to rush over to Michael Venn's potion stall to get some form of moral support, but realised that this would result in Venn learning of his troubles, because inevitably she would see him there and so come over to talk to him in front of Michael Venn. No, no, that was not a good idea. He was dreading talking to her, but it would be better to be on his own when she arrived.

However, his dreadful panic evaporated, because Eve didn't arrive. The girl in the green bodice was not Eve, but the same ginger haired girl he had met with her blond haired friend on an earlier occasion. Such was Callow's relief at this that he couldn't stop gabbling to her throughout the entire time that he served her. The poor young woman had probably been looking forward to a friendly chat with a young man of about her age and instead found herself listening to the nervous prattle of someone who appeared to have gone slightly mad. So as soon as she had got her change back in her hand she beat a hasty retreat leaving Adam Callow standing there wondering what it was that he had said that had driven her away.

Chapter 17

The fact that there was no actual statute law against witchcraft at the time (that didn't come in until later in King Henry VIII's reign in 1542) did not deter Prior Obscurant from convening a court to try 'the witch'. The court was a theological court and so there was no need for it to open its doors to the public. Prior Obscurant, or was it sub-Prior Grees, justified this by pointing out that the common people would never understand the finer points of canon law and, as they had so disgracefully shown at the recent dispensation of justice, could not be relied on to behave in a civilised manner either. They had to be excluded so that God's justice in His Court on this earth could be exercised without tiresome interruptions.

The trial, if one can call such a sham a trial, was to take place in the hall directly above the dungeon which had held master Frank Artless and more latterly brother Stephen La Roche, and now also held the poor woman charged with witchcraft. Novice-brother Adam Callow and his fellow novice-brothers, together with the more senior brothers were summoned to attend; as justice not only had to be done, but seen to be done and if not by the public at large then the monastery's brothers would be witnesses to it. Their attendance would of course also importantly serve to relieve those prosecuting and sentencing of their burden of responsibility - or was it guilt? - because if all present did not raise objection, it could and would be assumed that they also tacitly agreed with the verdict and sentence.

As we know, sub-Prior Arriviste Grees had been appointed to prosecute the case, novice-master Rodiron McBane had been appointed the Inquisitor and, now that the problem posed by brother La Roche was out of the way, Prior Obscurant had nominated a useless little toady by the name of brother Vartfish to act in the token role of Defence.

None of the novice-monks had been in this court room

before, so all except Adam Callow looked around with an air of awe, wonder and fear. Callow was still too numb to feel either awe or wonder, though we can guess possibly did feel a hint of fear at realising that this court room might be where he would end-up if ever his relationship with Eve Lilith was discovered. As much as he was trying to forget her, indeed forget all that had happened between them, he hadn't. She was still there in his memory; on the one hand all the cause of his troubles and yet on the other, although he did not wish to admit it to himself, the source of his previous happiness. He felt a hollow emptiness inside, an aching emptiness, as if part of something of himself was missing, a part which he both wanted and yet did not want in equal measure. Although his depression had gradually lifted during the weeks following the disastrous episode in the cave, it certainly hadn't departed from him yet and so the witch trial was, for Adam Callow, almost a welcome distraction; something which had nothing to do with him and so he would be able to lose himself in it and so forget his own troubles.

At the head of the room, facing you as you entered, was an impressive row of dark wood panelled seating set equidistant about a central throne. The actual seats could not be seen as they were hidden behind a lower section of panelling which acted as a screen to hide the legs of those seated behind it and provide support for the front of a thin sloping desk which extended along its length. It also conveniently served as a barrier to distance those who were seated behind it from that which was in front of it? As this panelling on each side of the central throne was divided into four sections it was reasonable to assume that there were either four individual chairs, one behind each panel, or that there was a single bench which was divided into four. Behind whatever seating there was and extending up the wall for a height of about two metres, was yet further panelling. All this woodwork was fairly plain. Yes, it featured some mouldings and beading to delineate the various sections, but other than that it contained no carved ornamentation. The lower section of the central throne-like section projected forward and supported a lectern upon which could be set books of law and documents required for the case at hand. Much to Callow's discomfiture, and no doubt to the discomfiture of anyone unlucky enough to be brought before this court, its front panel contained a base relief carving of what might have been either a Bible, or more likely Church Penitentials, and a flagellum. Although this court was God's Court on earth, crucially it was on earth. It was not in Heaven. So whereas Almighty God had the power to forgive, His representatives on earth could not possibly dare to presume that the Almighty had delegated that divine responsibility to them!

But hasn't The Law and The Law Courts always had two purposes; yes, *two* purposes? The second one being the publicised one of the administration of justice, of fairness and impartiality, the acknowledgement of wrong doing, the punishment of the wrongdoer and so possibly some form of redress and closure for the victim. However, these laudable aims were never those which originally brought about the concept of The Law. The first purpose of The Law, that which is rarely if ever talked about but none-the-less is that which caused it to be created, was the need for the rich and powerful to have a set of rules which they could impose on the less rich and less powerful; rules which subsequently became laws, which they could use to maintain their positions of wealth and power. These laws, made by them, did not and still do not apply to them. Phrases, such as 'the law is handed down,' point to the fact that there is nothing democratic about it. Laws are not made 'by the people for the people.' They are made to protect and preserve the position and status of the rich and powerful; not for the benefit of the common people. All the common people have to do is obey them. So The Law being seen to be done is vital in reinforcing this fact, publicising this message, and so applies now just as it did in Adam Callow's day. However, we can speculate that Adam Callow was not thinking about the finer socio-philosophical aspects of this when he was looking at the carving of the Penitentials and flagellum on the front panelling of Ecclesiastical Court Throne!

The upper section of panelling to that same throne which would be behind the central sitter, was set slightly forward of that on each side of it before rising to the same height and finally finishing off with an ornately carved gable, somewhat reminiscent of that which might be seen on the west facade of a cathedral. Indeed, this triangular section was even capped with a large beautifully sculpted, if somewhat gruesome image of the crucifixion, so there could be no doubt that this was a theological court and not a secular one.

To each side of this no doubt deliberately awe inspiring display, and running parallel to each of the sides of the court, rose several rows of benches. These too had a wood panelled screen in front of them. These three sets of furniture thus left an open central area between them, rather like the floor of an arena; flat and walled all round, thus presenting no hope of escape for whoever stood there waiting for the lions? Callow, Venn and their four fellow novice-monks were seated on the first bench on the left hand side, at the farthest point from the main wood panelled seating area, or 'the bench' of this courtroom. Although somewhat remote from the action, which would obviously all happen at the other end of the hall, none-the-less, by nature of being on the front bench, they did have a pretty good view.

As soon as all were seated, those involved in the case commenced to file in. One group, led by sub-Prior Grees, again dressed in his finery and followed by two other Obscurant cronies, and finally McBane, passed in front of The Bench so as to enter their domain from the left hand side. Prior Obscurant, resplendent in a finely embroidered cope, made his way to his central throne from the right. He was followed by the useless Vartfish and three other personally selected yes-men. All wore their cowls forward so it was almost impossible to see their faces. Did Adam Callow, or more likely, Michael Venn, think it odd that they so obviously did not wish to be seen administering

God's Justice; a justice supposedly so pure that it might be suspected that they could succumb to the sin of pride at having been selected for such a worthy task? But no, these men appeared more ashamed of the task that they were about to perform than proud of it, with each keeping his face well hidden.

There was a small amount of quiet conversation going on amongst the brothers, rather like the murmurings heard from the pews before a church service commences and as is the case with such a service it becomes apparent when the proceedings are about to start, and so no signal had to be given, the room simply fell silent.

Prior Obscurant's usual loud and prophetic sounding voice emanated from his cowl as he opened the court session,

"By the power that hath been vested in me by Almighty God, I declareth that this Court of the Priory and Monastery of Saints Paul and Augustine is now in session. This Court shall be presented with evidence by the Prosecutor for our faith, our church and our Priory and Monastery of Saints Paul and Augustine ….," and the Prior's cowl turned in the direction of sub-Prior Grees as indeed he said, "….. by our Holy Prosecutor".

Having introduced the prosecution for the case, the zeal noticeably faded from the 'impartial voice' and it continued in a vein which might have been appropriate for a speaker who was talking about dung on the underside of his shoe,

"….. and defence for the accused presented by brother Vartfish," with barely a nod in the direction of the luckless brother who had in fact been personally selected by Prior Obscurant for this unenviable task; no anonymity for him! Brother Varfish's qualifications for this role will become apparent as the events of the trial are recounted.

Then back at full volume,

"They that art present at today's court will listen to the evidence as it is presented and will pass judgement at its conclusion. Should there be any points of Canon Law that requireth clarification, the members of this Holy Court may consulteth me and I, with God's wisdom, will advise. May the Almighty God guide us in our deliberations. Bring up the accused!"

The cowled Grees signalled to the cowled McBane, who left the hall and a few minutes later returned with ….. the witch. McBane took her to the centre of the floor and stood her there, faced on all sides by a blank wall of dark hard wood panelling and an equally blank wall of dark cloth cowled staring male eyes.

Callow had to admit to himself that at one stage he had entertained silly ideas of a witch being some supernatural, or semi-supernatural being dressed in strange clothing, perhaps with a cat and possibly a besom. Even after his conversation with brother La Roche when he had wondered if he might have been misinformed about witches, he had still been unable to shake off a lingering doubt that a witch was, well, not really human. However, now that he saw the virtual skeleton clad in rough sackcloth standing in front of him, he began belatedly to grasp why brother La Roche had referred to her as 'this poor woman'.

Poor woman indeed; she looked absolutely broken. Callow did not have a good view of her and could not see her face because she was facing Prior Obscurant and 'his bench'. He could see that her hair was unkempt and unwashed, that her shoulders were hunched and her head bowed. Indeed, her whole body was hunched and shaking, and she was obviously having difficulty standing. She held her arms crossed in front of her and her dirty nailed fingers clawed nervously at the flesh of her emaciated forearms. There was also something else about her pose, that of being as near as it was possible to be of being fetal whilst standing up, which suggested that something horrible had happened to her. 'And to them it was given that they should not kill them, but that they should be tormented five months; and their torment was as the torment of a scorpion, when he striketh a man.' But the individual standing before that court was not a man, but a woman. What tortures had she endured? What torment had she suffered? And whatever it was, it had been inflicted by the Church, by those who supposedly believed in a tolerant, merciful and loving God? 'And in those days shall men seek death, and shall not find it: and shall desire to die, and death shall flee from them.'[87] She certainly looked as if she desired to die. It would be a release for her.

"Rose England", boomed Prior Obscurant.

Who? thought Callow. It can't be! Oh Good God no, not Rose! It couldn't be her. She looked nothing like ….. Suddenly Adam Callow was wide awake and in the middle of a nightmare! He felt the nausea welling up in him and slumped forward resting his head in his hands trying desperately not to retch. Oh dear God, what was going on? This can't be real! Rose England had been his teacher when he was younger. She was a friend of his mother's, a friend of their family, a lovely woman. How could she possibly be a witch? This was madness, total madness! But ….. Oh goodness! What had happened to her, happened to the attractive proud woman he had known? The semi-skeleton standing in front of the court nervously clawing at her arms looked nothing like her. What had they done to her? They? No, Callow realised, it wasn't *a they*, but *a who*, and without having to think further could guess that the answer to his question was that sadistic fanatic, Rodiron McBane. What had that perverted maniac done to her?' Anger welled up in him along with an urge to attack McBane, but was almost instantaneously extinguished by his need of self-preservation and so he sat there and like the others present, pulled his cowl forward and wallowed in cowardice and shame. So much for

---

[87] Revelation 9: 5 - 6

Callow thinking that this witch trial would present a welcome distraction from his personal problems! No, all it was doing, indeed all it could do given his personal knowledge and relationship with the so-called witch, was to add to them.

"Rose England," said Prior Obscurant again, "You are accused of being a witch, of witchcraft and of heresy. How durst you plead?"

What was left of Rose obviously managed to say something, but Callow couldn't hear what it was.

"Prosecutor, will you presenteth your case to this court," said an imperious Obscurant.

The Sub-Prior stood and addressed the court,

"This ...." he sneered in his high pitched whine, whilst indicating the wreck of a woman standing in front of him, ".... this wretched woman stands before us today accused of being a witch and of practising witchcraft."

"Objection," bleated the toady brother Vartfish.

Goodness! Perhaps Vartfish wasn't as toady as all thought him to be, as this unexpected intervention certainly took most of those present by surprise and a brief murmur rippled round the courtroom. Venn looked at Callow as though he was about to say something, but obviously thought better of it.

"Yes, brother Vartfish," said Judge Prior Obscurant with such a tolerant voice that some must have wondered if the man inside Prior Obscurant's cowl had miraculously been transformed into a different being altogether.

"Are not the offences of both being a witch and witchcraft, offences which should be dealt with by the secular courts and not theological courts such as this one?" mumbled brother Vartfish nervously before sitting down both rather too hastily and, to those who knew him, without showing any real sign of fear at having challenged the authority of the Court, or of challenging Prior Obscurant, who remained sitting on his throne, a cowled picture of tolerance, justice and fair play.

"This stinks," whispered Venn, unable to restrain himself any longer. "What are they up to?"

"Prosecutor," called Prior Obscurant. The omission of any instruction from Prior Obscurant confirmed Michael Venn's suspicion that whatever it was that they were up to was known to at least the pair of them. No doubt there hadn't been any need to inform the luckless brother Vartfish why he needed to ask his question. Without any further ado sub-Prior Arriviste Grees launched into,

"The Court will be aware that our beloved saint, Saint Thomas Aquinas, has after years of painstaking study, theologically linked maleficium, or, as it is more commonly known, sorcery or witchcraft, with heresy. And heresy, heresy against our true faith and this Church, most certainly is within the jurisdiction of theological courts. So it follows therefore that a witch and the crime, indeed the sin of both being a witch and practising witchcraft, may be tried in this court."

"Thank you for your clarification, Prosecutor," said the impartial, though evidently well pleased Judge.

So that was their game; justifying their right under Canon Law, to conduct this trial, even though strictly speaking it should have been conducted in a secular court.

Sub-Prior Grees continued for the Prosecution in his high pitched whining tone,

"The case before this court is a classic case of the heinous sin and crime of maleficium, a crime so foul and blasphemous as to be outwith the bounds of normal law and so decreed as crimen exceptum. The recognised authoritative text on these most heinous acts is the treatise Malleus Maleficarium[88] as written by Henricus Institoris[89] and if the court permits, I will use this as my guide."

Prosecutor Grees looked in the direction of Judge Obscurant, whose cowled head nodded approval.

"This text also confirms that maleficium is heretical and contains the legal and theological arguments prescribing why it is that witches must be eradicated from our society. Furthermore," he squeaked, "it also prescribes the approved inquisitorial practices in order that this may be achieved. With this court's permission I shall call the Inquisitor for this case to ascertain whether the recommended procedures, [90] those as prescribed for cases of crimen exceptum, were followed.

"This woman", continued Grees, indicating the accused with a fat moist hand, "is accused of being a witch and practising witchcraft. It is well known that she sold herbal potions. What perhaps is not so well appreciated is that they were un-Christian herbal potions; indeed potions concocted with the assistance of Black Magic, potions produced in collusion with the Devil, in collusion with Satan himself! It is also known that on occasions

---

[88] Commonly known as the 'Hammer of the Witches'. St Thomas Aquinas' writings are the main source for Section 1 of this text, that of establishing an essential link between witches and the Devil, though his writings are cited in all three sections.

[89] Heinrich Kramer, a subsequently discredited German Catholic priest who published this work in Speyer, Germany in 1487. However, at the time Pope Innocent VIII referred to him (in his capacity as Inquisitor for south Germany) and his co-author Jakob Sprenger (in his capacity as Inquisitor for the Rhineland) in his Papal Bull 'Summis Desiderantes affectibus', as 'beloved sons'.

[90] Which included torture as a means of obtaining confessions.

she hath slain infants yet in their mother's womb[91] and that she hindered men from performing the sexual act and women from conceiving, [92] all of which are expressly forbidden under Summis Desiderantes affectibus of 1484."[93]

At this point Prosecutor Grees evidently had noticed that his voice had risen a little too much as he had enthusiastically enunciated the charges to the court, so he lowered it and slipped back into a pseudo-Biblical style of speech to conclude with,

"It is known that the Devil useth women, because he knoweth that they love carnal pleasures ...."

Upon hearing this Callow must have recalled the pleasure visible on Eve's face as she sat astride him in their love-nest just off the Hartstane road. Oh goodness! Was she, Eve, not only a she-devil, but also a witch? Had he been seduced by a witch, a disciple of the devil himself? Oh why had he been so stupid and so weak willed as to be taken in by her? But ..... no, Rose couldn't possibly be a witch .... could she? So was Eve? Or could they both be? Instead of Callow's earlier doubts gradually fading at the back of his mind, all resurfaced and came crashing back down on him. Had he been fornicating with a female disciple of the Devil? Was his soul damned? Would he be cast into the bottomless pit to suffer everlasting torment? And then, what he had been desperately trying to forget, the accident in the cave, also resurfaced. Was the child dead, or would it be born deformed and so would the world learn of his disgustingly lustful and sinful ways? Oh dear God! What could he do?

"..... and he taketh them as his disciples in a pact in which they renounceth Christianity and devoteth themselves to Satanism," continued the porcine Prosecutor Grees. "Their allegiance is then licentiously sealed with sexual intercourse

---

[91] Abortion

[92] Contraception

[93] A Papal Bull of 5 December 1484, issued by Pope Innocent VIII, sometimes referred to as the 'Witch Bull of 1484'

with one of his demons, or even himself! The very Devil himself!" explained Grees, his squeaky voice rising as he did so.

Venn looked at Callow as if to ask, 'How does our sub-Prior actually know this?' But Callow, with doubt and fear rising in him, was too preoccupied with his own newly awakened problems to engage with Venn on this subject, being far more concerned with knowing if Eve had actually had sexual intercourse with the Devil himself. And if so .... oh .... Oh dear God, what had he (Adam Callow) done?

"May I now calleth upon the Inquisitor to testify?"

The Prior Obscurant cowl nodded approval, after which Inquisitor McBane stepped forward on to the floor.

"Inquisitor, do you confirm that you have interrogated this woman and confirm that you have done so in accordance with the procedures recommended and prescribed for cases of crimen exceptum?" asked an earnest Arriviste Grees.

"Aye. Aye, I do."

"And will you tell the court what it is that you learned," responded Grees with an almost theatrical flourish.

"The woman has sinned, and sinned grievously, an' so had buried her sin deep inside her. Aye, so deep that she was denying it even to herself. However, with the methods at my disposal, and with God's help," he added, "I was able to assist her, to confess to some of her sin."

The sub-Prior started again, "This court will observe that this woman, Rose England, is not a young virgin. She is of an age when most women would be properly married, yet she is not. Neither has she taken Holy Orders. This is indeed unusual .... very unusual," he added, after a short pause. "Inquisitor, did you inspect this woman Rose England and ascertain whether or not she was a virgin?"

"Aye, I did, and she is nay."

The two appalling statues in the novice-monks chapel dedicated to Saint Bibiana and the Virgin Mary, coupled with the ice cold water filled brick bath in McBane's cell in which he could 'quench the heat in himself of every vice,' might well lead us to presume that McBane took his work, especially as an inquisitor of women, 'very seriously'. So it was not at all impossible that poor Rose England may well have been a virgin when arrested and that McBane had considered it his Christian duty as the Inquisitor to ensure that she did not remain so. Indeed, as she was accused of being a witch, which in McBane's eyes would be the same *as* being a witch and therefore subhuman, he might have reasoned that this gave him a degree of carte blanche regarding how he extracted a confession from her, and if his first chosen 'line of enquiry' didn't produce the desired result, there was also the use of the so called 'gynaecological instruments' at his disposal to both ascertain virginity and be used as part of the 'prescribed procedures' for obtaining a confession in cases of crimen exceptum. Callow, who had nearly regained control over the latest storm of doubt that had just hit him, felt his stomach turn as these possibilities joined the maelstrom of horrors coursing through his mind.

"So she is not a virgin and she is not married. How can this be?" questioned sub-Prior Grees, his voice rising with his question. "I will tell you!" he squeaked. "It is because she is married to the very Devil himself; that is why! She has had debauched and bestial sex with the very Devil!"

Yes indeed, she probably has, thought an emotionally drained Callow. Oh poor Rose. What has that heartless brute of a man done to you? He felt sick. Sick with his own lot, sick at what might happen to Eve and her baby. Sick with what that might mean for both of them. Sick at the thought of what might have been inflicted on Rose and sick with frustration and shame at his own inaction. But what could he do? He was just a young novice-monk, what could he, Adam Callow, possibly do against the power of the institution vested in those sitting on The Bench in front of the court? Rose had been accused and so was already condemned. Nothing could save her. He was, at present, seated on the 'safe side' of the court's dark wood panelling. If he didn't wish to join Rose out there on the floor, all he could do was sit, listen and watch. 'There won't be any qualms about throwing either of you onto the fire if they feel the need to. So you keep your heads down ....'

"Will you tell this court of her confession, Inquisitor?"

"As I said, I felt she was burying her sin inside herself and so, after ascertaining that she was not a virgin even though she is not married, I introduced her to the chevalet."

"What is the chevalet?" whispered Callow to Venn.

"I'll tell you later," Venn whispered back.

So it was only later that Callow learned that the chevalet was a wooden horse, the body of which was triangular in shape with its thin pointed edge uppermost and running along its spine. The naked victim with legs straddled on each side, was then lowered on to it. Sometimes weights were attached to the feet, though often body weight alone was enough to make a female victim confess to just about anything. And indeed Rose had, as McBane went on to explain,

"She then confessed to all her crimes and to all her sins. She confessed to being a witch and practising the evil art of witchcraft. She also confessed that she had renounced Christianity and devoted herself to Satanism, and she further confessed that she had both had depraved sexual union with numerous demons and had willingly indulged in lascivious ravishment by the very Devil himself. And she confessed that in exchange for her renouncement of our True Faith, the Devil had granted her supernatural powers."

A gasp at the atrocity of these confessions went round the

courtroom. How could so much unmitigated depravity be concentrated in one woman? And with the shock of this revelation came the associated fear as all realised that this female devil incarnate had spent her life living in amongst them and so at any time could have used her evil sexual wiles on them to lead them astray and into a life of sin and so eternal damnation. However, not all thought this. Many knew her better and knew of her work and so knew the falsity of McBane's statement, realising that anyone trying to endure the agonising pain being inflicted on them by a chevalet would confess to anything put before them that might result in a cessation of the pain, and so for them the gasp was not at the atrocity of the confession but at the atrocity of how it had been obtained. Even our naive young Adam Callow had doubts about McBane's claims as he had had some experience of McBane's methods and, as has already been mentioned, the so-called witch had been a personal friend of his family for as long as he could remember and had never shown any inclination to devil worship throughout that time.

So why was there this barely disguised venomous hatred of women by so many of the cowled, faceless, True Believers? Hadn't the likes of Obscurant, Grees, McBane and those in their camp had mothers, or sisters? Had they been appallingly abused by women when they had been children, so as to grow into manhood with raw misogyny flowing through their veins? Or was their hatred driven by their own sexual frustration? A frustration brought about by their ludicrously elevating sex to the status of The Cardinal Sin and so anything relating to it, which of course included women, had to be abhorred? Yet, because sex is a perfectly normal and reasonable human desire it could not be simply denied, simply be abstained from, because that would not give enough reason or justification to the individual for such action. For those who forced this illogical and unnatural doctrine on themselves, the simple exclusion, the 'choosing not to' was not enough, so the sexual urge, women and the temptation that they presented had to be regarded as abhorrent, the work of the Devil, and so had to be hated, simply because these were the very things which those who chose to impose these constraints on their lives probably wanted more than anything else! And if they did not hate, then their will would weaken and they would be tempted, and so would be led astray. 'So he hates the real truth for the sake of what he takes to his heart in its place.'[94] Although we can be certain that they would never have admitted it, wouldn't any of these religious fanatics have been a lot happier and more contented with their lives had they had the warm, soft, loving embrace of a woman?

And," mused Joe breaking off from his story and looking round the table at us, "it is not just men who behave like this. These days the male / female roles have all the appearance of having been somewhat reversed, with hard-boiled misandrist women accusing and thus condemning men without trial. OK, we are not literally burning men at the stake these days, but are sending their reputations up in smoke. What motivates these man-haters? 'All men are potential rapists.' Would these women, just like their male medieval counterparts, not be a lot happier if they had the love and embrace of a loving man? What were the medieval males, and what are the modern females, afraid of? Is it the simple, but oh-so-difficult step that we all have of taking the risk, of daring to commit? As Saint Jerome said all those years ago, 'What necessity rests upon me to run the risk of the wife (or, read husband) I marry proving good or bad? It is better to dwell in a desert land, than with a contentious and passionate woman (or, read man) in a wide house.'[95] Did those men, and do these women, really want to live in an emotional 'desert land' with their dried-up emotions, sexual frustration and cold, hard hearts?"

Joe was quiet for a minute, while he let this observation of

---

94 Saint Augustine, Confessions, Book X:10
95 Proverbs 21:19 and Against Jovinianus, Book 1:28

his sink in. Then he continued his story.

"Thank you Inquisitor," said Prosecutor Grees. He licked his thin pink lips with a small pink tongue before continuing with, "This woman who standeth before this Holy Court is a witch. Of that there can be no doubt as her guilt is established by her own confession. I need say no more."

And with that, Prosecutor, sub-Prior Arriviste Grees sat down.

"Brother Vartfish, desireth you to say anything in the defence of the accused?" asked Judge Obscurant in a manner which suggested that Vartfish had better not 'desireth', and so, perhaps needless to say, brother Vartfish did not 'desireth' to say anything in defence of poor Rose England.

Poor indeed. Horribly violated, humiliated and mentally and physically broken, she stood shaking in the centre of the open floor, surrounded on all sides by a wall of dark wood panels and rows of cowled faceless men in dark priests habits, all looking at her with unseen eyes and passing judgement on her for crimes that she had not committed. Alone. So totally alone in the centre of that wood walled arena; an arena where the 'True Believers' throw 'angels' to the lions, and leave their mauled souls spread out on the dry floor.

A horrified, numb Adam Callow looked on. This place was a mad-house. Did he now appreciate why St Bibiana's patronage, that of the mentally ill and insane, had been given to the novices' chapel? Stephen La Roche's, 'But don't you two get any foolish ideas! There won't be any qualms about throwing either of you on the fire if they feel the need to. So you keep your heads down and keep your opinions to yourselves.' came back to him. No, the stark reality was that any intervention on either his or Venn's part would achieve nothing other than getting themselves killed as well. Not that Adam Callow was feeling brave, far from it. He felt absolutely dreadful about what was happening, as well as sick at both his own cowardice and his powerlessness to intervene. Indeed, and it seemed like the powerlessness of anyone to intervene. 'We establish the rules not you, all that is expected of you is to obey them.' So who had given these religious fundamentalist maniacs the power they had over the lives of others?

"It is the moral duty of this court to root out and extirpate heresy, malevolent sorcery and those who practice it," announced the revolting squeaky voice of Arriviste Grees who was back on his feet again.

"Does it not say in The Book of the Covenant, 'Thou shalt not suffer a witch to live'?[96] So, my fellow brothers ….." he turned first to his right and then his left, looking at each of those on The Bench, "….. it is our heavy duty, for the welfare of society and the welfare of this Church of the True Faith to find this wretched woman guilty and sentence her to death by burning, as this is prescribed as the only certain remedy against the evils of heresy and witchcraft."

The porcine Prosecutor then sat down and there was a moment's silence before Judge Obscurant spoke.

"Fellow inquisitors, will you each raiseth your right hand if you findeth the woman guilty."

And of course all did, even Vartfish, who was supposed to be defending Rose raised his right hand, though this action might have been a nervous reaction and so more to do with his simply copying everyone else rather than anything to do with self-preservation or his opinion on her guilt.

"We art unanimous," boomed an evidently satisfied Judge Obscurant. "The accusation of witchcraft and blasphemy against Rose England is foundeth proven. She is guilty!"

Guilty! The word echoed round the cold, unforgiving, stone walls of the courtroom.

---

[96] Exodus 22:18

Guilty! What did they, those who did not conform to the prescribed laws of a society expect; no matter that those laws had been formulated and enacted by a self-selected, perverted and bigoted elite?

Guilty! Had there ever been the slightest possibility that the verdict could be otherwise?

"The witch will be taken from here and burnt," the Judge solemnly informed the court. "Inquisitor, taketh her away!"

McBane stepped forward and with a gnarled hand took Rose roughly by upper arm and dragged her away.

And that was it.

The cronies on The Bench collected their papers and books and filed out. After they had left the other monks, including Adam Callow and Michael Venn, also made their way out of the hall. No one said anything. The only sound was that of shuffling sandalled feet on the stone flagged floor. There were probably those in the hard-line camp who felt that justice had been done, that there would soon be one less witch in the world and so there was no need to comment on it, but there were also those who felt that the whole business was absolutely appalling and were silent because they knew only too well that La Roche's unexplained death might so easily be visited on them if they raised objection or had done anything to stop it, and so their cowardice and complicit guilt weighed heavily on them.

Chapter 18

Inevitably the market day came when Adam Callow had to meet up again with Eve Lilith. Perhaps fortunately for Callow, he was busy arranging produce on one of the trays behind the trolley as she approached. So it wasn't until the last minute that he saw her and hence had no time in which to experience his usual nervous jitters.

"Hello Adam," she said.

"Ugh …. hello Eve. Er, How are you?"

"Better now," she replied.

"Oh, good?" said Callow hesitantly, not really understanding what it was that she meant by 'better now.'

"You'll be pleased to know, I lost the baby," she said, unable to hide the acidity in her voice.

"I'm sorry. I ….."

"No you're not. It is what you wanted, isn't it? So now you are free. Free of your child, free of me, free of any responsibility. You've had your fun and ….."

"Eve, it's not like that."

"No? So what is it like then?"

"It's ….. I just think that ….."

But how could he explain why he had decided to break from her? Explain how what they were doing could not continue for all the 'reasons temporal' that he had gone over in his head a thousand times, as well as all the 'reasons spiritual' that he had also gone over just as many times. And now, in addition to the foregoing, how could he even start to describe what he had witnessed at the trial of Rose England? The imprisonment, the abuse, the being condemned for something which he (Callow) was sure, well fairly sure, because he hadn't fully shaken off the nagging doubt he had about her being a witch, that she hadn't done? How could he explain his sense of guilt at the unfairness he felt at this when he knew that he and Eve had probably done everything that they would be condemned for; the fornication out of wedlock, the gaining of pleasure from their acts, their committing these on days when they should not have done so, etc.? If those fanatics had done what they did to Rose, what would they do to Eve? Venn's explanation of the chevalet came flooding back to him along with feelings of nausea and horror. He wouldn't wish that on any woman and so even though he didn't want it to be so, he found his heart going out to Eve. In his own immature way perhaps he did still love her, but he also knew that he had to stop doing so, even though his emotions were in fact telling him otherwise.

And what would they do to him? Visions of McBane with a knife and a bucket, and his privates being nailed to the monastery gates. Oh God! Just how could he start to explain to Eve the theological conflict between the flesh and the spirit? How on the one hand he loved being with her, enjoyed her company and yes, enjoyed her body; and yet on the other so conscious that those temporal heavenly pleasures were driving both of them deeper into sin and closer to eternal damnation, when she was so evidently uneducated in such matters? How could he even start to tell her all that was at stake? At stake! Oh no! Why did that expression, with all its appalling connotations have to come into his mind? Rose was going to burn tied to a stake! Would they, Eve and he, also burn? Burn in this world and burn in the everlasting flames in the next? No, no! What they had done had had to stop.

Then to Callow's surprise, Eve's tone softened.

"We don't have to be enemies, do we?"

"No," said Callow in relief, whilst also belatedly realising that, yes, as cruel as it sounded, her loosing the baby did in fact solve all the problems that having a child would have brought with it, and so these, thankfully, were now behind him. Possibly things were, in an unexpected and strange way, working out? He could almost feel the weight being taken from him. All would be well. So no, there was no need to be enemies. They could part on friendly terms.

"Could we meet up again …. like we used to?"

"No, er no," mumbled Callow in alarm, realising that having got this far he didn't want to go back to the life of sin from which he had been trying to escape. No, he mustn't go back to that!

"No, not exactly like we used to," she said, noticing Callow's alarm, "but just for a talk, just like friends," she went on to explain with a winning smile, the small black diamond between her pale pink lips hypnotically attracting Callow's almost vacant eyes.

"Well …." Oh how he wanted to kiss those lips …. wanted to put his arms round her and hold her warm body close to him. No, no! He must not …. but there could be no harm in just meeting …. just meeting for a friendly chat …. surely?

"Good. That will be nice, Adam. Will next Saturday afternoon be alright? At our usual spot?"

"Yes …. alright." replied Callow, his mind now, in spite of his desire for it to be otherwise, focused on Eve's lips and soft, ivory skinned shoulders and so completely forgetting that Saturday was the day when Rose was to be burned and that his attendance at that was obligatory. Thus Adam Callow meekly - or was it weakly? - failed to break his ties with Eve Lilith and agreed to meet up with her again.

The market came to a close and Adam Callow packed up his stall and went back to his monastery. He had met Eve, hadn't he? Or had his meeting up with her again, just been a dream? No, it hadn't been; he had met her. She had told him that she had lost the baby. So now all that had happened between them was just between them and if they both kept quiet about it no one need know. It could remain thus; just between them. He could carry on his life as a monk, just like Saint Augustine had done, and all would be well. But, oh God, what of his soul? He'd been so preoccupied with temporal matters, he'd forgotten that. What would happen to his soul? Was he already damned, or could he somehow redeem himself like Saint Jerome had tried to do, somehow try to claw his way back from the pit of flames that currently awaited him, claw his way back to his previous state of innocence? But what exactly should he do? He couldn't confess; certainly not to McBane! So what could he do; what were the options open to him? No, he mustn't panic. One step at a time. If he could part with Eve on friendly terms that would stop the continuing sin. Then he must follow Saint Augustine's path, or was it Pelagius' path - oh which one was it? - and earn salvation by his own efforts? Never mind which. The first step was to stop the sin. With that behind him, he could then concentrate his efforts on salvation. But in order to save himself was he to just abandon Eve? Simply to leave her standing alone in the centre of an empty floor like Rose? If he left her, who would care for her? Would she be torn to pieces by the faceless lions of the Priory and Monastery of Saints Paul and Augustine? As much as he knew he had to dismiss Eve from his emotions, he couldn't. His head told him one thing and his heart told him the opposite. Unanswerable questions and doubt and fear, kept running through him. One minute his thoughts were on a sense of duty to, and yes, there was no denying it, the soft warm delights of Eve Lilith, and the very next, those soft warm delights were rudely replaced by a vision of a grizzled, grinning McBane carrying a bucket with hammer and nail in hand! Then he was back to Eve again. Oh goodness, why wouldn't this mad emotional merry-go-round stop?

Chapter 19

"As you can probably guess," Joe said to all of us listening to his strange and now tragic tale, "by this time my faith in any rational explanation for all that had happened during our family visit to the tree-root cave off the Hartstane road that day and what had subsequently happened to young Harry, was, like young Adam Callow's, also wavering badly. There seemed to be rather too much evidence linking what Harry had claimed he had seen and heard spoken at the cave with the story that I was reading for there not to be some sort of a connection between the two. Furthermore, I had seen the female ghost moth with my own eyes and I couldn't get the feeling out of my head that it was a bit too much of a coincidence that we should have met nurse Senoy on our way to the cave, her indirectly warning about any such visit, and then that she was now one of Harry's nurses.

Elizabeth and I had only just finished a late breakfast when nurse Catherine phoned us to say that they expected Harry to come round from the anaesthetic shortly. The journey down to the town and hospital was uneventful and in what seemed like a remarkably short time Elizabeth and I were walking along the now partially familiar corridor to the reception area where we met nurse Catherine. She told us that Harry hadn't come round just yet, but if we wanted to we could wait in his room. She thought it would be nice for him to see us when he did come round. I left Elizabeth chatting to her and went on to Harry's room where I met nurse Senoy.

"Hello," she said in her usual bright and cheery manner. She then continued, "I hope you don't mind my asking while there are just the two of us; Harry did go into the cave didn't he?"

"Yes," I answered. "How did you ….?"

"Oh, it's hard to keep little boys out of caves," she replied cheerfully, before adding in a more serious tone, "And did his mother?"

"Yes. Why do you ask? And how ….?"

"Ah. I thought so ….. but I wasn't absolutely sure."

"But why …..?"

In the light of what I've just said, you can guess my head was racing. OK, perhaps nurse Senoy's guess about Harry going into the cave was a reasonable one, but why did she ask? And why did she ask about Elizabeth? Before I could say anything, she continued in her usual breezy manner,

"Harry is safe and he'll be just fine now. He is her child after all so there is no need for me to look after him further. But I am afraid …."

"Of what?"

"No, not of what, but for you."

"Me?"

"Yes. I am sorry."

There was a slight pause before she added, "Harry will be coming out of the aesthetic at any minute and I must go now. It's been nice meeting you, Joe."

"And you," I replied in a somewhat numb tone as my mind was racing to try and make some sort of sense out of what I had just thought I'd heard.

"Thanks for looking after Harry."

"Not at all," she replied, "That's why I am here, and now my task is finished I will leave him in the capable hands of nurse Catherine who will be along shortly. Goodbye," she added. "Harry is a lovely boy."

And with that she left the room, closing the door quietly behind her, leaving me wondering precisely what it was that I had just witnessed. Have you ever had a conversation with someone who'd obviously mistaken you for someone else and had assumed that you knew all that they were talking about? Well, that's how I felt just then. I hadn't a clue what nurse Senoy had been on about. Well, OK, I could make some partial sense of some of it, but her choice of wording was not only odd but also extremely disconcerting. Was I correct to infer that our visit to the cave was somehow linked to Harry being in hospital, even though the medical evidence suggested otherwise? And what had Elizabeth's going into the cave got to do with anything? And then there was nurse Senoy's slightly ominous, 'not of what, but for you.' So was I to presume that all was not over yet and that somehow I was also already, or going to be involved?

Elizabeth, who had obviously finished her conversation with nurse Catherine, joined me in the room and as she did so Harry stirred and the amulet on a chain about his neck which nurse Senoy had given him, became briefly visible. I started to move closer so as to get a look at it.

However, Elizabeth's, "What's that he's wearing?" stopped me. "I'll bet it's that nurse."

She started walking towards Harry with, I presumed, the intention of removing the amulet, but as she did so Harry started to come round from the anaesthetic and so very inconsiderately for his mother, turned and placed his arm on top of the bed covers, thus effectively shielding the amulet both from view and his mother's hands.

"Don't you think you should let him decide what he wishes to wear?" I suggested, and perhaps unwisely added, "It will probably be sooner than either of us wishes it to be when other women are giving him things. He won't remain a little boy forever."

Elizabeth glared at me. I considered what I'd just said as a statement of the obvious. Namely, to suggest that in due course Harry would wish to leave us, that other women would start to feature in his life, so why Elizabeth's unwillingness to accept this and her hostility towards nurse Senoy? At that time the latter still eluded me and I think, only became clearer later.

Harry came round from the aneasthetic and as he did so nurse Catherine joined us in the room. We all had a bit of a chat and I am sure Harry was pleased to see us. However, he got tired quickly and at a certain point we adults decided it was best that we leave and let him get a bit of sleep. We made to go out of the room, but Elizabeth decided that she wanted one last moment with her little boy and so returned to his bedside. Nurse Catherine and I made our way to the corridor.

"Just before you came in," I said, "I had a chat with nurse Senoy and she said …."

"Nurse who?"

"Nurse Senoy," I replied, "she's been looking after Harry with you. Have I got her name right?"

Nurse Catherine looked at me blankly.

"I don't know," she said. "But I don't know a nurse Senoy. As far as I know there has only been myself looking after Harry."

"Oh." I said, realising that my earlier suspicions about my not fully understanding all that had been going on were not as ill-founded as I had thought them to have been, "and you wouldn't know anything about the Ghost Moth that has been in Harry's room?"

"Ghost Moth?" she repeated, smiling at me, "No I wouldn't. Indeed, I don't think I would know one if I had seen it and I haven't noticed anything in there that shouldn't be."

"Bright orange yellow wings, about so-big," I indicated with my fingers.

"No. Sorry. Why do you ask?"

"Um. I'm not sure really. Maybe something to do with a girl called Lilith, Eve Lilith, I think. I am still trying to work it out."

"Best of luck. Will you be visiting tomorrow?"

"Yes, that's our plan."

And with that Elizabeth joined us and the three of us walked to the end of the corridor, at which point nurse Catherine went her way and Elizabeth and I made for the car park. Perhaps needless to say, I didn't tell Elizabeth about my conversation with nurse Catherine.

Even when back home, I couldn't rid my thoughts of the strange and disconcerting happenings at the hospital. Nurse Catherine so obviously didn't know of nurse Senoy. How come, when I had seen and spoken with her, as had Elizabeth? Indeed, Elizabeth had been barely able to conceal her antipathy towards her. The more I thought about it, the more uncomfortable I became. I like things to be explainable and logical, you know. And yet what seemed to be happening appeared to be anything but explainable and logical. I made a mental note to have a closer look at the amulet that nurse Senoy had given Harry as soon as I had the chance, and in the meantime decided to push on with reading the tale that was now looking to be at the root of all of this, in the hopes that it would make things a little easier to understand. As much as logic suggested that Harry must have had his cerebral cavernous hemangioma malformations before visiting the tree and cave with us that day and that it was just an odd coincidence that the first symptoms of it should have shown up that night, I have to confess that there was a part of me that didn't quite buy into that coincidence theory. Unfortunately, that ghastly looking tree with its roots resembling a skull screaming in anguish and despair, did tend to drag one's reason off into a world of imaginings and speculation rather than allowing it to inhabit the world of logic, and as a result I found myself drawn to push on with reading the story to find out what, if anything, had happened at that cave.

To my surprise and I have to confess somewhat to my annoyance, my dear wife Lillibeth, had other ideas in mind.

"Joe," she purred in my ear, "come to bed. You can read your book when Harry comes home."

Didn't she realise why I wanted to read 'my book'? However, after my initial reaction to her suggestion, it occurred to me that finishing the tale that evening perhaps wasn't so important, because if there had been any connection between what had happened to Harry and the story of Adam Callow and Eve Lilith, perhaps it was no longer relevant as Harry's operation now had all the signs of having been successful. Indeed, the fact that one of his nurses had just indicated that afternoon that her presence was no longer required seemed to confirm this. Furthermore, I had found no real hard facts linking what Harry had claimed he'd seen and heard in the cave with his subsequent and was it in fact, purely coincidental illness? All we'd had was Harry's account, and given that he must have been ill at the time, that, with due respect to Harry, was probably a little bit suspect. So I remained fairly convinced that the story of the Ghost Moth was, as I had originally thought, just a story. However, as it had certainly hooked both Elizabeth and myself for a bit, I had to admit it was a pretty good one.

"Joe," said a departing Lillibeth from the open doorway to the living room, "Are you coming?" And, just in case I had not understood, she let slip one side of her dressing gown.

Of course I had no objection to her renewed interest in our marriage as any change was most welcome after the 'big freeze' we had been through ever since we had moved. Although I wasn't complaining, and does any husband worry about the 'why' when his wife is amorous, I couldn't help but wonder what had brought about the dramatic change from 'ice maiden' to 'red hot lover'?

So I left Adam Callow agonising over the fate of his soul and dutifully went to bed.

Chapter 20

"Whatever peace Adam Callow did manage to find after foolishly agreeing to meet up again with Eve Lilith; it was cast to the winds on the Saturday morning when Prior Obscurant announced that,

"Those followers of Satan that I hath told you about (in Münster, Germany), those that hath turned their town into a pit of vice and fornication, turned it into a new Sodom and Gomorrah!" The arm was in the air and the bony index finger extended. "The Almighty God hath intervened on the side of the righteous and hath drawn their strength from them and the Devil's own disciples[97] hath been captured, tried and found guilty of their sins of heresy, fornication and adultery. They hath been duly executed and, as a warning to all, their bodies hath been set in iron cages and hoisted up the spire of the Church of St Lambert where the birds of the air will feast on their flesh." And in case anyone had any doubts about where the birds of the air resided, the fanatical gaze of Prior Obscurant rose heavenward to follow the direction of his arm and pointing finger, which were still raised aloft to indicate this.

Oh, and yes, I think we can safely assume that McBane was paying particular interest to this announcement and no doubt was already speculating as to how he might introduce an iron cage into his repertoire! This gruesome piece of news must have added considerably to the horror of the daytime nightmare that was afflicting poor Adam Callow, because now, he not only had to contend with the prospect of having his genitals nailed to the monastery gates, but also the additional prospect of being placed in an iron cage and hoisted up whatever building the revolting Grees and sadistic McBane thought fit!

As always, Prior Obscurant had been selective with his

---

[97] John of Leiden, Bernhard Knipperdolling and Bernard Krechting

dissemination of news, there being no mention of why the established church waged war against the so-called rebels, or that the town was almost starved into submission. So Callow and his fellow novice-monks and most of the senior monks were unaware that the so-called rebels had taken the Biblical claim that all men were 'equal under God' a little too literally; namely, by asserting that wealth should be distributed equally. Anabaptists had flocked to the so-called 'New Jerusalem' both to be re-baptised and so become 'The Elect of Heaven', and yes of course, to share in the redistribution of wealth. However, the male death toll in the subsequent siege had resulted in there being three times as many women of marriageable age as men by the time their original leader, Matthys was killed (he whose privates had been nailed to the gates) and John of Leiden took over. John of Leiden evidently recognised an opportunity when he saw it, legalised polygamy and took sixteen wives to himself. For hard-liners in the Church and particularly those who wished to be amongst the one hundred and forty four thousand, such as Prior Obscurant, who was theologically unable to justify one wife let alone sixteen, this descent into debauchery provided public reason enough to justify the siege of Münster and the resulting loss of life even though it was not the real cause of the siege. The real cause was of course money and power, as the Catholic Church was far more interested in preaching about equality than it ever was in actually doing anything to bring it about. Money and power had to remain where they rightfully belonged. The status quo had to be restored. As ever, fornication and debauchery were well recognised sins which got the public hot under the collar back in those days just as they do today, and so no doubt it was deemed better to publicise these and not to mention anything about clawing back wealth and power to the Church. So officially it was for the aforementioned heinous sins, together with the catch-all crimes / sins of heresy and blasphemy that the three leaders had been publicly executed and their bodies hoisted up a church steeple in iron cages as a warning to others with similar ideas.

Whereas Adam Callow would have realised that technically speaking he had fornicated (had sex outside of marriage), he had not taken sixteen wives. All he had done was have an affair with one woman and he was pretty sure she wasn't married. So at the very worst, this was concubinage. Even Saint Augustine had sinned more that Adam Callow had, as Augustine had had at least two mistresses, one illegitimate child and had walked out on the woman he had promised to marry. Our Adam Callow now knew that Eve wasn't going to have a baby and he hadn't promised to marry her either. Surely, he reasoned, though without any real conviction, he ought to be able to survive this?

Survive this, what? What exactly was it that he had to survive? 'The foremost temptation that the Devil places in the path of man, is woman!' Yes, that was it. Survive this being tempted, this being led astray by a woman. Why, oh why had he ever agreed to meet up with Eve again? Adam Callow, you fool! The weight of his sin hadn't become any lighter; it was still dragging him down into the pit. His soul still remained soiled. He could never be one of the one hundred and forty four thousand, because he was no longer a virgin, having been defiled by a woman. He was lost, a lost soul and he would burn, just as poor Rose England was about to, only she would be burning in what for her remained of this life, whereas he, Adam Callow, would burn for eternity in the next!

Would Rose's burning purge her of her sins, so that in fact her soul might enter Purgatory rather than Hell? But what exactly had been Rose's sins? Yes, Callow had heard them mentioned at her inquisition, but when they had been extracted by McBane using torture in the form of a chevalet, or worse, how much could any confession be relied on? Had she really had sex with numerous demons as had been claimed? Certainly she had been an attractive woman, he could remember that; but not married, and he could remember that also. So if she had not had sex with a husband and was not a virgin, who had she had sex with? Although part of him found it impossible to accept that Rose could be a she-devil and witch, her lack of virginity and unmarried status was not the norm and so there was left a large uncomfortable space for doubt. But then Eve wasn't married either and she'd had sex as Callow knew only too well. And he knew that she enjoyed sex. So, if as had been claimed, Rose was an unmarried she-devil …? Oh goodness! And all of Adam Callow's old doubts came thundering back. Did this mean that Eve was also in fact a she-devil? There was no doubting that she had tempted him into having sex with her just as her namesake Eve had tempted Adam in the Garden. So if she was a she-devil, had he had sex with …. with a female disciple of Satan himself?! Oh good God! He *would* burn! He knew it! He would definitely burn! He tried to calm himself and to this end resolved that he must occupy himself, keep his mind off this wild speculating and be more calm, be more positive. Saint Augustine had managed. So he, Adam Callow, would also manage …. but .... stay positive.

However, staying positive was far easier said than done, because as he and Michael Venn were making their way back from the priory church following Prior Obscurant's missive on the sins being perpetrated in Münster, Venn took him to one side and told him that he was leaving the monastery.

"You can't," said a frightened Adam Callow, "You can't leave me. You can't leave me in this mad-house."

Michael Venn looked at his friend and must have noticed that the fresh faced youth with whom he had set up a vegetable stall at the start of the year, had lost all his youthful innocence, joy and enthusiasm. The face was thinner, the cheeks more hollow and the eyes nervously restless and set in dark sockets. This was no longer the face of a young man looking at the world with optimism, a young man looking forward to his life stretching away in front of him. It was more the face of an animal well and truly caught in a snare, unable to escape and certain in the knowledge that it was about to die.

Michael Venn must have noticed the terror in his friend's utterance, 'You can't leave me. You can't leave me in this madhouse,' because he took hold of Adam Callow's hands and said,

"Do you remember our talks, Adam; you, me and brother Stephen?"

"Yes, of course. Of course I do," replied Callow.

"Then you will remember me telling you about the life of St Paul, about his saying, 'When I was a child, I spake as a child, I understood as a child, I thought as a child.'[98] and my saying that men must learn to stop behaving like children, must stop thinking that they don't have to take responsibility for their lives, stop thinking that God, like their parents when they were children, will pick them up, dust them off and so save them from themselves and miraculously transport them to live in some Paradise of their imagining. It won't happen! Our individual salvations are in the hands of each and every one of us, Adam. *Your* salvation is in *your* hands.

Do you not remember that we discussed that Heaven is not 'up there' nor Hell 'down there,' as the likes of Augustine, Jerome and Obscurant would have it? They are not places we literally go to. They are states of mind, or rather states of existence. We each carry our own heavens and hells with us in our hearts. Remember Adam, 'if we love one another, God lives in us and his love is made complete in us.'[99]

That is the route to Paradise."

Of course Michael Venn must have realised that Adam Callow was carrying a hell of his own in his heart, but as to whether he knew precisely what a hell that was, how it was driving his friend almost to the edge of madness, we don't know. However, Michael Venn could not live Adam Callow's life for him, he could only love him, offer him advice from his

---

[98] 1 Corinthians 13:11
[99] 1 John 4:12

heart and trust that he would appreciate this, see the value in it, hold on and work his way through whatever it was that was troubling him.

"There is no limit of one hundred and forty four thousand, Adam. And no, we do not have to be virgins with the seal of God in our foreheads either, in order to experience Paradise. The Heaven envisaged by the likes of Augustine, Jerome, Obscurant, et al, where one's soul is miraculously cleansed of its sin and one basks for eternity in Paradise is nothing but a promise of redemption for lazy sinners; those who choose not to redeem themselves. It is both ...." and Michael Venn could not resist letting a slight smile cross his face as he then said, ".... both a devilishly tempting concept which conveniently provides the Church with a means of having a hold over the population on the one hand and, on the other, extracting money for the forgiveness of sins and the issuing of a passport to Heaven; a gentle form of extortion. However, we do not and will not receive true redemption by inaction or simply paying for it. We have to try to redeem ourselves. We don't have to be saints; all God asks is that we do our best and His seal is in the foreheads of those that try. As you walk this road of life, Adam, should you stumble on the road, do not expect an angel to come and pick you up and put you back in the nest[100]. Only you can save yourself by your own actions, and you can. I know you can, Adam."

Callow had never had his friend speak to him that way before, almost as though he were a child, and so stood in front of him, slack jawed and wide eyed. This was not the questioning, the debating Michael that he knew. This was a resolute and absolutely certain Michael, a Michael who now seemed years older and so much wiser than him. Whether Adam Callow actually understood and absorbed the advice of his friend is debatable. In his troubled state he probably totally

---

[100] St Augustine: Confessions, Book XII: 27

misinterpreted it and took what he had said as his knowing about him and Eve. Why else would he (Venn) have said anything like 'we do not have to be virgins with the seal of God in our foreheads', 'we do not have to be saints', 'should you stumble by the wayside', or 'only you can save yourself'? So had Michael Venn known about he and Eve all along and had said nothing, and this was his way of suggesting that somehow he, Adam Callow, needed to find a solution to the problems which beset him? Should he tell his friend all about his relationship with Eve? Should he open his heart to him? Oh that he could, because he so desperately wanted to tell someone! So desperately wanted not to keep his secret all to himself. Tears welled up in his eyes and he found himself so close to relinquishing the last vestige of self-control that he retained. All he wanted was peace, to be away from all the troubles which were crowding in on him, peace, warm still peace, where his tortured soul could rest. Yes, just like Augustine and Jerome, Adam Callow so wanted his soul miraculously cleansed of its sin and transported to bask for eternity in an innocent state in Paradise! So much so, that he was unable to formulate anything like an answer, or response to Venn's entreaty to redeem himself and instead heard his friend say,

"Wish me luck Adam, and I will do the same for you."

"Of course I do," replied Callow blankly, because although he was hearing his friend's words, his thoughts were, as we have learnt, elsewhere and so their meaning was passing him by, "but, but when you are leaving and why."

"Very soon," answered Michael Venn, who then somewhat enigmatically continued with, "Suffice it to say, I am called to move on." No doubt Michael Venn had his reasons for not divulging too much, and we can speculate that even if he had told Adam Callow precisely why he was leaving down to the last detail, it would have made little difference to Callow whose troubled and confused state of mind would have remained just as troubled and confused. Staying positive, as Callow had told himself he needed to do, was so much easier said than done and would have been hard enough for him even if his mentor, brother Stephen La Roche had still been alive, but he no longer was, and now his friend Michael Venn was also leaving him. Adam Callow could feel a void opening in front of him. Who could, or would be able to replace the stability provided by these two stalwarts in his life?

"Thanks for being my friend Adam, and I am sure we will meet again some day." And with that Michael Venn put his arms around Adam Callow and embraced him. He held him close for a few seconds before simply turning and heading off down the passageway without looking back, leaving a dumbstruck and numb Adam Callow standing in his wake. By the time Callow came to his senses Michael Venn had disappeared from view. Several of the senior monks had passed him and were now between him and his disappeared friend. He made a half-hearted attempt to chase after Michael Venn, but realising he was never going to catch him, gave up and walked slowly and disconsolately back to the cloisters and so to the vegetable garden. It was only when he arrived there and had sat himself down on one of the benches that he and brother Stephen La Roche had used to share, that the full impact of Michael Venn leaving his life really started to hit him. The sickening emptiness he felt almost devoured him from the inside like some hideous beast that had hatched in his stomach. A numb, featureless misery filled him. Although he shared a dormitory with four other novice-monks he realised that he hardly knew them, whereas precisely the opposite had been true of brother La Roche and novice-brother Venn. These two had been like a father and brother to him. He and they had shared their intimate, intellectual and possibly heretical discussions with each other, and so the bond of trust that had been established between them quite simply eclipsed any relationship with the other novice monks. Suddenly, Adam Callow found himself feeling horribly alone.

Chapter 21

When the appointed hour came round on the appointed day to burn the witch, a black habited and heavily black cowled procession of monks made its sombre way from the monastery and out on to the Market Square. As had been the case for the public flogging, sub-Prior Grees, dressed in his formal attire, followed the young crucifix-bearing novice-monk Peter Lamb. McBane followed him. Immediately after McBane, were Callow and now after Michael Venn's departure, the three other remaining novice-monks. Behind them were the senior monks. The black hooded procession filed slowly out to witness the legalised killing by burning. Were these the people who believed in a loving caring God, a God who had created man in His own image, a group who preached tolerance and love of their fellow man, charity and forgiveness, a group whose self-proclaimed task was to spread the Word of God and His son Jesus Christ? A nervous and frightened Adam Callow must have been wondering just how it was that he had got mixed up in this nightmare. What was he doing walking out dressed in a black habit and cowl; the uniform of faceless, heartless killers?

A large pyre had been built. Projecting out of its top was a round stake. A rough wood ladder led up from the cobbled square to the top of the pyre. Off to one side of this was a small raised platform. No doubt McBane had taken a fiendish delight in supervising all of this. The villagers stood behind armed guards, who formed a large circle round the pyre and platform, though several metres from it, and also flanked a route from it to the dungeon in which the witch, Rose England, was incarcerated. Prior Obscurant and sub-Prior Grees didn't want any rebellious behaviour of the crowd upsetting their orchestrated demonstration of Church power and control. There was going to be no sliding into the decadence seen in Münster in this village; not on their watch!

There was some restlessness in the crowd, some booing and jeering which suggested that the grizzly proceedings were about to start; and indeed, they were. Two prison guards appeared half dragging and half carrying the witch, an emaciated Rose England, who all too obviously was barely able to stand, along the guard flanked corridor towards the foot of the pyre. McBane stepped forward to meet them.

Rose was dressed in a simple sackcloth smock. Callow looked at her and was not sure if he would be sick, or was simply feeling too numb to react and do anything. He saw her grey, drawn face surrounded with unkempt dirty hair and noticed to his surprise that she didn't appear to be afraid. Possibly she now saw death as a release from the hell that McBane had been putting her through, or perhaps her ordeal had been such that she was already in a state of madness and so not actually aware of what was happening and what was going to happen to her. But to Callow's horror he realised that there was also one other possibility; the possibility that in fact she was a witch and that the flames of Hell held no fear for her!

As much as he tried to reason that she was not a witch, and he recalled that he had heard La Roche refer to her as 'this poor woman' which suggested that he (La Roche) did not see her as such, Callow could still not completely drive the idea from his mind that she might just be one. What he did know was that he didn't know women at all and the more he thought about it the more convinced he was that Eve Lilith had tempted him, both with her feminine charms and then with wine, into having sex with her. Oh goodness, he'd had enough warnings about this both directly from his Prior and also his novice-master, as well as indirectly via the writings of both Saints Paul and Augustine, and of course Saint Jerome. Indeed, Augustine's experiences had in many ways mirrored his own, so if Callow needed an example to reference, Saint Augustine was it. Augustine had been tempted into becoming 'more a slave of lust than a true lover of marriage'[101] as he had worded it, and the more Callow thought about his entanglement with Eve Lilith the more obvious it became to him that she had been tempting him into becoming one as well. Who would ever have believed that such a nice looking young woman like her would behave like a sexually depraved .... well .... who would have believed? Yes, Rose looked a dreadful sight right now, but how had she behaved, how had she been when the world did not have its eyes on her? Was she as sexually lascivious as Eve? And why wasn't she married, as most women of her age were? Had she led men astray, tempted them into licentiousness and away from attaining their places in the purity of God's Celestial Kingdom? He didn't know. However, such was Adam Callow's mental muddle and preoccupation with she-devils and witches and their leading men astray that it never crossed his mind that there might just be a totally different reason why death held no fear for Rose.

The crowd was roaring and jeering. Whether this was because they wanted to see a witch burn, or because they were of the opinion that the incumbents at The Priory and Monastery of Saints Paul and Augustine were about to burn an innocent woman, wasn't all together clear. There were many who knew Rose was a kind soul at heart and that she'd done her best to assist those less well off financially and intellectually than herself. And there were those who thought she was an angel. However, she had been outspoken and openly critical of what she saw as the pretentiousness and hypocrisy of the ruling group in the Priory and Monastery and had singled out Prior Obscurant and his sub-Prior Grees for some particularly harsh criticism, and so possibly, some reasoned, it was hardly surprising that they were now, now that they had the chance, getting their own back. Then of course there were those in the crowd who didn't know Rose well enough, only knew of her outspoken and critical nature and so were inclined to believe the

---

[101] St Augustine, Confessions, Book VI:15

charges of blasphemy and heresy that the Church had levelled against her.

Sub-Prior Grees and his young cross-bearer reached the small raised platform. The youth took the cross around to the side of the platform and the sub-Prior ascended it via some small steps at its rear. Novice-master McBane took up his position at the base of the ladder set against the pyre. The two prison guards all-but carried their charge up the ladder, placed her back to the staff and bound her to it. They then descended the ladder, removed it and took it away back along the guard-lined passage.

Sub-Prior Arriviste Grees raised his Bible in his right hand and the noise from the crowd subsided.

"This woman," he commenced in his effeminate high pitched voice, "has been tried, and found guilty, by a unanimous verdict, of being a witch, practising witchcraft and blasphemy. She has confessed to all the charges. She has confessed to partaking in sexual acts with both demons and the very Devil himself!"

There was a gasp from the crowd.

As sub-Prior Grees was making his speech one of the prison guards had returned with a burning pitch torch and had handed it to McBane.

"Her soul is damned!" continued to squeak the sub-Prior, "and as is decreed in 'Malleus Maleficarium', such maleficium is so vile and heinous that it can only be categorised as crimen exceptum." There was nothing like a bit of Latin gobbledegook to bamboozle the ignorant peasants! If Latin was used, it followed that the crimes must be terrible and hence that sub-Prior Grees, one of the educated elite of the Priory and Monastery must be right, and hence that the institution of the Church must be right. The simple villagers knew their own ignorance. Most could not read, let alone write, they had no comprehension of foreign languages, no knowledge of law and so had to take everything on trust from those who did know these things, did understand these things. However, the boos and jeers from the crowd suggested that perhaps that trust was breaking down and that although they did not know precisely how, none-the-less had a gut-feeling that they had been and were being deliberately bamboozled.

Holding his Bible aloft, the fat, little sub-Prior said in a high pitch whine,

"God's Justice be done! Burn the witch!"

Novice-master McBane plunged the torch into the dry brushwood at the base of the pyre.

Adam Callow looked on, hardly able to believe what he was seeing. Smoke started to emanate from the top of the pyre and swirl around the Market Square. People started coughing and wiping their eyes, but it was not possible to refrain from looking at the fire for long, as the hypnotic horror that it represented drew all eyes to it. This was not an ordinary fire, it was not just wood that was being burned. Suddenly the flames started to take hold and rip up through the body of the pyre. Smoke and ash curled skyward and then a fickle wind blew this into the crowd who spluttered and coughed. Then a few seconds later it was the turn of the black cowled monks to try and shield their eyes and attempt to avoid coughing as the wind whipped the smoke in their direction.

Adam Callow wiped his watering eyes and through the smoke managed to see Rose still standing, well, hanging would be a more accurate description, from the central stake on top of the burning heap. Part of the sackcloth smock she was wearing had caught light and a flash of flame at one side of her head removed her hair from that side. Probably like everyone else present, Callow continued to look on, mesmerised by the surreal horror of what he was witnessing, unable to tear his eyes away from the ghastly sight right in front of him.

Up to that point not a sound had come from Rose, but suddenly she screamed out in what appeared to Callow to be an extremely loud voice,

"Beware the pale horse Obscurant, for his name that sits on him is Death, and Hell follows with him," and then after a brief pause, added, "Come and see!"[102]

Callow was not the only one to turn his head towards the stone balcony after hearing this direct address to Prior Obscurant and so would not have been the only one to see the Prior stand and pale faced, leave the balcony. God's Prior might have argued that there was no further reason for him to remain, might have argued that what all had just heard were the last blasphemous utterances from a wretched creature who deserved no more than to burn. However, no doubt many thought differently, especially as Rose's dying curse appeared to confirm their belief that she was in fact an angel after all.

The wind died for a minute and so the vertically rising smoke blocked everyone's view of her and as it did there then followed a blood-curdling scream, which gradually died away until the only sound remaining was that of the roar of the flames. The angel had left this temporal life and 'gone before'. No, she most certainly was not one of Prior Obscurant's one hundred and forty four thousand, but most present thought that she stood a far greater chance of 'opening a seal' and of her soul gaining admittance to God's Celestial Kingdom, than ever would be the case for the religiously fundamental and fanatical Prior Obscurant.

Then the wind picked up again and blew the grey smoke into the crowd with the result that Callow and all his fellow monks could see the blackened, burning body of Rose England hanging from the stake silhouetted against the bright brimstone yellow and orange flames. A hideous vision of Hell on earth.

---

[102] Revelation 6:7-8

'Oh dear God,' Callow must have thought, 'is this what Hell looks like?' The horrific image lasted just long enough to sear itself into his consciousness; a vision of the unquenchable and everlasting flames of the spiritual Hell, the Hell to which his damned soul was most certainly destined.

However, that ghastly vision was short lived, as the wind once again smothered the black cowled monks in smoke and ash; only this time the smoke did not smell of just burning wood, but also the vile stench of burning flesh. This was the smell of Hell on earth. Adam Callow was lucky as he and his fellow novice-monks were at the far end of a row and so as remote from the inferno that was devouring the witch - or was it the angel? - Rose England. However, so revolting was the smell that Adam Callow could clearly hear the sounds of retching coming from the body of monks nearer to the fire on his right.

Across the square he could see the villagers trying to shield their eyes and noses from the smoke and smell. Children had buried the heads in their mother's skirts and were nervously stamping their feet. Yes, even young children were being forced to witness this horror! Several of the crowd were openly being sick. Even some of the guards were finding it impossible to maintain a stoic composure. One suspects that it would have been sub-Prior Arriviste Grees, who realised that it would not be wise for the monks to be seen in such obvious physical distress in front of the villagers at the burning of a blasphemer, heretic and witch - they were after all supposed to be witnessing God's Justice and so should not be showing signs of being as revolted by it as the villagers so obviously were. Grees placed an arm on the shoulders of young Peter Lamb, the crucifix bearer, who was being sick beside the small raised platform, and bade him pick up the object of his office and proceed back into the monastery. The other monks followed on behind in a reasonably orderly fashion glad to leave such an appalling spectacle and retreat into the safe confines of their monastery.

Chapter 22

The importance of La Roche's warning to both Callow and Michael Venn, 'there won't be any qualms about throwing either of you on the fire if they feel the need to. So you keep your heads down and keep your opinions to yourselves,' was now so horribly clear, though whether it had really registered with Adam Callow was another matter. Since the death of his mentor, brother La Roche, and the departure of his friend, Michael Venn, Adam Callow had become acutely aware of being apart from his fellows, unable to communicate with them, isolated, like a walking lost soul. The ghastly spectacle of the burning of Rose England was seared into his brain and the temporal and spiritual problems associated with his relationship with Eve Lilith had not gone away either and were constantly tormenting him. He felt all-but dead to the world and what was going on around him, and had no idea what to do. In spite of the assurances and entreaties of his departed friend, 'There is no limit of one hundred and forty four thousand, Adam,' 'No, we do not have to be saints. All God asks is that we do our best,' Adam Callow's grip on reality was slipping away from him.

Prayers passed and so did lunch. Although he hardly tasted the food, he did at least notice that he was not the only one to have lost his appetite, but such was the weight of his troubles and the horror of the burning seared into his mind, that he nearly forgot that he had arranged to meet Eve, and it was only as lunchtime came to an end that he half-heartedly, suddenly remembered. Somewhat surprisingly, his immediate reaction to remembering this was one of joy; it would be nice to see her, to be with someone with whom he could share his intimate thoughts and to get away from the insanity, the madness of the monastery. However, this initial joy was almost instantly replaced with fear, as so many of the problems in his life stemmed from his relationship with her; his relationship with a she-devil who had so very nearly led him astray, led him off the straight and narrow path. No, these problems had not gone away. They were still there; still unresolved, and so it was with very conflicting emotions that he set off to meet with her.

As soon as he set foot outside the monastery gate and saw the still smouldering pile of ash, all the horror that he had seen, heard and smelt that morning came flooding back to him. Oh good God! Whereas he realised that he had to get out of the living nightmare he was in, whether this rendezvous with his ex-lover, Eve, would help, he had absolutely no idea. Yes, part of him did want to see her, but just as fervently part of him did not. She was one of his problems, so going to meet her did not appear, even to Callow in his present state, to be a wise idea. However, he desperately needed the company of someone with whom he had some sort of relationship, and just as desperately needed to get away from the monastery and the madness that it represented. He just wanted out! Wanted out of everything, wanted to be free of all the problems in his life, and so to Adam Callow, walking out of the monastery gate seemed right then to represent that. But Adam Callow's personal hell was not 'down there,' as Michael Venn might have said, but within himself. So whereas he left the monastery gates behind him, he had not left his personal hell behind, and so the naissant positive spring in his step soon faded and he trudged disconsolately up the stone road to his rendezvous.

The bank of Rosebay willowherb, or as it is also known, fireweed, came into view. But it was early autumn now and so gone were the beautiful soft bright pink flowers and green leafed stems of summer and in their place were .... were flames! The autumn leaves of the fireweed were now a sea of bright red and orange flame burning out of the very earth. Hell itself was sprouting up all around Adam Callow, its flames evidently so hungry to claim his corrupted soul. In horror and fear he turned away from the fireweed and looked at the trees on the other side of the road only to find that their soft greenery had changed to flaming yellow and orange. The whole world was alight! Everywhere he looked there was fire. Was there no escape for him? Was Hell opening its doors and the very Devil himself waiting there, waiting to claim his soul? The smell of the fire that burnt Rose England filled his nostrils and the vision of her body hanging from the stake and silhouetted against the dancing yellow and orange light came back to haunt him. No, don't close your eyes. Keep them open. However, it made no difference whether he kept his eyes open or closed, all he saw was flames, flames from the bottomless pit coming to sear his flesh and burn his soul.

Fortunately for Adam Callow's sanity not everything was burning. Thank goodness. He noticed that the fire stopped at the drystone wall which bounded the road, though still at some distance from it. On the far side of the wall was a field of soft golden undulating grass; a soft rippling golden field of Heaven. Yes, Paradise was there; visible, but out of reach. Unattainable, over there on the far side. Oh why could he not reach it? Why was he on the side of the wall which had a hard stone road surrounded by fire that would burn one's soul before it was plunged into Phlegethon; 'where souls, well boiled, give vent to high pitched yells'[103]? Why was he being shown but denied Heaven? Oh dear God forgive me! Of course he knew why Heaven was being denied him, though did not wish to acknowledge it, and so could surmise where his 'hard stone road' was leading. However, was turning and going back, back to the insanity and madness in the valley actually a realistic option? All Adam Callow could do was what we all have to do; go on. We can't go back in life. We can't turn back time. It is no use our thinking, 'I wish I had'. That time is gone. We, like poor Adam Callow, make our decisions and have to live with them, for good or ill. All any of us can do is go on. And so Adam Callow continued up his hard stone road and eventually arrived

---

[103] Dante, The Divine Comedy, Inferno, 14:100 (Phlegethon; The River of Fire)

at the entrance to the tunnel of now, flaming yellow birch trees which led through to the small grass covered natural amphitheatre. Here he momentarily halted as irrational fear gripped him; but fortunately he could see the green grass and sunlight at the far end of the tunnel, and so steeled himself and walked through the fire and thence out into the clean and still green space beyond; a space where the ground was soft beneath his feet, a cool, sweet smelling breeze blew on his face and a clear blue sky arched above his head. Perhaps Heaven was still within reach?

As he had half expected, Eve had arrived before him and had already spread her blanket on the floor of the small cave. She smiled at him as he approached.

"Hello Adam. I'm so glad you did come. I thought you might not."

"Hello Eve. No, I ….." but Callow didn't really know what to say.

"Come. Sit down," she said, gently patting the blanket.

With her black hair tumbling over her smooth, bare, ivory skinned shoulders and down her back, she looked both stunningly beautiful and dangerously, indeed, she-devilishly dangerously tempting! However, in Adam Callow's then current state of mind sexual temptation wouldn't have even registered with him, but she was tempting none-the-less, as a warm, understanding angel who could look after and care for a damaged soul. That afternoon Adam Callow's angel was wearing her golden coloured bodice with a yellow blouse beneath and bright yellow orange skirt; a golden angel. But those same colours were also the colours of flame, the colour of Hell fire! So from which kingdom had Adam Callow's angel come and had she come to save him, or claim him?

"We can be friends, can't we?" she said with the hint of a purr, patting the blanket again. "Please join me, Adam."

And he did. The pair of them sat side by side, saying nothing, each wrapped in their own thoughts, though the truth be told Adam Callow's thoughts were more numb blanks of either nothingness or despair, rather than anything resembling formed thoughts.

"Will you have some wine with me, Adam? For old times sake?" she asked in an attempt to break the silence between them.

"No, I shouldn't," he replied, his memories of the past suddenly appearing to crash in on the present.

She laughed, "I remember you saying that when we first came here."

Yes, and look where that got me? thought a cold, hollow Adam Callow. What was he doing sitting here on this blanket with this woman? This woman who had already given him so much trouble. Why was he here? Of what was he thinking? He'd already broken with her, so there was no need for him to be here. So why was he? Oh Adam Callow, what are you doing? What …..?

"And we had such a nice time, Adam. You loved me then," she added, but with no edge to her voice; it was simply said as though it were a straight statement of fact. She looked at him with big soft brown eyes; eyes holding back the hurt she felt inside? He though continued to avoid her gaze, still unsure of why he was there and what he should do. However, there was no denying that it was nice to hear her voice, to hear the softness in it and feel, was it the warmth in it? And so gradually he felt the ice within him begin to thaw.

"Yes, alright," he replied, and she poured him a drink of wine, visibly brightening as she did so, realising that at last she might be getting through to him, that she, Eve, might get her Adam back. She reclined herself on one elbow, so that she was facing him. He remained sitting upright and facing the view, his mind feeling tired, numb and exhausted, and his heart heavy and cold. They drank their wine in silence, but gradually it was no longer that cold, deliberate, rejecting silence, and he began slowly, painfully slowly, to feel more at ease in her company.

"Did you attend the burning?" she asked tentatively.

"Yes," he replied, but was still unable to let all that was pent up in him flood out. "Yes, we all had to. It was ghastly."

"How dreadful for you," she said and reaching out took hold of his hand.

He turned and looked at her. Oh goodness, she was beautiful …. and kind …. and right then Adam Callow needed a kind friend as he had never needed one in his life before. The earlier suspicious death of his mentor Stephen La Roche and sudden unexplained departure of his friend Michael Venn had left him feeling lost, confused and empty. And then the burning of Rose had probably shocked him far more than he had realised as he felt cold all through, felt as if he wanted to cry but had no idea why. His heart felt as if it might burst, he was so desperate for something, something to fill that dreadful void that he felt within himself, someone to hold on to, someone to help ease the burden of the lonely turbulent world that he was currently inhabiting, someone to share with. As he lay on the blanket with her, he slowly realised that in spite of all she had put him through, the only person who could provide him with the love and human warmth that he so desperately lacked and needed, was her. But could he open his heart to her again after all that had happened between them, and just as importantly, should he open his heart to her again? Couldn't they just be friends, like he was with his sister? Why was that so impossible? Yes, like that; that would be fine surely? The load began to ease from his shoulders and some much needed warmth returned to his cold heavy heart as he joined her, likewise reclining on the blanket. He smiled at her somewhat weakly, not knowing how to proceed and perhaps a touch ashamed of his own lack of inner strength and earlier coldness towards her. She smiled back at him and stroked his face. Yes, he knew, knew in his heart that he needed her, but he was at the same time frightened, frightened to his very core of precisely that, of needing her, needing a woman. She moved a little closer and put her hand on to his shoulder,

"Kiss me, Adam," she said quietly.

And Adam Callow found himself, in spite of all his earlier resolved good intentions, putting his arm around her, drawing her to him and kissing those delicious pink lips.

Just that, the simple act of a kiss, seemed to melt the ice within him and pour soothing balm on to the sea of troubles which tormented him. He lay back on the blanket feeling the relief flowing through him as Eve, his Eve, lying on his chest, ran a playful finger across his lips. The world ceased to look quite as dark as it had. 'Our individual salvations are in the hands of each and everyone of us, Adam.' Perhaps there was a way through, a way out of his current situation? He had absolutely no idea what his individual salvation might be, but at least the possibility of finding it appeared right then to be opening to him. That first tentative kiss became a second, and soon the second a third, each one longer, hotter, more passionate than its predecessor. And then suddenly there was no time to fiddle with lacing on bodices or to undo cords. She hurriedly pulled up Callow's habit and her own skirt, sat on top of him and all the previous tension and stress drained from him and was replaced, even though he was breathing hard, by a sense of peace, a heavenly sense of peace, the sublime peace he had missed and had been longing for.

He clasped his hands on to her rounded rhythmically moving hips and smiled up at her, pleased and content that she was enjoying their coupling the same as he was. Oh how he had missed her! Missed their closeness, missed their intimacy. No, it wasn't just sex. It was the being of 'one flesh,'[104] the ultimate expression of human togetherness, the being of one with another person and so creating a whole, a sense of completeness, and it was that which Callow realised he had missed. The being alone, being half of something when the other half was not there, of not sharing, was a lonely way to spend one's life, for indeed, 'it was not good that the man should be alone.'[105]

And with the contentment, a lightness entered him and it crossed his mind that it was strange seeing her thus, still partially dressed in her gold bodice. In their haste one side of it had come loose along with the blouse and one of her breasts was almost exposed. Her raven black hair was tumbling like a small dark waterfall over her white skinned shoulders. And then he thought, it was probably strange for her to look down at him still clothed in his monk's habit and the thought of the picture they must have made made him laugh.

"What are you laughing at?" she asked.

"Us," he replied, "Us still half dressed like this."

"Never mind that," she gasped. "Take me Adam. Have me and make me pregnant."

What?!

'Make me pregnant!'

The peaceful, blissful and contented world to which she had taken him suddenly shattered into a thousand fragments as the cold reality of what they were doing crashed into his consciousness! How could he be plunging himself back into all that he had tried so hard to escape; the whirlpool of fornication and sin and all the temporal problems associated with them? What was he doing?!

---

[104] Genesis 2:24
[105] Genesis 2:18

'And behold, there met him a woman with the attire of a harlot, and subtil of heart.' Oh no! Had she deliberately lured him there on false pretences? 'She caught him, and kissed him' with those lovely pink lips, with that almost hypnotic dark diamond at the their centre where they didn't quite touch. 'I have decked my bed with coverings of tapestry.' Was a blanket so different to a tapestry? 'Come let us take our fill of love.' Yes, it had been her that had invited him to join her on to the blanket and had 'with the flattering of her lips she forced him. He goeth after her straightway, as an ox goeth to the slaughter.'[106] Oh Adam Callow, you fool, you fool! How could you not remember that, 'The foremost temptation that the Devil places in the path of man, is woman.'? Still you have not understood! You poor blind, stupid fool, and now you are going …. going to the slaughter!

"No! Get off me!" managed Callow in a terrified, strangled voice.

"Make me pregnant again, Adam. I need a child," she implored, panting urgently as if she had not heard what he'd said, or was it that she had read his mind and the urgency she expressed was about her obtaining his seed before it was too late?

Pregnant. No! Not again. He could not go through all that again. The fiery pit was beginning to open beneath him and he could feel himself sliding into it, sliding down under the weight of his lust and carnal sin.

"Get off me!"

"Have me Adam. Take me! Make me with child!"

Oh dear God! How could he have been so mistaken? She must be the work of the Devil. Help me! A she-devil is upon me; a she-devil dressed in a golden yellow bodice …. golden yellow? …. gold gilt sackcloth? …. with silky black tumbling

---

[106] Proverbs 7:10-22

hair bouncing with each thrust on white smooth skinned, bare shoulders and an all-but naked breast .... where had he seen this before; the head thrown back and mouth open in the throws of sexual ecstasy? .... and the woman Adam Callow found he was looking up at was suddenly horribly oh-so-familiar. Yes! That dreadful sculpted wooden statue of St Bibiana in the novice monks' chapel! He'd looked at the thing every day for the past several months, so why hadn't he noticed the likeness between Eve and that statue before? 'But isn't that how the devil works; to make what is temptation seem to be anything but, to make the victim feel secure and safe so they don't realise what is happening until it is too late and their soul is undone?' So had this she-devil who was on top of him right now, disguised herself as a saint to confuse him, seduce him and lead him off the straight and narrow path to the Divine Celestial Kingdom?

Then in quick succession another revelation hit him. Eve? Eve Lilith? Oh goodness .... that name, Lilith! That also now sounded horribly familiar. Oh Adam Callow, how could you not recognise it? Lilith; a sexually wanton she-devil, a dangerous demon who steals babies in the night! But it was broad daylight and .... her name was Eve? How could she be both Eve and Lilith? And there was also something terrifyingly familiar about this as well! Wasn't there .... wasn't there also speculation that Lilith was in fact Adam's first wife and not Eve; God having created Lilith at the same time as Adam and from the same dirt, and not from his rib, which He subsequently used to create Eve? And hadn't Lilith left Adam and coupled with .... yes, with Samael?

Samael!

Having left the nightmare of the monastery, Callow must have felt as if he had simply exchanged that for another as he remembered that Samael was another name of Satan. Satan, the very Devil!

And hadn't that Lilith told Adam, 'I will not lie below, for we are equal to each other inasmuch as we were both created from the earth.'[107]? And now she, she who had coupled with the very Devil himself, was on top of him screaming at him to make her pregnant! The horror of his situation was suddenly startlingly apparent. He attempted to push her off but, flat on his back, was unable to get a purchase on anything. Oh dear God, he would be dragged down, he would surely burn, and not just in this life but in the unquenchable flame of the next. Merciful God, help me! Help me!

"I must have a child! You must give me a child," the she-devil was now screaming at him.

He tried kicking his legs to her evident delight, and tried reaching her with his hands, but she pulled back from him and pushed his hands away so he could not get a hold on her. 'And I looked, and, lo, a Lamb stood on the Mount Sion, and with him a hundred and forty four thousand, having His Father's name written in their foreheads.' Oh Dear God, would he end up with his genitals nailed to the monastery gates and his dead body hoisted in a steel cage up the tower of the Priory Church? He had to somehow stop this, somehow get this lascivious lust-driven she-devil off him.

"Make me pregnant you useless priest! I need a child."

"No! Get off me, you …. you," and then, in whimpering desperation, "Leave me alone."

But hadn't his Biblical namesake, when he'd had the headstrong Lilith as a wife, also given up and gone crying to God after she had left him saying, 'Sovereign of the universe! The woman you gave me has run away'[108] and God had had to assist the weak Adam resolve his marital problems by sending three angels, Snvi, Snsnvi and Smnglof, to find the wayward woman and bring her back to him? Three angels ….? 'Do not

---

[107] Alphabet of ben Sirach (Alphabetum Siracidis, Othijoth ben Sira)
[108] Alphabet of ben Sirach (Alphabetum Siracidis, Othijoth ben Sira)

expect an angel to come and pick you up and put you back in the nest.' Was that what he, Adam Callow, was expecting, expecting an angel, expecting to be saved? The last conversation that he'd had with Michael Venn resurfaced in his mind, 'His seal is in the foreheads of those that try.' Yes, he must try, and to this end he managed to raise one knee and brace his foot against a boulder on the cave floor.

'And no man could learn that song but the hundred and forty four thousand, which were redeemed from the earth,' screamed in his head. 'These are they which were not defiled with women.' Oh merciful God! Yes he was defiled, but was he *so* defiled; defiled *beyond* redemption? The hideously grinning faces of Obscurant, Grees and McBane forced their way into his consciousness.

"I need a child!" the she-devil was screeching at him in her now desperate bid to achieve her so desired pregnancy.

The image of Obscurant raised its prophetic arm and pointed to the Celestial Kingdom. That of Grees said something in its high pitched squeaky voice about sin, fornication and he (Callow) being damned and destined to burn in the fires of Hell for all eternity. And finally the image of a grizzled, grinning McBane raised the bucket and knife! Callow could feel himself sliding into the bottomless pit, dragged down by the weight of his sin, could feel the mire of lust and fornication beginning to close in over his head and hear the voices of the damned getting closer and louder. 'Only you can save yourself,' said the steady voice of Michael Venn; and so Adam Callow summoned up all his strength and gave a last huge upward thrust, which initially thrilled Eve until she realised what he was up to and found herself tipped sideways and falling.

And she fell with a dull thud and lay still beside him.

All was quiet. It was over.

Callow was still flat on his back gasping from the physical

exertion and from fear. The whole incident had only lasted a few minutes, but he was bathed in cold sweat. Gradually a sense of relief spread over him, though relief from precisely what he wasn't quite sure, but he'd managed to avert something; something that had been trying to drag him down, down into the abyss. However, whatever that something was, the danger was now past and so he lay there as warm relief began to flood through his veins and his breathing gradually returned to normal. After a minute or two he was able to push his black habit back down over his pale naked thighs and so recover a bit of dignity.

Yes, all was quiet …. too quiet …. much too quiet.

He lifted himself up and looked at the she-devil lying on the cave floor and noticed that she was lying very still. Oh goodness, it had been close, too close. Indeed, much too close; 'For her house inclineth unto death, and her paths unto the dead. None that go unto her return again.'[109] But he had prevailed, was still in the land of the living and he hoped had saved his soul. The raven haired, ivory skinned woman lay sprawled, partly on her side, half on the blanket and half off, facing him, with her eyes open and staring at him. He reached across and touched her, but she did not move.

"Eve?"

He scrambled to his knees ....

"Eve!"

…. and leaned across her and rolled her onto her back and it was then that he saw the gash in the side of her head and the pool of blood soaking into the floor of the cave where her head had been lying. Oh goodness what had happened? Of course he knew; her still open eyes staring at nothing told him that, but he couldn't fully grasp the reality of it, that she was actually dead.

---

[109] Proverbs 2:18-19

Yes, she was, the she-devil was dead. A mixture of relief and horror swept through him. Relief that the danger was passed and he hoped his soul was now safe, but also horror that she was actually dead. But how? And it was only then that he saw the blood covered sharp corner of one of the cuboid rocks that was present on the cave floor. She must hit her head as she had tumbled from him? Oh no. No! Why did this have to happen? Her staring eyes seemed to bore into him even though they were actually looking vacantly at the roof of the small cave. Her, 'Oh God. Look what you have made me do,' said earlier in their relationship must have come back to him with a vengeance. But he hadn't meant to kill her, he'd just wanted .... She had been trying to steal his seed and drag him back down into a vortex of sin and fornication, so he'd had to stop her. He'd had no choice, had he? He'd had to get her off him. But why this?

Adam Callow sat slowly back on his haunches and tried to take in the new reality, a reality that had changed so dramatically in just a few minutes, but like any of us he was unable to grasp the magnitude of what had happened and so subconsciously distanced himself from it. Had Prior Obscurant been right all along with his advice that 'the foremost temptation that the Devil places in the path of man, is woman!'? Why had he, Adam Callow, not appreciated it? Why had he been so blinded by the delights of the flesh and base carnal lust? Fortunately, oh so fortunately, he had seen the error of his ways and just in time, but ….. but and now this! However, now was not the time to dwell on this he told himself; the earlier inner emptiness, loneliness, self-pity and fear having been replaced by adrenalin fuelled shock. His soul had been saved. The she-devil was dead. He felt strangely in control, in command of his life. What was it that now needed to be done?

He closed her eyes and remained kneeling beside her still feeling slightly sick, weak, and in spite of feeling more in control actually without any real idea of what he ought to do. Then he rearranged her blouse and the golden yellow bodice to cover her brazen semi-nakedness, rearranged her beautiful golden orange skirt so it didn't look so crumpled, and brushed off some of the dirt on it. The blood was still running down the side of her face where her skull had been punctured by the fall and was soaking into both her beautiful silky hair and the ground beneath; her evil life force draining into the soil. 'For dust thou art, and unto dust shalt thou return.'[110] There was no doubting that she was dead.

Then it occurred to him that of course she could not have a Christian burial. No, a she-devil most certainly could not expect that! It was .... simply not possible. In which case, she could be buried anywhere in a suitable piece of unconsecrated ground and this he realised meant that there was no need for him to tell others, tell them of what had occurred, relate the details of the sin that she and he had been indulging in and no need to tell them why he'd arranged to meet this wanton woman for their last rendezvous. The whole debauched story need not come out. He wouldn't have to lie about it. No, he could simply not mention it. That was not a lie. After all, what could possibly be gained by everyone knowing? If they did, she would certainly be excommunicated after having been branded a concubine at best, or, more than likely, a whore, or a witch, or a she-devil, and none of those possibilities would result in her getting a proper Christian burial anyway. And furthermore, this course of action would also prevent his being mistakenly arrested for murder should they (Prior Obscurant, sub-Prior Grees and novice-master McBane) not realise that the dead woman was a servant of the Devil as Rose England had been. His simply not mentioning the incident would eliminate all the explaining, all the shameful explaining. So he wouldn't need to justify his actions to anyone. No, telling all was not necessary, and so very obviously could only make matters worse. He would have to bury her himself and make it as proper and fitting as he could for someone of her standing. That was what had to be done and

---

[110] Genesis 3:19

all that was necessary now was that he set to and do it.

And so it was that in this state of shock Adam Callow finished tidying up the body of Eve Lilith and the contents of the cave, and then headed back to the Priory and Monastery of Saints Paul and Augustine for a pail of water, a shovel and a crucifix.

<u>Chapter 23</u>

On the walk back to the monastery Adam Callow initially thought of little, his mind was focused on what he had to collect and what he had to do, but as the shock of what had happened gradually subsided other thoughts began to creep in.

He most certainly hadn't intended or tried to kill Eve; her head hitting that rock was pure chance, simple bad luck. It *was* an accident. All he had wanted was for her to cease …. cease what? Cease using him to make herself pregnant? To stop her from involving him in what it was that *she* desired, but he didn't. But wasn't that what Eve, the Biblical Eve, Adam's second wife, the one who had been created from Adam's rib, had also wanted of her Adam, to involve him in what *she* had wanted, and why *she* had tempted him with the fruit of the Tree? Yes, God had made woman 'bone of my bones, and flesh of my flesh so that they shall be one flesh'[111] after He had observed and stated that it was 'not good that the man should be alone.' Whereas to be company for the man may have been the justification given, it was evidently not the reason why God had made the woman, because He made both His women, the first woman, Lilith, and the second woman, Eve, want children. And if this was the case, why were Saints Augustine and Jerome, and now Prior Obscurant and his ilk suggesting that men and women were supposed to lead celibate lives? Although Adam Callow hadn't contributed much to the discussions between brother La Roche, novice-monk Venn and himself, perhaps some of what had been said had made an impression on him, because he went on to ask what would have happened if Adam and Eve had obeyed God's commandment? Would they still be living in the garden, subservient and childless? Or was it in fact God's Will that they did disobey Him, ate of the tree and so were banished? And if this was so, why was Prior Obscurant

---

[111] Genesis 2:23-25

suggesting that 'the foremost temptation that the Devil places in the path of man is woman,' if in fact God wanted the man to be tempted by the woman that He had created? Was men and women being together and enjoying each other in fact what God had wished, *was* in fact God's Will?"

"We might," suggested Joe, seemingly breaking off from his story, "think Adam Callow's confusion relatively simple to ours' these days when, as a society, we suggest that on the one hand it is wrong for a man and woman to have an affair, yet on the other euphemistically call the child resulting from that affair 'a love-child'; a description which all but indicates that the affair was not so morally wrong after all and also, unfortunately tends to imply that children born within wedlock are not 'love-children'. It is the new child and the woman's right to have it that over-rides all other considerations, including the possible wrecking of two marriages and damage to the entirely innocent children of same. Of course it is the fault of both adult parties to the affair and possibly their spouses, and none should duck their responsibility, but doesn't it behold all parties to retire, as gracefully and quietly as possible? However, all too often the woman cannot do that and more often than not, will want to 'dish the dirt', publish a 'kiss and tell' article in a national tabloid regardless of the damage it does to innocent third parties, all because she was unable to secure / hold onto her man and have her child with him. 'Hell hath no fury like a woman scorned!'[112]

However, whereas the having of an extramarital affair still carries a degree of moral opprobrium, this is completely overlooked when 'the other woman' is a surrogate mother. In these circumstances 'the other woman' becomes a Bilhal to the wife's Rachel and her 'Give me children, or else I die'[113] again suggests the woman's right to breed, to have children, overrides

---

[112] William Congreve, The Morning Bride, Act III, scene 2
[113] Genesis 30:30

all other considerations and that no morality can stand in the way! This over-riding desire to breed is the very essence of being female. That is what the female does. Is it any wonder therefore that the male, the man Adam, and all that have followed him down through the ages, have had difficulty coming to terms with this? And is it also any wonder that the early saints when trying to link the morality of their religion to this primal need in women, have become intellectually unstuck and so have almost inevitably seen women as the sex that leads men astray, seen them as the temptresses, the harlots and she-devils? It couldn't have escaped Callow's notice that both Lilith, Adam's first wife who had been made from the same dirt as Adam, disobeyed God, and ran off and coupled with the Devil, and that Eve, Adam's second wife, even though she had been made from a rib of Adam's, likewise disobeyed God, ate of the fruit of the tree and brought about her and Adam's banishment from the garden. So was it that the desire to breed, to reproduce, was so strong in the female, in the woman, in both Lilith and Eve, that it over-rode any instruction on God's part for things to be different? And if this was so, then had Adam Callow's Eve, Eve Lilith, been a she-devil or just a normal amorous woman?

And if we accept Michael Venn's proposition that the Creation Story is an analogy, are the Biblical Adam's two wives, Eve and Lilith, embodiments of two extreme traits of women? Possibly not the extremes, because Eve did dare to take the fruit; the need to reproduce sweeping any thoughts of caution aside. The extreme would be the Eve who did not dare, the one who is submissive and if not actually liking, at least needing an Adam to dictate her life for her because she does not wish to choose it for herself. Or possibly this Eve is one who retires from life, afraid of men and pretends that she prefers intellectual pursuits; her books, her causes, her seeking after bodily cleanliness and health, mindfulness and submissive spirituality, over the having of children; the passive Eve. And then at the other end of the spectrum is the Lilith, the fiercely independent woman, almost to the point of recklessness, who feels she has no need of men other than perhaps for pleasure when the mood suits her, and who, as a consequence, does not have children and / or derives little or no pleasure from them, but on the other hand subconsciously realises that a vital part of her femininity is missing because in fact she does need both men and children, and so hates her need of a man, and hence hates men; the misandrist Lilith.

Might it then have occurred to Callow that if the Eve and Lilith in the two stories could represent two contrasting female traits, perhaps the Adams in the two stories, were not one and the same either, and in fact also represented two different male traits? Was it perhaps simplistic to presume that one Adam represented a rather pathetic Adam who is afraid of life, wishes to retire from it and cocoon himself in things of the mind; to quest after knowledge, learning or spiritual enlightenment, pretending to himself and others that these are higher, more noble, perhaps closer to God, and using this acquisition of academic knowledge as a shield against the rough, rude baseness of normal life, the staple of normal mortals; the world outside? The Adam who, because he is afraid of living, is likewise afraid of women but knows that part of him wants them, but because he cannot form a relationship with them, hates his desire for them and hence hates them; the misogynist Adam? And so does the other Adam possibly represent what might be described as the alpha male; square jawed, 'strong in the arm', and some might unkindly add, 'and thick in the head', the archetypal hero, who thinks nothing of recklessly galloping in on his white charger to rescue a damsel in distress, or even disobeying a god and taking her out of the safety of Paradise to the trials and tribulations of an unknown world which lies beyond?

Adam Callow stopped walking and stood on the road staring ahead but unable to focus on anything. Had he got it all so wrong? But it wasn't he who had made the linkage between sex and sin. This had been decreed and written down by the likes of Saints Paul, John the Divine, Augustine and Jerome amongst others. It was there in black and white and had been taught to him by those in the monastery. Had they, all of them, got it all so wrong?

What he also observed in himself was a somewhat guilty sense of liberation which he had first felt earlier after realising that Eve was dead. No, he certainly hadn't wished her dead, but he realised that, as cruel as it sounded, her death removed all the temporal and most of the spiritual problems from his life at a stroke. Perhaps it was his sense of being 'unburdened' that had given him a new and clearer view of the world. His problems hadn't entirely gone away, but he felt as if he was better able to pull them into focus, instead of them all being one jumbled mess piled on top of each other. However, whereas on the one hand he had to admit to feeling a sense of relieve at Eve's death, he also felt sadness and couldn't help but wonder just why did she, 'his Eve', have to die? Why had God allowed that to happen? Couldn't he (Adam Callow) and she have had their relationship without all the temporal and spiritual problems that came with it? Was her death God's punishment to them for their sinful ways? But, and this brought our Adam full circle and back to asking why, if God had made man and woman desire each other, had their desires been deemed as sinful? But even if they were sinful, why was her punishment death, whereas his was .… being left without her?

"Oh, Eve," he sighed world-wearily to himself, throwing his head back and looking up at the sky as if seeking an answer - a divine answer? - but none came and so, after a brief pause, he continued his trudge back to the monastery.

When he arrived there he looked at the still smouldering pile of ash which was all that remained of the pyre which had consumed Rose England. What was wrong with these misogynistic men? Why did they hate women so? Were they so afraid of them that they had to concoct tales of witchcraft and brand them as whores and she-devils? Had he, Adam Callow, been as gullible as the rest, and believed those tales; the tales of men presented as though they were the Word of God? Possibly he had, but whatever the truth, it was too late now, both Rose and Eve were dead.

Chapter 24

Perhaps surprisingly, given what he had been through, Adam Callow's mind felt quite calm and lucid as he passed though the monastery gates and thence into the cloisters; the corridors around the quadrangle where, just under a year ago, his indoctrination had started. 'If ye are to becometh one of the blessed one hundred and forty four thousand, then your lives needeth to be wholly, yea wholly spent in your devotion to God. There can be no middle way!' had boomed Prior Obscurant back in those early days.

'Wholly spent in your devotion to God,' doesn't sound like an unreasonable expectation to be made of one just entering the priesthood. However, these were the words being used to describe how one might become one of the 'blessed one hundred and forty four thousand', those that would enter the Celestial Kingdom, those that would join God in His Heaven, and so the words carried a much heavier charge to them than might reasonably be expected, as they suggested that all other aspects of life must be excluded. Something La Roche had told him back in those early days came back to him, 'I don't think God is vengeful and cruel.' No, this could not be right. God would not bar men from Heaven just because they were not virgins. That was ludicrous, and it was also assuming that Heaven was a physical place 'up there', whereas his friend Michael Venn had suggested that Heaven was in fact more to do with one's soul and lay inside each and every one of us and had cited a quotation from John to justify this.

With these thoughts turning in his mind, he walked from the cloisters and made his way to the vegetable garden, where he collected a shovel and pail from the tool shed. He filled the pail with water from one of the small tanks. Then he stopped and surveyed the garden, La Roche's Eden on earth, the garden in which he (Adam Callow) had spent so many hours and learned so much about the wonders of nature. His eyes took in the fruit trees, the raised beds of vegetables, the irrigation system that he had just used to fill the pail, and while doing so recalled brother La Roche's comment about the grass amphitheatre where the three of them (Venn, La Roche and himself) had had their discussions, 'It's been a while since I last visited it and I would like to see it again before ....' We might reasonably ask if, at this point in time, Adam Callow had already realised where his destiny was leading? Was he now visually taking in the garden as if for the last time, as if he, like La Roche, also realised that he might not see it again?

There was one further item he required; a cross or crucifix. Where might he find one that wouldn't be missed for a while? Yes, he realised, the novice-monks chapel had one. It was a gruesome and gory sculpture in wood, but it would serve, and as the chapel was only used first thing in the morning and last thing at night, it would not be missed for a while.

Taking the pail of water and shovel with him, he made his way along the slype to the semi-subterranean chapel dedicated to Saint Bibiana. Upon entering the chapel he set down the pail and leant the shovel against the stone wall. The polychrome wooden crucifix appeared larger than he remembered. Oh yes, he had looked at the thing everyday, but it's strange how one doesn't consider the size of an object accurately until faced with the task of transporting it. He walked across to the small altar passing between the tastelessly erotic sculptures of the two saintly ladies. Then he lifted the carving off the wall and held it against himself, measuring it, before placing it on the stone flagged floor.

Although he had never looked in the cupboards beneath the altar and had presumed that they contained religious accoutrements, he was not surprised upon opening the first to find McBane's leather thonged scourge or flagellum. Discovering it there must have brought back some unpleasant memories; memories of when he was 'instructed' by McBane that women and sex were sinful. There was nothing else in either cupboard other than a few spare candles. Callow held the flagellum in his hand and then turned and looked at the two kitsch statues. Whereas we might speculate on Callow's thoughts about the relationship between these three objects, what in fact caught his eye were the two burning candles which lit the two wooden effigies. Holding the handle of the flagellum in one hand and the individual leather thongs in the other, one by one he burnt several of them off. Possibly he derived a degree of pleasure, or sense of revenge or justice at doing this, but destroying the implement was not his objective. When he had removed enough of the thongs, he tied them together to form a cord and this he attached to the wooden crucifixion sculpture before placing the whole thing beneath his habit and the cord around his neck. It wasn't perfect, but as he would also be carrying a shovel in one hand and a pail in the other, and as all knew he worked in the garden, he thought it unlikely that anyone would notice his rather bulky and lumpy habit.

However, instead of proceeding out of the chapel, he removed the cross and placed it on the floor, took up the shovel and walked across to the statue of Saint Bibiana. At the cave he had suddenly noticed the similarity between this statue and Eve; the same tumbling raven black hair over ivory white skinned shoulders, back and breast, and so bizarrely clad in gold gilt covered sackcloth, which had so resembled Eve's beautiful golden orange skirt and golden yellow bodice and .... and she was dead. No, not Saint Bibiana, though she obviously was dead, but Eve, his Eve. Eve was dead. Was it that cursed statue, depicting the lustful, licentious nature of the female, that had helped to subconsciously cement the she-devil concept in his mind? And so was it that statue, along with the continual brain-washing of the monastery, that had led him astray from a perfectly natural human path which involved women, and on to a so-called 'path of righteousness' which supposedly led to some divine celestial kingdom of Prior Obscurant's imagination? Although vestiges of his earlier calmness were still with him, Adam Callow found his heart filling with loss, grief and a horrible sense of having been callously deceived. He raised the shovel and, with tears running down his face, brought it down on, and then repeatedly smashed at the kitsch sculpture until it lay a splintered mess on the chapel floor. Then he turned and did the same with the equally tasteless statue of the submissive Virgin Mary.

A hollow Adam Callow stood there leaning on the shovel, belatedly realising that what he'd probably had was a lovely, loving woman who had wanted him so much that she wanted him to be the father of her babies. What greater compliment can any woman pay a man, or for that matter any man pay a woman? So why had he felt he couldn't marry her? Why had he seen her as socially beneath him? Her clothes had always been of the finest material and beautifully tailored, so logically she must have had money to afford them and he recalled, it was she who had purchased the wine without any mention of its cost. They had never spoken of each others' families, other than when she had quite rightly, and he had to acknowledge that, reprimanded him for his superior attitude. So in fact he had no idea of her background. Was his reaction simply some sort of defence on his part, to pretend to himself that she was beneath him, so he might use this as a pretext as to why he could not, or rather should not, become too involved with her?

Or, on the other hand, was his reaction to her brought on by her demanding, narcissistic nature? She knew she was beautiful and so was tempting to men, and so had she been using her sexuality to both satisfy her desire to breed and her desire for the material things of this world? He couldn't help but recall that she hadn't been the least bit interested in his dilemma concerning the perdition of his soul. No, everything had had to be what she wanted, what she desired. Were all women selfish like this, to a greater or lesser extent and if so, was it any wonder why Jerome had taken Theophrastus' text to heart in his diatribe Against Jovinianus?

And woven into these conflicting views was the monastery's institutionalised attitude to women and sex. Callow realised however that Obscurant and his bigoted like did not have to make things up. All was already there, observed and written down by those that had contributed to the Holy Book and by those who had subsequently gone on to officially establish the religion and its rules. So why did those men, who were so fearful of women and sex, hold such sway in the establishment of the religion and Church? Of course ordinary men liked women, desired women, wanted to have sex with women. God had made them thus and made women to induce and then ful-fil those needs in men, so that men in turn would, by implanting their seed, ful-fil the God-given need in women to breed. So why had God also created the contradiction of 'the Flesh lusting against the Spirit and the Spirit against the Flesh'? Why had He created woman to be so desirable to man, so tempting on the one hand and yet so attention seeking, selfish and demanding of him on the other, and by being so, make the man feel that the woman is taking his soul?

Taking his soul.

Yes, that is what the devil does. He takes your soul. So was it that man resented being tempted into a life of marital servitude as so eloquently described by Theophrastus back in the fourth century, that women were so easily cast as she-devils? St Paul's, 'For the flesh lusteth against the Spirit, and the Spirit against the flesh: and these are contrary the one to the other: so that ye cannot do the things that ye would,' which Callow had heard so many times and had taken as being indicative of male misogyny in the religion, was, he now realised, perhaps not so much that, but rather a simple statement of how things stood for a man.

And how did things stand for the man, Adam Callow? Had he loved Eve in spite of the fact that she, a woman, would steal his soul and lead him off the straight and narrow path to the paradise of personal freedom, and instead shackle him to a life of marital servitude? And in exchange for what? An occasional glimpse of heaven which he would never be able to grasp and hold? A heaven which, like a rainbow, is stunningly beautiful but untouchable, or a heaven akin to a tantalisingly brief glimpse of a mountain top momentarily seen through a gap in the clouds? Yes, Heaven is there. It can be momentarily enjoyed. He had experienced it in all its beauty and wonder, but he could not hold on to it. So is it in fact 'there', there geographically; something 'up there' where we 'go to', some fairytale paradise replete with angels, harps and ambrosia? Or, is 'the kingdom of God within you,'[114] as his friend Michael Venn had explained? In which case is Heaven what you choose it to be; a glimpse of that mountain top, a beautiful summer day smelling of the scent of Meadowsweet, the peace felt when the woman of your dreams is lying in your arms? If so, neither he, nor Prior Obscurant, nor any of the one hundred and forty thousand virgins with the mark of God written in their foreheads could, or would ever reach it definitively because one can never reach an ideal, an aspiration, a dream of a world high above mortal man. So had the brief glimpses that Callow had had of Heaven not been in this semi-subterranean cold stone walled chapel supposedly dedicated to the finding of God, but in a stone walled cave up on a hillside just off the Hartstane Road and with that woman, Eve, who now lay dead on its floor?

Thus Adam Callow came to realise that he probably had loved Eve and had been prepared to sin in order to be with her, just as his namesake had also sinned by tasting the forbidden fruit so that he might stay with his Eve, even though he knew that it went against God's instruction to them and hence that his action would bring punishment on himself. So was God's instruction just a test? No, not a test that He knew they would fail, but a test to ascertain their loyalty to each other? The woman's, Eve's, innate desire to multiply and fill the earth that God had implanted in her would of course over-ride any such

---

[114] Luke 17:21

interdiction. However, as the man, Adam, had failed to hold on to his first wife, Lilith, she who had been made as his equal, made from the same dirt as he, possibly what God needed to ascertain was when the man, Adam, was forced into having to choose, would he choose to obey God and desert his mate, or would he choose to stick with her regardless of the consequences? So had God been merely testing the man, to see if he was made of strong enough stuff to look after and care for the woman and their resulting offspring? And if this was the case then he, Adam Callow, sickeningly realised that had failed. Yes, he knew others had deceived him, but even that knowledge did little to mitigate the shame he felt at his lack of courage to pursue what his heart had told him all along.

Adam Callow looked down at the smashed fragments of the two wooden statues and wondered how anyone could have pretended they were venerating the women depicted whilst degrading them in such a manner; making them out to be no better than wanton whores? What warped fantasies of a perverted misogynistic mind had resulted in these as art? The devils he realised, were not only outside the monastery walls in the guise of women waiting to lead men astray, but also within its cold stone walls, with hearts that were as unyielding and cold as the stone that surrounded them, too afraid to go out into the real world and meet women. So they had locked themselves away and pretended to themselves and others that they knew God's wishes and intentions better than He did, thought that their self-imposed masochistic life of abstemiousness and celibacy, coupled with a distrust and hatred of women was for some bizarre reason what God desired! How had they forgotten that God had also created woman, and created women with the specific intent that men and women should share their lives together? And how had they thought it their God-given right and duty to thrust their warped view of life onto others?

Oh, how had he been so misled? His friend Michael Venn had seen the falsehood in their teachings and of course so had his mentor Stephen La Roche. Why had it taken him so long to tear the veil from his eyes? He rearranged the cross beneath his habit, placed the knotted leather cord around his neck, took up the shovel and pail, and walked out of the monastery.

We might ask if, as a result of destroying the two effigies and stealing the polychrome-on-wood crucifixion, he had burnt his bridges at the same time? And if this was so, then it seemed unlikely that he could return to the monastery after this. Did he have a plan? This also seemed unlikely. Far more probable was that he was simply reacting, reacting to circumstances, reacting to what he found around him. He hadn't gone into the chapel with the intention of smashing the polychrome sculptures. He'd gone there to collect the wooden crucifix and then, once there, saw the two carvings and it was only then that all that they represented finally hit him. He recalled how on various occasions it had struck him that he knew his Eve from somewhere without realising that she had so resembled the St Bibiana statue and hence had concluded that she was a she-devil who had modelled herself on someone or something as part of some evil plan to lure him off the true path. Perhaps though, this was simple coincidence and she, as a woman, had been doing nothing more than her Biblical namesake had done to her Adam and every woman has done to every man ever since, namely, tempting him into, well, was it sin, in order to secure him and have children? In which case might every woman be a she-devil, not necessarily because she is a devil, a disciple of Satan's, but simply because every man knows that his desire for her will, in effect, result in the ruination of his freedom and result in his foreseeable future being consigned to that of marital servitude? But then again, was it just coincidence that Eve resembled the St Bibiana statue, or .... or alternatively might we ask, was it just coincidence that Lilith resembled the St Bibiana statue?

Adam Callow arrived back at the grassy amphitheatre and walked slowly back over it to the little cave. We can speculate that he may momentarily have toyed with the vain hope that what had happened had in fact not happened and that when he arrived all would be well. But of course what had happened, had. Eve was still lying there in her beautiful golden orange skirt and golden bodice, with a hole in her head where her blood had leaked out and into the sandy soil which formed the base of the small cave. He looked down at his beautiful Eve and felt as if his heart might break. However, he had a job to do, a duty that he owed her. He must give her the best burial that he could.

It seems unlikely that he ever debated where he should bury her; inside the cave simply seemed to him to be the logical place. However, to do this he had to take her outside so as to give himself enough room to work. So after he had set down the various items he had taken from the monastery, he gently dragged her out on to the grass outside. Then he washed her and re-arranged her clothing better. These were emotionally painful tasks. Waves of loss, regret and blame welled up in him and there were times when he was close to tears and breaking down as a result, but in a contradictory state of near-bursting emotions on the one hand and a purposeful numbness on the other, he was able to continue until all was done.

Then he put down the cloth and pail of water, and took up the shovel. It had never occurred to him that the base of the cave could be solid rock beneath its sandy surface, just like the rock that formed the cave itself. Luckily it wasn't, and surprisingly and fortunately, was composed of relatively easy to dig sand. Of course we can assume that Adam Callow had never dug a grave in his life and so had no idea what he was doing or how to do it. Initially he worked far too quickly and wasted a lot of effort. It was hard work for a puny specimen such as he, and he had to keep stopping to give his arms and particularly his aching back a rest. However, eventually he had dug a hole which he thought looked large enough and deep enough. Though could any hole ever be deep enough to bury his love? He then collected Eve's body and in as dignified a manner as possible, dragged it and placed it in this rudimentary grave.

The one female love of his life, the woman who had helped him glimpse heaven on this earth, lay in the bottom of the sandy hole fully dressed and, perhaps not surprisingly given her naturally pale complexion, looking as if she might have been asleep. Oddly, thought Callow, she didn't look dead. The only damage to her was the hole in the side of her head, and that was facing the rear wall of the cave and so not in this last picture that he had of her. She was beautiful, even in death. And oh how he wanted her not to be dead! Oh how he so wanted to hold her in his arms, to feel her physical warmth against him and her emotional warmth flood through him. 'I love you Eve Lilith', 'Yes I know you do'. Why did he have to lose her? Why had she been taken from him? Why?!

But he wasn't finished yet. The numbness returned. He turned and picked up the shovel and started to gently move the soil in beside her, and then place it on top of her until at last she was gone from his sight. It was easier then, easier when the task became an abstract one of piling up soil on a long narrow mound rather than covering up the body of his beloved Eve. That task complete, he went and collected the carved wooden crucifix that he'd taken from the chapel. He held the thing at arms length and looked at it. Goodness, it was a ghastly representation, as tastelessly gruesome in its depiction of the crucifixion as the other two statues had been blatant in their eroticism. Temptation, lust and desire, resulting in sin and guilt, and hence masochistic suffering, abstinence, celibacy and martyrdom. Why? What was so wrong with simple love, tolerance, peace and kindness? Why did everything have to be taken to such ludicrous extremes? Why was the simple middle ground so difficult to tread?

Callow took the cross and pushed it into the earth at the head of the mound. By this stage he felt so numb as a result of holding in his emotions that he had no idea what to do next, and stood there feeling both physically and mentally drained. Yes, he realised, he must say a prayer. So he knelt down behind the cross and said one. Perhaps we should not intrude on his private grief and so not speculate on what Adam's last words were to his beloved Eve?

When he opened his eyes, he noticed that a beautiful orange and yellow moth had alighted on the hideous crucifix. He looked at it and wondered where it had come from, as he hadn't noticed any moths ….? Orange and yellow, he observed …. the same colours as her dress. A numb sadness welled up inside him. Why? Oh, why this? Then he stood up and walked out of the small cave into the autumn sunshine, and as he did so something delicate brushed against his face. He turned and looked up, and saw the roots of a small tree which was growing right on the lip of the cave roof and saw that some of its roots were hanging down in search of soil and water in order to cling to life; a biological simile of what Adam Callow was desperately trying to do? Desperately searching, desperately trying to find how to live a life which accommodated perfectly natural God given desires, such as physical love for the other sex, in a world which felt like a desert to such things. Why couldn't his relationship with Eve Lilith have been simpler, easier to understand. Why couldn't they have loved each other openly? Why had their relationship been deemed to be that of fornication and hence sinful, and as such condemned and so had to be conducted secretly and in fear? Had it not occurred to those who pronounced on such matters that it might just be that it was the Spirit that was wrong and not, as was assumed by them, the Flesh? How could it be *so* wrong to love and enjoy a woman and yet be right to live a life of self-imposed abstinence and celibacy? Were they mad or was he?

And now, what should he do? By this time he had realised that he couldn't go back to the monastery; there was no doubting that he had burned his bridges regarding that option. He also couldn't go back to his family; his departure from the monastery would be regarded as 'in disgrace' and so returning to them could only bring shame on them. No, he realised, he and Eve were outside society now; outside The Garden. Outside, like his namesake and his Eve had found themselves after they had eaten of the tree. But Adam Callow's Eve was dead. So unlike his namesake, he was alone; so totally alone. Hence his question became not so much one of, 'what should he do?' but more one of, 'what could he do?'

The view across the valley that he, Venn and La Roche had looked at back in those so hopeful days of summer, was that evening bathed in the orange glow of .... of the flames emanating from the fiery pit? Was that his destiny? Had it always been so? Had his die been cast from the very beginning? Yes, he had tried to change the course of his life, but fate, or was it a devil in the guise of a very beautiful she-devil, that had always dragged him back to this path of perdition? He simply didn't know with any certainty any more, and it was that lack of certainty that nagged away at him. Unfortunately, he couldn't forget her 'so obvious' loose blouse that fell open to tempt his hungry gaze, the prepared blanket, the wine, the urgency with which she had straddled him and her undisguised selfish desire for pregnancy and a child, and so marriage. Had he really ever had a choice? And then the ghastly vision of Rose's charred body hanging from the stake, silhouetted against the flames of 'a hell on this earth' came back to haunt him. Where was hope in such a world; a mad illogical world of conflicting desires and blind, insane belief?

He looked up to where he had been told Heaven was located and saw dark grey clouds galloping across the sky; four dark grey horses with their bellies lit with the blood red flames from the Hell that was opening for him. However, if 'the kingdom of God is within us' rather than external to us, then so must Hell also be within us. So, was what Adam Callow was seeing an external manifestation of his inner torment, his inner hell? And did this lead him to conclude that the three saints whose lives Venn, La Roche and he had discussed, might likewise have actually been living with, indeed wrestling with their own personal hells? Hells brought about by the chances of their birth, their sexual orientation, their own failings, their own inabilities to handle their lives and rise above whatever it was that was dragging them down, dragging them down into their own pits of everlasting torment? And was this why they not only sought, but desperately sought to find a way out, to find some respite, some rest from their torment, desperately sought some peace for their troubled souls, desperately hoped against hope that they would be redeemed, would find salvation, would be saved? Did our Adam Callow realise this and so did he also realise that he, like they, was now trapped in his own hell of his own making? Had he, whilst worrying about the imaginary Hell as described by others, failed to notice that he had been inexorably walking into the very real one of his own? A hell where he had killed, albeit unintentionally, the female love of his life; the one person who he now realised had made his life feel complete, made him feel whole. Killed her because he could not reconcile perfectly normal and perfectly reasonable human physical love with the insane dictates of a religion preached by those who, because of their own perverted beliefs, abhorred this. A hell where not only had he lost his love, he had along with that, also lost all hope, lost all faith in what his mad world appeared to believe in. Oh he had tried, he'd tried so hard, but at every turn …. and he was just so tired, so very tired.

A hollowed out and ruined Adam Callow looked out across the grassy amphitheatre in front of him to the valley beyond bathed in the orange red glow of the setting sun. On the face of it a tranquil scene of late autumn evening beauty, but also a scene of impending doom, because although serene and calm, it was slashed by the long dark shadows being cast across it, growing shadows, darkness gradually eating up the light, just as the darkness in Adam Callow's soul was gradually eating up the last vestiges of any faith and hope that remained there. Was this how the world would end; the sun, together with its comforting and so necessary life-giving light, warmth and hope, slowly slipping below the horizon to be replaced with cold darkness, a 'darkness visible'[115] and terror?

"Why?! Why?!" he screamed in hopeless anguish and despair at the still oh-so-beautiful but deaf world in front of him.

He stood there broken, defeated, numb and totally exhausted with it all. The only thing he craved was peace; rest and peace for his tormented soul. If Adam Callow had ever needed an angel to pick him up and put him 'back in the nest, so that he might live and learn to fly'[116] it was then. But, as his friend Michael Venn had suggested would be the case, no angel came.

One of the cuboid boulders lay not far from being directly beneath the overhang to the cave. A numb Adam Callow rolled it nearer, climbed on it, unfastened the cord around his waist and threw it over the projecting rock so that it passed behind the little tree; the little tree that was on the edge and fighting to hold on to life. Perhaps that little tree saw a future? However, Adam Callow, who was also on the edge, did not see one in this world, only one in the next with his beloved Eve. 'Where you die, I will die, And there will I be buried.'[117] He fastened the cord around his neck and stepped off the boulder. And so the little tree through no fault of its own, other than simply being there, was cursed."

[115] John Milton, Paradise Lost, Book 1
[116] St Augustine, Confessions, Book XII:27
[117] Ruth 1:17

Chapter 25

"And that was where this story of The Ghost Moth ends," Joe said as he closed the book and placed it on the table.

"However, it is not where the full story ends, or where my tale this evening ends.

About a year after the death of our Adam and Eve, King Henry VIII of England broke with the Church of Rome and established the Church of England. He then set about with his dissolution of the monasteries. The local history books tell us that the Priory and Monastery of Saints Paul and Augustine was closed at that time, obviously without any resistance from the triumvirate of Prior Obscurant, sub-Prior Grees and novice-Master McBane. We can imagine Prior Obscurant dying in somewhat disillusioned old age, though no doubt still blindly holding on to the self-evident (to him) knowledge that he would be amongst the one hundred and forty four thousand. Sub-Prior Arriviste Grees had no doubt seen the change coming and we can imagine that he was quite happy to adapt his faith however necessary to fit the prevailing religious climate both for his own self-preservation and his continued progress up the greasy pole. And novice-master Rodiron McBane? For all we know he might have ended up as chief torturer and axeman at the Tower of London; there would always be a job for one who loved his nasty line of work.

However, in my opinion, far more important than those three, is Michael Venn, who seems a strange, almost enigmatic character, being both young and yet wise beyond his years, at the same time. What might have happened to that young, or not-so-young man who seemed both knowledgeable and radical about theological matters? His views most certainly did not accord with those of the Church at the time of this tale and one suspects probably didn't accord with those of the subsequent new Church either and one also suspects that they may well not accord with those of today's Church. Indeed, the Church still retains a huge problem with sex, still regarding it as 'the sin'; a dreadfully unfortunate legacy of the influence of those early saints that has still not been shaken off in spite of the fact that, as Michael Venn had pointed out, Paul treated the subject far more sensibly and open-mindedly in his various epistles. We can also guess that Michael Venn would not be pleased to learn that the Church is still clinging to the concepts of Divine Redemption, and Heaven as a place you can 'go to', and hence still suggesting that regardless of the lives we all lead, good or bad, we all stand a chance of actually 'going there' and having our sins forgiven and being blessed with the innocence of childhood, even though both Luke and John make it abundantly clear that 'the kingdom of God is within you,'[118] and hence that we do have to actually *do* something! Of course, men and women are lazy and so much prefer someone else, a saviour, to do the work for us. So the concept of Jesus having done the hard work, so that we might gain access to Paradise without any real effort on our part, is bound to be more appealing than us having to do the hard work ourselves, to actually make changes to our lives and the way in which we treat others, in order to achieve our desired salvation. However, trying to 'sell' the notion that it is up to each of us to choose by our actions whether we end-up living in our own Heavens or Hells is not so easy. Hence we can speculate that Michael Venn's view of us actually choosing how we should live our lives would never have any real 'sales appeal,' either then or now. Unfortunately, we don't know what became of him because he simply - enigmatically? - disappears from the tale. However, as he seemed a wise and pragmatic young man, we can only hope that he didn't end up tied to a stake on top of a burning pyre, or give up on life like his friend Adam Callow. Who knows, perhaps he went on to fight the good fight in another place and time?"

"Well, it's nice to know that at least one of the good guys

---

[118] Luke 17:21

may have survived," said Susan.

"Yes," concurred Bill.

"And I am afraid," said Joe smiling to himself, "that even with that little extra titbit, we are still not quite at the very end of this tale; not just yet. Now then, where do I start on this last chapter?

Some of you may remember that in the late autumn of the year that Harry, Elizabeth and I visited the tree and cave, we had some very severe storms. One of these, I learned later, did in fact bring down that bizarre dead and accursed tree, and because its roots were so integral to the cave beneath, when it finally did fall, it brought down the roof of the cave as well as some of the rock of the adjacent cliff face. The fallen tree has of course been cut up and removed, and so if you go to that little natural amphitheatre today and you knew nothing about the tree and cave, you would never realise that either had existed. All there is now is a pile of rocks and a small depression in the centre of the curved wall of sandstone.

Although I have mentioned Lilith in the tale at various points, perhaps we need just a little more detail on her? I am not sure if I mentioned that the three angels who were dispatched to bring the wayward woman back to her Adam were named as Snvi, Snsnvi and Smnglof; each name a bit of a mouthful to our ears. The story then goes on to explain that these three caught up with Lilith in the middle of the sea and threatened to drown her if she did not return with them. 'Leave me!' cried Lilith, 'I was created only to cause sickness to infants.' However, the three angels continued to insist that she return with them, but she would not and, in return for them letting her go, made her swear to them, 'Whenever I see you or your names or your forms in an amulet, I will have no power over that infant,' and it is suggested that it is for this reason the three angels' names are written on the amulets of young children, so when Lilith sees their names, she remembers her oath, and the child recovers.' You have probably already guessed that the three angels name's are translated as Senoy, Sansenoy and Semangelof. So now is any of this beginning to sound familiar?

Just in case some of you don't know," Joe continued, "Elizabeth's and my marriage ended in divorce."

"Oh, I am so sorry Joe," said a distraught and embarrassed Susan.

"Don't worry, Susan," Joe reassured her. "I am well over that. The emotional hurt fades, but the events, the facts, stick with one and strangely remain as if they were a story that had happened to someone else, not oneself.

I suppose if I am honest," he mused, "I had lived a bit in denial of the fact that our marriage had a time limit on it, and also have to confess that I totally missed the what now seems so obvious connection between Elizabeth's apparent renewed interest in it and our visit to the tree and cave that day. However, it wasn't just her mood or attitude toward our marriage that changed, it was almost as if her entry into that cave resulted in her taking on a different personality altogether. Of course, at the time, I was worried about Harry, and as I said earlier in this tale, certain aspects and events only became clearer later. So no, when it came, Elizabeth's announcement that she was leaving me was not entirely out of the blue. However in spite of that, her new hair style and colour, tumbling silky waves of raven black, just like a shampoo advert on the TV, and her newly purchased yellow and orange dress, was a surprise and unfortunately confirmed what nurse Senoy had tried to warn me about at the hospital;

'But I am afraid….'

'Of what?' I had asked,

'No, not of what, but for you,' nurse Senoy had replied.

"And Harry is coming with me," stated a newly assertive Elizabeth.

"Lillibeth, don't you think we should ...," I managed, before she added,

"He is *my child*!"

And that wasn't all, because as both young Adam Callow and myself had been warned by Theophrastus, she then continued with,

"And I will be taking the car, *and* I want *my* share of this house."

"But where will you …?"

"Don't worry yourself, Joe. I've arranged everything," she replied, before proceeding to load already packed suitcases into the car, along with Harry, and drive off. The whole business only took a few minutes. Fortunately, I did manage to say goodbye to Harry before he got in the car and from him gained the impression that he was just as surprised as I was. It all seemed so unreal and happened so quickly. Yellow orange dress, tumbling black hair and 'my child'; were these things just coincidence? After their whirlwind departure, I just sat for several minutes in a bit of a daze wondering if I had dreamed the whole thing.

Joe looked round the table at us before adding,

"Although I have tried to stick with the facts, you'll appreciate that my story is nonetheless a personal recollection of how reading the tale of The Ghost Moth, coupled with the various incidents that I have related and the people involved, struck me at the time. I make no pretensions to it being a full and comprehensive account, and yes, am sure that a certain amount of personal bias has crept in. This has been *my* story after all!

Well, that's it.

The End," he said, with a flourish.

Those of us listening to Joe's story in The Red Grouse that

evening just sat there in silence feeling a mix of surprise and embarrassment at his candid conclusion to it. Just what do you say when someone openly describes the breakup of their marriage? Never mind that it happened several years earlier. Such a thing was, indeed still is, a private matter. So there was a somewhat awkward pause, with all of us trying on the one hand to take in the tale that Joe had just told us and on the other, well, to be honest, not really wishing to hear any more.

"But you and Harry are back to seeing each other," said Bill, breaking the spell. "I had quite a long chat with him in the village only last week."

"Oh yes. Everything is fine now between Harry and myself. For the first few years things were a bit difficult as I had very little access to him during that period. Inevitably though, he grew up and, as might have been written in The Ghost Moth tale, 'became as one of us.' When he left school and went off to university we started to see a lot more of each other. These days he usually 'comes home' as he calls it, to see me once or twice a month.

I cannot say the same of his mother though, as I haven't seen her since that day she walked out. The last I heard," he added with a slight chuckle, "was that she had flown off over the ocean to join her Samael and live in a location which is a lot warmer!

END.

And did you enjoy this story?

If you did, could you be so kind as to post a review (it need only be three or four words), or just your star rating, on any or all of:-
Amazon.com, amazon.co.uk, Goodreads and Bookbub or any other platform you choose.

Thank you. And as a favour for yourself? Well, now you know what my stories are like; possibly try another one?

Thank you for reading.

More information can be found on my website, and you can follow me on social media, via

https://www.linktr.ee/lesliegarland

Acknowledgements

Although this tale is a work of fiction, a work of my imagination, nonetheless many have both wittingly and unwittingly contributed to it. So to all of them, I am much obliged to you for providing me with material, ideas, snippets, etc., all of which are necessary for the writing of a story. My gratitude is also posthumously due to Aud, my late wife, who provided me with the necessary space to write, the much needed words of encouragement along the way and for proofreading the final manuscript. I must also not forget all the advance readers who have taken the time to read my work and post their oh-so-necessary reviews and words of encouragement; thank you all. And finally I must thank the team at Noble Legacy Publishing for their editorial ideas, behind the scenes efforts and the superb cover picture.

About the Author

Leslie Garland is the author of The Red Grouse Tales series. His stories blend history, faith, and supernatural suspense, exploring the mysteries of belief, temptation, and ancient evil. They have been both Book Excellence Awards Finalists and achieved Readers' Favorite 5-star status.

He lives in Northumberland, England, UK., is inspired by folklore and the landscapes around him and is currently working on various new tales.

Also by Leslie Garland:-

- The Little Dog
- The Crow
- The Golden Tup
- The White Hart
- The Red Grouse Tales: The Little Dog and other stories.
- The Bat
- The Blue Horse

Visit www.lesliegarland.com for further information

Published in Collaboration with Noble Legacy Publishing

www.noblelegacypublishing.co.uk